Scribe Publications
THE ITALIANS AT CLEAT'S CORNER STORE

Jo Riccioni was born in the UK to an Italian father and English mother. She worked in Singapore and Paris before settling in Sydney, and she has a master's degree in literature from Leeds University. Her short stories have been read on the BBC and published in *The Best Australian Stories 2010* and *2011*. Her story 'Can't Take the Country out of the Boy' has been optioned for a short film.

THE ITALIANS AT Cleat's CORNER STORE

- JO - RICCIONI

SCRIBE
Melbourne • London

Scribe Publications Pty Ltd
18–20 Edward St, Brunswick, Victoria 3056, Australia
50A Kingsway Place, Sans Walk, London, EC1R 0LU, United Kingdom

First published by Scribe 2014

The epigraph is taken from *Four Quartets* © Estate of T.S. Eliot and reprinted by permission of Faber and Faber Ltd. The quotation on p. 14 is from 'Italia, Italia, o tu cui feo la sorte' by Vincenzo da Filicaja. The quotation on p. 88 is from *A Room with a View* by E.M. Forster, reproduced with the permission of The Provost and Scholars of King's College, Cambridge, and The Society of Authors as the E.M. Forster Estate. The quotation on p. 236 is from 'Sea-Fever' by John Masefield, reproduced with the permission of The Society of Authors as the Literary Representative of the Estate of John Masefield.

Typeset in Dante MT by the publishers
Printed and bound by CPI Group (UK) Ltd, Croydon, CR0 4YY

National Library of Australia Cataloguing-in-Publication data

Riccioni, Jo, author.

The Italians at Cleat's Corner Store / Jo Riccioni.

9781922070883 (Australian edition)
9781922247391 (UK edition)
9781925113020 (e-book)

1. Immigrant families–Great Britain–Fiction. 2. Italians–Great Britain–Fiction.

A823.4

This project has been assisted by
the Australian Government through
the Australia Council, its arts funding
and advisory body.

Australian Government

scribepublications.com.au
scribepublications.co.uk

In memory of my mum,
Pat Riccioni (nee Waiton)
1940–2007

Dimmi chi sono, non mi dir chi ero
(Tell me who I am, not who I was)

Italian proverb

A people without history
Is not redeemed from time, for history is a pattern
Of timeless moments. So, while the light fails
On a winter's afternoon, in a secluded chapel
History is now and England.

T.S. Eliot, *Little Gidding*

PART ONE

Leyton
1949

The first time she saw them, they were mending the gate on Henry Repton's land. She was cycling to Leyton on her way to Cleat's and had reached the top of the hill that was good for sitting upright and freewheeling. She might have missed them, coasting at speed as she was, the hedgerow budding thickly on either side of the lane, but as she rounded the corner at the dip, there they were, two of them, their heads bent together over the broken gate, tools in their hands. One had his face obscured by a shock of hair, slick and jet as a raven's wing. They both stood up as she flew by, and she couldn't help but glance back over her shoulder to see the shine of their brown faces and forearms in the clean light of early morning, their neat, compact waists as they straightened. One of them put his fingers to his mouth and let out a high-pitched whistle.

As she pedalled towards Leyton, she could no longer see them, but their voices hung in the air, foreign words rolling over one another, rapid and restless and no more meaningful to her than the chatter of pebbles in the brook after a downpour. Afterwards she heard a laugh — she guessed it was the whistler — loud and playful, cutting the morning in two, and then she heard no more.

'Eye-ties,' Mrs Livesey fired across the counter, as Connie raised the blind and flipped the *Open* sign in the window of Cleat's. The string bag on Mrs Livesey's arm danced under the trembling shelf of her breasts. Connie finished buttoning her serving coat and said nothing. Mrs Cleat was resting her flour scoop on the countertop, fixing her customer with small, hard eyes, like a hedgerow animal disturbed. After a moment, she motioned Connie towards the sacred domain of the new Berkel compression scales, presenting her the scoop with both hands, like a sceptre. It had been Connie who had talked Mrs Cleat through the instruction booklet and the complexities of the weighing grid when the scales had first arrived, but this was a detail Mrs Cleat chose to forget, except in times of urgent distraction. She rounded on Mrs Livesey.

'Eye-talians?' she demanded, perhaps more greedily than she'd intended.

'Eye-ties, that's what I said. Back again. For farm work. Paid this time.'

'I see,' said Mrs Cleat. She cast her eye past Mrs Livesey as if down an imaginary queue of customers at the counter. Connie could tell she was peeved that a farmhand's wife, and a shabby one at that, had the advantage of such news. Mrs Cleat prided herself on being the most informed woman in the Leyton and Parishes Christian Ladies' League, not to mention the Greater Huntingdon Amateur Operatic Society. She was the one to whom others came precisely because she did *not* gossip. Mrs Cleat gave *updates*. It was true that most of the village placed her version of news not far below the hallowed authority of the BBC. But Connie knew, from being in the shop with Mrs Cleat five days a week, that these *updates* had to come from somewhere, and that somewhere was largely countertop gossip.

'I see,' Mrs Cleat said again, buffing the new Formica with a cloth.

'Apparently, Henry Repton told one of his WOPs there'd always be work for him on the farm if ever he wanted it. Well, that's done it. Eye-tie's come back and brung the whole ruddy family. Get that.'

Even from behind, Connie saw the change in the set of Mrs Cleat's shoulders, the marginal shift of her hips. She would not be told, least of all told what to *get*.

'You do read the newspapers, don't you, Janet?' she said in her Christian Ladies voice. Connie smiled: Mrs Cleat knew very well that the only newspaper they'd ever sold Mrs Livesey was a royal-wedding edition two years ago. 'They say there's no jobs on the Continent. And anyone who's got one is wheeling their wages home in a barrow.' She proceeded to ply Mrs Livesey with the paper packages Connie had placed on the counter and topped them with an air of worldly superiority.

Mrs Cleat enjoyed regurgitating the casual items of global news that Mr Gilbert shared with them when he picked up his morning *Times* on the way to the schoolhouse. No doubt she felt that this snippet, opportunely recalled, redeemed her somewhat in the face of Mrs Livesey's scoop.

'That's all well and good, but what about our boys?' Mrs Livesey continued. 'It's their jobs these WOPs are taking.' She re-adjusted the loaded bag on her arm, her cleavage rising ominously.

'With respect,' Mrs Cleat said, the words again stolen from Mr Gilbert, who often used them as a gentle precursor to correcting the ill-informed, such as Mrs Cleat herself, 'I hardly think your Derek will want a job mucking out pigs on Repton's farm. And even if he did, he wouldn't do it for twice the money Repton'll be paying them Eye-talians.'

Mrs Livesey pulled her chin to her neck. 'Well, Eleanor,' she said, 'I knew you liked your opera singing and whatnot, but I didn't think you were such a ...' She scanned the shelves, searching for the answer as if it might be hidden among the tins of Vim and boxes of Rinso. 'Well, such a ... a bloody WOP-lover, that's what,' she finally gave in. 'In the book, if you please.'

Mrs Livesey began to heave herself about when the sight of Connie, who was opening the ledger, evidently put her in mind of a more sophisticated line of attack. 'How's your Aunty Bea, dear? Still grafting away at the Big House?' she asked. Her tone suggested Connie's aunt was a manacled slave of the Reptons' rather than their paid housekeeper. 'I'm sure Bea Farrington's memory isn't as short as some people's hereabouts.'

Mrs Livesey's nostrils still glistened from the early walk across the fields, and the tip of a rogue canine tooth pressed onto her lower lip even when her mouth was closed. Connie was reminded of the hounds at the Hamerton Hunt: harmless creatures in the yard, but killers on the scent. 'I'm not sure what you mean, Mrs Livesey,' she replied, although she suspected she did.

'Poor Bea. Working alongside prisoners in the war is one thing, but having them back in peacetime to rub salt in your wounds is another. I'm surprised your Uncle Jack still lets her work up at the Big House, seeing as how them Eye-ties was the death of his own brother.' She glanced at Mrs Cleat, smugly gauging her response to this rather clever equation. 'Monte Cassino, wasn't it, where Bill Farrington fell?'

Connie closed the ledger and returned it to its shelf under the counter.

'I don't know ... that is, my aunt and uncle don't really speak of it,' she said. 'Anyway, she wouldn't see the Italians much — farmhands don't have any call to go inside Leyton House.'

'Give her my sympathies,' Mrs Livesey said, as if Connie hadn't spoken a word. She gave a last triumphant sniff in Mrs Cleat's direction before she headed for the door, the squeak of her rubber boots and the tinkle of the bell sounding oddly discordant behind her.

Mrs Cleat, agitated, took up the broom and began to sweep the dried mud left in Mrs Livesey's wake. 'WOP-lover ... *WOP-lover?*' she argued with herself. 'Even if I was, which I'm not, she could have at least used the proper word. Connie — what's that *word* Mr Gilbert uses?'

Connie shook her head. She knew exactly the term Mr Gilbert sometimes used about himself, but she also understood the repercussions of educating Mrs Cleat.

'Ah, that's it,' Mrs Cleat said, propping up the broom and appearing fortified by the efficacy of her own memory. 'WOP-lover, indeed! Still, you can't expect the likes of Janet Livesey to know a word like *Eyetaliphile.*'

Connie began to look out for them on her way to and from work, squeezing her brakes and forfeiting the thrill of coasting round the bend at the entrance to Repton's in the hope that she might catch sight of the Italians. But a week passed and the single sign of their existence was the thin line of smoke from the chimney of the crumbling gamekeeper's cottage. She took to stopping in the greying light after work, dismounting and pushing her bike up the hill towards Bythorn. After the strictures of Mrs Cleat's shop, she usually enjoyed the challenge of pedalling up the rise, the perverse sense of release she felt from the pounding of her heart, the sweat breaking over her skin. But the walk allowed her more time to survey the squat, derelict building across the fields; to conjure them from the dusk, somehow bright and radiant, the light of a foreign sun in their hair, the sheen of it in their skin.

It was several weeks after Mrs Livesey's news when Connie got off her bike at Bythorn Rise and saw a figure at the edge of the field. She recognised the taller, broader of the two Italians. He was staring at the hedgerow, standing very still. She made out a bundle of papers in his hands, a battered notebook perhaps, and saw that he was marking something in it. Unseen herself, she became lost in the act of watching him, until his head darted up, aware of her. Confronted with what she had been wanting all along, she felt exposed, somehow found-out, and she quickly got back on her bike and cycled up the rise. But when she reached the top of the hill, she couldn't help glancing back. He was standing in the same spot, unmoving, vigilant as a nocturnal bird waiting for night to settle.

The next evening after work, the sky dimmed early with rain. She had forgotten her mackintosh, and by the time she got to the gate of the farm, the downpour had begun and she was already wet to her skin. She stopped to switch on her bike lamp, and as she did so she caught sight of him again in the gloom of the hawthorn, oblivious to the rain dripping from his fingers, or from the slick of hair flattened against his forehead. They peered at each other, the space between them still, save the liquid tick of the hedgerow. She was about to raise her hand to him when he turned his back and began to stride up the hill towards the cottage, leaving her shivering in the leached light.

'Teaching them, that's right.' Mr Gilbert nodded, reaching for the *Times* that Mrs Cleat held rolled like a baton on the counter. 'I'm enjoying it immensely. Purely selfish motivations, you know. It's such an opportunity for me to practise my rickety Italian.' Despite his pleasantries, Connie could see in Mr Gilbert's restless stance his eagerness to be gone.

The other end of the newspaper was still pinned in Mrs Cleat's fingers. 'So they have no English at all, the sons?' she asked.

'Oh, they're doing admirably. Their father's been teaching them, but they need a greater vocabulary and instruction in grammar. That's where I've offered to help.'

Mrs Cleat gripped tighter. 'And Repton gives them the gamekeeper's cottage in return for labour? He doesn't actually pay them, I hear?'

Mr Gilbert resigned his hand from his *Times* and exhaled. 'I certainly hope that isn't the case, Mrs Cleat.' Connie recognised this sigh, the lowered tone. She had become familiar with it at school, the way he corralled his temper, allowing rebuke to merely glimmer at the edges of his voice. After a series of thunderous village teachers all trained in the same ear-twisting, chalk-hurling method for extracting terrified rote, Mr Gilbert's patience and enthusiasm, not yet beset with the jading of middle age, had been easy to idolise.

'But I've been told on good authority they don't have any special skills,' Mrs Cleat persisted.

'On the contrary. They were farmers themselves in Italy. No experience with machinery but, regardless,' Mr Gilbert smoothed a thumb and finger over his eyebrows, 'I believe we outlawed slavery in 1772. Such an arrangement would be rather illegal, don't you think?' His eye caught Connie's and glinted conspiratorially.

Mrs Cleat straightened her shoulders, affronted. 'Of course. Of course it would, Mr Gilbert. I'm merely repeating what others in the parish are saying.'

'Then, with respect, perhaps it would be better not to?' The bell clattered as he opened the door sharply. 'Loose lips, Mrs Cleat ...'

'The war is long over, Mr Gilbert,' she sang back to him, leaning over the counter.

'... can still sink ships,' he called from the pavement beyond the bay window, lifting his hat and offering them his most charming smile, as he always did. Mrs Cleat ignored it, busy digesting his meaning. The fist of one hand was still around his *Times*, while the other wiped the counter absently. Connie hovered nearby.

'Oh, now look! Connie, run this up the school,' she finally huffed. '*Loose lips* ... I'm sure I don't know what he's implicating. These intellectuals ... theorising and setting the world to rights, but they'd forget their own heads if they wasn't screwed on!'

Connie caught up with Mr Gilbert as he was entering the school gate. He half sighed, half laughed. 'Am I to be interrogated about them every morning, Connie, before I'm allowed my newspaper, do you think?'

'About the Italians?'

'Si. La famiglia Onorati.' The foreign words rolled off his tongue fluently, luxuriously, and she felt for a second she had peeked through a door into another world.

'So beautiful ... the Italian ... the sound of the words, I mean.' She became annoyed at the heat in her cheeks.

'Oh yes. *The honoured ones* ...' he said in a deep theatrical voice, raising his eyebrows at her. 'It's what it means — their name. Rather ironic, don't you think, given what they must have seen, what they must have been through to settle for living in that bloody pigsty of Repton's?'

She didn't know what to say. Even now she still felt awkward when he invited her opinions, as one adult to another. Four years ago they had sat in his empty classroom, preparing scholarship papers for St Bernadette's College in Benford. Now, thanks to Aunty Bea, all she prepared was his grocery account.

'Do you think … I mean, have they had it that hard — the Italians?' she asked, rather ashamed to show her ignorance to the one person who had seen her potential.

'I suspect so. But it's behind them now, I suppose. Nobody wants to go back to that time.' He smiled at her. 'War's about the future, not the past, isn't it?' Yet as he tapped the newspaper to his hat in farewell, she sensed that he had no faith at all in what he'd said. She nodded her assent, but it was no more than a habit, and she was angry with herself afterwards for not asking him more.

Had the war been about the future? She stood at the gate of the school, feeling like she had lived through those years half dreaming, unconcerned with the games of grown-ups, and was now slowly awakening. She had barely any idea of what was beyond Leyton. Once, she had gone as far as Benford on the bus, simply so she could imagine rumbling through the countryside while practising conjugations from a Latin primer, jumping off at the wrought-iron gates of the Victorian school, inclining her head and laughing under the red facade with those pale-haired, doe-legged girls.

'St Bernadette's? That *Catholic* school all way over in Benford?' Aunty Bea had asked Mr Gilbert as if he had been proposing to send her to the fire and brimstone of hell itself. She hadn't changed out of her housedress, her cheeks ruddy from carpet-beating at the Big House, the plain silver crucifix winking on her flushed throat. In the corridor Connie had chewed at a quick until it throbbed, listening to the escalating symphony of their exchange.

'The uni-*ver*-sity, you say? And what kind of learning would she be doing at this uni-*ver*-sity of yourn, Mr Gilbert? Something for the war effort?' Her deliberate use of the article — as if there was only one university, like the Odeon, the grubby picture house in Wellsborough — her purposefully obtuse questions, her thick Leyton accent had made Connie grind her teeth in embarrassment.

At least Mr Gilbert hadn't played to Aunty Bea's fool. 'She's full of potential, Mrs Farrington, and with young men still enlisting she has more chance of matriculating than ever before. You know as well as I do what that can open up to her. But the war won't last much longer.'

'Won't it, now? They said that four years since, didn't they? Still, don't reckon it affects your life much, not here in the schoolroom.'

'Christ, Beatrice!' It was the first time she had heard Mr Gilbert truly raise his voice. 'Kids need an education even in wartime. Teaching *is* my war effort.' There was a pause, the clearing of a throat, the awkward scuff of shoes on the flagstones.

'Thank you for your special attention to Connie, Mr Gilbert, but we Leyton folk has simple needs. You might be better off spending the time with one of your London kiddies.'

'Beatrice.' Connie heard the sadness in his softened voice. 'I might have come back from Town with the evacuees, but I was born here, as you well know. I think I have a good idea what Leyton people need.'

But it was Aunty Bea who had emerged from the school-room first, straightening her scarf, her expression flinty, as it always was when the Lord's name had been taken in vain. In one glance both Connie and Mr Gilbert understood: Connie would not be going to St Bernadette's. Aunty Bea couldn't fathom why anyone would want to leave Leyton, to leave the life God had given them, unless, of course, it was to enlist and defend that life. Mr Gilbert, in her mind, was doubly damned for leaving Leyton in the first place and then for running straight back from London as soon as the war allowed him. As for Connie's future, Aunty Bea had, in her parochial wisdom, secured it well before that interview. She started at Cleat's within the month. The sight of her in a white serving coat, snipping rations coupons, instead of milking cows or scrubbing other people's floors, sometimes caused Aunty Bea to bite down on her lip with suppressed pride when she came into the shop. Such was her satisfaction that she had done right by her sister's child.

Connie pulled on the low wooden gate of the schoolhouse, feeling its familiar grumble along her arm. Four years on and she felt even more of a child than she had at thirteen, more ignorant and blinkered, as if everything she knew about the world, about the war, about life, had been reduced to the shelves of Mrs Cleat's shop. At least Mr Gilbert had provided her with a view beyond the hedgerows of Leyton, even beyond England. He still lent her books and journals, but her favourites were the museum catalogues of the art he had studied in Paris, Florence and Rome when he was not much older than she was now. She followed the thumbed pages, the sculptures and frescoes, the naked warriors and gods in dramatic poses. She traced them by the light of her bedside lamp and felt guilty for thinking less about their mythical and biblical stories than about their breathtaking bodies. Once, she had found a photograph, slipped between the pages of a Baedeker: an olive-skinned man dressed all in white, standing on the steps of a fountain in some square of luminous marble. His face seemed to reflect that glow, lit with an expression that suggested to her the excitement of possibility, of the limitless future stretching out before him. On the reverse side was an inscription in fading cursive:

> *Italia, Italia, o tu cui feo la sorte*
> *Dono infelice di bellezza, ond' hai*
> *Funesta dote d'infiniti guai,*
> *Che in fronte scritti per gran doglia porte*

She had gone to sleep memorising the words night after night without understanding them. They came back to her now, an incantation conjuring that other world of youth and beauty and possibility, as she heard Mr Gilbert's voice: *La famiglia … La famiglia Onorati.*

As she neared Cleat's, the prospect of the dim counter, and the dimmer Mrs Cleat, slowed her pace. She felt like she could keep walking, past the shop, past the Leyton signpost in the lane snaking down the hill, south towards London, towards Dover, towards anywhere but Leyton. Leyton, where the low grey sky was a lid over the single file of the high street, unchanged for generations. The squat buildings of stone and brick seemed as naive as a toy village, she thought, living out the pretence, the replica of a life. She should keep walking. She *could* keep walking, in the same way her mother had done. But then where would she be?

She caught her reflection in the shop's bay window across the road: her thin skirt, dun cardigan buttoned to the neck, the flat leather lace-ups on pale legs, that cottony frizz of copper hair. She felt like she might be swept away on the faintest gust of wind or disappear under the vigorous buff of Mrs Cleat's counter cloth. In the passing chug of the morning post van, the smudge of her was gone, and she was left staring at the chipped lettering of the window: *Cleat's Corner Store*. The mere sight of it made her feel ordinary.

Her mother had christened her Marylyn — a name she had perhaps intended for billboard lights, a name that would go places, a name too grand for the rollcall of Leyton Village School. It was the only thing her mother did give her, a token gesture that Aunty Bea believed was better packed in the suitcase of her sister's other pretensions when she left Leyton on the number 11 bus. *Legs Eleven*. It was painfully fitting. Connie remembered the shabby glamour of her mother's silk stockings, her red shoes gaudy beneath her coat, a pheasant feather in her hat attempting finesse. The shoes, she recalled, had rounded toes embroidered with roses, and heels that clicked like a flamenco dancer's — too quick, too restless for the lanes of Bythorn. She had held her mother's hand at the door to Aunty Bea's, like they were popping in, dropping something off. But once inside, her mother had shaken her free and stood smoothing a thumb under her lips, examining her reflection in the hallway mirror. 'It won't be forever,' she heard her tell Aunty Bea in the kitchen. 'Your lives are ... well, better suited to it. You've got this house. You've got Jack. Jesus, Bea, you've even got Christ!'

She had often wondered why her mother's life wasn't better suited to keeping her, but no one had ever offered a real explanation. She had heard the word *divorce* mouthed over the lips of teacups, or whispered above her head as if it was a disease and she was carrying it. But her father had already been gone so long that all she could remember was the uneventful click of the door, his trilby bobbing past the kitchen window, the scratch of his shoes on the pavement outside, while her mother militantly flicked through the pages of *Britannia and Eve*.

At Aunty Bea's stern little terrace in Grimthorpe Lane, she would sit waiting for her mother on the stone wall that ran along the front of the workers' cottages. *Mary, Mary, quite contrary*, the lane kids chanted, wringing the colour from her name and chalking it into the village playground. *Where did your mother go?* And in her head she would sing, *With silver bells and cockle shells and pretty shoes all for show*. But the shoes, once they had gone, never came back. Aunty Bea kitted her out with a sturdy pair of Church's boots, combed her hair for nits, and scrubbed her with carbolic soap until she was as shiny as a new penny in the collection plate on Sunday. And she renamed her Constance. That was what they needed in their lives, Aunty Bea said. In Bythorn, where the mud from the fields coated everyone's steps, life had no room for red shoes.

For several months Connie saw the Italians at a distance: a bent spine among the sprouting sugar beet west of Leyton House, the back of a head juddering along the ridge in a tractor, or a shadow in the lit window of the cottage at dusk. But she had learned to tell them apart, even from afar: the broader shoulders, the thicker, blacker hair of one brother; the more confident, graceful energy of the other. She had hoped their paths might cross as she cycled home from work and they walked to the schoolhouse for their lessons with Mr Gilbert, but she only ever saw them on the bridle paths between the fields. She guessed this shortcut must have saved them two of the four miles of road between Bythorn Rise and the schoolhouse, but they still reached Leyton in the dark and left in the dark. And the less they were physically seen in the village, the more their presence seemed to intrude, fuelling ridiculous anecdotes and hushed speculation over pints in the Green Man, in the same way that Axis spies had done during the war. The shop never failed to provide her with daily titbits of misinformation and wild rumour, which she did her best to disregard but which piqued her curiosity even more.

'No, not one letter,' she heard Agnes Armer, the postal assistant, telling Mrs Cleat one afternoon in late spring. The smell of keck and hawthorn carried in from the hedgerows through the open door of the shop.

'Not a single letter from the Continent,' Agnes continued, clicking the word neatly on her tongue. Connie was rearranging tins of Carnation along the back wall and took a while to tune in to the conversation.

'After all these months, not a word from anyone in their own country?' Mrs Cleat asked, her eyes busily scanning Agnes's for evidence of a chink in their glacial blue.

'Mm.' Agnes rolled a blonde curl around her forefinger, as if she had already lost interest in the topic. She had been two years above Connie at school, a girl conscious of her own prettiness, and its power when combined with an air of languid self-assurance. Even in the playground, Connie had seen first-hand how one crack in that temple of bone china wielded the same force as any broad-fisted, pimple-faced bully.

Connie had applied for the postal assistant's job. Aunty Bea had huffed that she could hardly see how tearing off stamps was any different from tearing off rations coupons. But Connie had thought it was the closest she might get to leaving Leyton, handling mail that was at least going somewhere else. Agnes, however, had returned from London with a secretarial diploma and some French mascara, and Mr Tonkiss, the postmaster, was a lost man. For Agnes, the job was apparently a *fill-in* until she decided what she wanted to do with her life *back in Town*. Two years on she was still in Leyton.

'Not one letter. Don't you think it strange, Agnes?' Mrs Cleat prompted again.

'Well,' Agnes replied. 'I really don't like to comment.'

'All I can say is,' Mrs Cleat continued, heedless, 'Henry Repton must be giving them Eye-talians all they need because they haven't as much as stepped foot inside this shop.'

'Have they not?' Agnes glanced at Connie and let out a closed-lipped laugh that might have passed for a cough. 'Perhaps you need to start stocking Chappie, Mrs Cleat,' she said.

'Chappie? You mean the dog meat? In the tins?'

'Mm,' Agnes murmured. Connie could not tell whether she was more amused at the information she knew or how badly Mrs Cleat wanted it.

'And?' Mrs Cleat urged.

'Mm … I'm not sure I should say.'

'Well, Aggie Armer, spit it out or don't.' Mrs Cleat stood erect and indignant, tired of being played. 'What's dog meat got to do with the price of eggs?'

Connie rubbed her nose with the back of her hand. She knew that Mrs Cleat could still remember Agnes Armer holding up her sticky hand for mint humbugs before the war. It was unlikely she would let herself be reeled in by Agnes's adult artifice just yet.

'Mr Watt over in Clopton told me the older boy bought two cans of Chappie from him last week.'

'*And?*'

'Well, I've never seen a dog on the farm, have you? Mr Repton keeps all his hounds over at Hamerton ever since Mrs Repton got bitten by that bitch of Fossett's before the war. Not likely Mr Repton would let the Italians have a dog then, is it?' Agnes paused to let Mrs Cleat catch up, then added with a change of tone, 'Supposed to be very resourceful cooks, the Continentals. They say the WOPs at the camp in Sawtry could make a meal out of anything.'

Agnes stood before the counter and smoothed her hands down the front of her flannel skirt, with the assuredness of a woman ten years older. She blinked at Connie as unnaturally as a doll. Mrs Cleat was still confused. Connie became aware of her pulse beating in the dip of her throat, a heat spreading through her chest. *Stop it*, she wanted to say. *Don't* — but the words didn't seem to make any noise in the space between herself and the untouchable Agnes.

Agnes raised her eyebrows into thin arches and left the shop with her packet of tea, the smart clack of her patent shoes a counterpoint to the lazy tick of the afternoon. Mrs Cleat gazed after her, buffing the counter distractedly. When she spoke, it was not to Connie, but to rehearse the news as she now understood it. 'I see. Well ... dog meat ... from a tin. Even in the war we didn't stoop to that. *Really*, it makes your stomach turn ... almost savages. How can Repton let them live like it?'

Connie listened, feeling weak. She would have to hear the story pieced together and regurgitated by Mrs Cleat to half of Leyton, to witness her embellishments and emphases, finely tuned to the tastes and opinions of each customer. It might not have occurred to Mrs Cleat, as it had to Connie, that if indeed the story was true, the Onorati boy couldn't understand the label on the tin and had bought the meat by mistake, on the basis of price alone. But such an explanation would not concern Mrs Cleat, who knew that it was sensation, not sympathy, that kept half her customers coming into her shop.

By the time spring was nearly done and the light lingered up on Bythorn Rise, Connie had become familiar with those parts of the farm where the Onorati brothers could most often be seen.

She began to suspect that the taller of the two boys also looked out for her, so often did she find him at some occupation — or none at all, as if waiting there in the late afternoons.

One protractedly grey day after work, she rounded the corner of Repton's as the sun finally broke the blank sky. The light had that renewed quality of dawn about it, and as she got off her bike, she held up her face, enjoying its meagre heat on her skin, the goosebumps it raised on her forearms. When she opened her eyes again, he was standing two steps away, on the other side of her bicycle. She flinched, and the shudder of the handlebars made the bell ting, a lingering, artificial sound among the hum and purr of insects in the grass before the hedgerow. She tried to arrange the expression on her face, not wanting to appear shocked, but he had already backed away from her.

'It's alright,' she said. Then, not knowing what else to say, she blurted a stiff 'Hello.' He didn't answer, and she was wondering whether she should get back on her bike when he nodded and reached to open the gate. From over his shoulder, he motioned to her: a downward scooping gesture, almost the opposite of beckoning, but clearly intending her to follow.

She wasn't sure. She wasn't sure about him or what he might want with her, so she hesitated. He stood patiently at the gate, and in his face she saw no flirtation or playfulness, no assumption or judgement in the making, just a child-like invitation to see what he had to show.

She let her bike fall into the verge and walked towards him. He looked down at her shoes, her ugly practical lace-ups, and as she grabbed the gate from him he pointed at a pair of wellies sitting behind the post. Had he planned it all then, this meeting? She didn't know whether to feel flattered or alarmed. Such a strange thing to do: to think about her shoes in the mud of the bridle path. His own boots were caked with fresh clods layered upon the dried. She couldn't imagine any of the village boys thinking of such a thing. Everyone had muddy shoes in Leyton, except perhaps Agnes. She left her lace-ups in the grass and followed him, slipping around at first, until she got her feel for the oversized boots. He led her along the emerald wheat, up around the rise to a field left fallow. They were closer now to the outbuildings of Repton's farm: the two chicken barns to their right and the gamekeeper's cottage backing onto the spinney to their left, before it the gentle rise of another paddock, where Repton's horse grazed lazily.

Halfway along the hedgerow, the boy dropped to his haunches. Instinctively she copied him, like they were playing a game, and as she did he reached out towards the maythorn laden with blossoms and nudged back a jagged branch with the cuff of his shirt. The petals released a faint cherry scent as they fell like snow across their feet.

Deep inside the hollow of the hedge was a nest, neat and tight, with four brown eggs. A fifth, in the centre, was broken, the wet blue chick recently emerged. She couldn't help catching her breath even though she had run wild in the spinneys and hedgerows, had prodded and plundered a hundred nests growing up. But this act of discovery was so simple, so long forgotten, that it took her by surprise. With a dirty wrist, the boy pushed back his hair. It inched again to the bridge of his nose, so luxurious in its sheen that she felt the urge to touch it, as she had the eggs in their nests as a child. She watched the way he drank everything in: the spectacle of the newly hatched chick; the precision of the nest; the twitching female on her stump, sending out her creaking alarm; the dull, self-contained eggs. There didn't seem any need to speak, to disturb something already perfect. So they stayed quiet, until the bird gathered the courage to hop in increments back to the nest and dance on its edge, ruffling her wings.

He let the branches fall back and they stood facing each other in the hedgebank. As she tried to think of what she might say to him, something he might understand, she felt rain on her face, and saw the grey that had re-formed across the evening sky. He led her back to her bike, both of them slipping in their haste as the rain became heavier and the mud of the bridle path got wetter. She reached the gate, where her shoes should have been, but she could not find them in the drooping grass. The downpour became a pelting mist as she searched, and it was only when she felt something cover her back that she realised he had gone to her bike and retrieved her mac. She pulled it over her head and finally threw the hateful shoes into her basket.

On the road, she stood in her muddy stockinged feet, her bike against her hip, the hood of the mac dripping before her. 'Thank you,' she pointed back towards the bridle path, 'for showing me the thrush's nest.' She articulated the words. He held his soaked hair back against his head and, despite the rain, considered her slowly. The skin of his forehead shone.

'It's a nightingale,' he said.

She opened her mouth to speak, but he continued, 'It will go soon.' He squinted at the dull sky, like he was searching for something. 'To the sun … to Africa.'

She felt ridiculous standing shoeless in the rain before him, understanding now that his silence all along had been from choice, not necessity. She hurried onto her bike, but hesitated, giving him the opportunity to speak again. When he didn't, she pedalled off without saying goodbye.

At the top of Bythorn Rise she stopped and glanced back. He was sitting on the gate, following her progress up the hill, still unconcerned about the rain. He might have always been sitting there, like some owl on the barn gable at dusk, unnoticed and all-seeing, shifting to the measure of his own, instinctive clock. She thought about his careful English, accented but not laboured, and her naive assumptions. She had equated his silence, his foreignness, with a kind of stupidity, as Mrs Cleat or Aunty Bea would have done. Of course the bird was a nightingale. He must think her dim, not knowing the common birds of the hedgerow that bounded her in on every side. She vaguely remembered a lesson where Mr Gilbert had traced their migratory patterns on the world map. 'From Leyton to London fifteen times over,' he had told them, and she had been filled with awe imagining a bird's-eye view of a vast London, not even able to picture a world that lay fifteen times beyond that.

She cycled over the crest of the hill but dismounted, bringing her bike around. She wanted to see if he was still there. She felt petty and ungrateful now and thought she should wave to him. But when she got back to the top of the rise, the gate was empty and he was nowhere to be seen, as if, with the calling crows, he had taken flight over the brooding spinney. She hadn't even asked his name.

Montelupini
1939

Lucio squatted on the battlement walls, studying the changeover from dusk to dark. In a few blinks, the colours of the mountains all around him would submerge, the blue of night pooling up from the valley. Far down the range, the rooftops of Gavignano, grafted on the hill, caught the last light and glimmered like a spun coin. It always made him wonder whether Montelupini was ever so dazzling at sunset, but he had never been far enough away to look back and see. The moon began to show him the details of night-time in the village: the huddle of mules stirring on the campo, the cat with the broken tail stalking the washhouse roof, a bat's shadow on the cobbles of Via del Soccorso.

Below him, at the Osteria Nettuno, the men were drinking and cursing at scopa. Through the beams of the pergola, he could make out the tops of caps, the pates of heads shining under the single bulb, the coins and cards tossed among the glasses.

'She's a beauty, my Valeriana. Purest Roman blood, see. No dross mixed in.' The voice of Urso, the butcher, was always the easiest to single out. Its bass was deep and hummed like a well. Lucio could see the spread of his colossal hands, the cards dwarfed inside them. 'I knew she'd give fine babies. But this bitch of a hand! Ma, que bruta!' He palmed the table.

The talk stopped and the play began. Cards were scooped and flipped in quick succession, until a round of groans rose into the night, cut with the growl of the butcher's victory. Lucio loved Urso's laugh, with its weight of cigarettes; the way he could feel it rumble inside him, like logs down the hillside. And he liked the butcher to win at scopa, especially when he played against his father.

'Nine of them, there were. Nine puppies, straight out, no fuss. Afterwards she looks at me, proud as if she was suckling Romulus and Remus themselves! Didn't you, my beauty?' Urso's hand went to the ears of the great hunting dog at his side, who answered by resting her head on his thigh. There was a shuffling of the deck and of feet beneath the table. Someone hocked noisily, and Lucio saw it arc towards the open drain.

'So, Urso, tell us about the puppies,' a voice drawled. 'Do they look like you?' There were sniggers and wheezes, the dull applause of shoulders and legs being clapped. It was Lucio's grandfather, the grappa already bolstering his voice. Lucio knew that, later, it would turn on Nonno Raimondi and have the last laugh, that his grandfather would be witless and blind as a whelp himself, mewling and puking in the gutter. And Lucio would have to help him home.

'Go on and enjoy yourselves, why don't you?' Urso said. 'But any good hunter can see she's a cane corso, like in the picture.' He raised his knee to make the dog sit tall, as in the bookplate of a Roman hunting scene he had framed behind the counter of his shop. 'Il Duce himself would be proud to have such a beast by his side.' He always said this when he was teased for indulging the dog, but Lucio thought it might be true. Next to the rangy curs chained to vineyards all around Montelupini, Valeriana was a gladiator among dogs. 'You only have to look at her to know the blood of Caesar's boarhounds flows in her veins.'

'Beh! And the blood of the Medici masters flows in mine,' Nonno Raimondi slurred, 'but it doesn't make me Botticelli.'

'You have to admit, though, the dog is like the one in the drawing,' Fagiolo, the innkeeper, called from the bar inside. 'Noble jaw on her.'

'Noble, my cock. Still shits in the street, doesn't she?' Nonno Raimondi was beginning to chew and drool over the words as if through a mouthful of torrone. 'Damn what the beast looks like! What does it do?'

'*Do?*' Urso said. 'What does any dog do?'

'Everyone in my family has to earn their dinner.' Nonno Raimondi belched melodiously.

'And most of yours too, it seems, old man.'

The osteria fell quiet. Lucio felt the brittle chill of his father's voice in his bones, like a winter wind off the eastern ranges. His words always carved a silence in the bar and seemed to hang alone in the night air. In the hush, Lucio heard Nonno Raimondi snorting back phlegm and shuffling to the bar to stew.

'Perhaps what my father-in-law meant to ask, Urso, was when the dog will be back at work again?'

'Back hunting, you mean?'

His father didn't answer. In the distant orchards of the Vigna Nuova a faint clang sounded, like chain links against a metal trough, and high up on the slopes of Montemezzo, Lucio thought he heard a wolf's bark.

Before she fell pregnant, he would spot Urso and Valeriana climbing up Via del Soccorso at sunrise with a kill: badger and rabbit, mainly; sometimes squirrel, which looked like rats when skinned and hanging in the window of the butcher's shop. Now and again there was a young boar laid out on the counter, which would stop the jokes at the bar for a while. But since the puppies, Valeriana had been out of action, and Urso's coddling of the dog had provided too much new material when the scopa hands were dull.

'Santa Lucia, what are you going to do with nine puppies?' Fagiolo asked, clearing the empty glasses from the table. 'I've got a big sack and a barrel of rainwater if you need them.'

Urso ignored the sniggers. 'I'll have to sell them.' He seemed regretful, but added, 'Cane corso fetch a good price at the Monteferro markets.'

'What kind of price?' Nonno Raimondi called through the open doors.

'More than you've got, Barilotto. Especially after that hand!' Urso swept the coins towards him. 'I'll keep one of them to make a hunting pair.' He paused, and through the pergola Lucio saw him glance uncertainly at his father. 'Actually, Capo, I promised one to your eldest boy.'

Lucio held his breath. He shifted along the wall so he could get a better view of the two men. Urso had let him handle the puppies at the back of the shop every day since they had been born, but the butcher had never said anything about giving him one. He understood now: Urso was speaking up for him, seeking the permission that Lucio would never dare ask of his father.

'What d'you say, Capo? Your Gufo could use a dog, eh?'

His father reached for his glass and drained it.

'What d'you think?' Urso asked again, more timidly now.

'What do I think?' His father's voice was flat, with that ominous tone he used to make people question themselves.

'Well, what would I know?' Urso shrugged and fanned the cards open and shut in his ruddy hands. 'It's just that he came by this morning before school. I'd asked him to make a likeness of Valeriana for me. You know what a skill he has with the pencil. You should see the picture he drew! I'm going to hang it in the shop.' He squeezed his fingers together and shook them upwards. 'A puppy, Capo, what's a boy without a puppy, I ask you?' The butcher was talking too fast. He laughed, but Lucio heard no rumble in it this time. There was only his father's silence and the scrape of chairs against the flagstones.

The two figures that emerged from the pergola stood under the streetlight before the entrance to Vicolo Giotto. His father seemed no more than a boy next to the butcher's bulk.

'I saw the lad with one of the pups, Capo,' Urso explained. 'It drew him out a bit, you know, put some sparkle in his eyes.' He waited for an answer. When it didn't come he breathed, '*Madosca*, you said yourself, the boy needs to come out of his shell.'

'And this runt is going to teach him to open his mouth more, to join in, make friends?' Lucio imagined the stiffness in his father's lips when he said one thing and meant another.

'Maybe,' Urso said feebly.

His father held his hands behind his back and squared himself to the butcher. 'Urso, we've had our recall papers for a reason. Albania's just the beginning. In a few months we could be in the colonies — pushing through Africa, even. War is coming, it's just a question of when Il Duce sees fit. And then who knows when we'll be back? That boy needs to grow up, be responsible for planting grain, bringing in fruit. He doesn't need to waste time on a puppy. You think scribbling his pretty pictures is going to help him put food on the table?'

'He's got a gift for it, is all. Like his grandfather.'

'A gift? Like Barilotto?' Lucio could see his father nodding slowly, but his voice was as tight as a wire. 'And that's what I should encourage, is it? Half-finished murals and blurred effigies all through the mountains? Spending all he earns on *models* and only ever bringing home the clap?' He flicked his head back towards the bar, where a liquid voice very much like Nonno Raimondi's had begun singing a stornello. 'Barilotto's gift is to turn everything to drink. And he even pisses that away at the end of the night.'

Urso cleared his throat and scratched at the back of his head. 'Understood,' he said. 'Understood.'

His father had this sway over men, twisting their intentions with his words, moulding them to his own purpose. They said he'd earned his nickname, Capo, the chief, as a boy; and even before he became the Fascist commissioner, everyone in the village — including Professore Centini, the mayor — went to him for advice.

'Listen, Urso,' his father said, his tone relenting. 'You want to give that boy something? Take him hunting. Show him some of the skill of it. That's what he needs.'

'Gufo on the hunt? You mean the courses up at Montemezzo?' His father didn't answer. Urso wiped a palm across his mouth. 'It's a bit early for boar hunting. They're still breeding, you know.' He seemed to fidget under his father's gaze. 'And the boy's still young. You sure he has the stomach for it? Gufo's … well, Gufo's the owl, isn't he? He's a loner, a watcher — those eyes of his taking everything to heart, you know? Now that Primo of yours, he's a different cut entirely. I can see him with a pike or a skinning knife.'

'Lucio's the eldest. He's eleven and it's time he acted like it. An owl doesn't just observe, Urso.' His father brought the back of one hand down onto the palm of the other, and the sound slapped against the battlement walls. 'It strikes.' Lucio saw his pale face tilt up to the lookouts. 'The boy needs to start earning that name.'

They began the climb up Montemezzo before sunrise. The first rays broke over the mountains, casting the woods first in silver and then in gold. A honeyed haze lingered in the trees and promised heat. 'Bastard horseflies up at the lake can bite like demons, even in autumn,' Urso complained. 'Best to be getting back before midday.' He glanced at Valeriana as he said this, and Lucio could tell he was thinking of the dog's hungry puppies, not horseflies. She darted between them as they walked the mule track, disappearing into the tall grass at its edge and emerging further ahead, all the while softly whining, her dugs swinging heavy underneath her. He wondered whether she was excited to return to the mountain, or fretting at leaving her babies so soon. Every so often she froze mid-step, her body cleaving the breeze, her nose wet, a shudder rippling through her sleek skin.

Urso clicked his tongue to her as he walked. He wore his corduroy hunting jacket, baggy and crudely sewn with leather patches at the elbows. Its pockets bulged and swung to the measure of his stride, and Lucio puzzled at their weight. His father was next, carrying a canvas bag of the butcher's slung across his back and strapped with a leather belt to keep its contents from rattling. From its top, a short section of rope had escaped, and it danced behind his shoulder as he walked. Lucio studied its russet patina, shiny from use, mulling on the inside of his lip until he could taste the blood in his mouth.

Valeriana crossed his path and stopped to sniff again the way they had come. 'Cammina. Forza, su!' the butcher coaxed, but when Lucio glanced up, Urso's eyes were not on his dog. They were on him. Lucio snatched his gaze away. It might have been easier if he hadn't liked the butcher so much. But he did: he liked the way Urso beckoned him into the shop to thrust a slice of guanciale in his mouth; the way his great jaw went slack as Lucio sketched the puppies; or how he grunted his satisfaction at the runt of Valeriana's litter burrowing with translucent claws to suckle beside the others. Lucio couldn't bear to disappoint his small, unspoken encouragements. But now, with his father there, he could feel his own failure before he had even begun. He felt it hanging over him even more than when he stood in line with the Balilla scouts at drill in the piazza. Boy by boy, battle by battle, they would shout out the chronology of Italy's military victories, and his father's attention would always hover somewhere nearby, restless, as Lucio stood mute, clawing a hole in the pocket of his uniform. It was even worse now, because at drill Primo was always there to yell over the void of him, appeasing their father with the jut of his chin. Urso was right. His brother should have been the one to come. Primo would have kept pace with the butcher up the mule track, asking all the right questions, discussing the lay of the grounds, what weapons they would choose. It was Primo who should have been there. They all knew it. Especially his father.

When they reached the plateau of Montemezzo, the chestnuts were tall and dense with yellowing leaves and fruit. They stood for a while, breathing hard from the climb. Lucio could taste the sweet rot of the forest on his tongue, the smell of autumn that had already arrived on the mountain. In the clearing they rested on a tumble of boulders, green with mosses and lichens. He expected they would take the path that sloped down to the lake and the tangled glades of the woods beyond. But instead they headed along the ridge, to the chain of caves where the grotto of Santa Lucia dei Boschi was set into the mountainside.

'She has the best view in the Lepini,' Urso murmured, nudging his head towards the saint in her chapel behind them.

Lucio stood next to him on the rocky outcrop, taking in the valley shaken out before them. Far below, the walls and rooftops of Montelupini seemed cold and strangely spent, cobbled as they were between the wooded hills that were beginning to glow like embers with the change of season. Even Valeriana was quiet, as if she too understood the sad majesty of summer's passing.

Lucio charted the year from this spot. In spring, he would escape the gangs of children playing football on the campo and climb there to trace falcons or griffons wheeling their lazy circles below him. The air was sharp then, the valley hard and clean as a pencil line, so clear he could see a shed feather if it spiralled down the range. In winter he came here to see the first snows, the mists swallowing up the village below, so that all he could hear were its muted mechanics: a discordant cowbell, the tick of a saw, the tock of an axe.

His father was rattling at the lock of the chapel grille behind them. 'Padre Ruggiero gave me a key,' he said. 'We'll ask a blessing for the hunt.' He motioned Lucio to follow him into the damp air of the cave, their steps echoing in the empty chamber. It felt odd to enter the chapel in the daylight, the hymns and candles and prayers of a hundred people replaced by the murmur of the woods. He'd only ever been inside at midnight, for the Saint's Mass in December. He would line up then with the rest of the village in the frozen night to kiss the feet of Santa Lucia and take communion from Padre Ruggiero. His father always led the procession, one of the litter-bearers honoured with taking the effigy back down the mountain to her winter home in San Pietro's.

The saint's statue stood at shoulder height. It was recessed into the rendered wall, the dim light through the gate catching the gold of her diadem. It glinted like hidden treasure, which

Nonno Raimondi told him it would easily have become, had the villagers not hung the grille across the grotto's entrance in the days when the caves were the hideouts of highwaymen. Lucio watched his father take a box of matches from his pocket and light two candles on the altar. He kissed the foot of the saint and settled into a pew. Lucio fell in line behind him.

He had been born on the saint's name day. His father often reminded him of it, as if that was at least one thing in his favour. No one in Montelupini doubted the special protection that Santa Lucia dei Boschi granted the village. On Sundays, the nuns taught every child how the Duke of Alba, at war with Pope Paul IV, sacked each town in the Lepini mountains, but could not conquer Montelupini's citadel, thanks to the Lady of Light. And during the great drought, when wells and washhouses through-out Lazio dried up, the spring below Lucia's grotto continued its determined drip, snaking through the mountain to feed the Fontana Nuova far below. Every family in Montelupini had a personal story of her intercession: children saved from malaria, marriages saved from infidelities, wine saved from souring.

But Lucio's love of the saint had always been material, not religious. He loved her because she was unlike all the other statues of sallow saints in the neighbouring churches, the pained Madonnas in their blue-and-white robes, languidly proffering the Christ Child. There was something human to their Santa Lucia: he felt it in the auburn curl of hair at her throat; the flesh tones of her cheeks and lips; even in her shawls, which fell in folds of burned orange, like real silk, about her feet. She was subtle and complex, and he saw in her the hand of an artist who loved man more than he feared God. To Lucio, that made her special enough.

They said every village had its sceptic, and his grandfather was more than happy to fill that role for Montelupini. 'Up your arse with Lucia,' Nonno Raimondi would slur whenever the saint's protection was invoked. 'This village is the shithole of Lazio, the thunderbox of Italy. That's why nothing comes here. *That's* what protects us,' he would call, raising his glass to the women gathered on the steps of San Pietro's with their candles and rosaries. 'Porca troia, Montelupini's so dull even the Spanish flu gave it a miss!'

Rumour had it that Lucia's grotto had been the undoing of Nonno Raimondi. The mural behind the effigy remained his last, unfinished work, tormenting him even now. Lucio studied the sketched-in lines of the temple at Syracuse, the partially painted tomb of Sant'Agata, the host of incomplete cherubs. The villagers claimed it was the saint's doing: Barilotto could never get the mural right because Lucia didn't want a drunk blasphemer working on her chapel. But whenever Lucio came close to the statue he could understand his grandfather's impotence. How could Nonno Raimondi's work live up to the mastery of it, drunk or sober?

His father muttered and sighed in the pew before him. Dead leaves had scuttled through the grille to rest in the aisle. Outside, Lucio could hear Urso and Valeriana, whose whines were growing with impatience. He felt he should pray: he needed the saint's help now more than ever, but he was not good at asking in the clenched, fraught way of his father, whose fervid mouthings seemed more like he was locked in mortal combat with God than asking for a blessing. Urso had simply touched the foot of the effigy, crossed himself and gone back to his dog. 'Yes, my beauty. I know. Yes, yes,' he could hear the butcher reassuring her in his throaty way. 'I'm going to miss you too.'

His words seemed to hover at the door of the grotto, like wasps circling before diving in for their attack, driving home to Lucio the real purpose of this detour to the mountain chapel, to the saint of his birth. His father wasn't asking a blessing for the hunt. He was praying for the coming war and for his son, for Lucio, to fill his boots and to step up to the mark while he was away. He wanted to tell his father he could do it, take care of the family, take care of everything, when he was gone. But the air in the chapel felt suddenly thin and insufficient, and he had to step away and find the warmth of the sun.

The light that bounced from the rocks outside made him squint. Urso had laid out the contents of his pockets and the canvas bag. There were two heavy knives with grooved bone handles, not unlike the ones on the butcher's worn chopping block. There were several coils of dirty rope, and two thicker blades each affixed to lengths of pole, making a kind of pike. Urso reached for one of these and went down on his knee before Lucio. 'Now, Gufo, courage! Your weapon, sir.' He shoved the spear into Lucio's hand, searched his face, and then laughed heartily. 'Don't look so worried, boy,' he whispered. 'Valeriana does most of the work. She'll sniff out a dozy spinosa or badger for us, and you can finish it off with your pike. Alright? Forza!'

Urso reached for the other spear and handed it to Lucio's father as he emerged from the chapel. 'Set?'

He nodded. 'In the mouth of the wolf!'

Urso grinned and finished off the saying for good luck: 'And may the wolf drop dead!' The starlings in the trees screeched at his growl. He clicked to his dog and set off at a pace Lucio hadn't thought him capable of.

They worked their way deeper into the wood with its rises and dells, its briars and fallen trees to be negotiated. Even his father seemed to struggle to keep up with the butcher's large and practised strides, as good as noiseless as he tracked Valeriana's tail forging ahead of them through the under-growth. Her whining had stopped: an expectant silence had descended on both the dog and her master. Lucio listened to the faint workings of the forest.

Without warning, Valeriana sprang into the ferns and vanished. For several minutes none of them moved. The only sound was the groaning of the trees, the distant chime of birdsong. Uncertain, Lucio kept Urso in his sights. With a jut of his chin, the butcher signalled the dog's whereabouts and cocked his head. As if at some secret signal, he started to run, coming to an abrupt stop at a tangled thicket of holly and young hornbeams. Valeriana had begun a fierce baying, and alongside it they could pick out the angry grunts and squeals of some cornered beast. Urso lifted his stick to thrash through the scrub, but the two animals burst forth, a young boar bolting towards them with Valeriana clamped to its ear. Lucio caught the flash of her bared teeth and the newly ruptured tusks of the boar. Within seconds she had it down, her massive hind legs firing the barrel of her body, so that he understood for the first time what she had been bred for.

'Get here!' his father shouted from Urso's side.

The butcher was bent over Valeriana, her tail in his fist, struggling to hold her back. 'Now or never, Gufo. I can't keep her from its throat for long,' Urso called. 'Forza! Su!'

It was the dream of running with legs of lead. Or the slowing of time so that all the details of a second pass as minutes. He was no more able to move than one of the giant chestnuts rooted all around him. He could hear the blood coursing in his ears, felt the pulse of it in his tongue. The faces of Urso and his father, flushed with adrenalin, glanced up at him and back at the boar, and he saw the disappointment gathering at their mouths.

When he finally reached them, the animal was panting and pumping blood from its belly where his father had driven his pike, pinning it to the ground. He circled Lucio now with slow, deliberate steps and raised his hand. Lucio flinched, but the blow didn't come. Instead his father reached for the spear and tugged it from the boar. Its scream caught Lucio like a fist to the stomach. He saw his father's clamped teeth, heard his animal grunt as, in one fluid stroke, he pulled the head of the beast against his thigh and drew a deep slit across its throat with Urso's skinning knife. The boar's blood let over the leaf litter of the forest floor and slapped across Lucio's boots.

Valeriana's whines were all that was left of the confusion. Urso kneeled over her where she had fallen, trying to stem a gash in her side. He kept up a constant murmur as his hands worked over the dog. 'Come on, my beauty. Up, up ... you've had worse than this. It's only a scratch from some angry little squire ... Up, now, up!' He pressed at the dog's torn belly with the canvas bag as if the wound was no more than a graze.

'Urso.' His father's voice was low. 'Move away.'

'No. It's not like that,' the butcher said. 'It's not like that, Capo.'

'Paolo, come away.'

It was the first time Lucio had heard the butcher's real name. And he knew then what his father was going to do.

'Go with the boy. Go tie the boar to the spears.'

Lucio looked at Urso. His cheeks seemed redder, the veins about his nose more broken when wet. His father told him to lead the butcher away from the dog, but instead he stood next to him and waited while he stared down at Valeriana. Eventually he pressed his fingers inside the great hook of the butcher's hand, hanging limp at his side.

'Gufo?' Urso said, as if he had forgotten all about him.

They turned away to the dead boar and Urso set upon it with a vengeance, binding its legs around the pikes with ropes so tight they broke the animal's skin. He knotted and yanked and knotted until they heard the short, high whine of Valeriana. The butcher fell still. A crow's caw ripped through the silence.

His father called and Lucio went to the tree where he stood, the dog's collar dangling from his hand. 'You and I will carry the boar down the mountain. You can manage that at least, can't you, boy?' He nodded, but his father had already stepped away, towards Urso and the boar.

Lucio forced himself to look down at Valeriana. The innards that peeped from the gash in her belly were glossy, seething like they were still alive. He thought of her head on Urso's lap in the osteria and considered it now, its jaw askew. He took off his jacket, laid it on the ground and pulled the dog onto it, tying the sleeves about her until her torn and bloody teats were hidden.

The trek home was laborious, with the boar hanging between them on the spears. On the flat he took most of its weight, being shorter than his father, but the struggle gave him some distraction from his thoughts. Urso trailed behind them, Valeriana laid across his shoulders, like quarry. They didn't speak until they reached the Viale Roma. There they parted ways, Urso going down to his allotment on the road to Monteferro, where Lucio imagined he would bury the dog. Lucio wanted to go with him, but his father and the butcher had already clasped fingers in a wordless farewell.

As they were climbing Via del Soccorso his father said to him, 'You think it covered your shame, giving your jacket to a dead dog?'

Lucio didn't answer.

'Perhaps when you have it back you can tell me whether the dog's blood is easier to wear than the boar's?' His father spat into the chalk of the road.

The beast swung between them. Lucio thought of Valeriana

on Urso's shoulders, her glassy eye and greying tongue. And he thought of his bloody jacket holding together her swollen dugs, full of milk for her puppies. It wasn't his shame he had most wanted to spare. It was Urso's.

Leyton
1949

Halfway through summer, Mrs Cleat had begun to leave Connie to tend the shop alone on Tuesday afternoons. The Leyton and Parishes Christian Ladies' League had been fund-raising since VE Day and were now in heated discussion with the Parochial Church Council over the status of what some considered a rather avant-garde mural scheme for St Margaret's Village Church. The idea of not having a say in such a controversial legacy to posterity, such decisions of high art and donor signage, terrified Mrs Cleat considerably more than leaving Connie in sole charge of her livelihood. Standing on the customer side of the counter in her hat and gloves, Mrs Cleat talked Connie through every emergency that might befall a Tuesday afternoon's trading. 'Now remember that catch on the meat slicer, Connie. I don't want blood all over my new Formica ... and keep a lookout for them didicoy ... Mrs Watt says she seen caravans up at Buckworth Wold and they're on the march with forged coupons, no less. Mind what I told you now. If in doubt —'

'— throw them out. Yes, Mrs Cleat, I remember,' Connie said in a grave voice. She had never once seen a gypsy shopping for groceries in the high street, or a forged coupon for that matter, and it amused her that the coupling of both rarities was the height of criminal masterminding in Mrs Cleat's head. The shopkeeper appraised her for a moment, her nose cocked upwards as if irony was something that could be smelled, like milk on the turn. Finally her attention flicked to the clock, and with a start she gathered herself together and hurried off to meet Aunty Bea in the memorial hall.

Connie let out a deep breath. These afternoons of independence had become like oases in the desert of her days. She could silence the bell and have the door wide open to the insects and the pollen-filled afternoon; she could hang up her white coat and serve at the counter with a tea towel tied about her waist and her hair free of its net; she could chat to the old Misses Penny, secretly slipping in whole biscuits and newly opened leaf tea among the barrel remnants and sack dust that Mrs Cleat offloaded to them *on special*. These short hours she felt as though she was breathing air into the corners of herself, that her existence might not be as paper thin as she had grown to believe. Inevitably there were consequences to pay on Mrs Cleat's return, but even they were worth the brief time she spent alone, exerting the addictive pleasure of her own will.

She was not the only person to enjoy the Christian Ladies' mural meetings. Mr Gilbert now collected his groceries in the hour between the school bell and Mrs Cleat's return. Connie dealt with the after-school flurry of children with hot pennies and coupons from their mothers, and in the lull that followed began to pre-empt Mr Gilbert's needs, navigating her way around his tastes and his ration book.

'New Government Cheddar in today. I've kept you the first cut. You might have it for your tea,' she called to him from her ladder behind the counter, having heard his greeting at the door. 'I've got your Branston, too, and some flour and tea.' She had her back to him and an arm reaching into the dim recesses of an upper shelf. 'And shoe polish … there, light brown.' With some effort she freed the tin from above the cartons and packets, and waved it triumphantly over her shoulder. 'Should match your Logues. I knew we had that colour somewhere.'

'Do you see,' she heard Mr Gilbert say, 'how she looks after me? And what attention to detail! Had you even noticed my shoes were tan … and rather worse for wear?'

He laughed and she turned her head, aware that they were not alone. One of the Italians was with him: the shorter, leaner of the two brothers. He stood behind the counter, his hands in his trouser pockets — almost brazenly, she thought, like he had been coming into Cleat's all his life. She saw his gaze travelling up her legs on the ladder, resting on the run in her stocking that she had stopped with nail varnish and tried to position under the hem of her skirt. She hurried down and felt the need to put on her white coat. When she had finished busying herself with its buttons, the Italian was still scrutinising her, without apology. He seemed mildly amused. She noticed his skin was golden and glossy as a nut.

Mr Gilbert waved a hand between them. 'Vittorio, this is —'

'The girl with the bicicletta … on the hill.' He brought a hand from his pocket and clenched it around an imaginary handlebar, whistling through his teeth.

'And you're the whistler,' Connie said. She started to dust off the scale, before feeling like Mrs Cleat and stopping herself.

'Oh good, you've met already,' Mr Gilbert said matter-of-factly, and he clapped the boy on the back, grinning. 'Splendid.'

The Italian tilted his head to the side. 'Victor Onorati,' he said. 'My name is Vic.'

'Oh, that's right. No Italian. He wants no Italian. *Everyting Inglish, Inglish,*' Mr Gilbert mimicked. His hand lingered on the boy's shoulder as they laughed, and their complicity caused a pang in Connie's stomach, like hunger, but for what she did not know.

'Vittorio here has come bearing gifts. We thought you might like to share them with us. Come for tea at the schoolhouse?'

'Me?' she said, and felt immediately stupid for it.

'Why not you? Vittorio keeps saying he deserves someone prettier than me to practise his English on, isn't that right, *Vic*?' The boy seemed unashamed at the comment, whether it was true or not. 'Come on, Connie. It will do you good,' Mr Gilbert said.

She sensed her neck and cheeks becoming hot. It wasn't just the compliment or the unexpected invitation. It was the Italian's composure, as if he already knew the outcome of this meeting and was interested simply in the manner in which it would unfold. She thought of the few village boys his age who came into the shop, often in pairs, their chummy bravado as they made a show of ignoring her while browsing the shelves, before buying what they always bought: five Woodbines or a tube of shaving soap. It felt seductive to be looked at so directly, to be examined quite patently as something desirable and worthy of attention. Before she had even thought through what would happen if she got home late without telling Aunty Bea, she found herself nodding.

'Excellent, then,' Mr Gilbert said, and began to collect the bags from the counter, thrusting them one after the other into his student's chest. 'Come along, Vittorio. If you seriously intend to become a Vic you're going to have to stop all that staring. It won't do around here, old boy — making the girls blush to their bobby pins.' He squeezed Vittorio behind the neck and she watched them leaving, waiting for Mr Gilbert to lift his hat at her through the bay window. But he passed distractedly, steering the boy by his shoulder, and Connie noticed an ease, a physical affability that she had never seen between two men walking on the streets of Leyton until then. A liveliness had settled in Mr Gilbert's manner, a brightness in his face that had not been there before, and for the first time she could see the man he might have been fifteen or twenty years ago, the man he might have been at her own age. She found herself curious about this change the Italian boy had effected in him, but she now understood the rankling in her stomach was not jealousy. It was apprehension. Staring through the bull's-eye pane in the shop window, she sensed something shift, some tiny fracture — as if she was at the centre of a kaleidoscope, and everything about her was on the cusp of something new.

Even without the invitation to tea at the schoolhouse, the hour between Mrs Cleat's return and closing time on a Tuesday was always the longest of the week for Connie. Mrs Cleat atoned for her sin of leaving the shop by having Connie perform penance on her behalf. This took the form of camphor-sprinkling, chalkboard-blacking, potato-sorting, and any other creative shop maintenance Mrs Cleat could devise to keep Connie busy, while giving her a blow-by-blow account of the battle for high art fought over teacups in the church hall.

When Mrs Cleat finally released her, wearing half the dirt of that morning's potato delivery, she felt she was tumbling into the schoolhouse like one of the grubby-mouthed lane kids. She stood on Mr Gilbert's doorstep, feeling ordinary, regretting her timid knock but too afraid to leave for fear she'd already been spotted through the half-open door. She heard voices, an air of tension from deep inside. Something slammed.

She backed down from the threshold, but as she hesitated, the door swung wide in the breeze and she saw straight down the corridor to the kitchen, where Mr Gilbert was hovering over a figure seated at his table. At first she thought it was Vittorio, until she saw the broader set of the shoulders, the coarser hair of the brother she had met in the rain at Repton's gate.

His head was thrown back, and a tea towel across his shoulder appeared to be stained with blood. Mr Gilbert glanced down the hallway as she was turning to leave. He hurried towards her, but instead of offering a greeting, he reached around and shut the front door. His jovial mood of that afternoon was gone and his face was pale.

'Should I go?' she asked.

'No,' he said. 'No, don't, Connie. I think it would be better if you stayed.'

In the kitchen, Connie saw Vittorio leaning against a dresser. He had a paring knife balanced in his hand, and he straightened and put it down as she came in. Across from him on the Aga range, something was frying, its fragrant steam tangible in the golden light of late afternoon. It might have thrilled her to discover Mr Gilbert's walled garden beyond the back door, which was open to the summer evening, or to find both Italians in the same room, among the unfamiliar aromas of the food. But the boy sitting at the table had his back to her, and as she came alongside him he stood so quickly that the chair fell behind him. Without picking it up, he strode away into the garden. Vittorio called to him in Italian, but his brother was silent, pacing the walls of espaliered fruit trees.

'Connie, sit down,' Mr Gilbert said. 'Talk to Vittorio for a minute.' He rummaged inside a kitchen cupboard and drew out an old Air Raid Precautions tin before grabbing a clean tea towel and stepping outside.

Vittorio had picked up the chair and was bending to clean something from the floor: it was a pool of broken eggs.

'Sorry,' he said. 'My brother …' He scooped the eggs and their shells into a cloth and juggled them, dripping, into the sink.

'What happened to him?' she asked.

He avoided her eye. His mood was so altered from their encounter in the shop that he was like another person. He took the frying pan from the Aga and lowered the lid back onto the plate. She waited.

'Nothing,' he said at last.

'It doesn't seem like nothing.'

He gave an empty laugh. 'Nothing. My brother does nothing and thinks too much. Me?' He muttered something in Italian under his breath. 'Me, maybe the other way round.'

Mr Gilbert's voice drifted in from the garden. '… stitches, yes … why ever not? … no, no … sit down …' She saw him bring the boy around on the grass, making him sit in a wicker chair arranged on the patio. His eyelid was nearly swollen shut, and there was dried blood around his nose, a split above his eyebrow and one in his lower lip, which he explored with the tip of his tongue. She looked back at Vittorio, but he was busy shuffling a wooden spatula into the contents of the pan.

'It's a waste, this eggs,' was all he said. 'Now it's too thin, the frittata. No good.' His lips came back to rest together, full as a girl's. He tilted the pan to show her. At the stove he began to slice through what appeared to be an omelette, but smelled like something else entirely. Around the kitchen counter were stalks of herbs and the skins of garlic, which she had seen listed in French recipes in *The Lady* but had never actually tasted. Next to the board lay the chopped remains of baby marrows, still firm and glossy green, and she wondered why they had been picked so soon. She couldn't remember the last time she had seen so many eggs in one pan. Aunty Bea wouldn't keep chickens because of her phobia about rats, and so they were stuck with their ration and the odd gift from neighbours, which was usually stretched into a batter or various bland and pasty puddings. She watched Vittorio at work in the kitchen, his hands quick and skilful in the orange light. She had never seen a man cooking before, and he seemed to her like some magical, slightly fractured version of his sex: the flawed character of a fairytale, fascinating but cryptic; or one of the Romanies she had once seen through the door of a vardo, scouring a pot, as she cycled past Penton Gorse.

'Who did that to your brother?' she asked.

'Lucio?' He spoke the name quietly, with a soft *sh* in the middle, as if he wanted to silence her.

'I'm sorry. It's really not any of my business,' she said.

He snorted. 'Of course your business. You want this bloody man at the table?' She wanted to smile, to explain the joke, but it didn't seem right when outside she could hear the low, fraught voice of Mr Gilbert as he tended to the boy's wounds.

'I don't think your brother expected me to be here, did he?' she asked.

'Lucio,' he shushed her again with the name. 'Always he's in the bad place, the bad time.'

He didn't offer anything more, so she edged towards the patio doors, intending to see if Mr Gilbert needed her help.

'He got in the way,' Vittorio said.

'Of what?'

He began getting plates down from the dresser. 'I wanted to give Mr Gilbert something, you understand? He never takes the money.'

'For your English lessons?'

He nodded. 'He say, *You cook for me. You cook me some Italian food, Vic. Is enough.* So I take some of the cracked eggs from Repton's barns. Hundreds of eggs we pack into the truck every day. Cracked ones, we send to the Big House. We never take and they never give.'

Connie had often seen the damaged eggs piled up in the stoneware bowl in Mrs Cartwright's kitchen at Leyton House. She also knew that those eggs didn't always end up in Mr Repton's afternoon teacake. Aunty Bea liked to say that Edi Cartwright would filch the Eucharist wine for the black market if she ever thought to go into a church

'We feed the chickens,' Vittorio continued, 'we clean the barns, we kill the rats, we pick the eggs. Even I see sometimes this Repton watching us — but never one single cracked egg he give to us. To him, my father is still prisoner.' His shoulders fell. 'In Italy, we had eggs … in England only this … this *dust.*' He motioned to the packet of powdered eggs on the counter.

They heard Mr Gilbert's voice again outside. 'I said sit down. Stay still.' Vittorio shook his head.

Connie tried to piece his story to the scene around her. 'Mr Repton didn't do that to your brother?' She was horrified at the thought.

'Repton?' Vittorio gave a short, disgusted laugh. 'Non ha i coglioni.'

She frowned. 'My father,' he went on. 'He see the eggs on our table. He think Lucio take them. *We must do everything right,* he says. *Everything right. No asking, no taking, just working …* working for this Repton until maybe we break our backs and drop in the mud.' His face had become closed as a fist. He turned to wash out the dishcloth in the sink.

Connie didn't know what to say and he kept his back to her, suggesting the conversation was over. She stepped outside uncertainly. 'Can I help, Mr Gilbert?' At once, the Italian jerked his head from the teacher's hands.

'Connie,' Mr Gilbert said, bringing the boy's face back towards him. 'I'm sorry about this mess.' She wasn't sure whether he meant the face or the ruined evening. 'Sorry you should have to meet young Lucio here in such a state. He needs a stitch or two, but there's no getting through to him.' He was applying iodine and gauze to the boy's split eyebrow, and he indicated for her to replace his fingers with her own, while he searched for a dressing that would fix it in place. 'Lucio, this is Connie Farrington. She works at Cleat's. I invited her over for a taste of Italy. This wasn't quite what I had in mind.'

They said no more while Mr Gilbert finished treating the cuts. She stood to Lucio's side, holding up the dressings and scissors, her arms obscuring his face. He still struggled with ragged breath, and his hands, spread wide over his thighs, were also cut and bloodied. The fine stubble of hair shorn at his neck was damp. She began to realise that even in circumstances other than these, he might not have acknowledged their meeting on Bythorn Rise. That afternoon now seemed contained and self-sufficient, completely unrelated to the shop or tea at the schoolhouse or seeing him sitting there on the patio, smelling of Dettol and sticking plaster. Even when Mr Gilbert was done, they looked away from each other, like they had a secret to guard.

Lucio stood up awkwardly, hovering about Mr Gilbert, and she felt compelled to return to the kitchen and give them some space. He spoke a few words to his teacher, but within minutes he was gone again, striding across the grass to a gate at the bottom of the garden. She saw him hesitate briefly on the threshold before slipping into the thickened light of the summer evening, which hung over the bridle path to Bythorn Rise. Behind him, the gate swung shut, and the handle clicked into its lock with a kind of inevitability that made her unaccountably sad.

Mr Gilbert seemed to sense it too, for Connie caught his troubled expression slackening with resignation. But by the time he had returned the ARP tin to the kitchen cupboard and washed his hands, he was jovially insisting on their planned dinner, fussing over napkins and glasses, avoiding any mention of what had occurred. He jabbered on about his time in Florence and Venice before the war, and Vittorio became more sullen and uncommunicative, retreating into his own thoughts the more Mr Gilbert talked. Connie imagined a different summer night from this, where she would have become heady on the fumes of the kitchen alone, set adrift between Mr Gilbert's stories and Vittorio's attentions. But that night had been eclipsed, and now all any of them wanted was for it to be over.

Finally Connie got up to leave. 'I have to,' she explained to Mr Gilbert. 'Aunty Bea —'

'Oh yes, Aunty Bea.' He winced in mock terror.

'No, really,' she said, laughing. 'She might have recalled the Home Guard to come and find me by now.'

On the doorstep, the evening air seemed to clear Vittorio's mood. 'Your bicicletta, it's at the shop?' he asked her. She nodded. 'I get it for you.' And before she could stop him, he had set off down the high street.

Mr Gilbert touched her arm. 'No. Let him go.' He had become serious, even unsure of himself. 'Connie, can you keep what happened tonight — to Lucio — between us? Mrs Cleat, you know …'

She was offended. 'You don't have to ask that.'

Mr Gilbert nodded his apology. 'He does it to protect Vittorio, I think. I suspect it isn't the first time. But you should understand that things have been difficult … complicated for them … and their father. You know, Connie, I don't believe in bad people, only bad circumstances. Do you see?'

He rubbed at his chin with his thumb. She was about to ask what he meant when he straightened. 'Ah,' he said, focusing beyond her in the direction of Cleat's.

Vittorio was riding her bicycle down the road, arms stiff and knees wide, teetering ridiculously, like a clown on a wire. As he gathered momentum, he began to make swooping curves, barely avoiding the wild verges on each side of the lane. At first she thought he was putting on a show. But when he reached the schoolhouse and she saw his frown, his bright cheeks, his open-mouthed concentration, she realised he was as serious, as determined, as any child.

'His first time, evidently,' Mr Gilbert said as Vittorio sailed past. She was mulling over his comment about circumstances, bad circumstances, and her own mother, her father, what she could remember of them.

'There's more to him than what you see, Connie.'

'Isn't that true of all of us?'

He looked at her properly, perhaps for the first time that evening. 'You really are an unusual young woman, you know. I'm not quite sure how you've managed to turn out that way, given —' He stopped. His eyes ran the length of the street. The deflected brilliance of the evening in the windows, the heightened chatter of birds in dusky gardens, did not quite mask the vague sense of curtains twitching. 'Well,' was all he said.

Vittorio returned, breathless, locking the brakes and jerking to a stop by the kerb of the schoolhouse. 'This bicicletta,' he called to them, lifting his leg over the bike frame and revealing the underside of his boot, a hole lined with newspaper at the toe. 'This Ro-yal En-field,' he articulated the bike's golden letters, shaking one of the handlebars as he appraised the racing green paintwork. 'How much you pay?'

Connie was torn between indignation and intrigue at his candour. It had taken her a year to save the four pounds and six shillings for the new bike. She'd had to squirrel away what was left of her wages after paying board to Aunty Bea, even keeping hold of her thruppences when the collection plate rattled past in church. And all the while, she would curse Uncle Jack's rusty old Raleigh, which slipped its chain and spat oil on her as she cycled to Cleat's, mortified by the wooden blocks he'd attached to the pedals because the seat was jammed at his height. She didn't know whether to feel sorry for the Italian or to laugh at the ease with which he thought he could come by such a bike. She wanted to impress upon him how long she had had to wait for this one token of freedom. But she only reached for the handlebar protectively.

He shrugged. 'I think I get one.' She opened her mouth, but when she looked from his cracked boots to his unfaltering eyes, she closed it again. He had such little doubt in himself, such guileless confidence, she almost believed him.

Connie rounded the corner of the rise, still engrossed with the events of the evening. At the crest of the hill, though, habit made her stop to look out at the gamekeeper's cottage. The sun had sunk below the clouds, and the barley and wheat rolling before her shivered in the breeze like the skin of some vast animal. She felt the shudder of it in her own skin and was about to cycle away when she caught sight of a figure at the edge of the spinney.

At first she thought it was Fossett, off to the Green Man after his rounds checking the young pheasants. But soon she made out the broad shoulders of Lucio Onorati, bent over, examining something in the rough before the trees. When he stood up, she saw in his outstretched fist an animal held by the hind legs. Squinting, she made out the sleek skin, the distended belly of Mrs Repton's pregnant Siamese. It twitched, like one length of overworked muscle, and the wind over the ridge teased its fur, the colour of fine sand, its darker undercoat glimpsed like a secret. She watched him run his free hand slowly upwards from the neck to the tail, and the cat seemed to settle. She thought of the press of spine under fur, the stretched sinew of its body, the green eyes glazing as they would when she stroked it. For an instant, the shape of them seemed one and the same to her, camouflaged by the silence and the fading light.

The cuff of his hand was quick and blunt, strangely un-surprising when it came. She imagined the muted crack of bone, like a twig under leaf litter when she walked in the spinney. He descended the fallow towards the brook, the cat limp across his back, nothing more than quarry now in one practised blow of his hand. She gripped at the handlebars of her bike, feeling disconnected somehow, as if she was the foreigner in her own world, not him. But after a while he was nothing more than a shadow, swallowed up by the huddle of sombre trees at the brook's edge.

Montelupini
1939

His mother sat cross-legged on the battlement wall, watching the piazza below. Lucio loved it when she climbed up and sat beside him, cross-legged, her skirts pulled into her lap like a girl. He loved it even when her fingers worried at the fabric of her hems and her lips were chalky and dry, her skin like wax in the glow of the coloured lanterns strung across the fountain. She was supposed to be in bed, resting, not climbing the walls of the old town barefoot at night to see the festival. But he knew that was precisely why she had done it. She rarely did what she was told, and she refused to indulge her illness or become a martyr to it, as so many women in the village liked to do with their own ailments. When she emerged from a seizure, Lucio could sense the physical relief in her, like the quenching of a desperate thirst after being trapped somewhere, scrambling and clawing her way back towards the light. And afterwards, after those deathly sleeps, when he would hold his fingers to her mouth to feel her breath, she seemed to wake doubly alive, the force of her will thrumming inside her, like a plucked string. He wasn't going to be the one to silence that, to bully her back to bed.

Below them the village was celebrating the grape harvest. Padre Ruggiero had blessed the crop, and Professore Centini was judging the ciambelle al mosto, made with the harvest's grape must. 'Poor Centini,' his mother said. 'He looks like he can hardly squeeze one more mouthful into that cummerbund.' It was true. The mayor, in full Fascist uniform, was puffing along the sampling table from one identical cake to the next, rubbing the waistband that held his gut as fast as a bilge hoop on a barrel. It didn't help that most of the bland cakes were destined to be scattered to the chickens: even the children in the village ran away when they were offered one. But the same recipe had been made at harvest time for centuries, and for the Montelupinese, tradition was more important than taste. Behind the mayor Fagiolo was playing his bagpipes, their strangled, reedy melody seeming to aggravate Professore Centini's discomfort.

'He should let Padre Ruggiero judge the ciambelle — he's got more room for expansion in that cassock.' Lucio felt his mother's toes flex against his leg as she laughed. It entertained him more than anything on the stage below.

Sometimes he thought his father wanted her to stay at home not to rest, but to be hidden away. Her seizures, when they came, had something animal about them, so debasing that they shocked the villagers, no matter how many times they had witnessed them before. The one that morning had been particularly bad. Padre Ruggiero was giving communion to the departing soldiers when her foot had begun knocking at the pew, the wood trembling with such force that someone shouted, 'Earthquake!' Her eyes became lost in her head and Lucio had laced his hands about her as she thrashed, foaming at the mouth like a rabid dog. When it was done, he laid her down in the nave, and they were both pale and wracked and wet from the urine that had soaked through her skirt. His father's face had stared back at him from the line of soldiers at the altar — a blank, vacant expression, as if he barely knew who they were.

The scientific in Montelupini took his mother's fits to be one step removed from lunacy. The women twisted a finger to their temples if she walked away from a good price at the market, or when she avoided the washhouse, preferring to beat her clothes alone in the stream at Collelungo. Others were more superstitious, protecting themselves with the two-fingered cornuto raised to her back and muttering about witchcraft. But the worst by far were the men at the osteria. Those same men who invoked every orifice of each other's wives and sisters and mothers-in-law as they damned their scopa hands found their mouths dry and empty when Letia Onorati walked past. They would fidget behind their cards, casting lingering looks from under their brows, and Lucio had learned to see in their eyes the reflection of his mother's mouth, her hair blacker than the lake on a moonless night, the curve of her neck as she balanced a basket on her head. When she walked away down Via del Soccorso, their raffia chairs groaned underneath them. And what Lucio detected in their faces was a mix of regret and relief, like they had followed the song of a siren and she had thrown them back out to sea.

'Santa Lucia,' his mother said, uncrossing her legs and sitting upright. 'Not yet, surely?' Lucio's grandfather was climbing the stage, with Polvere, the baker, not far behind. Nonno Raimondi had dressed himself up as a woman, his lips smeared red, a shabby wig on his head. He staggered in a pair of stolen high heels. Even from the battlements, Lucio could tell he was flushed and sweaty, both from a day's drinking at the osteria and from struggling with two enormous breasts of water-filled pig's bladders, jostling for freedom at the neck of his dress. Meanwhile, the baker wore the Sunday clothes of a suitor and was attempting to seduce Nonno Raimondi with a ludicrous length of salami and a sampling of his chestnuts. Lucio wasn't really surprised: nearly every celebration in the village degenerated into drunken skits or tawdry songs at some stage of the evening, but this was early even by Montelupini's standards. The audience, on their upturned crates, cheered and heckled nonetheless.

His mother got up. 'I can't watch. Your grandfather seems intent on outdoing his own idiocy tonight,' she said. 'Will you make sure he gets home?' Lucio nodded. She put her fingers in his hair and tugged fondly, but the piazza below drew her attention again. A silence had settled over the crowd, the shouts and laughter dampened as if by a winter fog. Even the babies seemed quiet. Lucio saw his father standing before the village, his hands clasped at his back. Behind him Padre Ruggiero had ordered two men to drag Nonno Raimondi from the stage, water trailing from one of the breasts that had burst inside his dress.

His father paused before speaking. He was wearing his commissioner's uniform: the black shirt and tie he had made Lucio's mother press for him that afternoon, even as he told her to stay in the house and rest. He brought his hands out from behind his back and ran a palm over his head before settling his fez over it. The tassel swayed hypnotically and it seemed, for a second, the only movement in the piazza. 'People of Montelupini,' he began, his voice carrying clear to the battlements. 'Montelupinese.' The word raised a cheer of solidarity, as it always did among the villagers. 'We've been celebrating the Sagra dell'Uva for longer than I can remember, longer than many older than me can remember.' He nodded respectfully at Padre Ruggiero and Professore Centini, who still tugged at his cummerbund.

'And yet,' his father continued, 'we are on the cusp of a new era.' There was a murmur of agreement. Lucio became aware of his own held breath, his awe at the way his father spoke in public. Vittorio had inherited this gift: it dazzled Lucio, the way they could both work a crowd, whether in the schoolyard or the osteria, gathering allies as swiftly and skilfully as sheaves of wheat in the harvest.

'Il Duce has already begun to lead us back to the glory of the empire. But rediscovering that strength requires commitment and sacrifice from us all. I, and the other men recalled to arms, are proud to perform our duty in the restoration of our great nation. And what better farewell could we ask than this festival? What greater reason to fight than to honour what we love: the traditions of our ancient culture?' His father paused to allow the crowd to cheer and clap, for his words to be shouted again into the ears of the old folk on their raffia chairs, for the women to cross themselves and mutter their prayers to Santa Lucia. Lucio heard his mother's breath beside him, saw her gaze drifting up to the mountains, which brooded like some prehistoric beast in the night.

'In the meantime,' his father began again, stretching his hand wide to the side of the stage, 'it falls upon our young Avanguardisti and Balilla to safeguard Montelupini. I know they'll do the job honourably, like true sons and daughters of the she-wolf.' At this, Professore Centini clapped his hands for two groups of uniformed boys to take the platform. Lucio spotted Vittorio in the middle row of Balilla, the only one among them who was bareheaded.

'Where's your brother's hat?' his mother asked. Lucio didn't answer. She knew as well as he did that Vittorio detested the fez and would go to great lengths to avoid wearing it. She had already sewed the tassel back on twice. 'How can Il Duce be

leading us back to glory if we look like monkeys on a pianola?'
Vittorio complained to the mirror when they dressed for Fascist
Youth meetings. On the stage, the angle of his jaw, pointed at
his father, showed what he thought of Mussolini's dress sense.

'He'll feel your father's belt over it,' his mother said.

'I think he'd take the belt over the hat.' Lucio saw her mouth
twitch in amusement.

He picked up his own fez, dusty and discarded on the floor.
He should have been the one to get the thrashing — always
playing truant during festival parades, never going on stage
with the other boys. Yet his father turned a blind eye when
he slipped away to the battlement walls: it was the one thing
they seemed to share, this unspoken pact, this understanding
that they would spare the village the pain of witnessing Lucio
squirming on stage.

Who could blame his father? Who in the village would
notice Gufo's absence when there was Primo to enjoy? He
listened to his brother open *Giovinezza*, singing a solo, his
mouth wide and certain, his chest expanded with breath. And,
like the rest of the crowd, Lucio could do nothing but watch
him: his shining skin, his eyes rich and promising as a newly
opened chestnut, his lips full enough to make grown women
blush. His body was wiry, already tight as a gymnast's, so quick
and agile that even the older Avanguardista boys could not
best him in a tackle at football, a climbing dare, a race on the
campo. The wages of the schoolyard proved it: a comb, two
half-smoked Nazionale, a straight razor, a dented tin whistle,
a jar of hair pomade — and a cigarette card of his namesake,
the world heavyweight champion Primo Carnera. Sometimes
Lucio studied these things, piled on the nightstand next to their
shared bed, like offerings at the altar of some juvenile god.
'You'll let me win it back tomorrow, won't you, Primo? Eh, Pri?'

the vanquished would call as they walked home from school. Vittorio would raise his hand lazily to them without glancing back, but the collection of treasures increased. The other boys were drawn to him as they were to matches or firecrackers: the potential to be burned part of the attraction.

When the anthem ended, the soldiers filed onto the stage, and Padre Ruggiero blessed them. Lucio scanned the crowd for Urso, but he hadn't come. He felt his chest ache with guilt. He had not seen the butcher since the hunt, not at the osteria and not at the shop, where Fabrizia tended the counter alone, as if her husband had already left. But at night, in the alley behind the butcher's house, Lucio saw the great bulk of his silhouette in the window, could hear the lowing of his voice within. He wanted to call out as Fabrizia pulled the shutters, call so that Urso's face appeared at the glass. But he flattened himself against the wall, nursing his regret alone in the dark.

'Are you worried?' his mother asked him.

He shook his head, looking not at her but at his father, full of assurance in his neat uniform. 'Are you?'

She didn't answer at first. Instead she unpinned her hair from its combs. The curls sprang about her shoulders like unspooled twine, so thick that they dwarfed her face and made her seem a mere girl. She leaned into him. 'You're here. Why would I be worried?'

He pulled up his knees and cupped his chin in a fist. They were both lying and they both knew it. But that was their habit; that was how they protected each other.

On the stage, Professore Centini had wound up his gramophone. Predictably, *Faccetta Nera* played as the soldiers marched off. *Wait and hope … the hour is near*, Carlo Buti sang in his unmistakeable tenorino. *We will give you another law, another king*. The words of the song, which Lucio had heard so many times, seemed suspended in the night above the piazza. He stood next to his mother and sensed her eyes swooping to the hills, skittish and restless as a bird's. She turned to him before she climbed down from the battlements, but her face did not show the apprehension or worry he had expected. It held something more alive and vital, something he could only compare with that thrill of release he saw in her after a seizure, that joy of being given another chance. He followed her progress down from the lookouts until he lost her in the shadows of Vicolo Giotto.

The Balilla boys and the recalled soldiers were dispersing among the people. As Vittorio jumped down, their father caught him by the hair and gave him a blow to the ear, sending him sprawling towards the fountain. But Vittorio merely brushed himself off and turned his back on him, striding into the crowd, where a huddle of boys received him at their centre, laughing and slapping him on the shoulders.

Lucio stared down at the fountain's cupola, decorated with garlands of wound vines. Its cascading pool of water was tinged red and orange and green in the light of the lanterns. The bronze figure at its centre seemed to sulk in the dimness. Something was different about the boy Cupid. Peering down, he saw that the god of love was sporting a cummerbund, and on his head, the tassel swinging jauntily over one eye, someone had cocked a Balilla fez.

It was past midnight by the time the piazza had emptied of people. Lucio heard the scratch of Fagiolo's broom on the cobbles, saw cigarette ends being brushed into the drain. He lowered himself from the battlement wall, hanging by his fingertips before landing on the pergola of the Osteria Nettuno.

'Porca miseria!' Fagiolo cried. 'Can't you use the street like everyone else?' The innkeeper jutted his chin towards the open doors of the osteria. 'Take him home, Gufo, will you? The Raimondi Gold turned to lead hours ago.'

Inside, Nonno Raimondi was on the floor, slumped against the bar. Polvere stood above him, legs wide and swaying as if balancing on a moving cart. 'Primo, my boy. Good lad, good lad,' the baker said, grabbing Lucio by the shoulder. 'Barilo,' he yelled, a cigarette dancing in the corner of his mouth and dusting his waistcoat with ash, 'your lad's here. Primo! Primo Carnera! Heavyweight champion of the world, eh?' He pulled on Lucio's head and attempted two quick feints to his jaw. The sudden exertion made the baker stagger: Lucio had to grab his arm and set him right again. His grandfather stirred at the scuffle.

Lucio was used to the mistaken identities, the banter, the same old stories. He'd heard them all before. Every night's conversation was new to the drunk. Sometimes, when the men were drinking his grandfather's grappa, Raimondi Gold, he felt like he was the only one left remembering. He bent to haul Nonno Raimondi up and caught the familiar scent of him — piss and ash and yeasty clothes. He held his mouth shut as he jammed himself under the old man's armpit in a practised manoeuvre. They danced for an instant, but when his grandfather got his balance, he pushed Lucio to arm's length, keeping a hand on his neck for security.

'Look at him, Polve, would you? Eyes all over everything and a face like thunder.' Nonno Raimondi reached for Lucio's cheeks and squeezed them hard so that his lips popped open. 'See that? That gap in his front teeth? He's a gypsy. Wild and wily, like his mother … like his grandmother.'

Lucio had heard this before too. On nights when the Gold

made his grandfather sentimental, his grandmother had been half Romani; other times she was descended from mountain bandits who had lived in the caves. His mother told him not to believe everything Nonno Raimondi said, especially things intended to bait his father, who thought gypsies and brigands were the curse of the last century, part of the peasant culture that held Italy back. But sometimes Lucio liked to think there might be some truth in his grandfather's claims. For on autumn mornings when they collected mushrooms on Collelungo and the scent of bonfires carried on the thin air, he heard his mother singing snatches of folk songs in the old mountain dialect.

Nonno Raimondi sniffed and let go of Lucio's cheeks. 'I tell you, Polve,' he said, trying to lay a finger along his nose to signal a great secret about to be revealed, 'this is the one to watch. This Gufo, here. Not Primo.'

'Doesn't say much for himself, though, does he?' Polvere shouted as if Lucio was deaf as well as silent.

'The mouth that is shut ...' his grandfather began grandly, then trailed off, forgetting the proverb.

'... catches no flies?' Polvere finished. 'But it won't get heard either.'

'By the saint's tits, Polve! This boy can say more with one look than you have in a whole lifetime.' But the baker had already rested his head on his arm, his eyes closed, and was dribbling on the bar.

Outside, Nonno Raimondi tried to wedge a cigarette behind Lucio's ear. 'Don't pay any mind to Polve, boy,' he murmured. 'When the Montelupinese talk, it's their arseholes that move. That's why they can't tell a crap from a Caravaggio!'

Lucio shuffled him towards Vicolo Giotto and stopped before the drain. His grandfather spread his legs stiffly and rocked, fighting with his fly. His piss, when it came, made a glistening arc against the wall. Lucio waited. There would be more. Nonno Raimondi sucked air through his teeth. 'Porco Giuda! I'm dying.'

He said the same thing every night, if he hadn't already pissed himself. A draught was scuffing through the alley. Lucio could smell winter on it. He knew his mother would still be up. She never slept until they got home.

'That's why I need to set it right,' his grandfather mumbled to the wall. Another spurt of urine wet the stones. 'We'll do it together ... Santa Lucia's fresco ... you'll help me, won't you, boy?'

Lucio nodded at him from the shadows of the alley. Nonno Raimondi hadn't been able to make the climb to the saint's grotto in years, but when he reassured him, the piss seemed to come quicker. In the morning he would have forgotten all about it anyway.

'Soon, yes? We'll do it soon ... I can sober up. I can still make it. My redemption, don't you see, Gufo?' He grabbed Lucio by the collar, suddenly urgent. There was an edge of real fear in his voice that Lucio had never heard before. He placed his hand over his grandfather's, and Nonno Raimondi slowly released his grip, turning back to the wall. Lucio saw him straining to piss, the effort tight in his jaw. A last meagre droplet fell, thick as blood on the cobbles.

'Porca puttana.' His grandfather swayed again, and Lucio wedged himself under the old man. They shuffled on, but Nonno Raimondi was slow, preoccupied, dawdling like he had forgotten something, seeming to Lucio for the first time more dotard than drunk.

'What?' he muttered. 'No, no ... you were five or six, maybe, the first time we climbed up there ... they thought you were addled in the head ... pazzo!' A laugh cracked in his chest. Lucio stopped to stretch his aching shoulder. A hum of remembering sounded in his grandfather's throat. 'We were a pair, you and me — the drunk and the mute. But I'd catch you with your little fingers in my paints and brushes, see?' His grandfather held his arm, not for support now, but to stop him walking on.

'Padre Ruggiero wanted that fresco finished for the feast day ... and the snow lying thick all through the woods, and the quiet ...' He stopped and cocked his head as if listening to their steps through the white forest. 'Cold as an unpaid whore that grotto was ... needed a few nips to get the blood back in my hands. But you? You squatted outside in the snow all morning. Wouldn't budge. You'd spied an owl in the chestnuts, remember?'

Lucio shook his head. He'd never heard this story before and he didn't recall the day at the saint's chapel. He remembered going with his grandfather to paint other frescoes or church panels sometimes, waiting patiently through the hours of preparation, hypnotised by the pencil lines and brushstrokes when they came, forgetting the image itself until it burst upon him like a magician's trick, confounding, yet somehow inevitable. But it had been a long time since Nonno Raimondi could keep a brush steady, a long time since his grandfather worked his magic.

'I had a rest, see. Just a quick siesta on a pew,' he continued, animated now, telling the story like he was back in the osteria playing briscola. 'When I wake up, Gufo's standing in front of me, brush in his hand and paint on his face. I jump up to the fresco and then I see it: knee-high to Santa Lucia — the owl on my mural. Holy Christ, it was so alive I thought it might spread its wings and fly through the chapel grille!' His voice crumbled and he coughed, hovering to inspect the phlegm at his feet as if he was reading a portent. 'Hard to believe it was you … so young for work like that. You have to wonder if something else … some darker spirit was involved.'

Nonno Raimondi pulled him close again, examining his face. Confused emotions seemed to blossom and wither in his grandfather's eye — awe, then fear, then … was it jealousy? Lucio couldn't tell.

'On the way back down the mountain, I found that owl dead on the path, like a bad omen The next day I went back and painted over its likeness. That's why, see?' His grandfather raised two fingers in the sign of the cornuto to ward off the evil eye. 'Better to be on the safe side, eh?'

'Be on the safe side if you went to bed, Papa, don't you think?'

Lucio glanced up to see his mother, propped on the window ledge above their heads. She sat very still, barely giving them her attention, as if they had disturbed her in some other more important vigil.

'I'm telling Gufo his story, is all,' Nonno Raimondi said.

'He doesn't need your fairytales and superstition. And he doesn't need that stupid nickname. What's the point of naming a child if this village insists on giving them another name?' His mother was in a black mood, blacker than her loose hair and even that, Lucio thought, made the starless night above her seem a lie. She stood and stretched out her arms beyond the window casement for a moment, before pulling the shutters smartly, unafraid of the clatter in the alley and the sleeping neighbours.

Nonno Raimondi wrestled a peptic hiss from his throat. 'A force to be reckoned with, that woman. Her mother used to sit like that on the sill.' His mouth fell ajar at the memory.

'She'd snap the shutters on me in that very same way.' He gave a rare smile, strangely fragile and rueful. 'But she was just a little bird, really … a little bird, waiting to be let out.'

'Keep track of the old man,' his father told them the next morning. They were in the cellar under the house in Vicolo Giotto. Lucio leaned against the walls of the bowed stairwell that smelled of mould and vinegar and overripe fruit. His mother and Vittorio were filling two baskets with clusters of grapes. 'If you leave him to it, he'll throw in the eating fruit and skimp the pressing to make richer vinacce for his grappa. And don't mix up the vinegar barrels.' He rapped on the casks. Leaving the task of winemaking in their hands seemed to trouble his father more than leaving them. Or perhaps it was a distraction, his way of not saying goodbye.

His mother didn't speak. She straightened and regarded the baskets brimming with fruit on the hewn floor of the cellar. His father hovered close beside her, and Lucio saw him reach for his mother's hand behind the folds of her skirt. When she avoided his touch, his father caught hold of her wrist, pressing his thumb into her skin, until he appeared to think better of it and pulled away.

Lucio had once thought there was no love between his parents. In the villages, marriage was a matter for the market-place, for trading goods and land. The Montelupinese had a saying: *On the scales, love is a lot lighter than potatoes.* And yet there were times, such as this one, quiet and fleeting, when he sensed his father betray something. It might have been love, but to Lucio it seemed more like a dull pain, some gnawing ache cosseted deep within. It reminded him of the way Nonno Raimondi looked sometimes when he held up a bottle of Gold to study its colour and concentration — that aching need, that terrible dissatisfaction blunting his gaze. Perhaps that was how his father loved his mother: compulsively, without joy, and hating himself for it.

His grandfather had passed out in the chair by the fire the night before. When Lucio brought the baskets of grapes up from the cellar, Nonno Raimondi was awake, leaning to spit in the empty grate. At the fireplace, Lucio took up the poker and stirred the ashes, careful to avoid the jangle of the iron. The first hour of the morning was always the most dangerous around his grandfather.

'I heard your father. Self-righteous prick,' he was muttering. 'What would he know about my grapes anyway? Wait till he's tasting weak Fascist beer and poxy Libyan whores. Then he'll appreciate my grappa and my daughter.'

With the toe of his boot he nudged at one of the baskets Lucio had set on the floor between them. 'He's asked you to take these up to the Don, has he?' Lucio didn't answer. He knew what was coming. His grandfather was the only person in the village who called Padre Ruggiero *the Don* like he was saying *the devil*. The grapes were the last of the eating fruit from the Vigna Alba, the smallest and sweetest of the harvest, picked even while the leaves were shrivelling on the vines. His father always gave them to the priest, and Nonno Raimondi couldn't bear it.

'I planted those vines, you know,' his grandfather said, raising his voice and angling his head towards the open cellar door. '*My* planting and *my* pruning — that's what makes them fruit so late.' He grunted and put up one foot on the edge of a basket, as though staking ownership of it. His hand, hanging from the arm of the chair, trembled violently.

When the others came up from the cellar, his father walked

to the fireplace and pulled the basket away, making Nonno Raimondi's leg clunk to the floor. 'Something to say, old man?'

Nonno Raimondi hocked into the grate again. 'I said, I used to bring those grapes home to sweeten my wife, not some paunchy priest.'

'So I understand,' his father said, like he was humouring a child. 'But perhaps if you'd stayed sober once in a while you wouldn't have needed to sweeten her. And you could have given the Church the proper share of the yields from *their* land.' Lucio saw his brother glancing between the two men, his face alight with the prospect of the argument to come. Their father glared at Vittorio and thrust a basket into his chest, sitting down to lace his boots. 'Don't fool yourself, Barilotto. Any work you ever did in that vineyard was for your precious grappa. Do you even remember what an unfermented grape tastes like?'

'And do you? Does your family? As soon as anything is ripe you offer it up to that fat friar like a good little serf.' Nonno Raimondi was surprisingly quick off the mark, given his state the night before. Lucio wondered if he'd been rehearsing a farewell speech of his own. 'All your talk about Italy and the *new era*, but in the end you're just like your father. You Onorati understand nothing but rules and work and duty. The Church's, Mussolini's — you can't live without someone telling you how.'

His father didn't look up. Lucio could tell he was furious, but it was not his way to let others have the satisfaction of seeing it. Instead he tugged at his laces and laughed. 'The biggest Communist pisspot and freeloader this side of Rome, and I had to make him family.'

'Lucia's tits, I'm a Communist now, am I? You want to work your fingers to the bone to widen the Don's arse? Be my guest.' His grandfather ran his tongue under his bottom lip. Yellow spittle had crusted at the corners of his mouth. 'Who was the freeloader when your father stole my vines from me, eh? Five generations of Raimondi worked the Vigna Alba and that son-of-a-bitch snatched it from me in a single game of scopa. *Onorati*, you call yourselves? Beh! Any honourable man would have offered me the chance to win back my land.'

'It's the Church's land, old man. Your family were only given the right to work it, remember? And my father didn't make the bet. Raimondi Gold did that for you.' His father's voice was dangerously calm. 'You pissed away your grapes. That's what galls you so much, face it.'

Nonno Raimondi lowered his chin and smirked at the grate. 'And what galls you is that you'll never be certain, will you?'

His father sighed. 'Certain of what?'

'Whether she married you for love or for the land!'

At that, their eyes darted as one to his mother, standing by the open credenza in the kitchen. She shook her head tiredly at his grandfather, but she would not meet his father's gaze. They were silent, apart from the soft wheeze of Nonno Raimondi's lungs.

It was an old, shameful grievance, the loss of the Vigna Alba to the Onorati, one that always reared its head at harvest time. But his grandfather had never pushed the argument so far before, had never sunk so low as to toss the slops of washhouse chitchat before his mother just to spite his father. The whole village knew that only the grapes of the Vigna Alba produced the vinacce essential to Raimondi Gold. The whole village knew that only Nonno Raimondi had the exact recipe for the grappa, passed down and guarded as it was by the eldest Raimondi heir for over two centuries. The whole village knew that in marrying Aldo Onorati, Letia Raimondi had got the vines back for her father. Everybody saw this — except perhaps his father, who didn't want to admit it. Lucio realised that Nonno Raimondi had played his trump card.

His grandfather pulled a bottle from his pocket and drained the last of it. He tossed the empty bottle in the grate without satisfaction. Lucio could see he would need to stay up very late that night to bring him home from the osteria.

'Come here, boy,' Nonno Raimondi grumbled. With a trembling hand he reached for a bunch of grapes from the remaining basket and held them along the length of his wrist. He blew on the fruit, twisting the cluster to consider their colour and shape, before laying them in Lucio's hands. 'Here. Give these to your mother.'

Nonno Raimondi's eyes were fixed on his father, who was putting on his jacket and kicking his kit bag to the door with one foot. As he threaded his arms in his sleeves, he looked up at Lucio with a face grey as stone. Outside, the clip of boots sounded on the cobbles. A man's voice called out. It was Urso. Lucio still held the fruit, plump and heavy in his hand. He hoped his mother might provide a clue, but she was staring through the window, her back to them, and she would not turn around. A loose grape fell from the bunch and rolled across the ashy floor towards the hearth. He felt a sense of panic at the loss of it, as if he was a shepherd seeing a stray animal separated from the flock. He glanced again at his father, at Vittorio holding the basket bound for Father Ruggiero, at his grandfather rattling the poker in the grate. He set the fruit in the centre of the kitchen table and stepped away from it.

The voice in the alley called again. His father slung his bag over one shoulder and paused at the door. He angled his head in the direction of the credenza and said something, but it was so quiet that Lucio wondered whether his mother could have heard, even if she'd wanted to. She didn't move from the window. Lucio heard the echo of boots in the stairwell. His mother's breath fogged the pane.

When he stood beside her, he could see Urso in the alley, clasping hands with his father. He had the urge to call out, to rattle the glass, but he felt as impotent as he had on the day of the hunt. He watched the two men leave, but only the butcher glanced back, raising the palm of one vast hand up to the window. Perhaps it was the shaft of morning light that made Urso squint, as if he was focused not on them but somewhere far beyond; perhaps it was the way his hand lingered in that lazy salute, or the momentary uncertainty of his step — but in that instant Lucio knew he would never see the butcher again.

Leyton
1949

Aunty Bea was poking a spoon into the pot, mashing the last life out of the tea, her silence deafening and indignant, as always. Connie let her fork idle like a pendulum over her tea plate and listened to the sounds of her aunt and uncle eating, cutlery scraping on plates, the exhausting perkiness of the clock on the mantel, the monotonous score of her own existence. She had tried to forget the image of the dead cat on the Italian's back, but it had bled into her thoughts, tingeing her moods subconsciously, the way ominous, half-remembered dreams did. She saw again the carcass hanging in his fist, a reminder that all of life hung on little more than a sinuous thread.

'I saw Sheba last week,' she said, surprised at the sound of her own voice. Aunty Bea replaced the teapot lid and barely noticed her. She was eyeing her husband dropping crumbs onto the *Evening Telegraph* laid on his lap under the table. For all his ungainly height, his white hair and rectitude, there was something puerile about Uncle Jack reading the paper at the dinner table. It always reminded Connie of the way the lane kids pored over the *Dandy* under the pew racks during the Eucharist. Now she was older, she sometimes wondered whether Uncle Jack's childishness was feigned, a ploy to win small victories over his wife. Aunty Bea huffed at him and slid a tea plate directly onto the newspaper, forcing him to stop reading and look up.

'Queen of Sheba, more like,' Aunty Bea said to Connie. She lifted her own plate and brushed under it with a palm. 'Where was that blasted moggy anyhow? I've had her ladyship wringing her hands all day and getting in the way of fetching out the silver just because she hasn't seen the precious blighter for a week. *It's a cat, Mrs R, I tells her. They go a-roaming. That's what they does.* Good riddance back to Burma or Siam, or whatever foreign place it came from, s'what I reckon.'

'I suppose she's worried because the kittens are due,' Connie said.

'Oh, I see,' Aunty Bea said, drawing out the words suspiciously. 'That's what this is about, then, is it? Did you hear, Jack? Jack!' She brought her teacup down on the saucer before her, like a judge with a gavel. 'I say, she's still angling after a blessed kitten.'

Aunty Bea had never let her keep a pet. Working dogs and ratting cats had litters all the time on the farms, but Connie had learned early on in her new life never to bring an animal back to Grimthorpe Lane. Aunty Bea's opinion of animals was informed by rural practicality, obsessive cleanliness and a literal view of Creation that was not uncommon in the villages, but which she had honed to a Biblical law all of its own. 'If God had intended us to have beasts as friends, he'd have given them hands and a mind to clear up their own *muck*,' she liked to say when Connie was caught petting the rag-and-bone man's mare as a child. She remembered Aunty Bea holding her hands under the faucet and scrubbing them with a nailbrush until they throbbed. Through the kitchen window she would see Uncle Jack spading the horse's steaming dung off the lane and onto his roses. *Muck*, Connie would mouth, splaying her raw fingers under the water. *Dirty, mucky shit and crap and cack*, she would answer Aunty Bea back in her head.

And so, surrounded by animals, she'd made do without a childhood pet, as if the war had put affection on ration along with everything else. But when Mr Repton up at the Big House bought his young wife the Siamese, she couldn't help but coddle the kitten, tease and lavish it with all her saved-up love, while Aunty Bea finished starching linen for the Reptons' weekend guests.

'Connie, darling, you haven't let her claw you?' Mrs Repton would call, bringing out the Germolene tin. She would shake her head, happy to suck at the scratches, but the cool, delicate touch of Mrs Repton's fingers, her falling curls, her smoky, exotic scent as she bent over Connie were so much more enjoyable than being brave. Aunty Bea would be furious when she saw the bite marks. 'That cat's the devil's spawn. Why she keeps it inside is beyond me. Ruddy hair all over the runners and fur balls behind the cushions.'

Mrs Repton adored the cat. It was rumoured she couldn't have children, and because of it the villagers allowed her to be decidedly soft in the head for animals. Connie often wondered, if it was that simple, why the same circumstance in Aunty Bea had led to feelings at the opposite end of the spectrum.

Her aunt sipped at her stewed tea. 'Don't even think about letting her ladyship give you one of them kittens. Don't you even think about it. If God had intended …'

Connie sighed, getting up to refill the milk jug so she could escape her aunt. 'I'm seventeen years old,' she said. 'I'm a bit past wanting a kitten, Aunty.'

'Well, why bring it up then?'

'I didn't.' She sat back down wearily. 'I said I saw Sheba last week, that's all. At the bottom of Bythorn Rise.' On the mantel, the Bakelite clock ticked on behind her. She had the urge to shout or swear, and found herself clutching for something equally shocking, simply to be listened to, to be taken seriously for once. 'I saw one of those Italian boys crack her about the neck.'

Immediately she regretted it. Aunty Bea snatched her hand from the teapot as if scalded. Uncle Jack shook his newspaper and raised his head, blinking at her steadily. 'What d'you mean?' Aunty Bea asked. 'D'you mean you seen him kill it?'

Connie tried to be flippant. 'I'm not sure. I could be wrong. It was dark.'

But there was no going back now. Aunty Bea wouldn't let her. 'And he done what, this Eye-talian?'

'I don't know, maybe it was Mr Rose or Fossett.' She had her aunt's full attention now.

'Well.' Aunty Bea pulled in her chin and lined up the tea things distractedly. 'There were no love lost between me and that cat, but I wouldn't've wished it that kind of harm.' She looked at Uncle Jack, as if he might have an explanation, before thinking better of it and continuing.

'Janet Livesey did say they were near as wild, them WOP boys ... like as diddies. Reckoned one of them were seen buying dog food in a tin. No doubt Repton's paying them very near nothing, and they'll eat any old thing, you know, them *Continentals* — horse, dog, donkey, anything with fur or feathers, they say.' She swallowed her tea with a grudging mouth like the milk was curdled. 'Makes my stomach turn.'

Connie took a slow breath and gazed out at the ripe evening through the kitchen window. She often wanted to have tea in the garden on these summer nights, but Aunty Bea refused to *eat bugs with dinner.* 'They're hardly savages, Aunty,' Connie said. 'The Romans had plumbing and heating when we were still living in mud huts. Besides, Repton's is overrun with rabbit and hare. Why would they kill a cat?'

'Righty-o, Miss I'm-nearly-eighteen-now-and-know-it-all. Would you listen to her, Jack? You tell her what them WOPs at Wood Walton liked to eat.'

But Uncle Jack remained silent, contemplating his fist balled next to his teacup. He didn't have to tell her. Early in the war she had seen two prisoners from the camp at Wood Walton squatting in the mud by the brook, the yellow circles on their backs appearing from a distance like twin suns rising in the bulrushes. Tommy Pointon came to school one day with a woven trap they'd given him. 'You put the seed down on the ground, see. The finch hops along, has a peck, you pull the string and *bang*! Down comes the basket.' He slammed his hand on the desk, grinning as they all jumped.

'But why would you want to pull a bird so little?' Mavis Darby had asked.

'Well, I wouldn't want to pull one as dim as you,' Tommy said, and all the boys laughed. 'They eat-a them. With-a their *macaroni*,' he sang. There was a stunned silence as they all wondered what part of a finch or thrush was worth the eating. Later Mavis had her comeuppance, running into the yard that afternoon and shouting that PC Ferris was giving Tommy Pointon a hiding for *frat'nising*.

'For goodness sake,' Connie said, beginning to clear the tea things, 'that was the war. They had to eat, like everyone else.'

'And you expect them Eye-ties to be more civilised now, I suppose? A leopard don't change its spots.' Aunty Bea folded her arms and adjusted her shoulders. 'I hope you're not setting your sights on them two boys, just because the likes of Mr Gilbert and *her ladyship* have granted them an audience.' She glanced at Uncle Jack again. 'Some of us remembers things.'

'What?' Connie said. 'What *things*? I don't remember anything because you never tell me in the first place.'

Aunty Bea sniffed and went to the sink. Uncle Jack offered only a vague shake of his head before looking back down at the plate in his lap. For once his complicit silence sparked her anger even more. 'See, you won't even let Uncle Jack speak!' She couldn't help herself. She knew she'd pay for it later. 'You treat us both like naughty children.'

'Don't you get that tone up with me.' Aunty Bea stood to face her across the table. 'Course he speaks.'

Uncle Jack rose to his feet, his chair making a drawn-out screech along the tiles. He shook a trouser leg of crumbs, gave a preparatory cough and lowered his eyes to Connie, like he might say something. But instead he retreated, vapid as a shadow, to the front room, where all that could be heard was the ghostly rustle of his newspaper.

'See what you've done?' Aunty Bea gestured after him. There was something childishly lost and regretful about her now. Connie studied her tiny frame, as neat and trim as Uncle Jack's was tall and gangling. With all her compact energy, she might still be young. Sometimes Connie had heard tinkers or gypsies at the door calling Aunty Bea *miss* or *petal*. She marvelled that they could not trace the years of disappointment gathered at her mouth, the cleft of regrets driven between her pale eyebrows. But exactly what disappointments, what regrets, Connie could never fathom.

'Happy now?' Aunty Bea said, reaching under the sink for a dustpan and brush.

'Happy with what?' Connie persisted.

Aunty Bea resurfaced, her cheeks rosy as chilblains, as if, like everything else, she had spent her life scrubbing them raw. The emotions that crossed her face were as varied and confused as an autumn sky. The clock on the mantel continued its perky tick. Connie reached across to her aunt and pushed back a tendril of hair that had escaped its pin. It still glowed partially red among the faded brown, like an ember in the grate. But at the touch, Aunty Bea's hand went up to her head self-consciously. Her expression cooled and the moment disintegrated.

'You're the replica of your mother,' she said. 'The Lord knows we done our best for you. But it's never enough, is it? Just like her, you are. Yearning after the fancy and faraway, always hankering after something, wanting more. Well, where did it get her?'

Connie knew better than to answer, but the image of the cat, the monotony of the clock, the scrape of Uncle Jack's chair, his retreating shadow goaded her on. 'I don't know, where *did* it get her? How would I know when nobody ever tells me anything?' She heard the whine in her voice and put her hand on her forehead to steady her thoughts.

'It led her down a path of sin, is all you need to know,' Aunty Bea said mechanically, 'and the wages of sin is —'

Connie was already out of the door and reaching for her bike, propped against the front of the house. Aunty Bea stood in the doorway, the dustpan brush trembling at her hip.

'Don't you dare turn your back on me when I'm talking of Christ.'

'You weren't talking of Christ. You were talking about sin and my mother, remember?' Connie breathed in the thick scent of the evening, gathering her patience. 'I'm going for a bike ride. I think Christ will be OK with it.'

'You be back before dark,' Aunty Bea said. She caught hold of the saddle as Connie pushed past, and lowered her voice to a hiss: 'Or don't you bother coming back at all.'

It was an empty threat, Connie knew, but one that had

never been spoken before, and the challenge it held made her breathless before she had even started to cycle down the lane. It was always talk of her mother, or the avoidance of it, that reduced Aunty Bea to her meanest self. Connie had grown up straining her ear to the rumours, of which there was never any lack in Leyton. There were whispers of dance halls in the West End and clubs in Soho, of GIs and disappointments. And one night, when she was supposed to be asleep, she had heard Aunty Bea telling Uncle Jack of *the bag of bones* she had visited in a bombed-out bedsit, where ten or so people lived sharing *that evil muck*. By then she knew that Aunty Bea wasn't talking about animal manure. Connie didn't need every detail, but as she got older, not being offered any at all became even more crushing. It was as if Aunty Bea believed the flawed blueprint of her sister had to be firmly kept under lock and key, for fear Connie would trace in it her own intrinsic nature. And Connie needed to be protected from herself at all costs.

She gripped at the handlebars, her mind so full that the bike seemed to carry her of its own accord, following its usual route. And so she found herself freewheeling down Bythorn Rise in the syrupy light, her arms clutched behind her head, the wet flick of insects on her skin. Her heart raced with the speed and the dare of not touching the handlebars; with the danger of falling, of hitting a stone in the road, of a puncture — anything to feel alive, to make something happen that might nudge at the endless coil of her days and nights, wound tight as a cocked spring.

At Repton's, the Burrell engine was still droning. Mr Rose and his threshing team were finishing the western acres, and as she swung round the bend at the bottom of the rise, she spotted the line of steam rising behind the ridge. She left her bike at the gate, fetched her book from the basket, and climbed the bridle path towards the Big House. As she walked, she picked out the familiar beat of the threshing drum, a sound that had always stirred mixed emotions in her: the excitement of the harvest and the sadness of summer's end.

She missed being part of the bringing in. Even as a six-year-old she'd helped with the harvest at Repton's; most village children did. She remembered whole gangs of them chasing the great beast of the Burrell as it thundered down the laneways, or darting behind the tractor and binder with sticks to beat the rats and rabbits as they broke cover of the mown wheat. By the time the war was underway, she was old enough to help the land girls with the stooking or with sewing grain sacks. Sometimes, in the early evenings, they'd stop to trace the planes as they rose sleek and pink-tinged from Molesworth, counting them aloud above the drone of the thresher. They would all be quiet after that, especially the women, their faces closed with thought. On those evenings, when everyone had gone home and she was waiting for Aunty Bea to emerge from the Big House, Mr Rose would let her climb onto the drum with him to sweep it clean of the loose grain, the chaff and the haulms. She'd listen to the last *hum, hum, hum* of the beaters, and the staccato of the final grains jitterbugging crazily in the open drum. 'Listen, girl ... you hear?' Mr Rose would say. 'That's gunfire of the fairies, that is. You reckon they's on our side?' And he'd laugh, his hair and lashes pale with chaff, his lips red and wet as he swigged from his hipflask.

Connie crossed the yard and saw the Burrell beyond the pig barns, the silhouettes of the gang still at work in the billowing dust. She recognised the forms of the Onorati brothers lifting sacks onto the tray of a truck. On top of the thresher, their father was bent over the drum. He was tanned and wiry and lean as a whippet, and his shorn hair, the particular curve of his back, made her remember the prisoners bent in the doorways of barns or cutting sugar beet on the ridge during the war. It surprised her now to think how little attention she had given them. Early on she had sometimes glimpsed them thistle-podding or hedging with a camp guard from Wood Walton. But even later, when they were billeted to live at Repton's, two or three at a time, Mr Rose seemed to keep them occupied, away from the permanent hands and land girls, as if he sensed some latent danger in them, like ratting terriers that had to be kept far from the laying hens. By the time they were driving tractors and freely roaming the yard at the end of the war, she had started at Cleat's. She spent less time at Leyton House, and her aunt, while she must have seen them, never spoke of it.

This was how the war had been for Connie — a series of small intrusions from some other world: streamers of silver foil descending like frozen lightning over the fields; the irregular comings and goings of evacuee children in the schoolhouse; the shocking animal cries of a land girl with a telegram; a gabble of American voices in a truck overtaking her bike. It was like the war had allowed her a peek through the gaps in the hedgerows to a world beyond the villages, but by the time she was old enough to wonder at it, to hanker after it, that world was gone, and everyone was back home replanting the rents torn in their enclosures. Sometimes Mrs Cleat would tut her disapproval as she heard of Yanks from the airbase getting rowdy at the Pheasant over in Upton. And now and again a customer would ask if they had any of those bulrush baskets the WOPs used to sell at Thrapston market. Other than that, it seemed barely a trace had been left behind of this foreign world in their own — until now.

She watched the Onorati boys among the threshing gang, enjoying the silent rhythm of their work against the droning engine. Even from a distance she could tell the difference in the shapes and movements of the two brothers: Lucio's strength, the steady, closed way he worked; Vittorio's limber energy, his drive to finish as quickly as possible.

At the back door of the Big House, she could see that Mrs Cartwright, the cook, had already left for the day. Through the window the kitchen table showed uncut bread and covered cold platters, ready for Mr Repton's supper. He didn't eat with his wife during the bringing in. His land stretched as far as Great Siding and he always rode out to check with each of his foremen on the progress of their harvest teams. Connie had expected Mrs Repton to be alone, but as she walked around to the side of the house, hoping to be spotted by her, she heard voices coming from the open window of the library.

'You've seen how he treats them, Harvey,' Mrs Repton was complaining, 'making them sweat for every scrap he tosses their way. They're still WOPs to him. And he always has that *air* about him when he's dealing with them.'

'What *air*?' It was Mr Gilbert. Connie recognised the vaguely bored, exasperated tone that siblings used with each other. It always made her envious, even of their bickering.

'Oh, I don't know ... it's that self-righteous look of the bountiful victorious, I suppose.'

Mr Gilbert laughed. 'Oh Evie, really.'

'He does! And I hate it.' There was an impatient jingle of bangles, the snap and flare of a cigarette lighter. 'Whenever I try to do something useful, like sending up food or spare furniture for that dilapidated shed he's got them living in, he puffs up about it, like I'm doing something untoward, *blurring the boundaries, old girl*, or some sort of nonsense.'

'Well, what on earth do you expect from Repton? He's hardly going to be inviting them in for cocktails, is he?'

'I notice *you* have.'

'I'm a mere schoolteacher, not the lord-of-all-he-surveys. Anyway, I wouldn't over-think Repton. It's simply economics for him. Where else would he have found such grateful workers for such paltry outlay?' Drinks were poured; a chime of crystal.

'But that business with the eggs, Harvey,' Mrs Repton persisted. 'I've a mind to march up there with a whole basketful of bloody eggs for the boys if they want them.'

'Now, that wouldn't be one of your best ideas.' Mr Gilbert had become serious. 'Aldo wouldn't want to accept them.'

'Why ever not?'

'A man with nothing still has his pride left, Evie. It simply costs him a lot more. Even Repton is perceptive enough to see that. The boys tell me their father's repaying him the cost of their passage, were you aware?' She was silent. 'God knows how long that's going to take them. Repton would have already factored that cost in their lower wages. So you see, Aldo's pride effectively indentures them to the farm for quite some time.'

Mrs Repton didn't answer. Connie heard the soft sucking on a cigarette, its smoke mingling with the evening air outside, sweet and dense with the last lavender. She thought she should turn and leave, but Mrs Repton began again.

'What happened to the wife — the boys' mother? Have they told you about her?' There were footsteps on the wooden floor, near the window. Connie didn't want to be caught out, but she didn't want to miss the answer either.

'They haven't said. And I haven't asked. I should think there's a good deal of the past they don't want to talk about and, quite frankly, we probably don't want to know. I'm more curious about their future, what they choose to do from now on.'

'Oh, Harvey,' Mrs Repton said, half reprimanding, half concerned. 'You're not, are you? Please say that you're not.'

'Not what?'

'Don't be obtuse. You know what I mean.'

The footsteps sounded again at the window. 'I'm only helping them, Eve. Christ knows they need it.'

Connie began to retreat, just catching Mrs Repton's reply: 'What is it with you, Harvey? You and Italians?'

'Connie Connie, is that you?' Mr Gilbert's voice halted her on the lavender walk as she retraced her steps along the side of the house. She turned to see him sitting on the ledge of the window, leaning out.

She lifted the book in her hand. 'I came to return it.'

'Well, come on, then. Don't dilly-dally there.' He waved her to the window and held out his hand for her to swing herself over the low sill. She obliged, glancing awkwardly towards Mrs Repton at the drinks cabinet.

'Look, Evie. Look what I've caught in my web,' Mr Gilbert said, his hands squeezing Connie's shoulders and propelling her in.

Mrs Repton crossed the room to take Connie's wrist in her cool palm, as if weighing it. Her grey eyes, Connie noticed, were changeful, and often had the hint of some other light about them. Now they were shot with green, like a cat's. The image of the Siamese grew large in her mind.

'I thought you'd forsaken me,' Mrs Repton said — not altogether teasing, Connie thought.

'I've been busy ... you know, at the shop.'

'I suppose you've come for more books rather than the pleasure of our company?' Mr Gilbert said, feigning indignation. 'What did you give her, Eve?' He took the book from Connie's hand, and his mouth twisted into a mischievous smirk. 'Ah, Forster. *Un Ingelese Italianato è un diavolo incarnato.*'

'Certainly true of you, Harvey, I should think,' Mrs Repton murmured over the lip of her glass.

'Ha! And what about you? Una Inglese Italianata? I'm certain you got up to as much mischief in Florence as I did.'

'Hardly. I had Mummy hovering over me the whole four months we were visiting you.' The curls gathered at Mrs Repton's neck shifted as she reached for another cigarette from the caddie. 'I had to point out to her that it was rather tricky trying to improve one's Italian without actually talking to anyone.' She perched on the arm of the leather chair, her eyes glazing as she remembered. 'It really was uncannily like the book. I might very well have been Lucy Honeychurch.'

Connie still felt awkward from eavesdropping. She didn't know that Mrs Repton had travelled, but the conversation between brother and sister seemed too private for her to ask all the questions she wanted to about Italy. Instead they fell quiet. When Mr Gilbert looked at her, she said, 'What about them?' She nodded to the window, towards the western fields and the distant drone of the Burrell, which at that very second cut out, amplifying the chatter of swallows roosting in the eaves, the noisy closure of the day.

'Who?' Mr Gilbert asked.

'The Italians,' she said. They both regarded her oddly, waiting for more. 'It's just that I looked up what it meant — what Cecil Vyse says in the book.' She indicated the Forster in Mr Gilbert's hand. 'I wondered if the saying works the other way round. You know, if the Englishman in Italy becomes a devil, what happens to the Italians in England?' She tried to smile, to show she meant it as a joke. 'Do you think they become saints?' But in her mind, images of the Onorati brothers — Lucio's bloodied face, the newly hatched nightingale, Sheba's carcass, Vittorio cleaning up broken eggs, the hole in his boot — seemed to run over one another, conflicting and unsettling. She knew then she wouldn't be able to say anything about the missing cat.

'Oh, Connie!' Mrs Repton rose from the chair and squeezed an arm through hers. 'You really are an absolute gem.'

'I told you, Evie.' Mr Gilbert tipped his chin towards Connie. 'She's definitely not government issue.'

Mrs Repton let her arms fall from Connie's and wandered towards the window. Beyond the lawns, on the incline west, the harvest teams were finishing for the day. They could make out figures walking along the ridge, the silhouettes of two men clearing the top of the thresher.

'Maybe you're right,' Mrs Repton said, almost to herself. 'People are inevitably changed by the countries they live in.'

'But an anglicised Italian?' Mr Gilbert mused. 'That would be a sacrilege.'

'Isn't that what you're doing, though, Mr Gilbert?' Connie said. 'Teaching them our language, our customs and manners?'

He considered her, a little surprised. 'I suppose I am, but I hope I never completely *anglicise* them ... Anyway, I couldn't possibly, even if I wanted to.'

'Why not?'

He studied the whiskey spinning in his glass and then drained it quickly. 'Because Italy is impossible to forget. It's a dream that haunts you all your life.'

She left them, giving her excuses about riding home in the dark. She hadn't wanted to go, but the visit had left her with greater and more interesting preoccupations than calling Aunty Bea's bluff about the curfew. The library at the Big House often had this effect on her: she always loved its dim, cool refuge; a world unconnected to Leyton and its mud, the rot in its barns, the bland patchwork of fields outside. As a child she had spent hours there waiting for Aunty Bea, spinning the old globe on its stand, thumbing through the volumes, imagining herself somewhere else, in some parallel existence. There she could escape the Connie she was and imagine the Veronica or Clarissa — even perhaps the Marylyn — she might have been. The ashen smell of the books alone was enough to fire her imagination. But that night, as she ran her eyes across the spines and listened to Mrs Repton and Mr Gilbert talk about their travels, their privileges, she had begun to scoff at herself. All the words in the library, she realised, weren't going to let her experience what they had experienced, or make the world any more possible to her. All their easy encouragements, their open-mindedness, the casual debate she sometimes heard between them about education reform, social liberation and the classless future made possible by the war: it dazzled her. And misled her — making her feel special, making her feel that she might achieve anything. If Mr Gilbert and his sister chose to ignore the mud of Leyton clinging to her shoes, it still did not free her from it. She knew this now, had known it for some time, but even so, she could not give up the seductive pull of their orbit, or the brighter, more stimulating version of herself that she became in their reflected glow.

These were her thoughts as she reached the track leading to Bythorn Rise. She was so caught up in them that she nearly missed the figure sitting on the gate. It was Lucio Onorati, still dusty, chaff in his hair, the back of his neck tanned and grimy to his shirt collar. As she came up behind him, he stayed slouched over, engrossed in some activity. She saw the journal balanced on his knee, the pages battered and curling from being rolled too often. One arm lay loose across them, abandoned as a sleeping child's, but the hand with the pencil worked away, precise in its grip, compulsive in its strokes. The same hand that had struck the cat, she thought. It altered him in a way that both fascinated and repelled her. She wanted to know why he had done it, but was frightened there wouldn't be any reason. She thought she might back away and climb the rise by a different route, but he had heard her now, thrusting his journal in his back pocket as he got down to open the gate.

'You look better.' It was the first thing that came to her. She touched her own eyebrow to show she meant his cuts, the yellowing bruises. He didn't speak. She stepped towards her bike, propped in the hedgerow. Lying in the tall grass of the verge was a dead hare, gutted and bound about its feet. Its orange eye bulged, its fur made glossy by the low light.

'He's a beauty,' she said, with a brightness that she didn't feel. 'Are your traps near here?'

He nodded towards the copse of trees by the brook in the east.

'Why down there? Why don't you set them on the farm? Mr Repton would be pleased.'

He adjusted his weight on his feet. 'We give those to Mr Rose. They belong to the farm.'

'What?' She nearly laughed. Mr Repton had never begrudged anyone a rabbit on his land if they could catch it. Even before rationing, it had been the boon of the farmhands and anyone who helped with the bringing in. The Reptons had certainly never been forced to have rabbit on their table, even during the war, not with over two hundred head of pig in Mr Repton's barns at Great Siding and an army meat contract in his pocket. 'Does Mr Repton ask for them back?'

He dug his hands in his pockets and glanced over his shoulder. She couldn't tell if he was hesitant or impatient. 'Not him … my father.'

'Your father makes you give the rabbits back?'

'We don't take anything from Mr Repton.' She saw him chew on the inside of his mouth.

'So you set your traps down there because it's common land?'

He waited, as if to obtain her permission. 'Mr Fossett gives me one tanner for six skins,' he said.

'A *tanner*?' she burst out.

He lowered his face and frowned. 'I said it wrong.'

'No, no. A tanner, a sixpence. You said it right. But Fossett should be giving you sixpence a skin. That's what everyone else gets, even the lane kids. You know, he sells them on to the factory in Benford for twice that?'

He lifted her bike from the verge and set it on the road for her. But she didn't take it, wanting him to tell her more. She noticed his fists, the dried blood on his knuckles and under his broad fingernails. He might have sensed her inspecting him, for he nudged the bike towards her again, backing to the gate when she had hold of it, and removing his hands to the small of his back to tuck in his shirt. He seemed flighty, like he might disappear again into the hedgerow or sail over the spinney. And she had so many questions. She wanted to pin him down.

'Why did you kill that cat?'

He stood before her in the dimming light, shifting his boots and glancing about him like a creature cornered.

'It was Mrs Repton's. Did you know?'

His lips opened slightly and there was something pained about him.

'It's alright,' she said, unnerved by his reaction. She couldn't imagine any of the villagers responding in such a way: the lane kids learned early in life that an accusation was always to be met with a corresponding attack, especially if guilty. She had never fully mastered this Leyton habit herself, even after all her years with Aunty Bea, the queen of accusations. 'You can tell me.'

He tugged on his rolled shirtsleeves, leaving them unbuttoned and flapping at the cuff. 'It's a mistake,' was all he said. She waited. 'Mr Rose, he makes me put the poison for the rats. I tell Mrs Cartwright to keep the cat in the house, but only the other woman was there. I knock on the window, but she ...' He lifted his hand and shooed Connie away with it, and immediately, in that single action, she recognised Aunty Bea.

'She sent you away.' Connie leaned the saddle to her hip and squeezed her hand on the back of her neck.

'I look for the cat,' he continued. 'But Mr Rose is getting angry, so I put the poison in the barns. The next day, I find it here. It's sick. Very sick.' He pointed to the spinney by the brook.

'You buried it?' she said. He nodded. 'You haven't told anyone else, have you?'

He seemed stilled by the confession. She studied the cut healing under his eyebrow, the nick in his lip. 'Your father ... it wouldn't be good if he found out, would it?'

He shrugged. 'It doesn't matter about him.'

She began to push the bike up the rise, glancing back at him to show he should walk with her. 'It won't be the first cat poisoned from rat bait in these parts. If you hadn't found her, no one would be any the wiser. She might have got into a fight with a badger or a fox.' She stopped walking. 'Let's leave it at that, alright?' But as she said it, she thought of Aunty Bea: *she* would never leave it at that.

He took the handles back from her, and she saw again his

fingers and knuckles, smeared with dried blood from handling the hare. He tried to wipe a fist against his hip.

'It's just blood,' she said. 'We're used to it round here.' She wasn't sure whether she said it for his benefit or hers. 'Hunting, cubbing, culling — it goes with the county. *Hunting*donshire?' She waited to see if he understood. 'You'll see. Even Mr Repton gets his hands bloody come November.' The lack of sentiment rang false in her, and she suspected, from the glance he gave her, that he saw straight through it. She tried to explain. 'Mr Repton's the master of ceremonies at the Hammerton and Thurning hunts. He carries the horn and bloods the new riders — if they catch anything, that is.' She was prattling on about a tradition that was impossible to explain to a foreigner, something so English, so formal and regulated, yet absurdly barbaric, she realised, seeing it from the outside. She tried to laugh but her voice stalled.

By the time they reached the top of the rise, the night had settled, still and moonless. She switched on her lamp and caught him in its beam.

'Remember what I said about Fossett. A tanner for each skin. More for foxes. And if you get a stoat, talk to me first … you know what a stoat is?'

He shook his head, the harvest dust still gathered on his lashes and eyebrows. She remembered Uncle Jack smoothing his thumbs over her own when she was little, holding her chin, his thumbprint in the soft hollow of her eye, grubby from the fields, or sometimes wet with tears.

Not knowing what else to say, she blurted out: 'Bonna see-ra.' The Italian words sounded misshapen in her mouth, like a child's Double Dutch. She let out an awkward laugh. His face showed no reaction. He hadn't understood. She felt hot and climbed onto the bike, about to push off, but something made her hesitate.

When she glanced up he was smiling. A gap between his white teeth opened to her for the first time, like an intimacy.

'Buona *notte*,' he corrected her. The grin fell away as quickly as it had appeared, and after it his gaze was fathomless as the black sky. He took up a position again on the fence at the top of the rise, soundless, shadowy, all-seeing. And she shivered as she cycled away, imagining him watching over his expectant traps hidden in the coverts.

Montelupini
1939

'Porca puttana!' his brother shouted at the top of his voice. 'I-am-going-to-die-of-boredom!' He was standing on the lip of Rocca Re, venting his opinions to no one in particular — to the haze that hung over the valley, to Montelupini dozing in the folds of the hills. Vittorio let out another bestial cry, wordless with frustration. It silenced the scratch of the crickets and made a pair of quail beat out their indignation from the scrub below. The limestone crag had many names, but since he was first able to reach it, Vittorio had called it Rocca Re, the King's Rock, as though the very purpose of its prehistoric formation had been for him to stand upon it and declare himself to the world. Lucio sat and listened, running his hand over the stone that jutted out beneath them. He liked to imagine the rock was a wave, rolling and crashing through the millennia at infinitesimal speed, too slow for human eyes. It comforted him to think that Rocca Re would still be inching its course over the valley, still alive and changing, long after everything they knew had turned to dust.

They always stopped at the rock on the way to Padre Ruggiero's summer house. His villa was halfway up Collelungo, built for clerical holidays in the cooler air and set among some of the best orchards in the ranges. The priest lived there for most of the year, preferring the estate over the more convenient but humbler presbytery behind San Pietro's. The Don, Nonno Raimondi told Lucio, wasn't the type of priest who took religion literally, who rolled up his cassock sleeves to bless the passata or thresh the wheat, as Christ himself might have done. And yet, the less accessible Padre Ruggiero made himself, the more the Montelupinese looked up to him — literally. Like Santa Lucia in her grotto, he was held in a kind of reverential awe, part spiritual, part feudal, and the villagers were always grateful for every small condescension he deigned to give from on high. Such as taking the trouble to ride his horse three miles down the mountain every day to give Mass.

Vittorio aimed his foot at the basket of grapes on the rock before him. 'How can you bear it?' he said. 'Being stuck here in Montelupini delivering fruit while everything exciting is happening miles away?' He let an arm fall in the vague direction of Rome. Lucio knew his brother had seen older boys in the Avanguardisti swaggering about, making similar complaints. He didn't tell him he should have been pointing south, to the ocean beyond the ridge of the mountains, south to Africa. 'Fagiolo reckons we'll be at war soon. That'd be typical. By the time we're anywhere near old enough, it'll all be over and we'll be stuck here like donkeys for the rest of our lives carrying fruit to Padre Ruggiero!' He snatched a bunch of grapes and began to eat them mindlessly.

'What?' Vittorio snapped. 'Lighten up, Gufo. Papa and Padre Ruggiero won't know unless you tell.' He snatched another bunch and threw it over. 'Go on. Be a devil.' Lucio caught them, but didn't eat.

'Nonno Pisspot's right, in a way,' his brother mused, through a mouthful of pulp. 'We sweated over them, we should at least be able to eat them.' He crammed more grapes into his mouth and fired the pips over the ledge like bullets. When Vittorio reached for another bunch from the basket, Lucio heard his hand strike something hard wedged underneath. His brother pulled out the bottle of Raimondi Gold and gave a knowing grunt. 'Bet Nonno didn't realise this was stuck in there. No wonder Papa let him have the last word.' He weighed the bottle in his hand before squeaking out the cork and taking a swig. Lucio watched him pull in his chin and snatch his breath, turning away to blink back tears.

Vittorio stopped up the bottle and tossed it to Lucio, who caught it just before it met the rock beneath them. 'Go on then, big brother. Better get a taste for it since you're the heir to the Gold!'

Lucio hated it when Vittorio started on this. His age was the one thing he had over Primo – eleven months, which he would have gladly handed over if he could, along with the dubious right to the secrets of Raimondi Gold. The grappa, which was popular as an elixir, fetched a decent price at markets all through the Lepini, and their mother relied on trading it to supplement their table, especially when the harvest yields were poor. Vittorio knew very well that Lucio sweated under the responsibility of learning their grandfather's methods, the pressure of knowing that everyone in the village thought Primo was the one who deserved the privilege, not him. But Nonno Raimondi refused to be swayed. 'I know what you're thinking,' he had told Lucio, 'but it's a Raimondi secret. There's too much Onorati in that boy. He only has to fart and everyone thinks they smell biscotti fresh from the oven. Primo will spin straw into Gold without any help of mine.' To Lucio this seemed the very reason Vittorio should be the one to make the grappa.

'Relax, Guf, I'm teasing. Don't look so worried,' his brother said, flicking a grape at him. 'How hard can it be? Nonno

Pisspot manages to make the stuff and he's barely conscious half the time.' He threw two more grapes into the air one by one, jerking his head to catch them in his mouth. 'You need to make sure he runs you through exactly what he puts in it a couple of times — the temperature of the still, how he knows when the head of the flemma has passed, stuff like that,' Vittorio added casually. 'He *has* shown you where he stashes his still, hasn't he?' Lucio didn't answer. 'Santa Lucia, Gufo. You need to pin him down, start asking questions. He's not getting any younger. Papa says the old soak could fall off the perch any day now.'

Lucio studied the limestone under his hand, the holes weathered into it like honeycomb. The whites of Nonno Raimondi's eyes were the same colour, almost the tone of the Gold itself. They became hard and narrow whenever anyone became too curious about the grappa and the Raimondi method. 'That's for me to know and you to drink,' his grandfather would growl. When Lucio collected him from the osteria some nights, Nonno Raimondi would pinch his cheek and slur cryptically, 'Gufo knows though, don't you, boy? The quiet ones have all the secrets.' The men would frown at Lucio in disbelief, unable to see in him the next great alchemist of Raimondi Gold. And outside, when they were alone, his grandfather would say, 'Tomorrow, eh Gufo, tomorrow. We'll do it soon.' But tomorrow never came.

'Don't even think about not asking him, Guf,' Vittorio interrupted his thoughts. 'You get onto him, OK? Or else I will.'

Lucio looked up at his brother mulling on the grape skins and spitting them out, like he was chewing tobacco. 'Do you think Mamma really married Papa only to get the vines back for Nonno?' he said, partly as a way of changing the subject, partly because he was thinking of his mother, the sound of her breath at the window that morning as she watched his father leave.

He knew what his brother's response would be: Vittorio rarely questioned the common knowledge of Montelupini, even when its logic was dubious. 'Yep. Everyone knows Papa got the arse end of the mule in that deal, but they say he was a fool about her in those days. Just imagine, if he'd married a Ronzoni or an Ippoliti girl we'd be ten times richer, and he'd probably be mayor by now.'

Lucio gazed at a remnant haze of summer heat pooling in the valley. 'We wouldn't be us, though, would we?' he answered, but his voice had no substance and felt like nothing more than the itch of cicada song in his throat.

'Come on,' his brother said. 'Let's get the Don over with.'

Padre Ruggiero was asleep in a chair on his verandah. Through the kitchen window Signora Mazzocchi, his housekeeper, called for them to take the baskets down to the cellar and not to wake him. The screech of her voice alone, however, was enough to rouse the priest.

'Ah, boys,' he called to them, folding back his rug. They approached him and ducked their heads.

Vittorio drew a shy smile from his repertoire. 'Sorry, Padre. We didn't mean to wake you.'

'Never mind,' the priest said, but as he replaced his biretta, its red tassel wagged at them like a reprimand.

'Papa sent us with the last of the grapes.'

He took the basket and felt carefully between the fruit. 'Yes. Good. Did they have a safe start this morning?'

Lucio knew very well that Padre Ruggiero had already been told every detail of the soldiers' departure before they'd even disappeared around the bend to Montemezzo. Signora Mazzocchi, who reported to the priest on every prayer and peccadillo of the Montelupinese, was not known as La Mula for nothing. She could make the steep track between the village and the priest's house faster than anything on four legs, including Padre Ruggiero's Esperian mare.

Vittorio lowered his eyes at the priest's question and didn't answer. Lucio heard him conjure a faint sigh.

'Well, Primo. Good boy, good boy,' the priest murmured, reaching for their shoulders and prompting them into a kneeling position. He placed a hand on each of their heads, saying a short prayer for the speedy return of their father. Vittorio whispered a fervent *amen*.

'He'll be back before you know it,' Father Ruggiero said, pushing their heads away as permission to rise. He reached down and pulled out a large bunch of grapes from one of the baskets. From it he pruned two stems of bruised fruit that had been crushed against the bottle. Lucio expected him to toss these to the ground and scold them, as he often did, for their careless packing. But instead he opened Vittorio's fingers and placed the weeping clusters in his palm.

'There. Now off you go, boys. Off with you! And make sure you help your mother. Signora Mazzocchi tells me there are still some late figs rotting on the tree in the Vigna Alba. But I'm sure Letia will manage the land very well without your father. She has you two to help her, after all. So I won't need to ask another family to take over, will I?' His smile was rigid and he did not blink.

They left him swatting at a fly, and passed under the trees of his orchards, taking the shortcut home. When they reached the chalk track, Vittorio broke into a run and Lucio struggled to keep up. On the stone platform of Rocca Re, his brother stopped and bent over, breathless. 'Prick … arsehole,' he yelled, his neck bulging with the effort of it, 'fuckwit!' A trickle of grape juice dribbled through his fingers onto his dusty boots. He jerked his fist up, knifelike and obscene, hurling the mashed grapes into the air. They stood for a while, and Lucio could almost feel his brother's anger crackling like static about them.

'Come on,' Vittorio said at last, gazing at the drop in front of them. 'Come on. Fuck it all. Let's do it … Do it. Jump!' The words became a chant in his mouth, something tribal, to satisfy the raging in his blood. 'Jump! Jump!' It had always been his dare, ever since they had first climbed there alone — to leap from Rocca Re into the scree twelve or fourteen feet below. There the mule track snaked back on itself, continuing down to the village. Jumping Rocca Re would have saved them walking time, but that was never his brother's motivation. 'Just to jump,' Vittorio would explain. 'Just to do it, that's why. To be the king of the mountain.' But he had never actually taken the leap. Not until then.

Before Lucio could put out a hand to stop him, Vittorio had flung himself over the ledge, his wild shriek the only thing left behind. Lucio teetered on the rock's lip, craning to see: his brother was lying on his back in the loose shingle, a rip in the arm of his shirt blossoming red, his eyes open but vacant.

'Primo!' Lucio cried. 'Pri?' A chill surged up his neck and through his hair. He heard a soft groan from below, and another that became a shuddering cough. Finally Vittorio surrendered to a belly laugh, writhing with it as he drew up his cut knees. 'Your face,' he wheezed between convulsions. 'Your face, Guf … peeping over the edge … like I was dead!'

Lucio sat down, his legs dangling over the drop, listening to the thrum of his heart through his whole body.

Vittorio brushed himself off, fingering the cut in his elbow.

'Come on then, Guf. Jump,' he called up. 'Do it. Do it! Challenge the king of the mountain!'

Lucio peered down at his brother's face — that grin like a spell, the creases at the corners of his eyes half-encouraging, half-critical. He got up and balanced on the edge of the precipice, feeling his fear in the grip of his toes, the weakness of his knees and stomach, the adrenalin that threw every detail into relief and made him weightless with anticipation. His love for Vittorio was exactly that contradiction: the soaring thrill of possibility and the crushing need to protect himself, to protect them both.

He pushed back his hair with his wrist and made his way slowly down the slope of the mule track.

That night Fabrizia, Urso's wife, was waiting for him under the battlement wall. Her legs were planted wide, her arms crossed over her brawny breasts. 'Come down,' she called into the night. 'Yes, you, Gufo. I know you're up there.' He considered the line of her broad jaw, the angry quiver of her shawl in the moonlight. The butcher's wife was not a woman to refuse. She grunted at him as he dropped down from the shadows into the piazzetta, but once he was in front of her, she hurried away towards her house in Via Allori, her shoes darting like fish under the oceanic sway of her backside.

At the door to her house she paused and sniffed, checking him over. He began to regret following her. Perhaps she was brewing one of her famous scoldings, like the time she stormed into the osteria and dished Urso their anniversary dinner straight onto the briscola cards. The other men had spluttered and sniggered, but when she was gone, the quiet left behind was the worst kind of reprimand, like the hot, grubby calm that follows a sirocco wind, and Urso had squirmed in his seat until enough time had passed for him to slink home.

'Well, come in, then,' Fabrizia complained, as if he had asked to follow her. 'I haven't got all night.' He had no idea what he was doing there. Inside the kitchen, she lit the oil lamp and motioned to the scrubbed table. On it was a basket with his jacket folded inside, washed clean of Valeriana's blood. 'Take it. There's a pork knuckle in there, too — for your mamma to make stock.'

He felt the urge to reply, but she waved her hand before her like she was shooing a mosquito. He picked up the basket and stepped back towards the door. As he passed her, she took hold of his arm. 'Urso —' She stopped and bit her lip. In the lamplight her skin was downy, pinkly veined about the nose and cheeks. 'He was quite specific about it,' she said. 'Told me it was you and only you who should have it, being the special one, the one to make it.'

He didn't understand. He wanted to ask her about Urso, to have her ease his mind, but she sucked in her breath and pushed him over the threshold.

'And make sure you bring that basket back,' she said. He turned to nod, but she had already shut the door in his face.

In the piazzetta of the old village he squatted under the streetlamp. The cat with the broken tail picked its way over the battlement walls. Draughts funnelling along the alleyways carried the chill of winter that night, and the men at the osteria had gone inside. He heard a cry of 'Scopone!' from within, followed by murderous yells and groans. The basket at his feet creaked. At first he thought it was the draught that made his jacket stir, but when he put his hand upon it he could feel warmth, a wriggling underneath. A paw jutted out from under the collar. He pulled back the fabric to find a puppy, stretching from sleep. It was tan all over, its ears too big for its body, its belly swollen with worms. Next to it was a bottle of milk and a glass medicine dropper, like the ones his mother used to measure out herbal tinctures to add to the grappa. Urso must have gone to her to borrow it, for no one else in Montelupini used such an instrument. He began to understand why he had never seen the butcher in the days after the hunt. He had been nursing Valeriana's puppies, keeping them alive with goat's milk, drop by drop, or trying to, at least. That was an indulgence the men at the osteria would never let him live down. So this shivering runt was all that was left of the seven, the lone survivor of the great cane corso's litter? It was so small that its entire body was curled within the circle of Valeriana's spiked collar. He fingered the rusted nails driven through the leather. Beside the collar lay the hard bone handle of Urso's skinning knife. He drew the blade out of its sheaf and weighed it in his hand. The puppy squirmed again. They had big shoes to fill. Both of them.

The donkey was discovered missing long before Nonno Raimondi. Lucio had thought he was at the osteria all night, but when he checked, Fagiolo shook his head.

'Barilotto's not been in all day.' The innkeeper rubbed at his chin, looking at the end of the bar, where Nonno Raimondi's stool was vacant. 'Has your mother checked up at Prugni?'

'There was a little widow in Gavignano he used to visit in the autumn,' Polvere called from his spot at the bar. 'He used to talk about her truffle pig, you know. And her big …' The baker cupped his hands before his chest.

'Santa Lucia, Polve, I think those days are past for the old boy,' Fagiolo said. 'He could hardly get his leg over a donkey, let alone …'

'Wouldn't stop him trying.' Polvere shrugged. 'I know Barilo.'

Lucio left them still debating and went home. His mother was on the floor, beside the crate where they had made a bed for the puppy, running its ear between her fingers and thumb. She glanced up. He hated to see the disappointment on her face as he entered alone.

'It's typical of him to do this to me.' She got to her feet and paced the kitchen. 'He's only got the one bottle of Gold in his pocket. I checked the cellar. He can't last a day on that. He should have been home by now.' She snatched her shawl from the back of the door. The lines of her face had settled from anger into worry.

Lucio picked up the lantern and followed her as she started along Vicolo Giotto, going down towards the vineyards, in the direction of Prugni. A young moon hung over them, weak and nearly transparent. His mother headed beyond the last plot and through a shortcut of waist-high grasses before joining the thin track where the rugged rise of the mountains began again. When she turned to him, her face was pale in the glow of his lamp, her hair loose down her back. She might have just risen from sleep. Or from death, he thought. He knew where she was heading: the single hoary chestnut tree that whistled its lament between the ruins of the old settlement. There, the eerie quiet of the ancient foundation stones made the villagers tell ghost stories of massacred Volsci, the mists clinging to the mountain, scented with the smoke of funeral pyres.

'He used to go to the ruins to drink himself to oblivion,' his mother said. 'He's crafty. He knows no one ever dares go up there, so he won't get disturbed or brought home.' Lucio looked at her. She dared though, didn't she? She had always been fearless like that. He sometimes believed it was her seizures that made her so. Walking constantly along an abyss would make any other track seem easy.

But the further they climbed, the more he realised they wouldn't find his grandfather there. At the top of the hill, they sat among the ruins to rest. The chestnut tree creaked and whispered to itself, and the lights of the village broke the night like shards of glass.

A scrabbling sound on the mule track below became footsteps. They saw the swing of a lantern rising over the ridge: Vittorio stood before them, his breath blowing thick and white.

'I've asked all over. Umberto Udine hasn't seen Nonno or the donkey and he's grazed his goats halfway to Carpeto today. Fabrizia was in the shop all day and didn't see him cross the piazza either.' He sat down beside them to catch his breath. Lucio saw the expectation in his brother's eyes.

'So?' Vittorio asked. He nodded encouragingly, as if the force of his own will might put the words he wanted to hear in his brother's mouth.

Lucio rubbed his arms. The sweat from the climb was chilling on his skin.

'Tell me that he's taken you to the grappa still? Tell me you've asked … that he's showed you.'

'Vittor,' his mother warned, but Lucio could see that even she entertained some fleeting hope.

'Tell me, Gufo,' Vittorio continued. 'Tell me you got it out of the old man.'

Lucio nudged his toe at the cracked casings of fallen chestnuts. Somewhere in the scree below, he could hear a gravelly cough, the disgruntled hock of a badger.

'Porca Giuda!' Vittorio cried. 'You didn't do it, did you? The one thing coming to you, the only thing you had to do and you fuck it up!'

'Vittorio, don't,' his mother said, and his brother growled with frustration. He snatched up his lantern and headed back to the mule path. 'Where are you going?' she called after him.

'To see if I can't find him before the frost does. I'll make the old bastard tell me if it's the last words he gasps.'

His brother's lantern disappeared into the darkness. He felt his mother close beside him as the temperature dropped even further, and the crust of moon froze in the vast lake of night.

'He was never going to teach you, you know,' she said. She crossed her arms about her and ran her hands along her shoulders. 'He's jealous of it. Jealous as a lover. He'll take it to the crypt. But that's his gift to you.'

He let the words sink in, checked the truth of it in her black eyes, and he felt guilty at his relief — the release from the burden of attention, of expectation, that the grappa would have forced on him. Could Nonno Raimondi really have understood that?

The badger coughed again. They heard its feral spit. He gazed out across the valley and knew where he would find his grandfather.

He reached the plateau of Montemezzo just before dawn broke. Vittorio was right: a frost had settled in the night. The undergrowth was encrusted with it, and for a few minutes, before the first stirring of the birds, he stood listening to his own pulse, and imagined that he was the only living thing in the stiff blue silence. Leaves stirred above him. There was the slow beat of wings among the branches, a night bird retiring. He came to the outcrop and the chapel of Santa Lucia as the first orange rays began to tilt between the trees. The donkey was tied up outside, her ears twitching. He put his hand on her, and she snickered and blew at him as if in reproach that he had taken so long. The grille door was ajar, the key still in the lock. He took it out and held it in his fist: Nonno Raimondi had kept a copy after all these years. The gate keened as he pulled it open. For a second, hope flickered inside him, like the candle burning at Lucia's feet.

Nonno Raimondi was sitting on the floor to the side of the altar, propped against the unfinished mural. His back was to the grille. Around him were his rags and palette, the unwound roll of his brushes.

'Nonno,' he called, but when he touched his grandfather's shoulder it was leaden, his skin washed in the stony grey that had been creeping from within him for months. Lucio prised the bottle from his hand, but it was not Raimondi Gold. He smelled the turpentine and oil mixture, already separated into its constituent parts. In his grandfather's other hand was a rag, and before him, on the altar wall, he had begun to scrub away at a segment of the mural. Lucio held his lantern up close to the spot. A section of column at the temple of Syracuse had been reduced to a muddy smear, the paint partially dissolved. He peered at it, squinting in the low light. Underneath it, he thought he could make out the ghost of another image: a faintly mottled variegation, as of feathers, and a round yellow eye that fixed him in its sights.

Leyton
1949

On the green, Uncle Jack was oiling the grass roller for its winter hibernation. Connie leaned against the wooden hut the Leyton cricketers optimistically called the clubhouse, and savoured the smells of summer: chalk and linseed oil, the old wood of a graveyard of stumps, the musty wadding of leg guards. It was also the smell of Uncle Jack, in her mind. Every Saturday as far back as she could remember, he had mowed and manicured the pitch for the Sunday game, even when there was none to be had. During the war, when the Parishes League was suspended and the Leyton Green was lucky to see a match a month — a motley affair made up of Home Guards, servicemen on leave and too-eager boys — he became even more obsessive in this ritual. He seemed to treat it as his personal war effort, as if national morale was reflected in the glossy nap of his flawless green, the pristine white of his bowling crease.

Connie came to help him on Saturday afternoons after work. As a child she had learned to hide in the clubhouse, knowing the alternative was Aunty Bea and the Christian Ladies in the memorial hall, lecturing on how to knit socks or bottle jam for endless bring-and-buys: Warships Week, Fire Watchers, the Red Cross. Compared with the complex world of female alliances formed over ration-book recipes, amateur operatic programs and, now, church-mural commissions, there was something simple, something restful, about Uncle Jack behind his roller. His patient, measured walk, the neat lift of his sprigged brogues, his self-contained purpose calmed her at times when it felt like Leyton was suffocating her every breath. Pacing silently beside him, trying to match his enormous stride on the flattened grass, was one of the most comforting memories of her childhood, one of the few that anchored her. She still liked to slip off her shoes and place her hand beside his on the rusty handle that stained their palms brown, listening to his soft wheeze as he worked, the legacy of the TB that had kept him at home during the war.

'You'd think the parish could chip in and get you a new one for next year,' she said, tapping the handle of the roller. With a practised shove, they leaned their weight against the clunking beast of it. The roller let out a prehistoric groan.

Uncle Jack exhaled, nodding towards the memorial hall. 'They got bigger and better things to raise money for than cricket,' he said.

Through the open door, they could see the clutch of women inside and hear their faint gabble.

'The Great Mural Scheme for St Margaret's,' she said. 'Anyone would think it was the Sistine Chapel the way they carry on.'

'Now then, Rita,' Uncle Jack murmured, but she could tell from the way he teased her that he felt the same. He rarely called her Connie. She suspected he'd been uncomfortable with the name change from the start but, rather than incurring the wrath of Aunty Bea, he had staged his protest by calling her a variety of nicknames, ever changing, sometimes tenuous, often clichéd, but always playing on that one constant as she grew up:

the undeniable fact of her red hair. Sometimes she was Greer, Rita or Bette, sometimes Lizzie or Your Majesty after the great Tudor Queen, sometimes plain old Red. But these multiple identities became an early security in her adopted life, the first sign of approbation, growing as they did out of his acceptance of her, his quiet affection.

She nudged him with her elbow. 'You reckon Rita Hayworth would be getting her hands dirty rolling the village green?'

He shook his head. 'Course not. The Yanks don't understand cricket,' he said, deadpan as ever.

From the memorial hall, a round of stagy laughter rang out. Connie recognised the sound of nerves fraying. The Christian Ladies were making the last frantic arrangements for Sunday's harvest fair. Mrs Cleat had closed the shop well before lunchtime that morning especially to set up the hall, and Connie had been obliged to help. Even then she had found the women in a frenzy of activity nearing panic. The stakes were high for this year's fair. The proceeds were going towards the services of Mr Harry Swann, the artist commissioned for St Margaret's murals, which, being a cause so close to home, had turned the modest fete into a gala event.

'They certainly got enough folk donating fare this year,' Uncle Jack said, as yet another family of villagers entered the hall, which was already full of flower arrangements and over-sized vegetables, jars of chutney and stewed fruit, cottage loaves and Battenbergs.

'Even Mrs Livesey brought an offering,' Connie said. 'A bouquet of carrots in a milking pail and two bottles of stout. You should have seen Mrs Cleat's face.'

'Nothing wrong with Janet Livesey's carrots. Sweetest in Leyton, I reckon.'

'Yes, but it didn't stop Mrs Cleat from setting them down

behind the sheafs of wheat at the back of the display. *Thank you kindly, Janet*, she says. *We can always rely on you for ... root vegetables.'* Uncle Jack's eye glinted as Connie mimicked the shopkeeper. *'Some people'll throw any old thing together to get in this hall and see Mr Swann's cartoons for the murals.'*

'Are they up, then, for all to see?'

Connie nodded. 'That's why there are so many donations this year. It was Mrs Cleat's idea — *exhibiting the high art alongside the harvest display.* She knew no one could resist having a nose at the sketches. But people could hardly show up empty-handed, could they?'

Uncle Jack gave a loose, knowing laugh and hummed, as if to warm up his rarely voiced opinions. 'That woman could get the devil to donate his horns if she thought it'd help her cause.'

'Mr Farrington!' Connie feigned outrage, channelling Mrs Cleat again. *'I'll have you know Mr Swann is an award-winning artist from the college in London, no less.'*

'Is he now?'

'Oh yes. His cartoons are most uplifting. They have the approval of the diocese itself, I should tell you.'

'And what exactly are these *cartoons*?'

'They're a die-rama of edificating episodes from Christian history — the flight from Egypt, the Garden of Gethsemane, the stories of St Margaret and St Dorothea. High art it'll be, but rendered to satisfy modern sensibilities. No one can accuse Leyton of lacking vision.'

Uncle Jack wheezed. 'Been memorising Mr Gilbert again, has she?'

It was Mr Gilbert who had secured the involvement of his friend Harry Swann in the Leyton mural scheme. Mr Swann was indeed an artist from the Royal College, but Mrs Repton had told her he'd been reduced to earning a living as an ad-hoc set designer in the West End. Despite apparently straitened circumstances, he'd only accepted the Leyton commission under the proviso that he could have free rein in the execution and interpretation of the murals — at least, as much as was possible within the approved religious framework.

'You're playing with fire, Harvey,' Connie had heard Mrs Repton warning her brother in the library. 'Hot-headed left-wing muralists with large egos don't mix with country parish committees.'

'Nonsense. Swann's quite aware what he's getting himself into,' Mr Gilbert replied. 'Besides, any artist would be a fool not to behave himself for the prospect of a year's continuous work these days, especially one with Swann's debts.'

'Any artist, *except* Swann,' Mrs Repton corrected him. 'That's why he has the debts in the first place. How many commissions has he actually finished?'

'When did you become such a stick-in-the-mud, Evie? Really, sometimes I think playing lady of the manor has knocked all the fun out of you.'

Connie had eagerly awaited the arrival of Mr Swann, whom she imagined as some kind of artistically tortured firebrand pacing the lanes of Leyton and upsetting everyone in the Green Man with his revolutionary opinions. But when by chance she cycled past Mr Swann on the road to St Margaret's one afternoon, she was disappointed to find him a reedy, rat-faced man wearing the clogs of a fen worker and a miner's cap.

'That Mr Swann,' Connie mused to Uncle Jack above the complaints of the oil-can. 'He's definitely not the religious type. He doesn't even seem that artistic, does he?'

Uncle Jack hummed again, considering. 'He's harmless enough, I 'spect. Nurses his pint at the Green Man against the best of us after a hard day. But he only has to open his mouth to show he were brought up on single malt, not stout.'

'But he hasn't got any money,' she said. 'I heard Mr Gilbert tell Mrs Repton.'

'I dare say. Money comes and money goes. But class is not so easy to lose, even if you try.' Her uncle paused. 'Bit like your Mr Gilbert ... parlour pinks, the pair on 'em.'

Connie was quiet. In contrast to the machine gun of Mrs Cleat's views, her uncle reminded her of a sniper, his words picking off their target, square and precise.

'Sketches aside,' he continued, 'be interesting to see what they actually get on the walls of that church.'

Aunty Bea and Mrs Cleat emerged from the hall, their heads inclined conspiratorially. 'I see those two are on talking terms again,' Connie said, indicating the two women to Uncle Jack. He began to bring the roller around in a wide arc. The ladies fussed with their hats at the door, then disappeared together down the high street. In the months of planning for the mural scheme, Connie had heard in excruciating detail both sides of the heated debate over fine art for St Margaret's. She quite understood why Mrs Cleat, with her operatic predilections, should prefer the dramatic stories of the Bible for the murals. But Connie found it quite odd that Aunty Bea, for all her fervent faith, wanted a series of memorial scenes of the war. The committee had finally taken a vote. Aunty Bea had lost by one count. For a while the village had held its breath: there threatened to be a schism among the Christian Ladies, the tremors of which were felt as far away as the Green Man, where villagers who couldn't tell a Raphael from a Rout's Cider had been heard professing their views on the matter. But the price of making a stand was too much even for Aunty Bea to bear. She reunited with the Christian Ladies, much to the delight of Reverend Stanton, who told Connie he thought his sermon on 'Holy Spirit, Community

Spirit' deserved the credit. She suspected, though, that her aunt couldn't stand to miss out on further decisions concerning the murals.

'Why d'you think Aunty Bea was dead set on war scenes anyway?' she asked Uncle Jack. He wiped his forehead on his sleeve, but remained silent. 'In the shop the other day, Mrs Livesey was going on about Uncle Bill and Monte Cassino,' she added casually, hoping she might trick her uncle into some kind of unguarded disclosure. But he only straightened and squinted across the green.

On the far side, partially obscured by the shade of the great oaks that edged it, a figure was sitting. She narrowed her eyes: it was Lucio Onorati. He was leaning back on a tree trunk, one forearm propped on his raised knee, the hand hanging across his body as if to shield the other, which worked hurriedly, secretly, across the pages of his journal folded back along one thigh.

'Looks like you're being watched,' Uncle Jack said at last. She caught herself peering, her mouth open, and she closed it quickly.

'I *am* not.' She prodded Uncle Jack in the arm. 'Might have spoken to him a couple of times, that's all,' she conceded. 'He hardly knows anyone here. Don't tell Aunty —' He shook his head to stop her. Uncle Jack wasn't one for explanations. It worked both ways — she hadn't really expected he would offer any answers about Uncle Bill either. It was his habit to avoid difficult questions, changing the subject or immersing himself in some task at hand, like he hadn't heard a word. This selective deafness infuriated Aunty Bea, which was perhaps the intention, and it often frustrated Connie, particularly as she got older. Nevertheless, she had grown up accepting that it had its benefits at times. So when she reached onto her tiptoes to kiss his cheek, she was surprised to hear him speak again.

'There's summat you should know. You might hear the wrong thing, see.'

'What?'

'It weren't Cassino. You know, Uncle Bill. It were after, in the Liri Valley ...' His eyes were restless, as if searching for the quickest route possible to what he needed to say about his brother. 'The Italians, they was on our side by then, most on 'em. But in your aunt's mind they'll always be no better than Nazis. I 'spect it's easier to blame someone, see, than accept the lame truth of it.'

Connie waited, but he didn't go on. Eventually she asked, 'What do you mean? What lame truth?'

He drew up the corner of his mouth in an impatient shrug at the words. 'Strafing. It was strafing, from American planes. That's how Bill died. Just being in the wrong spot at the wrong time. Not much glory in that, is there?' He ran a cuff across his dry lips.

'Uncle Jack,' she began, but he tilted his chin at her, signalling she should go and meet her friend. She bent down for her shoes on the grass and walked backwards a few steps, watching her uncle as he went inside the clubhouse. When she turned and began to walk towards the great oaks, Lucio Onorati was already gone.

The harvest-festival service was held in the memorial hall. Reverend Stanton had decamped all worship there so that Mr Swann could prepare the walls of St Margaret's for his murals.

'Don't let it be said that the people of Leyton can't accommodate the artistic nature,' Mrs Cleat told the Misses Penny on the steps of the hall afterwards. 'An artist of Mr Swann's calibre needs absolute quiet and the freedom to work whenever the creative urge calls.' What she had neglected to say, Connie knew, was that Mr Swann had made a contractual demand that no one enter the church while the murals were being painted. His frescoes were to be viewed by the commissioning committee only at key stages of their completion. Connie suspected Mr Gilbert's hand in this: it was his attempt to keep a lid on the inevitable gossip and village politics the paintings would provoke.

'Oh yes, of course,' Grace Penny said, agreeing with Mrs Cleat. 'And Mr Swann is working so hard. Fossett told us he'd cycled past St Margaret's well after last orders at the Green Man —'

'— and he'd seen the lights still burning in the windows —' Hope Penny broke in.

'— glowing like a divine visitation,' Grace finished. Her sister giggled. The Misses Penny habitually spoke over each other, until their timorous voices sounded as one. Connie imagined it was both the gift and the curse of sisters who had lived together for more than sixty years. She always listened to them with a fond fascination, as well as a pang of loneliness.

'Stage lights,' Mrs Cleat said in a raised voice, evidently pleased with the chance to show off her insider knowledge to the wider congregation vacating the hall. 'No miracles yet, Miss Hope. Mr Swann has brought his theatre lamps up from the West End. Artists must have their light, you know, particularly if the muse is inclined to visit at night.' In unison the Misses Penny gave their girlish laughs, but behind them Connie could hear more excited voices gathering around the figure of Mrs Stanton, who had hurried from the hall after Mr Gilbert. The reverend's wife, in her enthusiasm, had backed the schoolteacher into the memorial cross and was thrusting a roll of thick paper under his nose. Mrs Cleat's face stiffened: she could sniff out a drama at fifty paces, and Connie knew she would not be excluded from it for long. The shopkeeper broke away from the old ladies, parting the villagers with her intimidating purpose. Connie walked the Misses Penny to the gate and then skirted behind the memorial garden to offer Mr Gilbert what rescue she could.

'Well, who else could have done it?' Mrs Stanton was saying as he unscrolled the paper. 'It must have been Mr Swann. No one else in Leyton can paint like that.' She tapped the underside of the sheet as he studied it. Mrs Cleat intercepted Connie just as she was positioning herself at Mr Gilbert's elbow to take a look over his arm. Aunty Bea had already planted herself firmly on his other side.

'Perhaps he left it with the harvest donations last night before he went back down to Town,' Mrs Stanton added.

Mrs Cleat gave a tight cough and raised her chin somewhat grandly. 'Mm,' she mulled, considering the painting again, of which Connie could see nothing but the grubby margins where the paper had been taped to a board. 'Well, I expect you're right, Ivy. Mr Swann's obviously donated it for us to sell at the fair,' Mrs Cleat said, as if disappointed her opinion aligned with Mrs Stanton's. 'No doubt it'll raise a rare sum at our auction. Even more if we'd had the time to get it framed.' She tutted. 'Very generous of Mr Swann, no less. Very generous indeed.'

Mrs Cleat placed a hand on her hat and proceeded to weave through the departing congregation, eager to disseminate the news. Mrs Stanton sighed and took her place at Mr Gilbert's arm. Connie tried to peer around her, but the rouged netting of Mrs Stanton's hat obscured her view even more.

'Nice enough, I 'spect,' came Aunty Bea's voice from the other side of Mr Gilbert. 'Mind, I'm not one for hanging pictures of dead creatures over me mantel.'

'It's a still life, Beatrice,' Mr Gilbert said vaguely, engrossed in the artwork.

'Is it now? A still life?' Aunty Bea spoke with the superiority of someone who understood that a life study attracted the same dust and cobwebs as any other type of picture when framed and hanged. Connie prayed for her to stop there. She had heard Aunty Bea's views on art at the Big House when she helped at spring-cleaning. 'Who wants to stare up this enormous old goat's nostrils on the way to bed, I ask you?' Aunty Bea would declare, standing on the stepladder to clean the portraits along the wide staircase. To her aunt, the merit of an artwork always seemed in inverse proportion to its size, and the intricacies of its moulded frame where dirt could harbour. 'Least it's small,' she offered over Mr Gilbert's shoulder. Connie bit the inside of her cheek. How Aunty Bea could have ended up on a committee making decisions about church murals was one of Leyton's many ironies. Mrs Stanton moved to take her aunt's arm, and the two stepped around the memorial cross to search out Mrs Cleat, finally allowing Connie to see the painting in Mr Gilbert's hands.

It was an oil-on-paper, finely detailed and textured. She had read enough art books, and studied their plates, to know that it was in a realist style, not unlike some of the Pre-Raphaelite studies she had seen in catalogues in the Reptons' library. The subject was a large hare laid upon a hessian sack, its head at the unnatural angle of dead quarry, its orange eye the focal point of colour in the scene. Arranged about the hare, and bound coarsely with twine, were the hedgerow fruits of the summer's end: the drooping heads of elder, heavy with over-ripe berries; rosehips starting to shrivel; and the hearts of hazelnuts browning on the branch among brittle leaves. At the table's edge, the loose folds of a cloth were gathered under a skinning knife, soiled from use.

'My God, it's beautiful,' Connie said. It was true, but she also felt a creeping sadness work its way over her as she admired the study.

'Apparently it was left tucked among the corn dollies,' Mr Gilbert said wryly. 'It's not Swann's. I'm sure of it.'

'How do you know?' she asked, even though she was already certain of the painter.

'There's no signature. Swann signs everything, even his sketches, and these days he doesn't so much as pick up his brush without knowing he'll get paid for it. He doesn't *donate*.' He smiled at her. 'His artistic ego as much as necessity demands it, I suspect.'

She examined the hare again, the way the artist had caught the variations in the fleck and sheen of its coat, the veins of its translucent ears, the eye that was dead as a pebble.

'Besides, this is … it's not Swann's style … quite remarkable …' he continued, as if to himself. She waited for him to explain.

Mr Gilbert let out a guilty laugh. 'It's just that it's too good to be Swann's. Still, what's the harm, I suppose?'

'The harm?'

'In allowing them to believe it's his, letting them auction it at the fair. Swann won't care, especially if it helps pay his fee.' Again he held up the painting at arm's length and studied it, frowning. 'I can't think who could have done this.'

Without answering, she ran to the gate and took up her bike from the wall.

'Connie?' she heard him call, but she only held up her hand to him as she pedalled away, along the high street and out towards Bythorn Rise.

She kept a lookout for Lucio on the gate at the bottom of the hill, sitting in the spot that she'd begun to think of as his. She trusted he would appear eventually, either from the farm or from the copse of trees down by the brook. The sun shone on her face with surprising heat for once, as if summer had saved all its energy for a last struggle with autumn.

When she finally spotted him, he was approaching from the bridge, his clothes dripping and his feet bare, his boots strung over his shoulder. She found herself unexpectedly filled with a childish envy. He'd been swimming in the brook, while she had spent the glorious morning suffocating through the harvest service in the memorial hall. He came up to the gate and hung his boots over it, then climbed to sit beside her. With his wrist he pushed away his thick, wet hair. It stayed back from his forehead for once, making his face seem boyish and vulnerable.

She already knew enough about him not to expect small talk, so they sat together, listening to the chatter of insects in the tall verge, to the liquid song of a skylark in the stubbled field behind them. At last she tapped the rolled journal, dog-eared and grimy, that poked from his back pocket.

'You going to show me, then?'

He didn't move and she thought perhaps it was his way of saying no. But a second later he jumped down from the fence in one clean twist, took the rolled folio from his pocket, and handed it to her with no more thought than if it had been last week's newspaper. He leaned his back against the gate, letting his elbows rest on the top rung. She watched him close his eyes and angle his face up to the sun, just as she had done. She wondered whether she would ever know what was going on in his head.

The journal roll in her hands was nothing more than a wad of over-thumbed papers stitched crudely and bound to a fold of pliant leather. She unwound the string that seemed to hold it all together and smoothed open the scroll of pages. Inside, she leafed through a patchwork of sketches, things that were familiar to her scribbled alongside the foreign. She recognised the birds of the Leyton hedgerow, their nests and eggs, a muntjac feeding, sticklebacks in a jar, a pinemarten in the spinney. There was Mr Rose drinking from his hipflask and Fossett with a brace of cony on his shoulder. There was even a study of Connie herself, holding the handlebars of her bike. She hurried over this, afraid he might notice her vain fascination, but more afraid to see herself as he did. Among these subjects, which felt like meeting old friends wearing new clothes, she found the unfamiliar: the flaking belltower of some other church, a line of wooded mountains and the cut of a valley, a wide winged bird of prey viewed from above, the loose hair of a woman, a dog suckling a litter. There, too, was the hare she had seen lying in the verge when she'd met him coming from his traps. It was studied from various angles, but the style was the same as the painted version. She knew to come straight to the point.

'That painting you left in the memorial hall. They think it's Mr Swann's.' He opened his eyes but seemed in no way curious as to who Mr Swann was. Perhaps Mr Gilbert had already told him of the artist and the mural scheme during one of their lessons. 'They're going to auction it at the fair this afternoon.' He didn't answer, but lifted his chin at her in a vague acknowledgement. 'You should tell them it's yours. You should get the credit for it. Something as beautiful as that.'

He squinted at her. 'Beautiful?'

She realised she'd touched a nerve, and she felt the small seduction of seeing her opinion matter to him. 'I did think it was beautiful. But in a sad way. It made me think as much about death as it did about life.' He was studying her, and it seemed useless to lie, as if he already knew her thoughts anyway. 'Isn't that what life studies are supposed to do?'

'Maybe,' he said. He took up his boots from the gate and pulled them on, stamping the clods off in the road and then wiping the residual mud in the grass. The sight of him doing this — a habit that every villager in Leyton developed with no more thought than blinking or breathing — filled her with a strange despair.

'Why?' she asked him. 'Why are you hacking sugar beet and pawning rabbit skins when you can do this?' She jumped down from the fence to face him, the folio flopping in her hand as she held it up. 'There are so many places this could take you. You should be going to an art college somewhere ... Mr Gilbert could help you.'

He bent to tie his bootlaces.

'Don't you see what a gift it is, how lucky you are to have it? Something that could ... that could get you out of here?' She heard the quickening of her words, the panic in them, and it shocked her.

He took the journal from her hand and rolled it up again, jamming it back into his pocket. 'Let them think Mr Swann made the painting.'

'Why?' She didn't want him to go yet, but she didn't know how to stop him. 'Why did you do it at all then? Why bother showing off if you're simply going to walk away and let someone else take the credit?' Her disappointment had become petty and she knew it. She wanted to grab his wrist and hold him there, but he already had his back to her, reaching for the gate handle. 'It's dishonest. It's more or less ... cowardly,' she threw out.

'It's all I've got,' he said. 'All I can give — for the harvest fair.' At once she heard the quiet injury in his voice, but also the regret, the closely held embarrassment, like a child spurned by older boys for not understanding the rules of their game.

Her throat tightened as she remembered an image from that morning in the memorial hall. It was of Mr Rose bringing in the corn dollies, woven for luck as always by the Misses Penny from the last sheaf of wheat cut at Repton's. Every year, their arrival drew a murmur of delight and relief from the volunteers, tradition and superstition mingling to put the dollies at the centre of the harvest display. But that morning, Mr Rose had brought them not in his usual wooden crate, but in a sturdy basket, woven expertly from bulrushes — a basket of the kind, she now realised, she'd only ever seen Tommy Pointon showing off as a trap for hedgerow birds when they were children. She understood now: Aldo Onorati had made that basket as a donation for the harvest fair, and it too was the one thing he was able to give.

The gate wrung out a groan as Lucio pushed it open, and she thought the sound might have come from her. She was mortified. She hadn't been able to see beyond his talent to the sheer simplicity of his intention. The more she learned of them, the more the Onorati seemed an enigma to her. She wondered again at their past, a past that could make them so hungry for the paltry offerings of Leyton, the mean-spirited acceptance of its inhabitants.

'The fair,' she said by way of appeasing her guilt. 'Will you at least come to the fair, then? They roast a pig tonight. On the green. And there's a bit of music.' She watched his wet hair nudging back to the bridge of his nose, glinting slick as a polished boot in the sun. 'You could come with me.'

He didn't answer. She reached for her bike as an excuse to turn away and let the full weight of her embarrassment take over. When she glanced back, he was already making his way along the edge of the ploughed field in the direction of the cottage. She didn't know whether she was angrier with herself or with him. His journal wagged at her from his back pocket, but she wasn't thinking about art anymore.

'I did expect Mrs Stanton to find another shilling and outbid me at the last minute, but there,' Mrs Cleat said, holding up the still life and tipping her chin with such pride, as if she might have painted it herself. Connie watched the group of Christian Ladies gathered around the tea urn catch their breath and marvel somewhat dutifully. She suspected the painting was in fact too graphic for their tastes, but the auction for it had been the highlight of the fair: a quick-fire attack of bold bids that drew out into a skirmish between Mrs Cleat and Mrs Stanton, determined to gain ground on each other in halfpennies and farthings. When the hammer fell in Mrs Cleat's favour, Connie hadn't seen her so flushed and speechless since dancing a foxtrot with Mr Gilbert at the royal-wedding street party. She still glowed even now, although her ability to speak had clearly returned.

'The reverend's got paintings enough at the rectory for Mrs Stanton to admire, I'm sure,' Mrs Cleat said archly. 'And I so wanted a little study of Mr Swann's for myself.' Mrs Armer nodded her approval, but Agnes, elegant as ever, stared languidly beyond her mother, towards the shouts and laughter that carried inside from the green.

The afternoon was fading on the harvest fair, stretching into a red, furrowed dusk. The children, with their race ribbons and bags of half-eaten fudge, were being dragged home. In the centre of the green, the men had gathered for skittles and quoits while the light lasted, but Splice the Mice, Leyton's favourite harvest game, always attracted the biggest group. Connie could make out Derek Livesey on a ladder, his hands in the twin lengths of piping, ready to release the leather 'mice'. Behind the crowd, the beater would be waiting with a rounders bat to belt the mice as they fell through the pipes into the air below. She spotted Mr Gilbert exchanging coins in a huddle of men to one side.

Connie heard a hush descend across the spectators. Two smart thwacks rang out. Both mice had been hit, one after the other, fired in a clean line down the green. The villagers seemed to inhale as one. It was rare that anyone hit both mice consecutively, least of all this late in the harvest fair, when the vast majority of men had just emerged from an afternoon in the Green Man. The crowd opened up and the beater became visible, handing over the bat and rolling down his sleeves. She recognised Vittorio Onorati.

'Cocksure of himself, isn't he?' Agnes said over Connie's shoulder on the steps of the hall. 'He's certainly settled into Leyton without as much as a *n'er-you-mind*.' She was twisting a lick of newly cropped hair behind her ear. 'God knows we could use a bit of foreign colour, though.'

Agnes's hairstyle, short as a boy's, had caused quite a stir over the counter at Cleat's. Connie saw now that, far from being artless, it served to heighten Agnes's very female and very sophisticated charms. Before she had time to reply, she found herself being propelled down the steps and onto the green, her arm pulled through Agnes's as if they were sisters meandering through the crowd. Vittorio caught sight of them as they drew near, and he grinned — but not solely at her, Connie noticed. Agnes shifted her weight to one hip and a laugh fluttered from her.

Connie was crushed at being played so easily. As much as

she wanted to stay, she couldn't bear to talk to Vittorio in the shadow of Agnes, evidently searching for an introduction. Alongside her magazine hair and angled hips, Connie felt she was no more refined than one of the raw sugar beet that the Italians unearthed from the dirt of Leyton every day. And Agnes knew it.

Behind them, not far from the clubhouse, Mr Rose was overseeing the spit roast. As Agnes became distracted with the approach of Mr Gilbert and Vittorio, Connie withdrew her arm and crossed the grass, escaping to the glow of the brazier and the scent of roasted meat.

'Smell it?' Mr Rose said to her as she drew up to the fire. 'Not long now.' The sweet aroma of cooked pork had been wafting into the memorial hall for most of the afternoon, clinging to her clothes, so she could barely smell anything else. It was a tradition of the harvest fair that Mr Repton send down a pig and a keg of cider for the village. Later he would stop by the fire to personally thank the harvest workers, just as his father used to do. Connie knew that even Vittorio's champion effort at Splice the Mice would not hold the Leyton villagers from the prospect of free pork and cider for much longer, but she savoured the short reprieve from the crowd, listening to the hiss and crackle of fat on the embers.

On the other side of the brazier Fossett was tapping the cider keg. 'How's our little shopkeeper then? All on your lonesome?' he called to Connie. Without waiting for an answer, he took several swift gulps from his tankard, then pulled in his chin in a struggle to suppress a belch, which he lost.

Connie offered Fossett a pinched smile. Her bones ached in her limbs with a kind of desperate weariness. She would rather remain invisible, overlooked by the village, than be thought of as nothing more than Mrs Cleat's successor. And an evening witnessing Agnes work her charms by firelight seemed even less enticing to her than a conversation with Fossett and Mr Rose. She slipped away from the spit, back towards the memorial hall. Inside, her aunt and the last of the Christian Ladies were washing up the tea things, their silhouettes criss-crossing the kitchenette, their muted voices talking over each other behind the closed hatch.

She was thinking she might as well cycle home when she saw a figure edging the green from the road. It was a woman, her grey dress sheer and full-skirted, shimmering in the low light and making her face and bare arms seem all the paler. Only Mrs Repton could afford the New Look in the village. She was barefoot, Connie noticed, her white shoes swinging in her hand, and she seemed almost transparent in that airy grey dress. Connie thought of a seed clock blown in from the fields: one puff of the breeze and she might fragment in the night air.

Just as Connie was about to make her way towards her, Mr Repton appeared. He was considerably older than his wife, which was accentuated further by his size and solemnity. He was a barrel-chested man who looked his best in hunting pinks and shooting tweeds. Standing there in a shirt and tie, his hands free of either reins or gun, he seemed purposeless, somehow diminished, and Connie guessed that he knew it. He bent stiffly towards his wife, squeezing her arm and mouthing terse words in her ear, like a parent threatening a troublesome child in public. He glanced at the shoes dangling from her hand and turned to join his employees at the fire, leaving his wife alone.

Mrs Repton blinked slowly, her focus soft and glazed. 'Connie,' she said, 'Connie,' this time with relief, her fingers trembling as she took her arm. When she pressed her lips together, warding off tears, Connie led her around the green, far away from the light of the fire and the hall. They stopped in the shadows cast by the oaks along the spinney. Mrs Repton stifled a noise that seemed half sob, half laugh, and let her shoes fall to the grass. She searched inside her evening bag, hanging from her wrist. 'Odious. Odious events, you know,' she said, withdrawing a cigarette from a silver case. Connie helped her with the match.

'A keg and porker with the villagers of Leyton? What more could you want?' she said.

Mrs Repton laughed. 'Oh, not this. We've come from the De Veres' garden party at Kimbolton. Mind-numbing. Thankfully it's the last one of the summer. Then it'll be the endless round of autumn shoots and meets, I suppose. What joy!' Cigarette smoke curled over her lip and veiled her face in the night air. 'I'm sorry. As you can see, I've had too much to drink.'

She saw Connie watching her every move and cast a rueful smile. 'What I wouldn't give to be you, Connie. To have it all before me again. There's so much on offer now for young women, ever since the war. All you have to do is choose.'

Connie pulled away from her.

'What? Don't you think so?'

'What do you think's on offer to *me*, exactly?' she said, fighting to keep the irritation from her voice. 'Managing the shop for Mrs Cleat on Thursdays as well as Tuesdays, maybe? Or being allowed to use the meat slicer or sign for stock?'

Mrs Repton thumbed the end of her cigarette. Ash broke from it and fell between them. 'The world doesn't stop at Leyton, Connie.'

'Not for some people, perhaps.' Her eyes followed the cut of Mrs Repton's fine dress, the high white heels splayed on the grass.

'You're right, of course. For me it goes much further — all the way to Kimbolton and Hammerton. Aren't I lucky?'

Mrs Repton walked a few restless steps, her skirt sighing about her. 'You've still got the chance, Connie ...' she began, but she trailed off, her lips quivering, once more the scolded child. They avoided each other's gaze.

'I think I'll go to the car. Lie down for a minute.' Mrs Repton backed away, still unsteady on her feet.

'I'll walk you,' Connie said, putting out a hand to her.

'No. I'm fine, really.' She brushed her fingertips over her forehead. Across the green, the reedy sound of Bobby Keyes's clarinet could be heard above the villagers' chatter. 'Perhaps you could get me some water?'

Connie nodded. 'Sit down here and I'll run to the hall.'

As she headed for the buildings, she had the sense of something unravelling: she felt a strange responsibility, like being asked, as a child, to fetch Aunty Bea's knitting, only to watch helplessly as the needles fell and the stitches ran away. She had always seen a sadness in Mrs Repton, something that weighted her expressions at unexpected moments or gave an edge to comments she made in the library. But this had made her all the more beautiful, more complex and mysterious to Connie, who assumed it was particular to all well-educated and cultured older women. She had never thought that a life of ease and luxury, of opportunities, could ever make anyone truly unhappy. For Connie, Mrs Repton's sadness was like the ebony comb she sometimes wore when she dressed for dinner: a bland old thing transformed into something elegant, serving to highlight the gold of her hair. She could not accept the suggestion that Mrs Repton was in any way like herself — trapped by circumstance. She refused to allow it.

By the time she had avoided Aunty Bea's questions in the kitchenette, filled a cup with water and carried it back, Mrs Repton was gone. Connie realised she had expected it, and was even relieved. Still, she paced the spot for a while, as if Mrs Repton might return.

The moon had risen and the shadows were cooler, damper. A few feet away, she caught the glow of something in the rough before the trees. When she got closer, she remembered Mrs Repton's discarded shoes. She studied the pointed toes, the delicate heels clumped with turf, the very whiteness of the leather, like she had come across a pair of rare nocturnal creatures foraging in the spinney. She shook off her sandals and nudged her toes gingerly into a shoe. As she wobbled on one leg and reached for the other heel, she heard a voice. She swung around to see someone squatting against an oak trunk.

'God!' she said. 'How long have you been there?'

Vittorio nodded towards the shoes. 'Be careful. They might bite.'

She heard the amusement in his voice and flicked off the heels a little too quickly, stepping back into her sandals. 'They do bite I don't know how women can wear them. That's obviously why they take them off whenever they can.' She turned away, embarrassed, but had to press back a smile despite herself. He'd come looking for her.

'Didn't you like the fire?' she said. He shrugged and smirked at her, as if he knew very well what she was really asking. They heard Bobby starting a new song on his clarinet.

'*Far Away Places*,' she said. 'Do you know it? From the radio?' He shook his head. 'Bobby's in the Benford Marching Band, but he wants to get a jazz group together. He's good enough to.'

It was nervous chatter, from being there alone with him in the dark. He must have sensed it, for he got up. 'We can walk.'

'Where to?'

'Anywhere.' He pointed two fingers along the trees. 'Just to walk.'

They strolled to the accompaniment of unseen creatures beyond the oaks, woodpigeons snug in the branches overhead. She became aware of the cold, and the nutty smell of the mellowing hedgerows.

'Will you ever go back, d'you think? To Italy?'

He dug his hands in his pockets. 'Not now. Maybe one day. When I'm rich.' He flicked a coin and caught it with his other hand.

'Planning on making a fortune, are you?'

'Yes.'

She was surprised how serious he was, how certain, like it was already mapped out and would be happening soon. 'You moving on from hoeing sugar beet, then?'

He didn't answer at first, and she regretted her tone: he became restless, irritated. 'My father says we must wait seven years. Mr Repton can help us apply for English passports after that. Then I get a better job.'

'Seven years! It can't be that long, surely? Why can't you get another job now?'

'Mr Repton sponsors us. My father says we can't change. If we don't have papers they send us back to Italy. And then —' He stopped and pushed a foot against a tree trunk. His breath was short and angry. 'Then Lucio and I will be called by the Italian army — for service. My father doesn't want it. He wants nothing to do with the army, with Italy now. Not anymore.' His face in the shadows made his mood all the blacker.

'Don't you miss home at all?'

He hesitated before nodding, almost guiltily.

'What? What do you miss?'

'The sun.'

She laughed. 'Obviously.'

'The water.'

'The water? What, for swimming?'

'For drinking.'

'How can you miss water? Doesn't water taste the same wherever you are?'

He shook his head. 'In our village, high up, there's a spring that comes from a split in the mountain. It's cold in the cave where the water comes, and quiet. Like walking inside the rock. And when you drink, you taste the earth and the stone.'

She imagined the chill of it, the metallic water on her tongue. 'So what does our water taste like?'

'Here, it tastes different.'

'Like what?'

He started to walk again. 'Here, it tastes like sweat.'

They had come back to where they began, to where the white shoes lay discarded in the grass. He reached down to pick them up. 'But here, you can make money from sweat. Here, there are lots of chances for someone like me. Then, when I'm rich, I pay someone else to sweat for me. Same as Mr Repton.' He grinned and took hold of her hand, hooking the straps of the shoes over her fingers. And as he held her wrist, she had to look away so he didn't see the pleasure it gave her. Or the fear, like being too close to a flare — bright and dazzling but beyond her control, eventually leaving her with nothing but smoke.

She backed away from him, towards the spot along the path where she had propped her bike. 'When can I see you?' he called.

'You know where I work,' she said. 'It's not like I'm going anywhere either.'

She followed the track and found her bike. When she switched on the lamp and sat back in the saddle, she thought she saw the flash of a face, one she had caught before in her beam. 'Lucio?' But the face disappeared, the undergrowth stirring softly, a bird beating up to its roost, swallowed in the black boughs.

PART

TWO

Montelupini
1943

The afternoon was damp and claustrophobic. Lucio felt grubby vapours hanging like phantoms over the hills. A lacing of drizzle had begun to collect on his jacket and on the donkey's coat, visible as frost, and the trees dripped despondently. Ahead of him, Vittorio was as sullen as the weather. It was the first time their mother had allowed them to make the trading trip to Cori without her. The walk across the mountains took the best part of a day, and they had to stay in the town overnight, at a cousin's house. After the market, which had begun at dawn, their return journey seemed all the longer, not helped by the fact that their trade had been shamefully poor. Even Viviana hadn't managed to sniff out something for their supper to redeem them. She disappeared from time to time, only to re-emerge from the undergrowth, uninspired, her coat slick and darkened from the wet.

The buckle on her nail-studded collar jangled intermittently. It was the same one Valeriana had worn. Lucio had needed to pierce an extra hole in the leather to accommodate her smaller neck. She hadn't grown as big as her mother, but it still amazed him to see the beast she had become, to watch her keen muscular form as she hunted, a far cry from the runt that had once curled in his palms. She'd clung to life as a puppy, stubbornly, the way those who have death close upon their heels sometimes do, surprising everyone. And for that he had called her Viviana, the force of life. Now the name seemed doubly fitting: their past two harvests had been so blighted, their livestock so depleted, that Viviana did not eat the scraps from their table — they had become the guests at hers.

A scuffle in the scrub made the dog roll off a growl. She froze, then darted away. Vittorio scanned the wilting meadow, clicking his tongue and calling her name, 'Ia. Iana!' Within minutes the dog sprang from the shuddering grasses, throwing a spray of dirt into the air ahead of her. They caught an arc of fur, the flash of a white underside, and then Viviana was on top of her quarry, panting and whining, impatient for her orders. It was a rabbit, small and fat, pregnant perhaps. It seemed almost knowing in its stunned compliance. Vittorio pulled out Urso's bone-handled knife, and Lucio started to fuss at the straps on the donkey's load, trying not to hear the tug of the blade, the release of innards across the chalk path, the noise of Viviana as she choked them back.

'Better than nothing, I suppose.' Vittorio grunted and held up the carcass. From the corner of his eye Lucio saw his brother wiping the knife on the grass. Despite everything, he had still not managed to steel his stomach to hunting. It was not in his nature any more than it was in Vittorio's to pick up a pencil and trace the line of Viviana's ribcage, or catch the angle of her spine as she leaned into the breeze, her tail as straight as a whip. It was Vittorio who had trained her for the chase, and it was Vittorio who had stolen milk to keep her alive as a puppy. Lucio had stood by while his brother ducked into Berto Udine's goat pen to draw milk from two or three nannies in quick succession, had followed his leisurely walk down the

Viale Roma with the corked bottle warm inside his jacket, and had listened in silence as he called good morning to the women at the washhouse.

'Here, let me help you with that basket,' Vittorio would say to Signora Udine, Berto's own mother, lifting the load of washing onto her head and turning his grin on the women at their washboards.

'Get on with you, Primo,' some of them would say, tittering, while others fixed him in their sights and called to each other, 'Santa Lucia, what I wouldn't give to be fifteen years younger ...'

Lucio could hardly believe it was the same boy who set traps in the barn at Collelungo and casually mutilated rats and mice, just enough to slow them so the young Viviana could get a sense of the chase, a taste for blood. Or the same boy who could, without thinking, slit the neck of the dog's first live quarry — a badger, Lucio remembered. In the light of the lantern, the animal's blood had sprayed across his brother's cheek, and he had thought about their own blood, running in their veins: how different it was, how different things might have been had his father chosen Primo for that last hunt.

As they tacked down to join the path at Collelungo, a light flickered in the meadow by the Fontana Nuova.

'It'll be Corbellino,' Vittorio muttered. 'Coming to check his father's traps, no doubt.' The poor harvests and general shortage of meat had made anyone who could fashion a snare into a hunter these days. Corbellino was two years older than Lucio, a handsome, popular boy who had been elected leader of the Avanguardisti, an honour for which Vittorio was unable to forgive him.

'We can save him the climb. His traps are empty. I already checked them,' his brother said with unveiled satisfaction.

He held up the carcass of the cony. 'He can sniff on this if he likes. It'll be the closest he'll get to red meat tonight.'

Lucio said nothing, but the nearer they came to the yellow light, the more they realised it did not swing to the stride of a walker. It glowed static in the night, and gradually other lights began to appear around it. They smelled a fire and roasting meat, and soon became aware of a camp in the meadow. They could hear the clang of pots and utensils, the odd cadence of foreign voices, and intermittent laughter, boisterous and bold.

They descended the track from Collelungo, mesmerised by what they saw — uncertain, thrilled and indignant at once, as if they had come across a herd of wild stallions among the campo's mules. They stood in the shadow of the washhouse, watching the silhouettes of soldiers pass between their tents. Lucio strained to see their faces. Some were ruddy and plump-cheeked, no more manly than his own; others had pale skin and hair the colour of maize in the firelight.

He thought of his father and Urso smoking or playing scopa about a campfire in some unknown place. In his mind, their faces changed, replaced by those of Vittorio and Corbellino, Bocca and Rampichino, all the wide-eyed, glossy-skinned village boys he'd grown up with, telling jokes and playing morra and laughing in their Fascist Youth uniforms. The one face he could not see among them was his own.

The donkey snorted and sidestepped, and Viviana, who had been sitting patiently on Lucio's foot, got up and began to pace, sniffing the air. He pulled on Vittorio's sleeve and began to lead the donkey away, up Via del Soccorso. But his brother was slow to follow, reluctant to drag his gaze from the camp. When he finally did, he brooded the rest of the way home.

'Fagiolo said the Germans would come,' Lucio offered, wondering if he should have shared the information sooner.

'There's been a troop camped in Monteferro for a fortnight. I heard him telling Professore Centini.'

'So what?' his brother replied. 'They're only passing through. Even the bastard circus doesn't think Montelupini's worth the stop.' It was the sort of thing Nonno Raimondi would have said. But Vittorio's voice cracked, lacking conviction, and Lucio thought it wasn't the first time his brother — or his grandfather, for that matter — had sworn something they didn't believe.

As he undressed that night, Lucio asked Vittorio a question. 'What do you think they want here? The Germans?' But his brother wasn't listening. He was like this sometimes when he hunted: blinkered, unswerving, almost feverish with it. He wouldn't settle until he had what he wanted. But this time, Lucio didn't want to imagine what that might be.

Signora Mazzocchi steadied herself against the counter of the butcher's shop. Lucio had come in early to bring Fabrizia the pelt of the cony and some of its meat, and now found himself trapped there, the hatch blocked by Padre Ruggiero's housekeeper. She was red-faced and breathless, tripping over her words.

'Yes … that's what I saw, I tell you … right in the meadow by the Fontana Nuova … their intimates strung up like flags for all to see!'

Fabrizia glanced at Lucio and brought her attention back to cleaving the bones before her. They both knew Signora Mazzocchi must have trotted down from Padre Ruggiero's villa at the first glimmer of dawn, so she could be in the thick of the news as it spread through the village.

'It's indecent … improper. They're supposed to be the German army, not a bunch of gypsies … Is that rabbit there, signora?' she asked Fabrizia, as if to justify her presence in the shop, even though she clearly had no intention of buying meat that morning. Not that there was much on offer: Fabrizia's supply these days had been reduced to scrawny poultry, the underfed pigs and goats of villagers desperate for cash to buy basic provisions: oil, salt, more flour or maize to tide them over until the harvest. Spring was always the hungriest month in the mountains. Lucio brought her whatever they could spare from Viviana's quarry and she sold it in the shop, allowing them all a little cash to keep them in staples.

'I've already spoken to Professore Centini about it, of course — great bumbling oaf that he is. He says his hands are tied.' She exhaled peevishly, puffing out her lips and reminding Lucio even more of a mule. The constant simmer of her opinion seemed to bubble up and overflow with a hiss, like milk boiling on a stove. 'Let's hope Aldo Onorati comes home soon,' Signora Mazzocchi said, glancing pointedly over her shoulder at Lucio's mother, who had just passed the window and entered the shop. 'Centini is lost without him. Aldo would never have allowed Germans to camp right where our women wash their clothes. It's asking for trouble … How fresh is that spinosa at the back?'

Lucio knew his mother was used to the minor insults of the village women — talking of her business without addressing her, as if her condition made her deaf or mute, or plain stupid. But sometimes he suspected they did this for another reason altogether: they couldn't bear to look her in the face, to fall under her unflinching gaze, for fear of being exposed to her opinions, which they knew to be dangerous, or, worse still, might reveal the pettiness of their own.

'I hardly think so, Signora Mazzocchi,' his mother said. But she faced the window to the piazza, impatient to be gone.

'Hardly think what, pardon me?' the housekeeper replied, feigning surprise at being addressed. 'Do you mean your husband would not have managed these Germans better?'

'No,' she answered. 'I hardly think it's improper they should be camped there.'

'Oh?' Signora Mazzocchi flushed, seeming reluctant to be drawn into an exchange.

'Are we not in bed with the Germans now?' his mother said. 'They're going to be seeing our underwear at some point, don't you think?'

Lucio heard snickering from behind the counter. Fabrizia opened her mouth and took a deep breath in a half-hearted attempt to stop herself. 'How is your son, Signora Mazzocchi?' she said, her voice unnaturally smooth, solicitous. 'Has Angelo received his papers yet?' She picked up her cleaver, and the muscles in her forearms, round and solid as ham hocks, twitched.

Signora Mazzocchi stiffened. 'No. Well, I'll think about that spinosa. Good morning, signore.' She hurried out and the beaded curtain at the door clacked in her wake. Fabrizia's stomach made the butcher's block shudder as she laughed.

'How is it you know the exact thing to shut La Mula up?' his mother asked.

'The shop feeds me all the latest ammunition.' Fabrizia wiped her knife. 'Ah, she makes me sick with her *Il Duce* this and *our men* that, and all the while her son's dodging the call. He's been seventeen for the last three years. You know she's packed him off to family in Siracusa? Underneath it all she's hedging her bets that Mussolini won't last the spring. But the cheek of the woman, wishing Aldo home, like he could simply hop on a boat.'

His mother hummed a vague reply, her washing basket

creaking on her hip. Lucio stepped through the hatch to the other side of the counter. Fabrizia stopped what she was doing and looked between him and his mother. 'So it's true, then? You *have* heard something.' They didn't answer.

Every time a letter arrived from his father, Lucio felt guilty for it, for not missing him in the way that Fabrizia missed Urso, and he saw the same guilt mirrored in his mother's face. The letters had come regularly, at first — from Valmontone, then Naples, and later Tripoli. He noticed the way his mother read the thin pages, the way her eyes jumped over the words, as if searching for something she knew she wouldn't find there. She would leave the sheets in the middle of the kitchen table, perhaps hoping he and Vittorio might read something in them that she could not. But after a while, even Vittorio stopped talking about their father's desert postings, the day-to-day lives of the soldiers, the early successes of the conflict. As the campaign in North Africa began to falter — the facts relayed by Fagiolo's wireless, which picked up Radio Londra — they barely spoke of the letters, of their gradual tapering off and then their complete absence.

When they finally received news that his father had been captured in Bardia, it shocked Lucio less than the ease with which their lives continued in the face of it. The next day dawned just like the one before, and the one before that. They still had their work to do, the hours longer and harder, especially as his mother refused to let them leave school, making them catch up on their chores at first light and well beyond dusk. Yet the months and the seasons trickled on, like the streams in the valley that always found their course somehow, regardless of the dams and diversions the village children built across them. When he thought of his father now, he was but a presence below the surface, a ripple in a moving current where a boulder or log had toppled and sunk.

And so it seemed unfair that they, rather than Fabrizia, received the first news after nearly five months of waiting.

'You might as well tell me. I know you got a letter yesterday. Pettegola has already announced it.'

His mother dropped the basket on the floor and sighed. 'Poor Orazio,' she said. 'Pettegola might have saved him the trouble of riding twenty kilometres uphill.'

Orazio Sposi, the postman who rode from Monteferro on his bicycle once a week, rarely arrived before the contents of his letters. His wife, Giga Sposi, as postmistress of Monteferro, had access to one of the only telephones in the mountains, allowing her to call Professore Centini's wife at the town hall and appraise her of news well before Signor Sposi had even finished affixing his bicycle clip at the gate. The war had led Signora Sposi to see a certain national duty in her prying, and in recent years it was said the postmistress had cultivated a surgical hand with a steaming kettle and knife. Disseminating updates from the front and screening letters for anti-Fascist plots, she liked to suggest, were a contribution to the war effort. Everyone else, of course, saw her for what she was: a gossip, a pettegola.

'Is she right then? Has Aldo been sent to England?' Fabrizia set down her knife and rested her fists on the chopping board, clenching them until her knuckles turned white.

His mother nodded. 'He's been shipped from the camp in South Africa to Liverpool.'

Fabrizia crossed herself. 'Thank Santa Lucia. He's safe, at least.'

'They've put him to work on a farm, in the south some-where ... here, read it yourself. There isn't much. I suppose they're not allowed to say a lot.'

She laid the flimsy letter on the counter. Lucio stepped towards the door and Fabrizia's eyes fell on him, swimming with worry and hope — searching for something of Urso, anything. He shook his head at her, the slightest of movements, almost nothing at all. But she caught it. Her hand closed over the letter and the colour drained from her cheeks.

'Keep it,' his mother said to her friend. 'Read it later when you're alone.' She picked up her basket and headed for the door.

'Leti?' Fabrizia called, following them. 'Those Germans. They say they have money and food to trade for wine and grappa.' She cleared her throat, forcing herself to become the businesswoman again. 'They might be good for more than spying on our *intimates*.'

His mother smiled, and nodded her farewell. As he left, Lucio felt Fabrizia press something into his palm. Outside, he sat on the lip of the fountain and watched the new spring sunlight playing on the water. The slice of smoked meat was tough and dry, but it didn't matter. He chewed on it and tried to remember the last time he had tasted guanciale. Not since before the war, not since Urso had folded up a slice and thrust it in his mouth.

That afternoon he found his mother in the cellar, among the dwindling bottles of Raimondi Gold. They could count them now within a few minutes. His grandfather's chestnut barrels were empty. He and Vittorio had searched every cave and derelict stable between the Vigna Alba and Collelungo, halfway to Montemezzo, but they could not find where he had hidden his still and vats. So even if they could have muddled together a recipe, they lacked the equipment to make the grappa. Instead they traded their vinacce with a maker in Morolo, but Lucio could tell that the resulting grappa was nothing at all like Raimondi Gold. They sold it to a tavern on the other side of Monteferro and kept the Osteria Nettuno supplied from their original stores of Gold.

That first harvest after Nonno Raimondi had gone, his mother had sworn them all to secrecy, including Fagiolo. 'If Padre Ruggiero finds out we no longer know the recipe, he'll give the Vigna Alba to another family — the Ronzoni or the Ippoliti, someone he thinks can work it better now Aldo is gone. I know it.' She had searched Fagiolo's face a little desperately. 'Please, Michele.'

'You just have to ask,' Fagiolo said. She had taken his hand and pressed it in her own. 'You always knew, Rondinella, you only ever had to ask.' Lucio hadn't heard the name before. He always thought his mother had never been given a nickname. It was the supreme insult of the Montelupinese — to be so far below notice to deserve one, a ghost in one's own town. But this name caught something of the truth of her, he thought, something beyond her illness, her difference. *Rondinella*. She *was* like a swallow, quick and sleek and restless. But Lucio never heard the name mentioned again.

He sat next to his mother on the cellar steps, mentally counting the bottles, as he knew she was. 'Don't worry,' she said, nudging his knee with hers. 'If we manage it carefully, we can keep Padre Ruggiero supplied and still have a few bottles to sell. It will see us through.'

Through till what? he wanted to ask. Till the next meagre harvest, the next hungry spring, the end of the war ... or till his father came home? Nonno Raimondi's method was gone for good and it was his fault. In the village, rumours had started flying, and he was at the centre of them: he was too stubborn or too stupid to follow his grandfather's instructions; Barilotto had backed the wrong boy; just like in scopa, he never could pick a winner. Lucio could endure the talk, the stares and shaken heads as he passed. But what he couldn't stand was his mother sitting in the cellar, her tired optimism.

Before dusk settled, he went to Collelungo to feed the animals. He usually went alone. It wasn't a job his brother liked, but that night Vittorio said, 'I'll come with you. Iana can have a run in the meadow behind the stable. You never know, she might find a rabbit.' They hadn't seen rabbits as low down as the meadow since the war began, and Vittorio knew it. Lucio understood his brother wanted a reason to pass the German camp.

They started the climb by the shorter mule path. Vittorio's gaze kept straining out across the hill, in the direction of the washhouse, but it was too early for lights and they could barely make out the tents on the campo.

When they reached the stable, Lucio brought the donkey inside for the night and fed the scraps to their hens. There were only two left now; a fox had slaughtered the others that winter. He had seen the hole under the wire where it had dug, blood staining the snow, brindled feathers floating in the weak morning light as he opened the pen. Four of their hens lay limp, still warm, their heads crooked. The two that remained were huddling in the roost, darting their beaks nervously, recounting in disjointed clucks the whole sad tale. He wondered why foxes did this, massacred a whole brood to take one hen. Was it the confusion of the birds scattering in all directions as they sprang? Or did they get a taste for blood, for the sport of it?

He closed up the stable and noticed Viviana's tail weaving

through the meadow grasses, her nose emerging intermittently, like a ship's prow above the waves. The last pink light hung on the ridge behind Carpeto, but in the air there was a warm buzz that promised summer nights. It was an evening for lingering. He thought of his mother: she would have liked to sit next to him on a dusk like this, the rooftops of the village tinged pink, their glow siphoning slowly into night.

'Let's go,' he heard Vittorio calling from the edge of the track. His brother was standing with his back to the light, fidgeting as he peered down to the tents in the growing dark. Lucio watched him stride down the cobbled path, the alternate route back to the village, less steep but longer, passing directly in front of the washhouse and the German camp.

'Hold on,' Lucio said, 'I think Iana might have something —' but his brother had already disappeared around the first bend.

Lucio waited for the dog. Her tail was no longer visible in the undergrowth, but he didn't call for her. Instead he traced the shadow of the mountains creeping up the meadow, felt the pleasure of being alone in the last circle of sun crowning the hill. He closed his eyes. The hum and tick of the grasses was strangely mechanical; birdsong rattled in distant trees.

When the shot rang out, it was so loud that he felt as if the mountain had cracked and was trembling under his feet. He stumbled, his head pitching as it did when his father slapped him across the ear. The echo rang off the rocks, shaking the crows from the trees and making the chickens screech in the barn. His first thoughts were for Viviana, but when he heard her barking — the fast, excited bay she made when she cornered her quarry — he breathed again.

At the bottom of the dim meadow someone was squatting in the grass. Viviana was nearby, partly barking, partly growling. He thought it might have been Vittorio returned for them, but when the figure stood he saw it was a man, tall and broad-backed. In one hand he held up something long and thin, coiling slightly like an unwound whip. Afraid for his dog, Lucio began to run towards them. Viviana met him halfway, giving an uncertain whine. He slowed to a walk. The man turned to face him, and for a moment they stood in the dusk, looking at each other.

He was a soldier from the camp, jacketless, his grey shirt-sleeves rolled to the elbows, his collar open. Lucio noticed that his skin was beaded with sweat, and his hair, falling across his forehead, clumped together. He might have come from working in the fields, or logging timber, except that his polished leather boots were the finest Lucio had ever seen, unlike anything a Montelupinesi would own. In the half-light, with the mountains behind him, he seemed conjured from another world — one of the brigand fairytales his mother used to tell him when he was a child: the disinherited count who took up with bandits to take revenge on a tyrannical stepfather. As Lucio went closer, the whip dangling from the soldier's hand became a snake. He raised it higher for Lucio to see. It was headless, charred and blasted at close range.

'It nearly bit your dog,' the soldier said. Lucio didn't answer. He was busy gathering every new detail: the paleness of the man's hair shining like moonlight as the dark descended, the unexpected delicacy of the pistol that had made such a huge sound, the snake's shuddering carcass as the soldier motioned towards the dog.

'She's very beautiful. A good hunter, I think?' the German said, and Lucio became aware of the fluency of his Italian. 'I was watching her from the trees there, and I believe she could have taken it. But she's too handsome a dog to risk on a snake. You don't mind me stepping in?'

Lucio frowned, grappling with all the questions, the words that scattered in his mind. He reached for Viviana's collar to tug her away, even though he wanted more than anything to stay and listen to this man speaking with his foreign rhythms but familiar words, like listening to an old song played on an instrument he'd never heard before.

'Don't you speak?' The German's face was frank, open as an invitation. He holstered his gun and reached for Viviana. Lucio gripped her collar but the dog was calm, letting the soldier massage her ears. He felt a little betrayed: she had never taken to strangers before. When travellers passed them on the road to Cori, he always held her firm, sensing the low growl creaking within her, the rise of her hackles. He secretly liked this about her, felt comforted by it. But now she fawned under this man's touch like he was some long-lost master with offcuts of mutton in his pocket.

'What do you call her?' the German asked.

'Her name is Iana … Viviana.' Lucio almost started at the sound of his own voice, his mouth working as if it didn't belong to him.

'Viviana.' The soldier nodded at the dog. 'I think it's not the first time you have cheated death, is it, my beauty?' His eyes were grey, still as the lake in winter, with something knowing about them.

'She doesn't usually let strangers fuss over her,' Lucio said.

'Then I feel honoured.' The soldier laid the snake on the ground and rolled down his sleeves against the chill. 'I have two Weimaraner bitches back home. I take them out in the Schwarzwald near my house in Baden.'

Lucio listened to the German words slipped between the Italian. He had never known anyone who could handle two languages so comfortably. Urso's older brother, Cano, could say a few phrases in English when he was drunk. They were his only legacy of a year in New York, with the exception of a tattoo he had to cover for Mass on Sunday. He rolled the English words off his tongue by rote, like a child at the catechism, and his accent was so Italian he might have been speaking some remote southern dialect for all his audience knew. But this German seemed to move between the two worlds easily, as easily as he inhabited the space in the meadow, like he had been coming here all his life.

Lucio's gaze was drawn to the gun in the leather pouch. The German retrieved the pistol and held it up, flicking a catch on the grip and releasing the magazine. He lingered over the procedure, inspecting the loading mechanism and then the latch, but Lucio realised he wasn't checking the gun: he was allowing him a good look at it without the pain of asking.

He had never seen such a compact weapon. At the markets in Cori, he sometimes saw bolt-action rifles slung across a man's shoulder, once even with a bayonet still attached. Fagiolo had a hunting piece of his father's hanging over the bar in the osteria, dusty as the ancient carafes and demijohns that lined the top shelves. According to Urso, the traditional hunting etiquette of the mountains considered it bad form to use firearms in the chase — an insult to the skill of the true huntsman and his dog. Listening to their slurred debate from the battlement wall, Lucio knew well enough that such sentiments masked poverty with pride.

This pistol was sleek and neat, the grip the colour of polished walnut. It fascinated him, the beauty and the danger of this object that seemed to fit perfectly in the soldier's hand. When he looked up, he saw the German was amused. Lucio rubbed at his mouth with the back of his hand, wishing his brother was there. Vittorio would have asked all the right questions. Vittorio would have had the adult conversation he could not.

The German's fingers worked a latch at the side of the barrel and, holding the shaft, he offered up the grip. Lucio hesitated, but the soldier waited patiently for him to take it. The heft of the gun in his hand took him by surprise and he had to steady his wrist. He laid the weapon flat in his palm so he could touch the cold metal, run his fingertips over the grooved lines moulded into the stock. It wasn't wood, he felt now, but the same smooth brown material as Signora Centini's telephone. He cradled the gun before his chest. He would have liked the time to copy it, to make a sketch in his notebook.

'You're a man of detail and design, I see. As am I, given the choice.' The German took back the weapon and ran his thumb over the heel of it, seeming elsewhere. 'We've lost the light. Shall we walk back?'

Perhaps it was the way he picked up the carcass of the snake and clicked his tongue to Viviana, the way they began to walk, comfortable in their silence, that made Lucio finally venture a question.

'What did you hunt? You and your dogs in Germany?' He drew in the night air, and became conscious of the rise and fall of his chest as he breathed, the hum of the German's voice as they descended the hill. And, as he listened to his answer, Lucio thought of the next question he would ask him, and the next.

By the time Lucio and Vittorio were harvesting the first figs from the Vigna Alba, the German unit had moved into rooms at the town hall. From the orchard, they could see the rear balcony of the building, where Professore Centini and Padre

Ruggiero had taken to smoking cigars with the unit's captain, Herzog Schlosser. Captain Schlosser seemed to command an endless supply of goods from Monteferro, some of which had been luxuries in the village even before the war: real coffee, sugar and foreign liquor. Professore Centini appeared more than happy to sacrifice his mayoral office and reception rooms in return for some of these things, while Padre Ruggiero conferred his benediction on the Germans. They were both even happier still to silence Signora Mazzocchi's grouching — at least for the present.

'That woman will be the death of me, Padre,' Lucio heard the mayor complaining to the priest in the osteria one evening, before the place had filled up with its new foreign clients. 'Only the other day she was finding fault with German army-issue bread, saying there was no substance to it. If she'd known, she would have rather not traded her eggs. Was there anything I could do to get them back? Could I have a word with Captain Schlosser?'

'What, about her eggs?' Padre Ruggiero asked, incredulous. Through the beams of the pergola, Lucio could see his belly shuddering with laughter under his robes, his face red with amusement; yet he made no sound, as if that might demean him somehow.

The mayor lifted his shoulders and implored the priest with open palms. 'Eh, Padre? I ask you? Before the Germans, she's grumbling about having to tap her bread to get the weevils out. Now she says the German bread doesn't fill her up. What can I do? Some people are never happy.'

Padre Ruggiero shook his head sympathetically and drained his glass. Fagiolo stepped out of the bar and came to their table with another carafe.

'Still, business is good, is it not, Fagio?' The mayor lifted his glass at the innkeeper. 'Who doesn't like a full house every night?'

'Oh, I like a full bar,' Fagiolo replied, regarding them over his shoulder and wiping his hands down his apron. 'A bar full of Italians.'

Padre Ruggiero made a noise in the back of his throat as if to warm up his voice. 'That will come again soon, you'll see,' he said in a stately tone, full of authority and conviction. 'Rest assured, the Germans are simply here to help us with that.'

'Rest assured?' Fagiolo said. He was halfway to the bar, but came back to the two men, settling his weight on his good leg. 'Does this feel right to you, Padre?' He gestured about the tables under the pergola, to the chairs that would soon be occupied by soldiers of the Wehrmacht. 'Does it feel right for Germans to sit here playing scopa, while our men are lost in the deserts of Africa and the snows of the Russian steppe?' He laid his palms on their table and a little wine spilled from the glasses. 'And if Mussolini falls? If the Allies invade? Shall we still *rest assured* then?' He limped back inside to his counter, not waiting for an answer.

Padre Ruggiero fingered his crucifix. 'Northerners, were they not — Fagiolo's family?' he asked the mayor.

'Mm,' Professore Centini replied. 'I've heard it said.'

'But he *is* a party member?'

'Of course, Padre,' the mayor lowered his voice, 'although not until he had to be.'

Padre Ruggiero sighed. 'These northerners — there's always something brooding about them, something ... *pessimistic*, don't you find? I suppose that's what makes them susceptible to the Red Menace.'

Professore Centini fidgeted in his chair. The accusation of communism was a serious one in Montelupini, especially towards the man who served them drinks every night. Lucio had witnessed fistfights in the piazzetta for less. Despite his career in local council, Professore Centini never seemed to show any interest in politics, and always blushed when the topic was broached, as if a man's political views were like his bowel movements — a question of personal habit, somewhat beyond his own control and certainly not a matter for public discussion. 'I think it's more the sciatica in his leg, Padre,' he suggested, handing the priest a Mokri. 'It plays up in this weather.'

The padre grunted. 'Perhaps you're right, Centini,' he mused, exhaling blue smoke up through the beams of the pergola. 'There's no pleasing some people.'

Does this feel right to you? Fagiolo's words lingered in Lucio's mind as he climbed to the stable to feed the hens. Did it feel right when he met the German in the meadow at Collelungo or found him walking down the track from Montemezzo? He hadn't considered this before, or perhaps he hadn't allowed himself to. All he knew was that he felt happy whenever he saw Otto Hirsch, whenever he found him in the long grasses at dusk, watching the mountains. His blonde hair would catch the last light, and even on the hottest day there was something cool and pristine about him, Lucio thought, something delicate and secretive that shimmered, like a fish underwater.

Otto had told him he was a translator, serving both Captain Schlosser and some of the other officers stationed in villages this side of Monteferro. And yet, despite the job he'd been assigned, he rarely went to the osteria with the other soldiers in the evenings. He said he wasn't good around so many men, so much talk. After a day dealing with words, he liked to clear his head of them. There was no one who understood this as well as Lucio. They wandered among the trees behind the meadow, or sat on Rocca Re while Lucio drew in his notebook, Otto's hand on Viviana's back as she panted. Lucio had never considered whether it was right because it always felt so.

And yet he didn't tell Vittorio. His brother didn't go with him to feed the animals at Collelungo anymore. Since the Germans had decamped to the town hall, they had lost their exotic lustre for Vittorio. Instead he made a point first of showing no interest in the visitors and then of actively setting himself against them. The Germans became a focus for his impatience, his discontent, an outlet for his frustrations. Influenced by the talk of traders on their last trip to Cori, he took delight in griping about their increased numbers throughout the hill towns.

'Every time you look over your shoulder in Cori or Carpeto there's more crucchi,' he grumbled to their mother over his minestra one night.

She eyed him warily over the steaming bowls. 'Be careful what you call them, Vittor. There are plenty of people with food on the table because of the Germans.'

'And what about when their supplies run out? What will we all eat then? That's what I want to know.'

That was why Lucio didn't speak about Otto. Instead he took him to Prugni and, under the budding tree, he told him the legend of the plague settlement, and eventually of his grandfather and the lost method of Raimondi Gold. Otto whittled on the switch of a snare he was making, listening all the while without comment or judgement. And Lucio felt, perhaps for the first time, the sweet ease of unburdening himself.

One duskfall on their way down the Montemezzo track,

Viviana started up the baying that meant only one thing. As Lucio stood unmoving on the chalk path, Otto asked, 'Don't you want to find out what she's caught?' But Lucio was rigid with the fear of it, the shame of revealing this truth, this failing, to his friend.

Otto inclined his head in the direction of the noise. When he stepped forward, Lucio felt bound to follow him, pacing through the ferns and the newly sprouting undergrowth until they were beside Viviana. She had the prey under her paws, pinning it down, her muzzle at its throat. It was a spring leveret, still lean, bleeding from the neck where she had bitten it. But its orange eye, glossy in the dim light, was fixed upon Lucio, as expectant as the dog's growls.

He tried to free the words that were lodged in his throat. But he had become his eleven-year-old self, standing before the bleeding boar, his father's breath upon him once more. Viviana growled again as if to hurry him, but Otto caught her tail in his fist and reached down to snatch the hare up by the hind legs. It twitched and quivered before him. Lucio felt Otto reach across for his hand, cupping it in his own, running his palm slowly upwards so that he could feel the nap of the hare's skin, its sprung bones adjusting underneath, until he could sense its lengthening body and lax weight, a kind of forgiveness. Everything seemed distilled, concentrated in their hands. All Lucio could hear was his own breath behind his teeth; all he could feel was the pulse of blood in his fingers. When it came, the crack of bone against his hand was nothing more than a tiny part of night descending in the woods, the trees creaking as the wind pitched in the canopy.

He felt a gentle pressure on his shoulder. When he turned around, Otto had already gutted the hare and Viviana was licking at the bloody leaf litter.

On the way back to the village, the chalk path seemed to rise up to meet them, pale in the moonlight, pale as Otto's hair, as they descended side by side.

And Lucio wondered how it could not feel right.

Leyton
1949

'Black Jacks today, barley twists last week. Did they never have sweets at all in Italy, then?' Mrs Cleat cocked an eyebrow at Vittorio, who gave her a small smile.

'No, signora,' he said, lowering his gaze. Connie thought he would blush if he could master that reaction at will. With a breathy titter Mrs Cleat let some extra Black Jacks fall from the scoop into the paper bag, and Connie rolled her eyes at Vittorio.

Through the autumn he had become a regular in the shop, and Mrs Cleat liked to tease him about his sweet tooth. She had begun to call him Vic, and last week she'd made Mrs Livesey wait in the queue while she told him about the Benford Operatic Society's new production of *Merrie England*. 'I've been meaning to ask you, Vic, do you sing at all? No? That's a shame. Don't you think he'd make a perfect Sir Walter Raleigh, Connie?'

Sometimes, as the days got shorter and his work finished earlier, Connie found him straddled across her bike in the alley by the shop.

'Who you hanging about for, then? Signorina Cleat?' She mimicked his bashful smile and fluttered her eyelashes as she wrapped her scarf about her neck.

'Signor-a,' he corrected her.

'I thought you didn't want to speak Italian anymore.'

'Sometimes … it's useful.' He offered her a Black Jack.

She arranged her things in the basket of her bike and shook the handlebar, indicating he should get off. 'Well, if you're buying as many stamps as you are sweets these days, you'll never save up for that bike.'

He frowned at her, then slowly began to grin. The sight of it changing the shape of his eyes, his even white teeth against his brown skin, was so pleasurable that she forced herself to bite the inside of her cheek and look away.

'So, the pettegole tell you?'

She got on her bike, ignoring him.

'That I walk Agnes home?'

She set her foot against the pedal. 'I've got no idea what a pette-majig is.'

'Pettegole.' He opened and closed his hand in a beak shape and nodded towards Cleat's.

'You should know by now that everyone in this village knows your business,' she said, trying to push off even though he was still holding the handlebar.

'Agnes asked me. What can I do?' He sighed. 'There was no Connie to walk home.' He refused to let go of the handlebars, and she got down from the saddle and stood on the other side of the bike.

'Agnes is a beautiful girl,' he said. She raised her eyebrows, wanting to appear unaffected by such a frank comment, but this was the best she could do. 'But am I waiting at the post office for one hour to walk Agnes home?'

She folded her arms and tried her best not to smile. As she let him push her bike, she thought of Agnes and her patent shoes making their singular click down the pavement.

Along the high street, the light from the windows of the terraces fell across their path. The smell of woodsmoke was set into relief by the crisp winter air in the open fields. As they reached the start of the bridle path, the shortcut to Repton's, he dug into the pocket of his jacket and drew out a package wrapped in newspaper. He opened it partially and she glimpsed two hen's eggs, which he wrapped back up and placed inside her mac, folded in the basket.

'Are you sure?' she said. 'I don't want you ... I don't want anyone to get into trouble.' She was thinking of Lucio. She hadn't seen him for more than two months, not properly — only the outline of him cutting sugar beet on the ridge, or what she imagined was his silhouette passing the lit window of the gamekeeper's cottage. He no longer appeared on the gatepost, and his absence made her feel guilty, but for what she didn't know. She thought of the night of the harvest fair, the face in the darkened scrub. She still had Mrs Repton's shoes wrapped in a paper bag at the back of her wardrobe. She knew she should return them, but when she took them out, she always had the urge to bury them instead, just as Lucio had Mrs Repton's cat, as if there was something sad and regretful about them.

She had to ask Vittorio: 'How is your brother?'

He rubbed the heel of his hand. 'Lucio.' It was practically a groan. 'I don't know. I don't know where he goes anymore.' He seemed torn between the release of talking about him and the intrusion of it. Eventually he said, 'He fights. With my father. Always fighting. I think one day they kill each other.' He laughed, trying to make light of it.

'But why? Why do they fight?' She heard her voice straining. 'Is it about the cat?'

'What?'

She waved her hand vaguely and took hold of her bike again, wishing she hadn't blurted it out. 'Why do they fight?' she asked once more.

'Many reasons. Things from before. Even I don't understand.' He was dismissive, like it wasn't worth explaining. 'He stays away now, Lucio. He gets up with the sun and comes back with the stars. Sometimes he stays away all night.'

'But I see him on the farm,' she said.

He shrugged. 'He has to eat, he has to work. But at night …'

'Where? Where does he go?'

Vittorio cast his gaze over the hedgerows and spinneys. He seemed restless, impatient to move on from the tiring puzzle of his brother. He fingered her mac in the basket, where he had placed the eggs.

'Will you do something for me, Connie?' His face was animated again, his eyes glittering.

'Oh, I get it. The eggs are a bribe, then. What? What do you want me to do?'

'You are free tomorrow, Saturday afternoon, yes?'

She nodded.

'You come with me?'

'Where to?'

'To Huntingdon. You help me.'

'With what?'

'You help me,' he repeated, insistent as a child. 'I tell you on the bus tomorrow.'

She hesitated. She had no clue how he might need someone like her to help him, but before she could ask more he hurried on. 'Per favore, Connie?' He took her hand like he depended on her. She found herself nodding.

His mood lifted instantly. 'Brava. Brava la mia Concetta,' he said, and she wondered whether she was no more sophisticated than Mrs Cleat, to be played with a pretty foreign name, a romantic accent.

He walked up the bridle path, buoyant, still fixing her in his sights, and then he grinned again. She wished he wouldn't. She had to pull up her scarf to cover her nose, not to keep out the cold but to hide the heat of her delight from him.

On the bus, the squat houses of Leyton fell away behind them, as the road opened up between the ploughed fields. It was an afternoon of fragile blue sky, the leafless trees clean as paper cuts against it. Everything seemed laid bare. Everything but him.

'You still haven't explained why it is I'm swanning off with you to Huntingdon,' Connie said, shifting her leg to avoid the press of his on the shuddering seat.

'Swanning?'

She laughed. 'Yes, you know, like the bird … flying off … for no good reason.'

'I'm not a good reason?'

'Vic,' she warned.

'There is a good reason.' He seemed sheepish. 'I need you to help me.'

'But what with?'

'With the police.'

'The *police*?' She sat forward, panic setting in. She couldn't imagine how he'd become involved with the police, but she could imagine the endless recriminations this would provide Aunty Bea, the material it would give Agnes or Mrs Livesey if it got out.

He took hold of her wrist. 'It's not like that, Connie. I don't tell you because I'm scared maybe you don't come.'

'Well, you were right.' She tugged her arm away.

'Wait. Concetta.'

'Don't … don't treat me like that.'

'Like what?'

'Like I'm Agnes or someone.' She began to put on her coat as if she had the option of getting off the bus. 'Oh, but hang on. I get it now. I'm here because she said no, aren't I?'

'No, Connie. No. Listen. I don't even ask Agnes. I ask you because I know you understand. You're smart.' He tapped his temple with his finger. 'We have to go to the police station every month — me or Lucio or my father. We sign the police book for the foreign workers. You see?' She wasn't sure she did. 'They want to know where we are all the time. Like … like prisoners.' His mouth turned down at the word.

'So why do you need me to help you?'

He leaned back towards her, hopeful that she might be coming round. 'The constable there, he explains the rules to me. You help me understand, OK?'

'What rules?'

'The rules to leave.' He nodded as she began to realise what he meant. 'The rules to leave Repton's.'

At the Huntingdon police station, the constable on duty reached under the counter and brought up a flimsy registry with the letters *RA* inked on it in red: she guessed it stood for *Resident Aliens*. He set it on the counter without greeting Vittorio, as if he already knew why he was there and deemed it a routine unworthy of any further attention. Connie's presence, however, seemed to pique his interest.

'Can I help you, miss?' When she shook her head, he angled his chin towards Vittorio. 'Are you with him?'

'Yes, we're together.' The constable raised an eyebrow and

glanced at his colleague. The duty sergeant, sitting at a desk behind him, stopped scratching in his notebook and looked up with grubby interest. 'That is to say ...' she began weakly.

Vittorio, oblivious to the innuendo, signed the register. He slid it back towards the constable and directed his attention to the sergeant beyond, calling out, 'Please, you tell my friend again about the rules — for the foreign workers?'

The sergeant got up from his desk and stepped towards the counter. 'Steel harpin' on that, are we? He's a heedstrong one, I'll hand et t'eem, the young Wog laddie.' His Scottish brogue was so thick that Connie had to concentrate to be sure of catching every word, only having heard a Scots accent once or twice on the radio during a New Year's Eve broadcast. She understood now why Vittorio needed her help. 'I've explained et al' t'eem the last month no' gone, but ... well, hes English is no' so strong, es et?'

Connie fidgeted at the desk and fought a violent urge to laugh. 'My friend wants to know whether he's allowed to leave his job and get a different one somewhere better. He's been there nearly a year now.'

'Well, a whool year, es et? And already wantin' better?'

The constable, who was making tea at the back of the station, sniggered. Connie pressed her hand on the counter. She was beginning to see that the obstruction was not simply a matter of accents.

'Look, we'd just like to know his rights. His sponsor said he has to stay with him for seven years at least. Surely that can't be true?'

The officer cleared his throat. 'I've toold the young fella, as long as he has a letter from a sponsor and we only see hes face in here t'sign the register, we dunna care how he keeps heself ootta trouble.'

'So he doesn't have to wait seven years to change employers, then?'

The constable sighed and spoke slowly, as if Connie herself was the foreigner. 'Seven years is t'apply fer residency. He can change sponsors if he can get another. O' course, he could gae hoome … p'rhaps there's better back in *Italya*?'

They left the station and stopped at Cromwells for tea and a bun. Vittorio still hadn't understood what the sergeant had said, but before she would explain, she wanted to hear his reasons for leaving Repton's. He was reluctant at first, but when she pushed him, she was taken aback at the sudden emotion of his confession.

'He can pull out his hair and eat ashes, my father,' he muttered, shaking his head. '*England is the future*, he told us. *Machines for the harvest, machines to do the work of ten men. We can be something there*. But what are we?' He paused, like she might offer him a different answer. 'Slaves for Repton, that's all.' His mouth had become hard in his face, making him seem years older. She stayed quiet, not knowing what to say.

'In our village my father was better than podestà — do you understand? Like the mayor. Men came to him to stop arguments, to find answers; they respected him. We had electricity in our house, clean water. Now we live in a *stalla* — this animal shed, with a hole in the ground to shit. We work until dark, we sleep, and then we start again. And this Repton, we have to pay him for this! We have to pay him for bringing us to … questo cesso, Inghilterra. And he says we must stay for seven years with him, like this tractor or this truck, this machinery he owns. Maledetto bugiardo, figlio di puttana.' He pushed away his teacup, which rattled indignantly in its saucer.

The loud flourish of Italian words made a nurse at the next table cough and stir her tea. The waitress blushed, her mouth open. Connie put one hand to her forehead, blocking them both from her view, and with the other she put a finger to her lips.

Vittorio glowered, petulant and unapologetic as he turned his back to the room and studied the view through the window. In the reflection she saw him wipe his mouth against his forearm, as if to press back the words that threatened to keep coming. Connie's heart tightened with the injustice of it, with anger at the way he'd been misled, but she didn't know how to make things better, feeling culpable on Repton's behalf — on England's behalf. Finally, she leaned towards him. 'I can teach you if you like?'

'What?' he said sharply.

And she whispered, 'All the swear words you need.'

On their way home, a few villages out of Huntingdon, Vittorio became preoccupied, scanning the scenery as they approached Spalewick. Ahead was Edwards Garage, with its two fuel pumps beside the open road.

'There, see?' He pointed at the filling station as the bus pulled into the stop a short way off. 'I take the Hillman there to change the oil. Mr Edwards, he likes me. He says, *Vic, you a smart boy. You work hard.* He asks if I want to be apprentice to him — mechanic.' The word sounded complex and important in his mouth. He tapped his chest with a thumb. 'Mr Edwards pays me four times more than Repton gives my father. Four times! Now you understand this Repton?'

She couldn't quite believe how low their wages were, even by Mr Repton's standards. She nodded.

'Tomorrow, I tell Mr Edwards yes,' he said, as if she had given her approval.

'It's already lined up, then, the job? And you'll leave?' She tried to disguise the flatness in her voice by studying the view across the open fields. At thirty miles from Leyton, Spalewick was too far to travel by bus or bike on a daily basis. He would need to move, and how could she be indifferent to that? She had started to look forward to his visits, which punctuated the monotony of her day at Cleat's, and to finding him straddling her bike in the evenings after work.

'Mr Edwards has a room for me to live behind his workshop,' Vittorio said.

'But your father'll be angry, won't he? About you breaking with Mr Repton?'

He jammed his hands under his armpits. 'They live their life. I live mine.' He thought for a moment. 'First thing I do is pay Repton the cost of our passage — for all of us.' He scoffed. 'Buy back our freedom.'

His certainty made her envious. People in the villages were never that confident: they were practical, unambitious, stubbornly compliant because, she suspected, like her they thought little of themselves. He, on the other hand, had such self-belief, such a conviction of his worth despite the complete absence of privilege. How had he got it, this attitude that the world was his, and all he had to do was crack it open? Being around him, she felt pulled along in his wake, buoyant with possibility.

He noticed her examining him. 'What?'

She shook her head and felt the engine changing gears, the spring in the seat, his knee knocking hers again. And when he took her hand in his, she let him.

As they reached the Leyton turn-off, Connie looked back at the main road, feeling his fingers touch her hair, the strange inevitability of his hands at her face. She turned to him and, though she found herself answering, she wasn't thinking about the kiss, his tongue on hers. Instead she imagined staying on the bus, travelling on and on, far away into the drawing night, until dawn broke over the misty city inside her mind, peopled with older, more sophisticated versions of herself. It was a daydream she had often become lost in, but somehow, today, he'd made it seem unnervingly possible. She pulled away from him and gazed out at the dull cluster of buildings that was Leyton.

When the brakes of the bus hissed and the doors opened, she was ready behind them, preparing to jump off, anticipating the familiar handles of her bike, the effort of the cycle up Bythorn Rise. For she couldn't deny the tug she felt in the pit of her stomach, not from his kiss but from something else. Something forgotten, holding her back. And as she stepped onto the high street, she found she was relieved for once to hear the bus grumbling away, back towards the open road.

Montelupini
1943

His mother was calling him. She was on a ladder against the peach tree in the Vigna Alba, handing Lucio a basket loaded with fruit. He had been gazing at the soldiers on the back balcony of the town hall, smoking in the heady afternoon sun.

'Lucio, are you listening to me? I want to get these up to the padre as quickly as we can.' She shook the basket at him irritably. Since he'd finished school the previous month, he'd been able to join her in the fields and vineyards, sharing her workload. But Padre Ruggiero only seemed to expect more from them. 'He's heard from La Mula that they've been ripe for days. As if I wouldn't know a tender peach when I see one. I should have picked them hard off the tree to spite him.'

Lucio took the basket and passed her another, lined with fig leaves. She layered the leaves between the fruit to protect them. Despite her words, she did all the right things, everything she could to appease the priest. Her brown cheeks shone from the work, her skirts tucked up into her belt behind her. The stitching was coming loose at the side of her shoe and he made a note to fix it.

She was irritated more with Vittorio than with Padre Ruggiero, he knew. This was a chore she had set his brother, but they had argued again that morning, the same argument they'd had ever since Lucio had graduated: Vittorio wanted to leave school too, before his final year, but his mother refused. What good were books and reciting poems and useless dates, Vittorio demanded, if they were all going to starve to death? With the three of them they might turn over some of the meadow near the stable, increase their yield, and he would have more time to trade and hunt. But their mother was adamant. In retaliation, Vittorio did what he always did and swung to the other extreme. He refused all his chores after school and, when questioned, said Lucio should do them so that he could concentrate on the education that was clearly so precious. Lucio couldn't help seeing some truth in the argument and, wanting to keep the peace, had taken on his brother's work, which made their mother even angrier.

'I don't know what Padre Ruggiero thinks I do with my days,' she muttered to the branches. 'Sunbathing, maybe? Or swimming in the lake at Montemezzo?'

'Sounds like something worth doing on an afternoon like this.' It was a man's voice, close behind them. Otto Hirsch stood with his arms folded, gazing up into the tree. He must have spotted them from the balcony of the mess and come down through the orchards. Lucio saw his mother's face peer out between the branches. There was a leaf curled in her hair. When she saw the German, she jerked back behind a bough and busied herself picking more fruit.

'I'm sorry. I didn't mean to startle you, signora. I was only wondering if you and Lucio needed another pair of hands?' She didn't answer, but she shook out her skirt and brushed a hand over her hair before climbing down the ladder.

'I'd be grateful for something to do — a reason to escape the mess,' Otto added.

'This is Signor Otto, Mamma,' Lucio explained as he tried to take the basket from his mother. But she held on to the handle and waited, indicating she expected more from him. 'I ... We met at Collelungo. He saved Iana from a snake.'

'Did he?' his mother said, but instead of greeting Otto or shaking hands with him, she reached for her headcloth and began to twist it into a tight ring. Her eyes flickered over the soldier, more amused than suspicious.

Back on the balcony, the men in the mess had begun to call out to Otto, whistling and heckling in German. He adjusted his stance, palming the back of his neck and blocking them from his vision. There was something different about him, Lucio noticed, something uncertain: he had never seen his friend at such a loss before.

'I saw you from the balcony and thought I should bring this back,' Otto said, handing his mother a small package wrapped in waxed paper. 'You left it behind at the stream — when you were washing your clothes.' Lucio could smell the soap. It was his mother's turn to fidget. She looked at the package like he had handed her one of her underclothes or a loose stocking in public. Over on the balcony, someone whistled again.

'I'm sorry,' Otto said, glancing up at the men. 'I didn't think. They're bored, mischievous ... it's the heat, you know ... Perhaps I should go?'

Viviana had wandered over, wagging her tail and whining at him, and Otto bent to scratch her ears, relieved to have something to occupy his hands. 'I'm sorry. I'm not used to doing so little.' He let out an awkward laugh. 'It seems a lot of waiting around, this life of a soldier. I think I might go crazy if I stay up there any longer.' The words spilled out like a kind of confession.

Lucio's mother considered him briefly, before bending down to swing the basket of peaches onto her head.

'Please,' Otto said. And he held the handles until she let him take it from her.

'It's going to be a tough walk up the mountain carrying it like that,' she said, nodding at the way he propped the basket on his hip.

'Well, I could use the exercise.'

'You tell me when it gets too heavy, then.' She pressed her lips together, and Lucio caught her eyes shining, black as wet ink.

His mother walked ahead of them, surefooted and steady, her neck long, her shoulders square, as if she was still carrying the full basket on her head.

As they climbed Collelungo, Lucio listened to their cautious exchanges, simple things he had not thought to ask Otto before, things he had never heard his mother put into words either.

'How come your Italian is so good?' she asked.

'My mother was from Lucca,' Otto said. 'My father brought her back to Germany after they met. But she always spoke Italian to us when we were growing up.'

His mother eyed him over her shoulder. 'You don't look Italian.'

Otto laughed, shifting the load to his other hip. 'And you don't look like someone who could carry the weight of this basket halfway up a mountain either. But I'm sure you can.'

'All the mountain women can. We learn it very young.' Her voice was serious, but then she added, 'My husband says our heads are flatter than men's. So, you see, we're pretty good beasts of burden.' As she turned back, Lucio noticed the playfulness of her mouth, her sidelong glance. So did Otto, for his face seemed to come alive with it.

'Is that so? And where is your husband?'

She ignored the question, and Otto's expression darkened. 'I'm sorry, signora. I didn't mean to pry.'

'You're sorry a lot, aren't you?' It made him smile again.

When she began to leave the path and wander into the meadow, they stopped and waited for her. 'If you're lucky, at this time of year you can find wild strawberries in this spot,' she called. 'Tiny ones. Very sweet.' She bent before a copse of brambles, searching, and Lucio and Otto set down their loads.

'Nothing?' Otto asked, when she returned.

She shrugged. 'Sometimes someone else finds them first.'

'I hope it wasn't men from my unit,' Otto said. 'They've been told not to take anything from the local area … but sometimes they need reminding.' He picked up his basket. 'Once again, I'm sorry.'

'You can hardly punish them for taking a few wild strawberries, Signor Otto. Anyway, I doubt they got there before one of the villagers did. These days people are hungry enough to pick them green.'

Otto motioned at the peaches with his chin. 'Then where are we taking all this?'

'To Padre Ruggiero,' she answered.

'The priest? Why?'

'His land, his tree, his fruit,' was all she said.

At the path beside Rocca Re, his mother stopped. She asked Otto to wait for them on the outcrop. 'In our village, Signor Otto, women do not walk with men who are not their husbands — and sometimes not even with men who are, if they can help it.' She started her climb towards the priest's house.

Lucio walked backwards along the track beside her. 'Stay, Iana,' he said, and his dog collapsed in the shade of the brambles and began to pant in the last of the afternoon heat. He looked to Otto for confirmation that he would watch Viviana, but his friend's eyes were on the chalk track, the back of his mother's neck, brown and smooth as honey, the sway of her skirts as she turned the bend.

An army jeep was parked outside Padre Ruggiero's villa, a German soldier propped against it, smoking in the sun. He didn't bother to stand up when they approached. They'd seen the jeep and driver before when the priest was entertaining Captain Schlosser. They could smell brewed coffee — not the blend of acorn and chicory grinds that the villagers drank, but the sultry aroma of the real thing. Lucio saw his mother raise her chin, savouring the smell of it.

They walked around to the cellar door as Padre Ruggiero and his guest emerged on the balcony above them.

'... I find it a rather barbaric ritual, myself,' the priest was saying, 'but it's part of the summer festival and the villagers are very protective of their traditions. Your men might enjoy it. I'm sure they're in need of distraction.'

'They are, Padre,' the captain replied. His Italian was laborious and heavily accented, but doubtless good enough for socialising with priests. 'Thank you for the grappa. It's the best I've tasted in this area.'

'Not at all, not at all. The least I can do in return for your generosity.' Padre Ruggiero caught sight of them. 'Ah, Letia, my dear,' he called. 'Wait there, would you?' His mother sighed as they set down the baskets. These days they delivered their produce to the cellar and left as quickly as they could, avoiding the priest for fear of what he might ask of them next, what he might decide against them.

The two men appeared through the kitchen door, the captain with three large bottles of Raimondi Gold in the crook of his arm. Lucio sensed his mother stiffening beside him.

'Please, Hauptsturmführer. Take some peaches from my

orchard.' Padre Ruggiero flicked a finger from Lucio to the idling jeep, where the driver had extinguished his cigarette and was standing to attention. Lucio carried his basket back and loaded it into the vehicle. 'You won't find better peaches anywhere in the Lepini ranges, I assure you.'

Captain Schlosser reached down to take a peach, running his thumb over the downy yellow skin. 'A messy fruit,' he mused. 'Not so much to my taste. But the men will like them.' He tossed the peach back in the basket, where it bounced against the others and split its skin.

'I look forward to the festival,' the German said, folding his legs into the jeep. He put on his cap and tapped the dashboard, signalling the driver to leave. As they set off, Lucio saw the captain twist around, not to farewell the priest, but to glance again at his mother, who had bent to lift her basket.

When the soldiers had rumbled out of sight down the rutted road, Padre Ruggiero took Lucio's mother by the elbow and led her to the cellar door. 'Letia, my dear, as for the grappa. You must have noticed how my stores have become depleted.' He gestured in the direction of the jeep and the settling dust. 'I have my reasons, you understand.'

'What reasons would they be, Padre?' she asked, deliberately obtuse.

'Now, Letia, don't play with me. You know very well that times are … well, strained, to say the least. We need to remain on the best of terms with the Germans — as your husband himself would stress if he were here to guide you.'

'Well, he isn't here, Padre.' His mother took her basket into the cellar and they prepared to leave.

'We've all heard the rumours,' the priest called, raising his voice, so there was no mistaking the change in his tone.

His mother stopped and faced him again.

'They say there is no more Raimondi Gold — that Barilotto took his methods to the grave,' Padre Ruggiero accused, letting his attention settle on Lucio. 'Far be it from me to cast blame, but I must consider the best future for the land at the Vigna Alba, you understand? Besides, what would a woman need with hard liquor? In times like these it's a much more powerful bartering tool in a man's hands.'

With his mother's arm around him, they began walking away. Lucio could sense her breath quickening beside him, felt her fingers pressing into his neck. He picked up his stride, making her follow him so that she didn't risk answering the priest.

Padre Ruggiero continued to call out to them. 'Yes, I was speaking to Guido Ippoliti yesterday. He agreed you might be struggling with the Vigna Alba … but we'll discuss it some other time, perhaps, when you're not so hot and bothered from the climb? I'll come to your cellar.' They heard the satisfied shuffle of his footsteps climbing to the verandah. He had said enough.

On the chalk road, dust still hung in the air from the jeep. They rejoined the mule track and his mother hurried ahead of him, almost running, shaking out her headcloth with a snap. When she reached the bend, out of sight of the priest's house, she stopped. The brambles and shrubs on either side of the track were noisy with the tear of cicadas, the grind of crickets. Everything seemed alive with the evening's pulse, building to a kind of crescendo that seemed focused on a single movement: the tremble of the rag at his mother's side. It became an erratic jerk and he recognised the rigid set of her limbs, heard the choking in her throat before she folded in on herself. He ran as fast as he could, wanting to get there before she hit her head or broke an arm, a wrist, her teeth on the stony path, for he knew how breakable she was underneath it all. But his legs wouldn't move fast enough. In his mind he cried out, but no noise came. By the time he reached her, she was already limp on the ground, her seizure passed. Her head was lodged in Otto's arm, and he was pushing back her hair with the cloth, wiping away the spit that had foamed at her mouth.

Leyton

1950

The frail blue skies of that autumn continued into winter and brought bitter frosts. By January, the washing was brittle on the line, and Connie's bike growled at her in the mornings like something forced from hibernation. There was no prospect of Vittorio's visits anymore, and at work in the shop she felt so chilled by the ordinariness of her life that she feared someone would touch her and she might crack like the thin ice on the puddles.

'Good-looking one's gone, then,' Mrs Livesey ventured across the counter the week after Vittorio had left. 'Bit of a hoo-ha up at Repton's, Mrs Cartwright reckons.'

Mrs Cleat buffed the grubby smudges of Janet Livesey's fingerprints from her servery. 'Mrs Cartwright's already been in,' she snapped, looking beyond Mrs Livesey for the delivery van. '*Last* week.'

'So you heard, then? About Repton throwing him out?'

'*Mr* Repton did not throw Victorio out.' Mrs Cleat sighed impatiently. 'Mr Edwards offered him a place to live beside the garage. No point travelling all that way every day. Even you can see that, Janet, surely?'

There were rare occasions when Connie wanted to thank

Mrs Cleat, and now was one of them. They knew very well about the fight between Vittorio and his father, how Mr Rose had stepped in to break it up. Mrs Cartwright had done her work last week, reporting the yelling match in the yard, all the while eyeing off the shiny new round of cheddar beside the last desiccated wedge, and pandering to Mrs Cleat: 'I wished you'd heard it, Eleanor; you might have been able to translate, what with your opera Eye-talian.' Afterwards, when they were alone, Connie had told Mrs Cleat about Mr Edwards's offer to Vittorio, trying to give her more of an exclusive on the facts, to draw attention away from the fight. Mrs Livesey, however, was intent on tabloid sensation.

'I expect you know, then? About Mr Gilbert and the other boy — that strange one who don't talk?'

Connie stopped wringing out the mop in the back store and returned to the counter. Mrs Cleat struggled with a resentful look.

'Oho. I see you don't.' Mrs Livesey chuckled.

'Really, Janet, you'll have to be quick. We're expecting the delivery van.' But she held the packages on the counter with firm fingers.

'Well, Nurse Stokes says she were called out last Saturday night. Very late. To Mr Gilbert's. Says she had to stitch up that young Eye-talian's face.'

'Whose face?' Connie burst out. 'Lucio's? Lucio's face?'

'Is that him, then?' Mrs Livesey said. 'Didn't know you was on first names, like.'

Connie turned away and began to mop the lino half-heartedly.

'All bloodied up he were, like he'd been in the boxing ring.' Mrs Livesey's rogue tooth glinted on her wet lip as if she was in the audience herself, shouting for blood on the other side of the ropes. 'And Maggie Stokes says soon as it were done, up he jumps out the door and into the fields, no torch nor nothing, like a wild thing. *Well, Maggie, I says, they get like animals when they're worked up, these Medit-ray-nuns. All fiery and over-excited, like.* And Maggie says, *They won't last much longer in Leyton, Janet. Sleepy little place that we are.* And I 'spect we'll be well rid of them.'

The delivery van had pulled up outside, its diesel fug drifting into the shop. 'Hey-ho, I'll leave you to it, then,' Mrs Livesey said, picking up her packages. Mrs Cleat almost ran from behind the counter, intent on reaching the door of the van before Mrs Livesey could distract Mr Jellis with the news.

Connie steadied herself on the mop and stared at the bland high street distorting through the bull's-eye pane. Everything in her mind, by contrast, seemed suddenly clear. She wanted to see him. She wanted to see if Lucio was alright, and not only because of this news. She admitted now she'd been wanting it all along, to sit with him again on the fence, hear the scratch of his pencil on the paper, the rhythm of his breath, his reassuring quiet beside her. Despite everything with Vittorio, she hadn't stopped searching the fields at Bythorn Rise, hoping he would come. And that brittleness within her wasn't just winter, or Vittorio's departure: it was not seeing Lucio walking over the ridge, not seeing him clearing his traps by the brook or watching for her on the fence.

That afternoon, it felt like Mrs Cleat was fixing her hat and putting on her gloves and going over her list of instructions without end, until the time for the Christian Ladies' meeting came around. As she finally stepped towards the door, Mr Gilbert appeared on the other side of it. He caught sight of the back of her and hesitated on the threshold, but it was too late.

'Mr Gilbert!' Mrs Cleat scolded. 'There you are at last. I've made myself late for the Christian Ladies waiting for you.

Now, can you tell us please what happened last Saturday night?'

Mr Gilbert held up his palms, as if at gunpoint, and slipped past her to the counter. 'I know nothing, Mrs Cleat, I assure you.'

The shopkeeper prodded her hair irritably from behind so that her hat sat forward and made her appear even more eager for the news. She frowned at her watch, evidently torn between harvesting more information from the schoolteacher and sowing what she knew at the meeting. 'What do you mean, you don't know anything? I heard you called in Nurse Stokes to sew up that wild boy.'

'I did indeed, Mrs Cleat, but beyond the fact that he landed injured on my doorstep, I know nothing more. He tends to keep to himself … and I choose not to *pry*.' He greeted Connie in an attempt to end the conversation, but Mrs Cleat was undeterred.

'It's hardly prying to ask who did it to him. I would have thought you of all people would want to protect the young.'

Mr Gilbert's face dropped at this, as though Mrs Cleat had touched a nerve. 'He's not a minor. There's nothing I can do and he doesn't want my help.'

'Well, perhaps Mr or Mrs Repton —'

'Mrs Cleat, I've been meaning to ask you,' the schoolteacher interrupted, his voice now gracious as he walked to the hat stand by the door and handed her an umbrella. 'How do you like the murals so far? Is the committee happy with their progress?'

Mrs Cleat hovered for a second, suspicious, before taking the bait. 'As a matter of fact,' she said, putting her umbrella back in the stand, 'we were all quite amazed at the first viewing. The reverend, as you know, was none too happy about changing services to the memorial hall for so long, but he says he's quite encouraged at how fast Mr Swann is working. And the detail, the richness! Those cartoons didn't do it justice at all. Oh yes, we're all enamoured with Mr Swann — his work, I should say.' Mrs Cleat tittered.

'Yes, his work,' Mr Gilbert mused, giving her the umbrella again. 'I must admit there's a telling detail to some of it, a loving realism in the depiction of certain human figures, the natural backgrounds, rustic touches and so forth that is ... well, luminous.' He glanced at Connie, who had to bite her lip. 'Frankly, I hadn't thought Swann's work quite so transcendent.'

'Oh,' Mrs Cleat said, opening her mouth and then closing it again, blinking slowly as if trying to memorise something. 'Well, yes. Exactly so. I couldn't agree more. Well put.'

And Mr Gilbert tapped the umbrella, pulled the door and put his palm in the small of her back, guiding her down the steps. 'Give my regards to the Christian Ladies, Mrs Cleat,' he said, raising his hat to her.

'Yes,' she said, nodding vaguely to the umbrella in her hand. 'Yes, you're right. Best be on the safe side. Looks like rain.'

Mr Gilbert shut the door behind her and came back to the counter.

'*Transcendent?*' Connie said, raising an eyebrow at him. 'Really?'

'Well, how else was I supposed to get the old girl off the subject? I thought she'd never leave.' Mr Gilbert fell silent. His face became flat, tired.

'How is he?' she asked, unable to hold off any longer.

'He'll survive, I suppose.'

'But what happened?'

Mr Gilbert looked towards the window.

'Tell me,' she said.

'His father took to him with a belt. Lucio wouldn't say why.'

'Was it about Vittorio leaving? Is he taking it out on him?'

He rested his hands on the counter and rubbed at a knuckle with his thumb. 'I don't think it's as simple as that.'

Connie fidgeted on her feet, impatient for more.

'If it's any consolation, he broke his father's nose. Eve told me.'

She didn't know whether to feel shocked or satisfied.

'The little I learn about the boy,' Mr Gilbert said, 'the more I think ... well, the more I feel he goes searching for it, in a way.'

'Searching for what?'

'For arguments with his father ... for Aldo to hit him.'

'Why?' she breathed, incredulous. 'Why on earth would he want that?'

'A distraction, maybe.' He lifted a finger to his temple. 'From whatever's in there.'

They were quiet, both wrapped in their own thoughts. The shop creaked about them.

'Can't you help him, Mr Gilbert?' she said finally. 'He's ... there's something special about him. You should see what he draws —'

'What he *draws*?' Mr Gilbert paused. 'Connie, you should see what he *paints*.'

'So you know? He's shown you things?' He nodded. 'Then you need to get him into a school, an art college or something,' she hurried on. 'Don't you see? He can't stay in Leyton.'

Mr Gilbert shook his head. 'That, coming from you?' She ignored his question, and he sighed. 'Look, he doesn't want me to help him. I've already tried. Besides, he's ... well, he's involved in something now. Something I think will be good for him for a time, until he's more certain of himself.'

'What do you mean? What's he involved in?'

He considered her for a moment. She became aware she was leaning across the Formica, squeezing the counter cloth in her fist. She straightened and let go of it, but Mr Gilbert's face had softened. 'Perhaps you'd like to see for yourself?' he asked. 'Can you meet me tonight at the gate across the commons? It'll have to be late, I'm afraid. Say, ten?' She nodded, pushing the logistics of getting past Aunty Bea to the back of her mind. 'I know you'll keep it to yourself, Connie, won't you? It'd be better if no one else found out.'

'Found out what?' a voice called archly from the door. Neither of them had registered the ting of the bell. Agnes Armer glided up to the counter, bringing with her the smell of Yardley and damp wool. 'Ugh, it's started to pour.' She brushed off the sleeves of her coat. 'Well, how about you two with your heads together? Be careful. People might talk, you know.' Her laugh was flippant, but her pale, hard gaze crept over them, steady as a hoarfrost at dusk.

'Might they, Agnes?' Connie said, but Agnes only pulled a scarf from her neck with dramatic panache and dabbed at her chin with it. Connie suspected she was copying a move from a Bette Davis or Veronica Lake film, and was embarrassed that Agnes would attempt such a gesture in front of a man who used to tell her to blow her nose and go outside to play.

Mr Gilbert tipped his trilby in farewell and made to leave.

'Don't forget these,' Connie called after him.

He sighed as he reached back for his groceries. 'What would I do without you?'

Agnes pursed her lips.

'Very pretty scarf, Agnes, by the way,' Mr Gilbert said. 'What colour is that? Puce?' Connie saw the twist of his mouth and had to cover her own with her hand.

But Agnes had caught it and, holding Connie in a steady gaze, she sang out, 'Before I forget, Mr Gilbert, Vic sends you his regards.' She tugged at the cuff of a glove, smiling at Connie, who could practically feel the chill of it in her bones.

'I get my hair set in Huntingdon on my day off — it's the one decent salon this side of London,' Agnes explained. 'Vic kept nagging me before he left, *You stop in and see me Agnessa, you make sure*. You know what he's like when he gets his mind set on something.' She gave that airy laugh again and laid her coupon book before Connie with a precise flick.

Connie busied herself looking for the scissors. *Agnessa*. It was a nice touch. Really, Agnes should be an actress: Connie could see Vittorio's manner in her words, hear his voice, imagine his grin playing about that name. She tried to chase it away with an effort at brightness.

'What can I get for you, Aggie?' she said, but her voice piped reedily, the sound of Leyton trapped in the words, and she reached for her serving coat, buttoning herself up and wondering who she was trying to fool.

She slipped out of the house as soon as Aunty Bea and Uncle Jack had gone to bed. It was well after ten, but she trusted Mr Gilbert would wait for her. She carried her bike past the red glow of embers edging the drawn curtains, and set it down in the lane, switching on her lamp and letting the wheels make their *tick, tick, tick*. The afternoon showers had passed and the moon hung above Bythorn Rise, floating full in a glassy night, so bright she could see her own shadow whirring past the silver hedgerow. As she approached Leyton, she was relieved to see another bike lamp flickering near the start of the commons. She heard her name. 'This way,' Mr Gilbert said, holding open the gate to the path that bisected the open grassland. His breath hung white in the air. 'We're crossing to St Margaret's.'

She looked towards the dark mass of the church. The cypresses were inky black against the night, and the sunken tombstones were cast like flotsam adrift on the pearly shimmer of the commons. Mr Gilbert set off over the incline and she pedalled after him, noticing the harlequin glow of the leaded windows ahead of them, as though the church had been turned inside out.

They dismounted at the lychgate, and Mr Gilbert propped their bikes against the stone seat. She stared at the church, beginning to suspect what he was about to show her.

'Swann caught him in a back pew when he was working late one night. He showed up again the next evening … and the next.' Mr Gilbert cupped his hands and blew into them. 'When he came back from London, Swann opened the church up one morning and found the stage lights still on. Lucio was asleep on the scaffold. He'd taken up Swann's brushes and palette and completed the background to the first view.'

Connie pressed her fingers to her mouth, felt the woollen prickle of her gloves on her lips. 'What did Mr Swann do? Was he angry?'

Mr Gilbert exhaled. The trees behind the cemetery seemed to stir with his breath. She heard the soft questioning of an owl. 'Connie, when you see these paintings, you'll understand. There was nothing Swann *could* do.' He lowered his voice. 'He's no fool. The quicker he completes the project, the sooner he gets his fee, and quite frankly that's convincing enough for someone like Swann.' He paused, chafing his hands together. 'I did suggest he take the boy on as an apprentice but he hasn't the funds. Anyway, Lucio won't leave the farm. He doesn't want anyone to know, apparently, especially his father.'

Mr Gilbert took her elbow and they walked down the path towards the western door. She felt like she was breaking the law, visiting the church at night, even more so because Reverend Stanton and Mrs Cleat's committee had been allowed to see the murals only once and by special arrangement. As they approached, Mr Gilbert squeezed her arm. 'Not a word, Connie, alright? You can imagine how they would all react — the Christian Ladies, Reverend Stanton, the diocese — to think their church was being painted by ...' He opened his eyes wide. '... *the other side*,' he said melodramatically.

'The *other side*?' Connie nearly laughed. 'They're not that narrow-minded, surely? Even Leyton has to get over the war sometime.' But as she said it she thought of Aunty Bea.

Mr Gilbert stopped and turned to her. The light under the door spilled across his shoes but made his face shadowy and serious. 'Oh, they'll get over the war, alright. But what they won't get over is that Lucio is a Roman Catholic, Connie.'

She would have realised the Italians were Catholic had she given it any thought. But she'd only seen the Onorati as a product of the war, thought of them in terms of the war's divisions. Now she understood their foreignness ran even deeper. The villagers of Leyton didn't have a Catholic among them. It was an odd tic of religious history, of geography, perhaps. But when the lumpy effigy of Guy Fawkes was dragged from house to house on Bonfire Night, it was more than a tic that some villagers crossed themselves as they tossed their pennies to the lane kids and cried *burn the papist*. And as a child, she had seen itinerant Irish farmhands refused at the Green Man, Tommy Pointon's spit fizzing behind them on the pavement as the kids shouted, 'G'on and piss off, bloody bead jigglers.' In her mind's eye, she saw the expression on Aunty Bea's face, imagined the fury over the Formica if news got out about these murals.

The lock turned in the oak door and Mr Swann's thin frame appeared backlit in the doorway, his miner's cap still on his head.

'Swann,' Mr Gilbert said. 'Hasn't anyone ever told you to take your hat off in church?'

The artist grinned at his friend and removed the soggy end of a roll-up from his lips. 'Gilbert,' was all he said. He regarded them with blue eyes that might have been arrogant had they not been somewhat glazed. His mouth made a half-hearted smirk that gave the impression he found everything around him either mildly amusing or mildly distasteful, Connie could not tell which.

Mr Gilbert introduced her. 'Hope you don't mind, Swann. She's a friend of the boy's. She'll be very discreet, I assure you.'

Mr Swann put the wet cigarette to his mouth and sucked tightly, examining Connie. When he stepped back to allow them in, she noticed he was unsteady on his feet.

'Welcome to the house of God,' he drawled, pulling off his cap with feigned deference, 'better known as the school of Swann.' Connie had the urge to cover her mouth from the fumes of whiskey as she passed him. 'Don't mind if I pass you over to Botticelli for the tour, old boy, but I was rather hoping to catch last orders at the Green Man.' Mr Swann made an elaborate yawn and rubbed at his neck. 'Not sure how he does it,' he said, motioning to the scaffolding, on which Connie saw Lucio adjusting a rig of stage lights towards the eastern wall of the transept. 'Damned if the boy doesn't keep going all night. Like his life depended on it. Wish I could spirit him up to London to help me out with those bloody Drury Lane commissions' — he winced — 'a tad overdue!' He replaced his cap and smirked at Connie again, as if she had just stepped out of her clothes in front of him. She shouldered past and made her way up the nave towards the scaffold. Behind her she could hear him asking Mr Gilbert for *a spare quid*.

From the raised platform, Lucio was looking down at her.

The spotlights threw into relief the wiry tufts of stitches scything his eye, the blue that blossomed around it, the cuts in his nose and lip. He straightened and pressed his forearm to his chin, as though wiping sweat away, even though the church was cold as a tomb. The handles of the brushes in his fist ground together like teeth.

'Can I come up?' she asked. He set the brushes across an upturned crate and squatted on the scaffold so he could take her hand. She climbed up beside him, the heat of the stage lights warming her a little. He dropped her hand and they angled themselves away from each other, studying different ends of the mural.

He was working in the left of the view, on a bird taking flight between the branches of an ash. The wands of glossy leaves seemed to quiver as they drifted across the arch, and a feather shed from the bird's beating wings spiralled as if disturbed by a breeze, or by the bang of the door. The hoary tree trunk was a study in itself, the silver bark beset with patches of white and orange lichen, borers and beetles, and in one part, a shelf fungus that appeared so real she felt she might reach out and break off a white-tipped frill, the way she used to as a child, cutting through the spinneys on the bridle path to the schoolhouse. To her right, in the foreground, stood three women in robes of russet, sapphire and brown, one bent in grief, her companions regarding each other, their faces pencilled, as yet unpainted. A light caught the hand of one woman, clutching at the neck of her headdress. Her skin was chafed at the knuckles, thick-fingered — a worker's hand, the faint liver spots of age strangely familiar.

She felt the tremor in the platform as Lucio shifted his weight. 'Have you done most of this?' she asked.

He glanced at Mr Swann by the western door, where Mr

Gilbert was holding his hand up to them. 'I'd better see him to the Green Man. Back in a half hour, alright?' They watched the men go, their footsteps sounding along the gravel path, leaving nothing but the hum of the stage lights, the hollow breath of the vaulted space around them. Lucio bent to clean his brushes on a rag, but she caught him observing her as she considered the work again.

'There's so much here ...' She heard the sibilance of her voice evaporating with her breath in the cold air. She tried again. 'It's all so real, like it could move ... it makes me ...' But she couldn't find the words. All she managed was, 'It's too beautiful for Leyton.'

He frowned. The muscles in his jaw were clenched.

'Who are they?' she asked, indicating the figures.

'Salome and Joanna.' He angled his head towards the third woman. 'And Mary outside the tomb.'

She remembered Mr Swann's sketches with their descriptions in the memorial hall. 'I know that,' she said. Again she examined the hand clutching the cloth, lit by the sepulchral glow, realising it would be enhanced cleverly by light through the south windows in the day. 'But *who* are they?'

'No one.' He shrugged. 'Mr Swann's models. He does the figures, the faces.' He pointed behind them, to the western wall of the transept, where another scaffold stood before an unfinished scene. She could make out two figures before a wooded backdrop.

'St John and St Peter in the garden of Getsemaní,' he said.

'Gethsemane,' she repeated. She had always loved the name, and now the subtle difference of his Italian pronunciation.

'Look.' He grabbed the handles of a light and aimed it at the mural. 'You see Peter?' The faces flooded with colour and life, and she recognised Mr Gilbert's, the perplexed expression he wore in the shop when he had forgotten something. In the face of St John, she saw a rather noble, optimistic profile of Mr Swann himself.

She realised her mouth was open and she closed it. Lucio smiled at her, and she felt the blood returning to her face and hands, warm and tingling. 'Do the committee know? Have they seen this yet?' she asked.

'Mr Swann says —' He paused, a twist to his lips that might have been amusement. 'He says they must sell more jam and cakes if they don't like it. He has no money to pay models.' She grinned. Despite the little she had learned and seen of Mr Swann, she could imagine him saying it. And she could also imagine the uproar once Mrs Cleat and the Christian Ladies found out they'd be singing *There Is a Green Hill Far Away* to the image of the schoolteacher perpetually wondering whether he'd left behind his cheese ration. Not quite the transcendent aid to worship they might have had in mind.

She turned to him again. His face was in the shadow of the light shining on the mural, making his bruises seem all the worse.

'I haven't seen you for ages,' she said, the echo of her voice sounding too loud, too accusing in the silence of the church. 'I thought maybe ... did I do something wrong, was I too outspoken — about the picture?'

He frowned and pushed his hair back from his face with his wrist. 'No.'

She lifted her hand towards him, towards the curve of stitches at his eye, but he turned away and she let it fall again.

'Why are you doing this?' she said. 'I mean, for nothing. No money, no recognition. And the work at Repton's on top of it all. You should be going to art college.'

'How?' he said flatly, like he was going through the motions of a tedious argument. 'We still pay Repton money for our passage here.'

'There are scholarships. If you're good, they pay for you. Mr Gilbert could help you.'

'Not for people like me — not for aliens. Mr Gilbert says I need a British passport first. Only six more years to wait.' His laugh was sharp, ironic. 'It doesn't matter.'

'Why do you always say that? Stop saying that,' she said, and the force of it surprised her. She found she had grabbed at his wrist, as if to shake him. 'Look at this.' She thrust her other hand towards the walls. 'You need to get away. From Repton's, from Leyton. Can't you see?'

His eyes scanned the sweep of the ash branches, the dove's wing, the falling light in the garden at Gethsemane. 'I do get away,' he said.

'But they can't appreciate this here. Not in Leyton. Don't you understand? You'll waste away here.'

Her fingers still gripped his wrist, and he laid his hand on top of hers. 'I think maybe it's you who waste away here,' he whispered. But she couldn't be sure whether she heard the words or simply felt them, saw them forming in the cast of his black eyes. She snatched her hand away.

'Connie,' he said. For the first time, she heard the sound her name made in his mouth, like something new, a name too exotic for the lanes of Leyton. And she wanted it to reinvent her, to remake her somewhere else: in Gethsemane or Israel, Damascus or Egypt, Antioch or Cappadocia. But the door creaked, and when she looked about her again, she was still in the stony chill of St Margaret's Village Church in Leyton, Mr Gilbert observing them with ruddy cheeks and chapped lips, his bicycle clip attached to his leg, his trilby turning in his hand.

Montelupini
1943

The festival of Ferragosto took place on one of the hottest days Lucio could remember. Even at sunset, he could feel the heat of the cobbles through his sandals as he and Vittorio trailed back along Via del Soccorso towards the village. An irritable Professore Centini had caught them lounging in the cool air by the fountain and set them to putting up trestle tables and hanging lanterns down on the campo for the evening's celebrations. Now they were sweaty from it, and while the rest of the village made their way to the party, Vittorio had insisted on going home to change. They approached the village just as the sun slotted behind the hills, and Lucio could almost hear the stones of the houses, the church, the battlements sigh their relief. On days like this, the whole village held its breath for nightfall.

As they climbed the steps to the piazzetta, they heard laughter coming from the osteria: a voice, German and loud, crowing in victory. Under the single light bulb of the pergola, Lucio could see Captain Schlosser's head, throwing back the remains of his glass, and Otto, bent towards the cards on the table. They seemed to be the last ones left at the bar, finishing their game. The rest of the unit had sauntered past Lucio and his brother in dribs and drabs, making their unsteady way down to the festival, red-faced from an afternoon's drinking in the heat.

'Idiot crucchi,' Vittorio muttered once again. It was his favourite comment these days. He leaned against the entrance to Vicolo Giotto and eyed the two senior officers with disgust. 'Anyone would think they were tourists on holiday. Do you think they've even heard that Mussolini's behind bars?'

Lucio didn't answer. He had no doubt the captain knew, but if he'd received any specific orders following Il Duce's arrest, he was keeping them very close to his chest. He and his men continued to frequent the osteria as they always had, while behind his back the villagers fretted about the German re-inforcements arriving in Montemezzo and the larger towns, the hostile attitude of the new troops, and the withdrawal of courtesies and trading.

'Here we are, pussyfooting around them, like some unexploded bomb in the piazza, but all Schlosser does is sit in the tavern and get everyone drunk for Ferragosto.' His brother was right. If tensions had increased between the Germans and the Italians elsewhere, the captain's answer was simply to drink the edge off them. In a gesture of goodwill to the Montelupinese, he'd even gone so far as to procure a piglet through his connections in Montemezzo, so that the pig jousting — the highlight of the festival — could continue as it always had. The fact that most of the village would rather eat the beast than play games with it seemed irrelevant to the captain.

Vittorio kicked at the heel of his sandal, as if to dislodge a piece of grit. 'Well, if that crucco's so desperate to see the jousting, we'll give him a joust.' He entered the alleyway, but glanced back at Lucio from the shadows. 'And we'll be hanging a nice fat porker in the cellar by winter, you'll see, Guf.' He thrust his hands in his pockets and began to walk home. But Lucio, hearing shouts again from the osteria, lingered under the arch of Vicolo Giotto.

'Padre! Padre, tell him!' the captain was calling loudly, rattling his chair behind him as he stood to address Padre Ruggiero. The priest was labouring across the piazzetta in his heavy robes, having finished vespers at San Pietro's. 'Tell him, Padre. He must see the pig fight!' The captain motioned to Otto impatiently. His accent had become thicker with the drink and Lucio could barely understand him. 'I find the pig especially. Is good sport, yah?' He pulled out a chair for Padre Ruggiero, who sat down heavily and pressed his sweating face into a handkerchief. He had come, it seemed, with the purpose of escorting the officers to the festival — making even more effort than Captain Schlosser to ignore the tensions erupting around them.

'Yes indeed. You must see the pig joust, Signor Otto,' Padre Ruggiero said, when he had recovered his breath. 'It's quite a spectacle. And so generous of the captain to make sure we've been able to carry on our traditions in such lean times.'

Otto didn't seem drunk at all, and Lucio sensed from the way he sat, upright and awkward, that he was there under obligation. 'I'm sorry, Padre. I'm not usually such a bore. I have a terrible toothache, I'm afraid —'

'He needs a drink, yes?' the captain interrupted. 'I tell him, drink the padre's aquavit. Tomorrow I take him to Monteferro myself to —' He put the knuckle of his forefinger to his mouth and made a ripping noise in his cheek, mimicking the extraction of the tooth. He laughed, pushing a generous glass of liquor towards Otto. Even from where he stood, Lucio could see the unmistakeable colour of Raimondi Gold. The captain said something energetic in German and took a swig from a silver hipflask on the table.

'I'm not much of a drinker,' Otto apologised to the priest.

'Even so, the captain is right,' Padre Ruggiero said, eyeing the size of the glass that had been poured. 'The villagers use this grappa as medicine. It's known to cure all manner of ailments. Particularly good for toothache, as I recall. Still,' he took the glass and poured some of the liquid into another, 'you shouldn't overdo it.' He knocked back the contents in one gulp.

The captain clapped the priest on the shoulder. 'Komm,' he said excitedly and nudged the glass again towards Otto. 'Komm!' Otto took it up, while Padre Ruggiero gave him a slow nod, like a benediction. He put the glass carefully to his lips, but before he could drink, the captain had tipped it upwards so that Otto was forced to gulp the whole shot or wear it down his shirtfront. Captain Schlosser wheezed as Otto grimaced, the liquor coursing down his throat.

When the joke had worn off, the captain jumped up. 'Good!' he said, slipping the hipflask into Otto's shirt pocket and patting it. 'Now we see the fighting pig!' And he grinned at them, innocent as a boy on the way to a country fair.

Lucio didn't go home to change. Instead he tailed the Germans and the priest, catching up with Otto when he found him alone at the edge of the campo. He was inspecting the lanterns that Lucio and his brother had hung from the trees, along the grassy hillside where most of the villagers had spread themselves, chatting before the entertainment began. In the meadow stood a semi-circle of ancient stones set about a chalk pit, partially cut into the hillside — when and by whom, nobody knew anymore. The small amphitheatre was only ever used for the Ferragosto games, or by children who staged plays and enacted feats of gladiatorial prowess while their mothers were at the washhouse. Leading the captain, Padre Ruggiero had already threaded through the crowd to take up the low stone seats set about the arena, which were always reserved for him. Behind them the soldiers from the mess were loitering in groups, set apart from the Italians, talking in their staccato voices and sending out volleys of laughter from time to time, like a flock of crows.

'How is your toothache?' Lucio asked Otto. He could tell from the shine in his friend's cheek and the softer line of his jaw that the liquor was already working its magic.

'Practically gone,' Otto said, surprised. 'The priest was right about that stuff.' Lucio nodded.

'It's beautiful,' Otto continued, gesturing at the coloured lights in the branches above them, the torches around the ring that were beginning to brighten with the falling night. 'The people go to so much trouble. It must mean a lot to them.'

Lucio shrugged. He remembered Ferragosto as it used to be: the pig spitting on the roast, Urso and Polvere arguing over its basting; the tables where the women would serve orecchie di prete, newspaper cones of olives and nuts, and the freshly made crostoli and ciambelle. There was none of that now, only a cask of young wine that Fagiolo drew off and sold by the glass to locals, and by the jug to the Germans. Everyone had eaten before they came, he knew, unable or unwilling to spare anything for the communal feast that once was the heart of the celebration. Now everyone saved the best of their harvests to trade, and pride prevented them from bringing out the paltry remains they kept to feed themselves.

He spotted his mother on the grass bank, sitting with Fabrizia. She was watching them. Otto began to raise his hand to her, but she turned away from them to talk to her friend. As she moved, her hair fanned across her back. It was tied loosely at the nape of her neck in a single black ribbon. She had taken to wearing it this way recently. Lucio had heard women in the washhouse complain it was too girlish, disrespectful to her husband, but this didn't seem to concern his mother. He liked the way it looked. Under the light of the lanterns, the curls falling down her back reminded him of ink dropped in water.

He saw Otto's hand retreat, yet there was a satisfaction playing about his friend's mouth, as if he'd lost fifty centesimi but found a lira. 'I can show you the best place to sit, if you want,' Lucio told him. He led Otto away from the crowd, past the washhouse, and up the track in the direction of Collelungo. When they were well above the campo, they cut through the meadow and onto a ridge, finding a spot that offered a clear view of the action in the ring and the audience below.

'All-seeing and yet unseen?' Otto said, smiling at him.

Lucio saw his mother glance towards the hill that rose behind her. She would not be able to see them, camouflaged as they were in the dusk, but she knew him too well, knew all the placcs to which he removed himself. She shifted back around, ready for the entertainment, running her hand over the hair at her neck, her fingertips lingering on the knot of ribbon, as though she knew she was being watched. And she was: he noticed Otto's gaze focusing there too.

'I nearly forgot,' his friend said suddenly, coming back to himself. He reached into the folds of his jacket and pulled out a book: a rolled journal encased in leather. He gave it to Lucio. 'I made this for you.'

Lucio held the book in his lap uncertainly, his fingers brushing the supple nap of the leather.

'Yes, it's for you,' Otto said. 'To keep all your sketches together.'

He untied the leather string around the journal. The cover fell back, soft as cloth, but the paper inside was thick and blank and clean. The pages reminded him somehow of the past:

freshly drawn milk; a tablecloth of pale linen handed down to his mother, cut up long ago for shirts; the whitewashed walls of his grandfather's murals.

'Thank you,' he began, but Otto shook his head to stop him.

'Oh, and this,' his friend said. He dropped something from his pocket into Lucio's palm. It resembled a coin, but on closer inspection he saw it was a metal disc on a ring. He ran his thumb over it and felt the engraving. He couldn't read it in the dark but he could guess what was written there: *Viviana*.

'Where is she tonight anyway?' Otto asked.

'I had to tie her up in the stable. She gets too excited about the piglet.'

Otto scoffed a little. 'What do they do with this piglet that everyone's making such a fuss about?'

'It's a game. They play it every year. Two men at a time get blindfolded. They have to chase the piglet round the arena with brooms. The one who hits it most in five minutes goes to the next round, until they get a winner.'

'And what's the prize?'

Lucio shrugged. He thought it was obvious. 'The piglet, of course.'

'A rather bruised one, then.'

'The beaters seem to hit each other mostly,' Lucio said. 'Some people find it funny.'

His friend's grey eyes were steady under their pale lids. 'But not you?'

He didn't answer. He didn't want to say that he'd never been able to laugh at the game.

In the amphitheatre, the competitors were lining up — a motley collection of boys and weathered old men, their shirt-sleeves rolled about their arms. Vittorio stood among them, balancing barefoot on the low arena wall, brown and lean.

He seemed to have grown over the summer, inhabiting his adult body with a nonchalant confidence that made Lucio feel like the younger brother. Many of the Avanguardisti had joined up over the spring, and he was one of the oldest left in the village now. But Lucio knew he didn't count, not the way Primo did. He was not a crowd-pleaser, a favourite to win.

'My brother,' Lucio said, indicating Vittorio to Otto. 'He's competing for our family.'

'For your family?'

Lucio heard the question that he knew his friend was too tactful to ask: *And why not you?* He tried to explain. 'My brother's better at things like this — better in a crowd. He'll have the audience behind him. It makes a difference. You'll see.'

Otto seemed unconvinced.

'It's become more than a game now,' Lucio said. 'Alive, that piglet could grow to see a family through next winter and spring. Even dead, it's the best meat anyone's likely to get all year. Vittorio has the greatest chance of winning.'

In the ring, Polvere was handing brooms to the first two competitors. Professore Centini stepped into the arena between them, the piglet under his arm. Spooked by the cheers of the crowd, the animal began to struggle and squeal, forcing the mayor to drop it and abandon his attempt at a speech. The pig skittered to the centre of the ring, sniffing the air and twitching the bell around its tail. The onlookers called out its whereabouts and jeered at the seekers for clinging to the safety of the walls. Shamed, they ventured inwards, blindly swinging their brooms, until one managed to land a sturdy smack on the backside of the other. The crowd bellowed, terrifying the animal, which did a circuit of the wall and promptly defecated.

Lucio could see the Germans exchanging coins and cigarettes, placing hurried bets. The captain was finding the game immensely entertaining, shouting in German at the top of his voice, his cheeks ablaze. His collar was unbuttoned, and he had discarded his glass, which Padre Ruggiero had given him, in favour of swigging straight from a bottle of Raimondi Gold, set on the wall before them. Every time one of the seekers hit the other, he clapped the priest on the shoulder with such force that the tuft of his biretta quivered.

From the sidelines, Polvere called time, and it was Vittorio's turn to replace the loser in the ring. The baker swung a leg down into the arena and gave the piglet a stiff kick. It screamed ridiculously, and Vittorio managed to land a few hits on its rump before it squeezed between his legs, leaving him swiping his opponent about the ankles. Someone summoned an imaginative curse that invoked both pigs and mothers-in-law, sending ribald laughter through the crowd, even among the Germans who hadn't understood a word.

At the fifth changeover, Vittorio was still undefeated in the ring, and the captain had become so excited that he could no longer stay in his seat. Stripping to his shirtsleeves, he jumped ahead of the queue of contestants, instructing the baker to tie the blindfold about him. His men seemed to think this a splendid development in the festivities, but their enthusiastic toasts fell suddenly loud in the villagers' silence.

To the side of the arena, Vittorio and Fagiolo were exchanging hushed, urgent words. His brother, still blindfolded, set back his shoulders and raised his broom tentatively. He seemed to have become a boy again, a David next to the German's towering Goliath. He sidestepped about the ring, keeping the head of his broom low to the ground and cocking his head to listen. He made a strike, short and quick, catching the calf of the captain, who lashed out in response. Vittorio took a cuff to the ear and another to the arm, which sent him sprawling across the dirt. But within seconds he was up again, this time swiping the German about the chin and drawing blood. There was a cheer from the villagers. Padre Ruggiero shifted in his seat. The captain spat and laughed, undeterred, continuing to command the space as he tried to locate his target. When the pig squealed, he jabbed his broom, striking its head with the handle and stunning it. Vittorio caught the second thrust in the stomach and doubled over. As he reached for the ground, his hand touched the pig, dazed at his feet. He scrambled to grab it, but the captain kicked his hands away and snatched up the animal by a hind leg.

A roar went up from the Germans, drowning out the pig's screams. The captain held his arms wide in victory. Still wearing his blindfold and dangling the piglet before him, he began to club it vigorously with his broom handle. The clamour of the audience gradually faded until all that could be heard were the dull thuds of the wood on limp flesh, the captain's rasping grunts.

When he became conscious of the silence, he threw the scarf from his eyes. He shook the beast towards his men for approval, like it was a hunting trophy. The soldiers stood and removed their cigarettes from their mouths, hesitating before starting up a solemn and dutiful applause. Vittorio had also pulled off his blindfold, panting. The captain offered him a broad grin, a bruised hand, but his brother only wiped his face on his sleeve and pinned the German in his sights for a long moment. Captain Schlosser, perhaps coming to his senses, lifted the piglet between them and offered it up to Vittorio. Everything seemed suspended. A dog barked; a child began to cry. Vittorio cracked his neck and snorted through his nose, making a bloody expectoration in the chalk at his feet. He walked to the wall and jumped over it, leaving the captain standing in the arena, the mauled piglet dangling from his fist.

Lucio became aware that Otto had gone. He caught sight of him striding towards the ring. But instead of joining the men thronging about the captain, he cut across the ridge, walking briskly away from the slope of spectators on the campo below. Searching ahead of him to see what Otto had seen, Lucio could make out a figure bound for the mule track up Collelungo. It was his mother. The shape and the sway of her was unmistakeable to him. He knew she was hurrying away from the festival, away from all that ugliness, just as he wanted to, losing herself between the moonlit brambles without looking back.

He bent to pick up the journal Otto had given him, intending to set off after them, but he paused. Where Otto had sat, something lay across the flattened grass, thin and black as charcoal. He prodded at it with his toe, thinking it might be a lizard or a young grass snake, but the thing was inanimate under his foot. When he picked it up, he felt its softness between his fingertips, the lush texture of velvet. The ribbon was no longer than his hand, too short to have come unthreaded from a collar or a cuff, to have been tied about a woman's hair. It was no more than a remnant, an offcut — a memento. He ran the velvet over his lips and recalled his mother's curls.

When he straightened he saw Otto on the mule track, his pale hair attracting the moonlight like something metallic under water. Lucio slipped the ribbon inside his journal and turned his back to the mountain, making his way down over the ridge and towards the village.

They knew the war was changing. But only after the festival did they actually see it for themselves. One November morning, there was a foreign stillness to the air: it reminded Lucio of the partial eclipse he had once witnessed, hearing it long before he had seen it. The birds had started up their frenetic evening song, even though it was barely midday, and there seemed a heightened flurry of insect activity in the grass. Fagiolo's mules had skittered and whinnied in their paddock, and dogs barked at the breeze that sounded like a distant train. Then everything became mute, holding its breath, as the shadow inched across the meadow, and he had imagined a stony chill like the Angel of Death passing overhead. Even when the summer day returned — the mules bowing their heads to the grass once more, the ants busy circling his boot, as though it had all been in his head — everything seemed changed to him. He recalled he had shifted his foot fractionally and let it hover over the black line of the moving ant trail. He could hear his blood in his ears, the thin, shallow breath in his throat, the very small-ness of life all about him, clinging to its tenuous thread.

He remembered all this as they walked under the canopy of chestnuts lining the road to Cori. No birds sang, and the verges dripped with quiet. Even Viviana seemed spooked. The donkey, with its load of olives to be pressed, stopped dead and shook at its bridle.

'Cammina, su!' Vittorio grumbled. 'Useless beast's as lazy as Padre Ruggiero himself.' He put up a hand to slap it on the rump, but Lucio caught his wrist. 'What?'

They heard a rope creaking, the flies fizzing among the branches, paper fluttering in a scuff of breeze. The body had been there some days, they guessed, the face pecked at by birds, the stench as stunning as heat from an opened oven door. Viviana let out a hesitant growl.

'Jesus Christ and all the saints.' Vittorio swallowed hard. 'Fuck.' The feet of the hanging man were bare and blue as stone: someone had already stripped him of his boots and socks. Lucio noticed his gnarled toes — the feet of an old man, bunioned like Nonno Raimondi's had been. He ran to the ferns on the other side of the road and retched.

'Bastards,' Vittorio said. They squatted together with their backs to the corpse, staring vacantly into the undergrowth. It seemed to glimmer in the weak sun through the trees, with tiny points of light like early stars in winter. His brother reached out and picked up several bullets from the leaf litter, shuffling them in his palm and blowing on the casings until their unspent charges were revealed. He pocketed them, glancing at Lucio. Then, without speaking, he scoured the bushes with the toe of his boot, perhaps hoping he might find the gun that went with them.

'See what your German friends are doing now?' His brother motioned to the swinging body and looked at him as if he could barely contain the contents of his own stomach. 'You see, Gufo? You think no one sees you — Mamma and you at Collelungo, meeting that blonde one. The translator.'

Lucio turned away, but his brother caught him by the arm.

'Things have changed. Weren't you listening at the fountain? They're rounding up boys as young as sixteen. They say it's for the new Fascist army, but the talk is they're being sent to Germany, to work in factories.' He was staring at Lucio but his focus seemed elsewhere, on some other image. 'How long do you think it'll be before they get to us?'

Last winter, Vittorio had been cursing the years between himself and the older Avanguardisti, imagining the envelope from Rome, stamped with the axe and rods, bearing his own name. But now Lucio could sense other longings in him, other ambitions coming to the surface, crossing his brother's face like clouds changing the colour of the lake at Montemezzo.

Behind him the rope creaked softly. Lucio saw the paper

pinned to the old man's chest. *Harbouring Deserters, Possessing Firearms, Anti-German Activity*. It read as bluntly as a market-day list.

His brother glanced over his shoulder at the noise. 'Let's do the business in Cori and get out of here.'

The next morning they were silent as they followed the road home, the only sounds the donkey's lazy shuffle on the chalk path, the bullets jangling in Vittorio's pocket as he ran his fingers through them.

He thought of Otto. He knew his brother was right. Everything about his friendship with the German should have felt wrong. But it didn't. Walking through the woods of Montemezzo with Otto and Viviana felt more real to him, more precious than any memory he could conjure of his father. And seeing his mother watching them from the rocks as they dived and resurfaced in the lake at the close of a summer day, her mouth open, her laugh skimming across the water between the two of them, brought him more happiness than it ought to. As for his mother's lantern, which he would track from the battlement wall as it swung up the mule track to Collelungo, and the torch that winked its impatient answer along the ridge, he would only lower his head and squint, until they became no more than fireflies, flickering to each other as nature dictated they must, on the last balmy nights before autumn.

They turned in at Padre Ruggiero's to deliver his share of the olive oil. The priest was expecting them and came to the gate.

'Is it true?' he called before they had finished the climb towards his villa. 'Did they hang Giacomo Luigi?' He saw the answer in their faces and he crossed himself, mouthing a prayer before sizing up the two casks of oil. He pursed his lips, evidently disappointed with the yield, but continued on the subject of the hanged man. 'Still, Giacomo was a known

Communist. They even said he encouraged the formation of resistance groups. At his age, I ask you? I wonder he had the energy.'

He rested a hand on each of their shoulders. 'They'll be the death of us, these partisans — you understand that, don't you? The Germans will retaliate. You must see the danger that poses for normal, honest men and women like the Montelupinese?' They nodded dutifully, but Lucio saw Vittorio's shoulder inch away from Padre Ruggiero's hand. 'That's why I want you to promise that if you hear anything of partisan groups or the GAP in these parts, you come and tell me. Even if it's someone you know, even if it's a friend. Is that understood?'

They gave their word and Padre Ruggiero climbed the steps of his verandah once again. Eager to be gone, they headed below to store the oil, but as they re-emerged from under the house, Lucio saw the priest's jowly face still at the balcony railing, his pale eyes following them from above, scanning the shape of their jackets, their trouser pockets as they left his cellar.

'And Primo, don't forget,' he called, 'I'm expecting you at the head of the litter during Santa Lucia's procession this year. Your father would want it.'

Without turning, Vittorio held up one hand in acknowledgement, as Lucio had seen him do so many times to boys in the schoolyard. But with the other, his brother made the cornuto behind his chest and spat as he led the donkey down the hill. 'Go fuck yourself,' he mumbled.

They stopped at Rocca Re from habit. Lucio suspected it had become a superstition of Vittorio's: to stand on the rock and make his mark before passing. The donkey wandered into the meadow to graze.

'What are we doing, Guf?' his brother asked. 'I mean, what are we *doing*?' He paced the great stone overhang, the bullets ringing in his pocket. The valley dripped dully before them: pockets of mist wreathed the mountaintops and threatened to shroud what was left of the day, while the smoke of a bonfire rose in the bare orchards on the Prugni rise.

'I can't bear this waiting,' Vittorio continued. 'Everyone here just sits around and waits — waits for the food to run out, for the Nazis or Mussolini's thugs to round us up, for the Allies to arrive. What difference will it make? Someone else is always telling us what to do.'

Lucio shifted his hands in his pockets and felt the familiar stub of his pencil. He couldn't think the way his brother did. He wanted to study the twist of smoke in the valley, the scribble of trees on the ridge; to see the sun appear in the thinnest gap of clear sky above Carpeto; to witness the range fire up for an instant like it was dipped in copper.

'Well, I'm not sitting around any longer,' Vittorio announced. He drew out one of the bullets, holding it up in front of him. It winked, bright and complicit, as he positioned it on the ledge. He jumped back down to the path, returning with a rock the size of his fist in each hand.

'What are you doing?' Lucio asked. He felt a looseness in his stomach, the apprehension of what his brother might do next.

'I'm going to go back up to Cori. I'm going to join that gruppo.' He set down one of the rocks at his feet, and with the other he took a practice swing at the bullet. 'They've got eyes and ears all through these mountains. I heard Scarvacci say so when he was pressing the oil.' He squinted and pointed the finger of his free hand at the tiny golden casing glinting on the granite a few feet away. 'He said they wanted someone like me, someone who knows the passes through the ranges, who can travel quickly without raising suspicion.' He raised and lowered his chin, realigning the bullet in his sights. 'But if they take me, you'll have to forget that Primo ever existed. It's the price of a freedom fighter, see. I'll be Fulmine from now on, I've decided.' And channelling his new name, he released the rock at lightning speed. There was a metallic ring, the beginnings of a whistle; then the explosion bounced back at them from across the range, sudden and vast and unruly. Ravens rose to shred the echo with their caws, and a pair of quail beat out their applause from the scrub below. When the boom faded, a chip of rock crumbling at the precipice pattered down upon the brush and scree, the sound as soft and innocent as rain.

His brother was finally still, but Lucio saw his mouth beginning to stretch into that dangerous grin. Vittorio yelled, an indistinguishable word, half jubilant, half animal cry, and grabbed Lucio behind the neck with one hand. 'See?' he said, as if the lucky hit was a sign of divine approbation. He balanced on the lip of the overhang, his arms wide. 'Sono re!' he cried down into the valley, which still seemed to shiver with noise. 'Sono re!'

And at that moment, Lucio believed his brother really could be the master of anything he chose.

Leyton
1950

'Don't see why her ladyship's books are any better than them in the mobile library,' Aunty Bea was saying. She was buffing a silver platter in the scullery of Leyton House.

'I wish you wouldn't call her that,' Connie said quietly, pulling against the doorjamb, eager to get away from her aunt. 'The library here has ... proper books, a hundred times more than the library van.' The sneer behind her words was audible and she knew she would pay for it.

'Oh, I see. *Proper* books, are they?' Aunty Bea sniffed. 'Good thing I dusts all them *proper* books as everyone's falling over themselves to read.'

Her aunt was aching for an argument. She could tell by the set of her chin, by the way her eyes scanned, as though searching for a loose thread that she might pull to unravel her. Connie knew what it was about. Through the autumn, Aunty Bea had been content with Connie's avoidance of the Big House. There was always a note of satisfaction in her aunt's voice when she told Connie how Mrs Repton had been asking after her.

'And what did you tell her?' Connie would say.

'What d'you think I told her? I said you was too busy at the shop now for books and reading and such.' And Connie understood the message she was giving Mrs Repton: that the Big House and its amusements were a childhood pastime that Connie had outgrown.

So when she passed the scullery that Saturday afternoon, on her way to the library, her aunt's disapproval was as keen as a blast of winter wind down the hallway. Aunty Bea spat again on the platter as she polished it, and Connie couldn't help but imagine the gratification she derived from knowing Mrs Repton's dinner would be sitting on a film of her own saliva.

'Well, fetch us the pot before you go in, then,' Aunty Bea snapped. 'You can make yourself useful and take her ladyship's tea in for me.' Connie reached for the service and waited while her aunt prepared the tray, setting down a solitary cup and saucer. 'Tea for one, it is,' she added pointedly.

Outside, four or five rounds of gunshot sounded, making the scullery windows hum. Mr Repton and his shooters were discharging, their gaming ended for the day. Connie had seen the start of the shoot that morning on the way to work, stopping at the top of Bythorn Rise to watch Mr Repton at his peg, lined up with five other men in shooting tweeds, their twelve-bores raised to their shoulders, the spaniels' barks carrying across the fields like a dry cough. The beaters were in the spinney. She heard the tapping of the trees, the high-pitched *burrs* and *aarhhs* as they flushed out the birds. Some of them would be lane kids hoping for rewards of eggs or sweets, sometimes even a bird if Mr Repton's bag and his mood were particularly good. Behind the line of men she had seen the pickers: Fossett and Mr Rose, with their dogs. And there at the edge of the spinney, placed as a stopper before the dyke, was Lucio Onorati. Two birds creaked from the trees, fluttering diamonds spiralling upwards, and the opening volleys had sounded, cracking over the fields like they might bring down the sky itself. Lucio had ducked then: she'd seen it clearly. Even at that distance she could sense his whole body flinch, see his hand darting to cover his head. The rest of the party were oblivious, too busy scanning the air for the covey. But she had seen it. And afterwards, when the guns were cocked, she'd witnessed the way he'd straightened and stepped forward with the others as though nothing had happened. The wings of a rogue bird, shot wide of the spinney, fanned as he raised it by the feet from the wet grass. He corrected it, the head lolling at his hip, the plump body banging against his knee as he walked. The air was so sharp it seemed to sting her lungs as she caught her breath.

'Shoot's over, then,' Aunty Bea said, interrupting her thoughts. 'See his lordship's got the Eye-talians beating and bagging for him. Just as well. According to Fossett, his lordship can't make a clean kill if the game were hung in front of him. The Eye-ties'll have to finish them birds off for his bag by hand … like they did her ladyship's cat.'

Connie bit down on her lips. 'I told you,' she said, trying to keep her voice calm. 'I couldn't be sure it was the Italian. It was dark …' She trailed off as her aunt flashed her a smug look. 'You've told Mrs Repton, haven't you? About the cat?'

Aunty Bea shrugged. 'So what if I did? Not like they's anything to you, is it?' The heat rose across Connie's throat and she could not meet her gaze. Aunty Bea had found the thread and tugged.

''Cause if they is anything to you, my girl, you're on your own. You get your sights set on one of them bloody WOPs' — she paused, gathering her strength after the poison of the word — 'and you'll be making your own bed.'

Her aunt lifted the tea tray and thrust it at her. Connie was surprised to see that her eyes glinted with the beginnings of tears. Aunty Bea wasn't one for crying and didn't tolerate it in others either, thinking it self-pitying and weak. Connie had only ever seen her cry on two occasions: once when the telegram about Uncle Bill had arrived; and once on VE Day, which Uncle Jack said was from too much sherry, even though the tears had continued at the kitchen sink early the next morning. Until that point, she had thought that, like Mrs Cleat, Aunty Bea might come around to the Italians, to Vittorio's charms at least. But these were tears of bitterness, stubborn and blinkered. She knew now that the further she became involved with the Onorati boys, the further she was sure to drive the wedge between herself and her aunt. She shifted the tray to her hip and tried to soften her expression, but Aunty Bea ushered her impatiently out the door.

Connie walked the corridors, the tea things chiming, unsteady in her hands. She resented her aunt's threat but was also confused by it, and the closer she came to the library, the more these emotions mingled with the memory of Mrs Repton at the harvest fair. Connie had not spoken to her since that night, and her nerves fizzed in her stomach, making her feel queasy. She was certain there would be reproaches for not coming sooner, and she felt a fraud for making the effort now, when she had such an ulterior motive. She took a deep breath at the unlatched door, tapped it with her foot by way of knocking, and nudged it open.

Mrs Repton was curled on the window seat, gazing out towards the yard. Through the pane, Connie could see Fossett, Lucio and his father pairing up the braces, laying them in lines for the hunting party to survey as they drank their whiskey. An open book had slipped from Mrs Repton's lap, and her head, leaning against the window, had fogged the glass in a small circle. She didn't turn around and Connie thought she might be asleep. But as she approached, she saw that Mrs Repton's eyes were open, lit with that feline changeability, which seemed at once focused and elsewhere. The tea things rattled on the tray as Connie set them down. Mrs Repton started. A strand of her hair, lodged loosely in the ebony comb, fanned down into her neck.

'Connie!' She held out her pale hands and Connie took them. 'Why haven't you been? I thought perhaps you'd finally found your wings and we'd become too dull for you.' Her disappointment seemed genuine.

'Hardly.' Connie tried to laugh, but it came out weakly, almost a sigh. She squeezed Mrs Repton's hands and was surprised to feel their thinness in her own, to see her tired smile, her collarbone angular under a silk blouse. She slid her hands from Connie's and pulled out the comb. Her blonde hair fell stiff and awkward about her face as she set the comb between her teeth, running her palms along her neck to gather up the loose strands. Watching her, Connie felt an ache in her stomach, as if for something lost, something that could no longer be regained — like a child discovering that fairies were a fantasy, or a wonderful magic trick simply the sleight of an adult's hand.

Mrs Repton motioned for Connie to sit next to her. 'Only one cup?' Connie ignored her, arranging the tea things. 'I see. Your aunt. She never has liked you spending time with me, has she? Am I such a terrible influence?' There was mischief in her eyes. 'Is it because of her you stayed away?'

'No. Of course it wasn't.'

'Good then.' She got up from the window seat and crossed to the drinks cabinet, returning with two whiskey tumblers and pouring tea into them from the pot. After a moment, she went back for the whiskey and splashed some of that into each glass too. She handed one to Connie and sat back down with her own. 'Well, it's how they drink tea in the Middle East, isn't it? In glasses. We can pretend we're somewhere exotic, like Morocco or Egypt.' Laughter sounded among the shooting party in the courtyard. 'Well, almost,' she added.

Connie sipped at her tea, the fumes hot in her throat, her fingertips burning on the glass. She could see Mr Repton outside, his chapped nose and cheeks seeming all the angrier for the dullness of his tweeds, his tan garters as he walked the mottled line of pheasants and grouse laid out on the flagstones.

'So, why *did* you stay away?' Mrs Repton asked.

'I've been busy ... in the shop ... and ...'

Mrs Repton stared out the window. 'Oh,' she said, clearly disappointed at Connie's lack of honesty. She waved a hand in the vague direction of the bookshelves. 'Help yourself, then. Take whatever you want.'

Connie set down her glass. The strap of her satchel was still strung across her shoulder and she slipped it off. 'I ... I didn't only come for books. Not really.' She flushed as she opened the bag, as much because the battered satchel was still her one handbag as for what she was about to do. She took out the paper parcel and handed it to Mrs Repton.

'What's this?'

'I should have brought them back ages ago. I'm sorry.'

Mrs Repton opened the crushed paper. 'Goodness,' she said, pulling out one of her white heels. 'I quite forgot about those. How angry Repton was with me.' She gave a tremulous laugh as she replaced the shoe and scrunched up the paper in her fist. 'Here. You keep them. Repton never liked them anyway and I hardly need to be reminded of that night. You're probably the same size as me now.' Mrs Repton held up the bag, her eyes on Connie's scuffed lace-ups.

Connie frowned and shook her head slowly, before realising how ungrateful it seemed. But she couldn't help feeling insulted, her pride somehow injured, and she imagined for the first time something of what the Italians might feel.

Mrs Repton let the bag fall onto the window seat between them. 'I'm sorry,' she said. 'That was ... tactless of me.' She stood abruptly, her hand beneath the coil of her hair, her shoulders rising and falling with her breath. 'Of course, I should apologise for walking off and leaving you while you were trying to help me that night.' Her tone was hopeful, as if Connie might deny the need for an apology, the need to bring up again the unhappiness she'd cast before her that evening. And for a second Connie was tempted. It would be so much easier to say what Mrs Repton wanted to hear, to retreat to the shelter of the bookshelves and lose herself in the great atlas like she used to as a child. But she also saw Lucio bending in the yard to gather up the braces, the carcasses of the game swinging against his side as he walked to the stable, where Fossett was hanging them. And the light from the window showed a thin strand of grey hair, loose on Mrs Repton's shoulder, aggravating in Connie that residual sense of something magical that was now ordinary, of something innocent now lost.

'You were very unhappy that night,' Connie braved finally.

Mrs Repton gave a hollow laugh. 'Well, I was somewhat worse for wear, wasn't I?' She reached for a cigarette from the caddy and held it between her fingers without lighting it.

It was Connie's turn to stare out the window and show her disappointment.

Mrs Repton snapped her lighter. 'Really. It's not as bad as it seems.' She let her head fall back on her shoulders as she exhaled, gazing up at the high ceiling of the library.

Connie concentrated on the baggers hanging the coveys, Lucio transferring them between the courtyard and the stables.

'It was my idea, you know,' Mrs Repton said. 'Bringing the Italians back.' A faint smile played on her lips as though she'd seen through Connie, had understood the real reason she'd come. 'Aldo came to us from the camp in Wood Walton during the war, did you know that?' Connie shook her head. 'I could speak some Italian, so I was asked to help settle the billets on farms in the area. He barely spoke a word when he first arrived, even to the other prisoners. He'd been taken for dead, pulled from a mass grave in North Africa and sent to the military hospital in Cairo. When he got here, it was like we'd received only the broken pieces of him. But by the end of the war, he'd thrown himself into his work like there was nothing else. When I heard how bad things had become for the Italians after peace, I encouraged Henry to ask Aldo to come back.' She glanced at Connie, something culpable in her expression. 'I thought I was doing the right thing, you understand? Repton simply saw the economic advantage — he still does — but I honestly thought it would be a better life for them.'

She leaned over to press her cigarette into the ashtray. 'I know why you're here. Harvey has told me about the boy.'

'About Lucio?'

Mrs Repton nodded.

'Do you know then? Have you seen his work at the church?'

'Yes. He's very good. There's no doubt about it.'

'Good enough to be at art college, don't you think?' Connie could hardly keep the hope from her voice, and hurried on before she could lose her nerve, the whiskey giving her courage. 'That's where he should be, not wasting such a talent hacking sugar beet and mucking out pigs. That's why I came ... to ask whether you could help him. He can't get a scholarship until he's a British resident and that will take years. But if he could pay his way — if he had some money ...'

She stopped. Mrs Repton had lowered her head, folding her arms about her as if she was drawing all the parts of herself together. Her lips trembled, but whether she would laugh or cry, Connie couldn't tell.

'Do you really believe I have money of my own?' Mrs Repton said.

Connie was taken aback. She hadn't thought there was even a possibility Mrs Repton didn't have money. She knew the Gilberts had never been a wealthy family. There were rumours their father, once landed gentry, had been a gambler, and Mr Gilbert seemed to prove it: teaching was a necessity, not a choice, she knew. Still, he and his sister had the privileges of the wealthy: the education, the travel, the accents, even the assumptions. Everyone knew Eve Gilbert had married Henry Repton for his money, but it hadn't occurred to Connie that she would have limited access to it. Connie considered her: the clothes, the jewellery, the furniture and books. Everything around them seemed to shrink, to become like copies, a doll's-house version in which Mrs Repton was acting out only scenes of a life.

'Repton keeps me on an allowance, just as he does the Italians, Connie. Anything substantial I could get my hands on, he would immediately know was missing. Besides, if I ask him, do you think he's going to support losing another worker who owes him money? What did you expect — that I could simply write you out a cheque?'

The reproach in her voice made Connie blush. She had thought she would confide in Mrs Repton, adult to adult, but now felt nothing more than a child again. She wished she had gone to the bookshelves when she'd had the chance. 'I ... I didn't ask solely because of the art,' she said, as if casting for something to cling to in the wreckage of the conversation. 'Lucio needs to get away from his father. You see that, don't you?'

Mrs Repton worried her lip with her teeth. 'I don't think

Aldo means it,' she said, but she sounded weak, unconvincing. 'Harvey says there are things we don't know about them, difficult things we don't understand about their past.'

'So you won't help him?'

'I can't. Weren't you listening?'

'No, you *won't*. There's a difference.' Connie's jumbled emotions until that point seemed distilled now to anger inside her. She found her fingers fidgeting noisily with something on the window seat. It was the paper bag containing the shoes. She pushed it aside and Mrs Repton glanced at the white heels peeping out. Connie thought her face no longer seemed pale in the light of the window — it was grey, and her eyes were less mysterious than simply lost.

She stooped to pick up her satchel. 'I'm sorry.' She wasn't sure what she was apologising for: perhaps it was to herself, for her own naivety. She headed for the door, past the wall of books where she had spent so much time growing up.

'Connie … Connie, wait,' she heard Mrs Repton call, but she had already closed the library door, shutting her in with the ashen smell of the spines, the leather of the cigar chairs, the sweet smoky staleness of the drinks cabinet. And she began to run towards the scullery, slipping out of her lace-ups and into her mud-caked boots on the back step, breathing in the damp air, the washed-out light of the winter afternoon.

'Well, what *can* we do? Our hands are tied,' Mrs Cleat snapped at Mrs Armer over the sound of the bell as they hurried across the threshold of the shop. Connie shivered. Outside, the sky hung grubby and low, and particles of snow had begun to swirl about the street like blown ashes. Normally the advent of snow occupied conversations for an entire day in Leyton. But this afternoon an even greater event had occurred. Mrs Cleat and the Christian Ladies had met for a long-overdue viewing of the St Margaret's mural project. And by the look on Mrs Cleat's face as she tugged off her hat and gloves, it had not gone well.

'Connie,' Mrs Cleat implored, her arm outstretched, her hand flapping as she returned to the servery. Connie rushed to pass her the counter cloth, which Mrs Cleat immediately applied to the Formica with vigorous, frantic buffs. From the other side of it, Mrs Armer took up where they had left off.

'But Foreman Rose? As Saul? I ask you. That's surely taking the joke too far.'

'You don't have to state the ruddy obvious, Edith. We all know the only blinding light Arthur Rose ever seen in his life is the sun shining on that blasted hipflask.' Mrs Cleat wrung her lips together, evidently even more furious that the meeting had reduced her to swearing.

There was a low chuckle. Mrs Livesey was standing in the door in her wellies. 'Well, well. Mr Rose as Saul? Is that right?' she said, her rogue tooth glinting as she squelched to the counter. 'Sounds like every regular at the Green Man might make it onto the walls of St Maggie's afore long. I can just picture it: Fossett as St Francis.' She waved a hand before her face in mock awe, then laughed loud and deep. The bounce of her bosom reminded Connie of two beagle puppies she had once seen fighting in a sack. 'Very uplifting,' Mrs Livesey said.

Mrs Cleat and Mrs Armer stood transfixed. A reaction such as Mrs Livesey's was their greatest fear: that the grand mural project and, by association, the Christian Ladies' committee, would become a laughing stock. Connie could see Mrs Cleat searching wildly for a response.

'Of course, not being privy to the works, Janet, you won't have seen how much true merit they have, how really ...

transcendent they are ... not being on the committee and all.'

Mrs Armer kept her shoulder to Mrs Livesey, as if to stress they could never seriously discuss the murals with anyone who called the church *St Maggie's*. 'Mr Swann's work is exceptional, never mind the models he chooses. They're saying it's his most ambitious project yet. People'll be visiting Leyton to see the murals at St Margaret's for years to come, you mark my words.'

'Well, as long as we don't end up with summat akin to the circus. He makes most of his living painting music halls, don't he?'

'Music halls?' Mrs Cleat cried. 'He paints the sets at Covent Garden, I'll have you know!'

'Gardens, fairgrounds. All I'm saying is it might not be the kind of thing we want at St Maggie's.'

Mrs Cleat touched her fingers to her temples, and her eyes flickered shut.

'What can I get you today, Mrs Livesey?' Connie said brightly, and Mrs Cleat left for the back store, touching her arm as she passed and murmuring, 'Bless you, Connie, love.'

Connie had seen the four completed murals and knew that, as far as Mr Swann's models were concerned, there was worse to come. She had been sneaking out to visit Lucio late at night, and he had shown her Mr Swann's sketches for the view of Martha and Mary, their bodies the slender, elegant forms of robed peasants, but their faces strikingly similar to those of Fran Carter, the barmaid from the Green Man, and Mrs Livesey, herself a regular at the pub. Their heads were inclined in conference and Mary had her hand up, shielding her mouth as they talked. And the cup that Martha held, though painted terracotta, was decidedly reminiscent of a tankard.

She also knew that, save for the figures and their identifying objects, the murals — the fine detail of the backdrop, the landscape and its atmosphere — were mainly Lucio's work. When she couldn't sleep at night, or when her day at Cleat's had been especially numbing, she couldn't help but be drawn to the other world he was creating in the church. As she cycled to St Margaret's she would look for the candle in the south window, which he used to show her Mr Swann was gone, and if it was lit she would scratch like a mouse on the great oak door. Inside, she settled herself on a pew, lying along it to watch as Lucio worked in the spotlights. She was mesmerised as much by the paintings as by the intensity of his concentration: the hours of fractional movements, the self-contained expressions of someone who was elsewhere, carried away by his imagination.

And he took her with him as he travelled through the wooded backdrops of chestnut and beech, white oak and sycamore, through the details of their bare, snow-frosted boughs or the luminous green of their springtime leaves, unfurling across the masonry like he was turning the walls inside out. She witnessed him hide within their branches the tight nests of cuckoos or sparrows, beehives or solitary bats; or at their bases, amid the leaf litter and tangled brambles, tiny blossomings of strawberries or mushrooms, a hedgehog's snout, a scuttling pinemarten or weasel. Even his subjects' clothes had something alive about them, a teasing veracity that sometimes made her look twice to check she had not been mistaken: a stain on St Peter's cowl, the raw linen of his tunic, frayed at one cuff; a leaf caught in the folds of Martha's headscarf, her sandals worn to a hole at one side, Mary's caked with mud; the grey cracks in the heels of Saul's bare feet. Sometimes she would fall asleep to the buzz of the stage lights in the hollow space and the images would come with her. And when she started awake again, there they were, spread before her, even more alive and colourful than when they spoke to her in dreams.

She did not really care that the faces of Fossett or Mr Gilbert or Mr Rose peopled this world. After all, the diocese had allowed the early Christian characters of the Middle East, the saints of faraway places, to be painted strolling through England's green and pleasant land. Why shouldn't they, then, take English faces too? But what did sadden her was that Mr Swann, a clearly inferior craftsman, would take the credit for Lucio's work and then, with a flippant artistic joke, cause enough local scandal and ridicule to divide the village and sap their enjoyment of it. It was as though he wanted the whole project to blow up in his face, like he couldn't countenance this raw unschooled talent, even if the free labour allowed him to pay his debts all the quicker.

'How can Mr Swann live with himself?' she asked Mr Gilbert when she caught him on her way home one Saturday afternoon. 'It's not that he doesn't pay Lucio, it's the recognition.'

'I believe there has been a small amount of money changing hands of late — that is, if I can get to Swann before he gets to the Green Man.' Mr Gilbert gave her a sheepish smile. 'But the recognition part is tricky, Connie. Lucio doesn't want it any more than we need more fuss surrounding these paintings. Why not allow him to get his pleasure from the work in the way that suits him?'

'But what about the models? Mr Swann is having his joke at the expense of the whole village, and more importantly at the expense of Lucio's work.'

Mr Gilbert considered her. 'I see Lucio's not the only one with the perceptive eye.'

She turned away, impatient with his deference to her these days. Deep down his veiled compliments pained her, reminding her too much of the disappointment she'd become, not just to him but also to herself.

'You're right, of course,' he said. 'You know, I think the committee members were rather more offended at being left *off* the walls than at the choice of faces on them.' He chuckled. 'Swann was livid they'd presumed to dictate to him about his work, though. I had to practically carry him home from the Green Man afterwards, and now he's stormed back down to London to complete some theatre project.'

'What about the rest of the paintings?'

'He's given Lucio free rein over the final views. He told me the Leyton coat of arms and the insignia of the diocese would be his last paintings for the honourable sisterhood of ladies.'

'Really? And that's what he called them?'

'No. He said they were a mob of fishwives in hats and gloves. *But I'm not one as likes to tittle-tattle,*' he added in Mrs Cleat's voice.

'Someone's bound to find out though, surely?' Connie said, ignoring the joke. 'About Lucio, I mean. I'm amazed Mr Swann hasn't already let the cat out of the bag in one of his drinking sprees at the Green Man.'

'Oh, even drunk, Swann's no fool. He's too worried about not getting paid. And the joke with the models is merely evident to the villagers. Any outsider, even the diocesan inspectors, would see nothing but the biblical characters. A work as good as this will raise Swann's profile and get him more-lucrative commissions. He won't let an opportunity like that slip through his fingers.'

She looked at him incredulously. *The joke is merely evident to the villagers.* He said it as though Leyton didn't matter, as though Lucio didn't matter, and the one thing at stake was Mr Swann's artistic career. Through his snobbery, she realised what her own had been. *It's too beautiful for Leyton,* she had told Lucio, like the village was unworthy of such a gift. But who was she or Mr Gilbert to say who could and couldn't appreciate art, as if one needed class or education to admire it? She began to understand what Lucio might be about, how much more important it was for him to paint his murals right here, for people such as them, people like him.

'Don't write Leyton off like that,' she said.

'Like what?'

'Like we're all too uncouth and stupid for the grander business of art to really matter to us. Like it's all a bit of country amusement for Mr Swann, which happens to have turned out rather well for his career.'

She stopped to get on her bike. Mr Gilbert stood back to give her room, and she saw that he was smiling, almost like he was pleased. 'Connie, that's not what I said. You're putting words in my mouth.'

His measured tone made her think he wasn't taking her seriously. 'And what about Lucio? Doesn't he deserve more than the bargain you and Mr Swann have struck up between yourselves?' She found she was giving into her anger, feeling spurred on by it. 'You're no better than Mr and Mrs Repton really, are you? Making it seem like you're helping, when in fact you're exploiting him for whatever you can get.'

'Connie,' he said, shocked now. 'Why would I be involved in such a *bargain*, as you call it? What exactly am *I* supposed to be getting out of all this?'

She paused, her foot on the pedal, breathing heavily. 'Do you think I'm such a country bumpkin that I can't put two and two together? All those *special* friends you have that are always at the ready to do favours for you. Funny how they're never women, isn't it?' She laughed hollowly, and it was as though the sound came from someone else — Agnes or Mrs Livesey, leaning over the counter of Cleat's. 'I've seen the way you look at them, the way you look at Vittorio and Lucio … yes, and even Mr Swann too.'

Her breath shuddered in her lungs. She had shaken herself more than she had him: Mr Gilbert stared at her blankly, his shoulders sunken and his hands loose by his side. She waited, wanting him to deny it, to call her mad or a fool, to be outraged at her accusations. But they were both locked in the moment, regarding each other with new eyes.

'Connie,' he said faintly, but she didn't want to hear any more. She stood up on her pedals and raced towards Bythorn Rise.

By the time she got home, her anger had subsided into a crushing remorse. She had never meant for the conversation to become what it had, for her suspicions about Mr Gilbert ever to be aired. She felt ashamed that she had clutched at them and thrown them in his face, when really she wasn't angry with him about that: she was frustrated with herself and with Leyton and the way circumstances conspired to trap people there — perhaps even Mr Gilbert himself. That thought made her feel even worse.

Out in the open countryside, a fog had descended on the afternoon, directing her thoughts further inwards and increasing her sense of claustrophobic wretchedness. She propped up her bike and went to the shed in the back garden, where she knew she would find Uncle Jack.

'Pea soup,' he mumbled to her from the doorjamb, as he contemplated his thin blue line of Woodbine smoke twisting into the thicker fog beyond.

'Couldn't see five feet ahead of me coming up the rise. The bike lamp made it worse.' She stepped up beside him in the shed, its interior lit by a single bulb hanging from the centre of the roof. Her uncle had been halving seed potatoes on the bench and still had the knife in his hand. He took a puff of his cigarette and hummed quietly as he exhaled through his nose.

'I remember a day like this, once. Took your aunt to Skegness. Before we was married.' She listened to the flatness of his voice against the fog, the dampened warble of an unseen bird in the garden, suddenly close and then far away. 'We stood on the pier to look out at the boats, but all we could see was pea soup. Just like this.'

Connie folded her arms about her and tapped the lip of the threshold with her toe. 'I've never seen the sea.'

'Well, neither had we.' He nudged her shoulder with his elbow, and she half sighed, half laughed, taking the cigarette from him and holding it playfully to her lips. She fanned out her fingers and inclined her head on the doorframe with a dramatic, longing gaze.

'*I must go down to the seas again, to the lonely sea and the sky,*' she said in the plummy tones of a silver-screen starlet.

He chuckled and took the cigarette back from her. 'Steady on now, Bette. Plenty of time for all that.'

Her uncle went back to his seed potatoes, and it seemed little more than a moment ago that she had stood there with him in that very spot, performing the same task on a rainy afternoon last year. Time seemed on a loop in Leyton, she sometimes thought. The months passed, the seasons ran into one another, but nothing changed. She seemed eternally stuck in the waiting room of youth, wondering when her life would begin, and she feared that one day she might wake up and find that it had passed her by without her even noticing. She swallowed back a sob that threatened to rise in her throat and laid a hand on the top of her head, flattening back the wild curls of her hair that had turned to frizz in the damp.

Her uncle was watching her. 'So, you going to take me to the flicks, or what?' she said with strained buoyancy.

'The flicks?' he replied. 'Right enough the weather for it. If I can fight off that long line of young men you got queuing at the door.'

She laughed. 'Pretty certain last time I checked it was just you and me, Uncle Jack.'

'Is that right, Rusty?' he said. 'Then how come I seen a young fella shifting about in the back lane, asking after someone called Connie. Know anyone by that name?'

She saw he was serious. 'Who was it?' she asked. But she already knew. Only the Italians would avoid coming to the front door.

Uncle Jack nodded towards the old cart track that backed onto the garden. 'Probably still there is my guess.' His watery eyes rested on her, with a glimmer that was almost impish, before he was lost again in a swathe of exhaled smoke.

Beyond the back gate she could barely see as far as the hedgerow on the other side of the track. She heard the amplified tick of it in the stillness of the fog, and then realised it wasn't the hedge but something mechanical, like an engine recently shut off. 'Hello?' she called, and as she said it, headlights were illuminated and the swirling grey became yellow before her. She approached the car, stepping beyond the beam and making out the solid form of an old Austin. She heard her name and finally saw Vittorio's face grinning from the driver's window.

'You like it?' he asked. His face seemed delighted at the expression on hers.

'Whose is it?'

His smiled faltered. '*Whose is it*? What, you think I steal it?'

'No, of course not —'

He frowned, and then laughed as if it wasn't the first time the idea had crossed his mind. 'Get in.' She hesitated. 'Don't worry. It's really mine!' He thumbed his chest. 'Mr Edwards said I can fix, I can keep it. So I fix it. Come on.' He leaned across to the rusty passenger door, which stalled as he pushed it open. He shrugged at her. 'It's good. The engine is good. Come on. I show you.' She paused, glancing over her shoulder at the house. 'Connie, come on. I waited a long time to show you.'

She walked around to the passenger door and slipped in beside him. He grinned again, and she felt the shudder in the seat as he switched the ignition and the engine fired; the shudder under her skin, as if he had flooded her veins with life. He twisted towards her as he reversed the car back down the cart track, his cheeks shining, his eyes quick and determined. And she remembered the boy who had ridden her bike with the hole in his boot, his complete lack of doubt.

'Where are we going?' she said as they approached the top of Bythorn Rise. 'You can hardly see a thing.'

He pulled over at the top of the hill, where the fog was thinner, and they gazed out at it pooling in the dells below, shifting and changing shape as if the black fields were tossing in their sleep beneath it.

'Doesn't matter where,' he said, reaching for her hand. 'Some place. Any place. We go. That's what matters.'

Montelupini
1943

Lucio crept up the steps of the house in Vicolo Giotto and lifted the latch of the door as quietly as he could. It was well past midnight and, after his vigil on the freezing battlements, his skin tingled from the sudden warmth of the embers in the kitchen grate. He hadn't been able to sleep and had gone to watch for signs of his brother, imagining him returning up Via del Soccorso with the donkey that had, once again, gone missing. In his heart he knew he was wasting his time. Vittorio had already been absent three days, and Lucio understood he wasn't coming back. But the watching, the waiting, the hope seemed easier to bear than his regret at not having stopped him, not having gone with him.

The day before Vittorio left, they had checked the stable together, to see if the lost donkey might have found its way back. But the stable was cold and smelled of mildew instead of dung, empty as it was now of animals. A single prodigal chicken, which had stopped laying months ago, eyed them with an accusing look and pecked out an indignant complaint as they entered. Vittorio caught it quickly under his arm and it creaked, tired and worn as an old hinge.

'She must have been up in the eaves. Otherwise the crucchi

would have taken her when they stole the donkey.' Vittorio tugged the bird's feet to keep her still. 'She's hardly worth the effort. But,' he took her neck in a fist and pulled, 'better in our stomachs than those bastards'.' And Lucio watched him as he slung the carcass over his shoulder and rifled through the straw of the roosts in the vain hope he might find a long-forgotten egg.

'Nothing,' he said. 'And that's all there will be, if the only thing we do is stand around scratching our balls while the crucchi starve us to death.' He gave Lucio a look and thrust the limp bird into his chest.

'Where are you going?' Lucio called, but Vittorio was already on the mule track winding down to the village. He only raised his hand without turning back. And Lucio became that small, mute boy again, watching his brother jump from Rocca Re, feeling the desperate lure of the flame, the fear of being burned.

He should have stopped him. He should have gone with him. Or at least told their mother his suspicions, Vittorio's endless talk of the partisans, the contacts he had already made with members of the gruppo on their trading trips to Cori. But instead he had gone home and told her that his brother was only away looking for the donkey. He could save her the pain, the worry for a day or two longer, if not himself. But as his mother nodded, he suspected that she already knew.

When he got in that night, she was waiting for him, standing in the dark at the window overlooking the alleyway. Viviana was stretched out in front of the grate. Even she had given up her vigil for Vittorio by the door. He bent to scratch her between the ears.

'I'm sorry,' he said.

'What for?'

'For always letting things happen … never doing anything.'

She drew her shawl about her and stepped away from the window. She looked tired and pale. 'You really think you could have changed his mind?'

'I could have tried.'

She came and squatted beside him in front of Viviana. 'Vittorio was born bigger than his boots. He's always needed more than everyone else. It was just a question of time.' He looked at the worry set in her jaw, knitting her brow. She tried to smile, nudging him with her shoulder. 'The war can't do much more, can it? We haven't got a lot left to take.'

But she was wrong. The next day, Otto came looking for them at the Vigna Alba. They knew something was wrong when the jeep and driver idled at the gate in full view of the washhouse, where the women craned and bobbed their heads like curious birds. He stood under the skeleton of the peach tree, turning his cap in his hand and waiting for them to approach from the rows of naked vines. Viviana jumped up at him in her excitement, but he barely looked at her, his attention fixed on his mother.

Lucio sensed her begin to shake her head at him, slowly, as if to hold back some terrible truth he was about to speak, and Otto looked so miserable, so guilty and hopeless that Lucio expected him to get back in the jeep and drive away. But he took his mother by the arm, moving her behind the meagre cover of the peach tree.

'I have no choice,' Lucio heard him tell her. 'I only found out this morning — the order of a few hours' notice.'

'Where?' was all his mother managed.

'Valmontone. Then back to Rome.' She twisted the sleeve of his jacket in her fist. Otto lowered his face to her hair and breathed deeply. Lucio backed away but his friend turned to him. 'Wait. I want you to have this.' He opened Lucio's hand

and thrust into it a roll of lire, bigger than any he had ever seen. 'It's all I have now, but I'll try to send more, I promise. You're going to need whatever you can get.' Otto took hold of his mother's face again and his voice became urgent. 'Listen to me. You need to use it to buy as much food as you can now. Go to Cori. Buy anything that will keep. Then hide it away, understand? Somewhere the soldiers and the villagers can't find it. I don't know how long —' She nodded to stop him, straightening herself and pulling her hands away. 'We always knew there wouldn't be enough time, didn't we?' he said. 'We knew it would come to this sooner or later ... didn't we?' He glanced from her to Lucio again, seeming to clutch at some desperate hope that he, at least, might understand. Lucio nodded, but inside all he could say was, *Not now. Not this soon.*

'You're practising the snares I taught you, yes? ... Good ... And Viviana will always find something for you. You need to trust her. You should go further up into the ranges. Give her the chance ...'

His mother ran her eyes over Otto, some calm finality settling within them, as if she had already prepared herself in a way that Lucio had not. His skin was flushed with panic, and all the words he wanted to say only hammered in his head and evaporated as breath from his mouth. He heard Otto say his name, but he turned away towards Prugni, stamped black against the paper sky. He remembered Urso raising his hand to the window in Vicolo Giotto, and he couldn't hold Otto's gaze, for fear of seeing in it that soft focus, that vision of a future without him in it. He knew they would never see each other again. They all knew it.

His mother took hold of his wrist as they listened to the sound of the jeep fading along the Viale Roma. Her nails kneaded into him and he was grateful for the pain of it, the physical insistence of her beside him. Later, as they watched the bonfire they had built catching alight, the heat of it distorting the clean air, the charred skeletons of leaves floating like birds released, his mother doubled over. He caught hold of her, thinking she was having a fit, but she pushed him away, bending over to vomit. There was little to bring up, but the noise she made was like she might turn her insides out on the hard soil. He had woken to the sound of her being sick all the week before, in the quiet of the still black mornings as he lay in bed. And he had noticed that she ate her breakfast later and later, or not at all, as if unwilling to waste the food.

She stood up and wiped her mouth, looking at him for a while, her face waxy. She didn't tell him. She knew she didn't need to. But, more importantly, Lucio saw that she hadn't told Otto. He could see it in the angle of her chin, the way she pressed her lips together and dragged the black ribbon from her hair. He saw all her reasons in that look: what point would it have served, what would it have changed? She pulled on his hand to steady herself as she got up. Her fingers were cold in his, bluish and fragile as birds' eggs. He warmed them between his own and they stood watching their breath form and disappear, form and disappear, as insubstantial as the thin smoke of the fire caught up by the wind and lost in the vast blank sky above their heads.

PART

THREE

Leyton
1950

Connie slowed her bike at the top of the rise to survey the game-keeper's cottage. Set against the glory of the summer evening, it seemed even more squat and lonely than usual. Beyond it, the windows of Leyton House shone rosy gold in the low sun.

Below her, Lucio's gate was closed, vacant. She didn't know why she always expected to see him sitting there when she rounded the corner. He would already be at St Margaret's, working through the night, even on a Saturday, she knew. Yet the gate felt somehow empty now, without him on it.

At the bend, she saw Vittorio's new Ford Anglia. He had pulled up alongside the verge, and was leaning against the front wing, a heel propped on one of its tyres. The smoke from his cigarette drifted over his head and out towards the hedgerow. She straightened the front wheel of her bike, lifted her bare feet to the frame and let herself freewheel down the hill. The air was still warm and dry, thick with insects. She dared herself not to squeeze the brakes until she'd skirted the big pothole right opposite the gate, and when she had, she juddered to a halt a few feet past the car, skidding dramatically. Vittorio threw down his cigarette and caught hold of the handlebars. She was laughing as she dismounted.

'Why do you do that?' he asked. He pushed the bike petulantly into the verge, so it couldn't be seen from the road. 'Look at you now.' She touched her hair, stiffened and tangled about her shoulders, saw her white blouse flecked with the yellow remains of gnats and midges.

'What?' She shrugged. 'If you wanted perfection, you should have picked up Agnes.'

He groaned and took her by the shoulders, and she let him kiss her, impatiently. He was tired of waiting, she could tell, and not entirely satisfied when she got there. He never was entirely satisfied, she felt. And not just with her.

'Did you even bring shoes?' he asked.

She went to her bike and fished her sandals from the basket, waving them at him from a hooked finger. He opened the car door for her.

The Anglia still smelled new, and the vinyl seat always gave an indignant complaint whenever she got into it. As far as her interest in cars went, she'd always felt more comfortable in the Austin, with its slow, shabby grandeur, like a run-down stately home. But no sooner had Vittorio restored it than he accepted an offer from a sentimental customer at the bowser. Mr Edwards had been so impressed with his sales patter, he'd given him a loan towards his next car, a Hillman that was on the blocks, waiting for a driver who would never come home from the war, and whose widow was only too keen to be rid of the constant reminder. Vittorio fixed up the Hillman and sold it on for a Morris Eight and then the Anglia, until it seemed to Connie that whenever he picked her up at the bottom of the rise, out of sight of the twitching curtains of Grimthorpe Lane, his cars had transformed themselves overnight. He did take her out of Leyton, as he had promised that day in the winter fog. And at first she was thrilled by it. But as the months passed, she'd begun to realise that the places they went were not always the places she wanted to go.

The first time he had taken her to the Roxy in Wellsborough he'd made her dance, even though she'd warned him she didn't know how. The song was *In the Cool, Cool, Cool of the Evening*. Her hand was clammy in his, her steps self-conscious in her worn sandals, and she felt anything but cool. Thankfully no one was looking at her. It was Vittorio everyone wanted to see, in his sharp new suit and shiny Logues, his olive skin rich against his white shirt, the slick of his hair impossibly black. He seemed even more exotic, more foreign than ever, and the attention of as many men as women followed him around the floor, though for a different reason, she understood. Vittorio didn't appear to mind making enemies as well as admirers.

They were regulars now at the Roxy on a Saturday night, but she couldn't say she enjoyed it any more than she had that first time.

'Next Saturday, I take you to Huntingdon,' Vittorio said. He was thrumming the Anglia's steering wheel, and she knew something was coming.

'What for?' she asked as they passed Leyton House.

'For new shoes,' he said, as though it was obvious. 'Some good shoes for dancing.'

She had tossed her sandals on the floor of the car. Like all her shoes, she'd had them since the war, and deep down she probably disliked them as much as he did. But the buckle had been hanging by a thread once, for a day or two, and when she'd fallen asleep at St Margaret's watching Lucio paint one night, she'd woken to find it sewn back on.

'I don't need new shoes,' she said.

'Yes, you do. These ugly things,' he gave a sidelong glance towards the footwell, 'they make you look like —'

'They're good enough.' She didn't give him the chance to finish. She didn't want to hear.

'Madonna, it's not the war anymore, Connie. Let me buy you some shoes.' He was laughing at her.

She didn't know why she kept going to the Roxy with him or why he persisted in taking her. He could have had his pick of the girls there, and he danced with most of them all night anyway. She was used to the powder-room talk as she tried to spruce herself up behind the cubicle door, brushing away the inadequacy she always felt as soon as she walked into the hall with him.

'My God, if I don't get a dance with him tonight I swear I'm going to die,' a voice agonised on the other side of the stall that evening.

'With who? Mario Lanza?' someone else asked. She heard the lusty, honest laughter girls made when men were not around.

'You'll die anyway, when you hear that accent,' another voice broke in. 'He can talk about changing a gasket and make it sound like pillow talk!'

Connie, unlocking the door of her cubicle, wanted to laugh then, less at the girls preening in the mirror than at herself, remembering the effect he'd had on her the first time she'd met him. But, oddly, that was all she felt when she heard such talk — a kind of mild amusement. When he danced all night with other girls, when other eyes melted like butter at his grin, other waists twisted in his hands, she should have been jealous, she knew. But all she harboured was a kind of relief that she was spared the pressure, the terrible weight of expectation that came with his favour.

If she was honest with herself, the best part of Saturday nights at the Roxy wasn't the dancing but the intervals. Everyone left the floor to crowd the bar, and the band switched from their dutiful covers of dance-hall favourites to improvise a few jazz numbers. Bobby Keyes would signal the boys and, from the side of the stage, she'd follow the way they changed instruments, unbuttoned their collars; the way they freed themselves from the staid rhythms of the wireless hits, the expectations of the dancers, becoming conscious only of the music. In their focus and fervour she caught a glimpse into another, more colourful, more passionate world. It was the way she felt when she watched Lucio paint.

Sometimes she thought it was those brief intervals, more than being with Vittorio, more than the rest of the night put together, that made it all worthwhile. All the tiptoeing home in the early hours, contorting herself through the kitchen window, only to hear Aunty Bea's pert cough from the bedroom, the purposeful rattle of her bedside clock as she rehearsed her arguments, ready to shatter the deceptive peace of the morning. It seemed she and her aunt could barely get through the week these days without some petty squall of bickering and cold-shouldering that by Sunday morning had built to an ominous front of suppressed grievances. And the more they argued, the more Connie stormed from the house, skipping church and damning herself even more in her aunt's opinion.

Strangely, the one great accusation that Connie expected never came. The rumours in the village about Vittorio stringing along all the girls at the Wellsborough Roxy would have reached Aunty Bea's ears by now. And Connie had heard Agnes's name mentioned often enough alongside Vittorio's to know her own would easily stand in its place when she was out of earshot. But why her aunt had never thrown this at her in one of their spats, she couldn't fathom. She assumed it was being saved up for some final offensive of grand proportions.

Yet even that threat could not force her back to the sitting room in Grimthorpe Lane on Saturday nights. How could she go back to the stale sofa, bookended by Aunty Bea and Uncle Jack, intent on ignoring each other? How could she settle for Arthur Askey joking on and on until she wanted to dash the radio into the grate? She couldn't. Not now — now that she'd heard Bobby Keyes's band in the interval, now that she'd seen Lucio's paintings. Now that she'd peeked through the hedgerow and seen life in colour.

When the interval ended and Bobby announced the next set, couples began flooding back onto the dance floor. Connie pushed against the flow, retreating to the emptying bar. As she brushed past the file of dancers, she felt a hand tug at hers, pulling her towards the side tables.

'Where were you? I wanted to buy you a drink,' Vittorio said. His voice was low and intimate, but his gaze darted about the hall like she was a secret he was keeping.

She lifted her glass to him. 'I still have this one.'

He gave her that dissatisfied expression again. 'Why are you always sneaking away to watch Bobby Keyes?' He drew out the name ridiculously. His eyes were glazed, dangerous in their lack of focus.

'I like the music in the interval, that's all. You know that.' She removed her hand from his.

'You don't listen to music with your eyes.'

She could tell he wanted a fight. He always became jealous when he'd been drinking, especially of Bobby or Tommy Pointon — any of the boys she used as an alibi for going out at the weekends. He resented having to meet her at the rise, not being able to pick her up from the house. Sometimes she suspected this was why he was attracted to her: the obstacles, the hurdles he needed to jump to make himself acceptable, to be accepted. Other times, she thought it was because he sensed her withdrawing from him, because she didn't fawn on him as other girls did. She only had to be a little quiet in the queue at the Orpheum on a Friday night, to nod vaguely when he repeated himself, or be the last out of the ladies in the intermission, to find him fidgeting in his seat, searching out her fingers, her knee in the dark when she sat down. It was a novelty for him, this lack of attention, and the less she gave it, the more he wanted it. At first she'd enjoyed the power of it over him, but now she wasn't so sure.

'Connie, wait,' she heard him call as she threaded between the tables. 'I need to —'

'You need to ask me to dance, that's what you need to do.' Connie glanced over her shoulder to see Agnes cutting between them with a rustle of her skirts. In her white dress and good white shoes, she almost glowed, as though she was projected on a screen. She caught Vittorio's hand and led him towards the dance floor. Her eyelids flickered up at Connie as she reached across to leave her cigarette burning in an ashtray. Vittorio looked back, but his frown didn't last for long. Soon he was making a show of spinning Agnes among the couples, swinging her faster and tighter than anyone else, making her beam as she twisted into him. Underneath it all, though, Connie couldn't help feeling it was Agnes doing the reeling, winding him in like twine.

'They reckon that Ford Anglia's his fourth car in less than a year.' It was the barman, leaning over the wet mats to Tommy Pointon, shouting over the music. 'Where's he get the money, that's what I wanna know?'

'Not bad-going for a bloody WOP.' Tommy had his elbows on the bar behind him, his gaze heavy-lidded, trailing Vittorio around the floor. 'Fossett says he's well and truly wheedled his way in with Edwards at Spalewick. The old boy hasn't got any kids, see, and he's always been a bit of a do-gooder.'

'Christ, makes you wish we'd lost the ruddy war. I might be in Germany now being adopted by a rich Kraut.'

Tommy snorted and drained his drink. 'Cars. I tell you, there's bloody money to be made now petrol's off the book, and that WOP's onto it. He told me tonight, he's off down south. Edwards has a brother with two more garages near Luton. Wants him to manage one, he reckons.'

'Well, that's fine and dandy, I s'pose ... if you want to live under an engine. Still, I expect the WOPs don't mind a bit more *grease*, do they?' The barman sensed Connie listening and winked at her. Tommy didn't laugh.

'Looks like Agnes Armer bloody well don't mind, neither,' he said, unable to drag his attention from the dance floor. 'Money's money, mucky or clean.'

Connie dipped her finger in the top of her shandy and ran it absently around the rim of the glass. Sometimes, if it wasn't for Bobby's band, she felt like the Roxy was nothing but a younger, more energetic version of Cleat's Corner Store.

It was already past midnight when she got back on her bike at Bythorn Rise. Vittorio had given lifts to Agnes and Tommy, dropping them in the high street and then driving her very slowly towards the hill, trying to draw her into an argument about Agnes, baiting and goading her into some kind of reaction. She barely answered, and when he kissed her good-night she kept her mouth closed. He tailed her up the hill, but she didn't turn back or bat her arm at his flashing headlights, as she might usually have done. He pulled alongside her as she pedalled, creeping ever closer to Grimthorpe Lane, flouting her rules. She stopped, irritated, and found he was watching her with that grin.

'Don't be angry with me, Connie,' he said.

She shook her head tiredly. 'I'm not angry. You'd like me to be, but I'm not. You're the one who's angry because I won't play your games.'

'*My* games? You hide your bike in the hedge and you ask me to pick you up in secret, and *I'm* playing the games?'

She wouldn't look at him, but she guessed his grin was gone now. 'You know very well why I have to do that.'

From the corner of her eye, she could see him nodding. 'Yes, I know why. I'm not good enough for your aunt. Maybe I'm not good enough for you. I'm still a WOP, even to you, isn't that right?'

'Don't say what you know isn't true.'

'You don't understand, Connie. I'm going to be so much more. So much more than this.' He waved his hand towards the open fields, before gripping the steering wheel again. 'Sometimes, I think I go crazy waiting for all the things I want.'

The sheer force of his will shamed her. Next to him she felt insipid and weak, indecisive, non-committal. But most of all she felt a coward. She leaned into the car window and kissed him, full on the mouth this time.

'Will you come with me tomorrow?' he asked. His grin had broken across his face again, and she felt it wash over her, luxurious but somehow depleting, like a too-hot bath. 'I want to take you somewhere. Really somewhere, this time ... far away from here.'

What could she do but nod? What could she do but force from her mind the image of the church across the dark commons, the candle in the south window burning down to the sconce, the same as it did every night, so reliable, so unchanging?

She nodded, and she made herself forget the paintings and cycle back to Grimthorpe Lane, thinking only of the road out of Leyton, its straight line heading south.

He wouldn't tell her where they were going. All he said was that it was a long way and he'd had to wait for petrol to come off the ration. She'd imagined it would be south, perhaps even to the garage Mr Edwards's brother owned in Luton. But instead they headed east, on and on, emerging from the fens into leafy lanes, which she knew must be Norfolk. With her head out the open window, she smelled brine and heard the gulls, and peered through the hedgerows for her first sight of the blue horizon. She was restless as a child as they drove along the road, forgetting to answer Vittorio's questions, holding her breath until she caught the slow, mulling body of the sea.

The picture of it wasn't what she'd imagined at all. She'd always thought of a drizzling first encounter in the mist, an umbrella flipping inside out at the whip of the wind. Instead they walked across bright flats towards the water, shimmering like mercury pressed between the sky and sand.

'So, what do you do think?' Vittorio asked, but she didn't want to talk yet. She wanted more time to breathe it all in. He tugged on her skirt, and she stepped back as he slipped an arm about her waist. When she opened her mouth, the salty air felt like it would scoop out words against her will.

'It's marvellous,' she said. 'It goes on forever.' She pulled away from him towards a flock of gulls peppered across the sand.

'Connie,' she heard him complain behind her. 'Not this. I'm talking about Luton. The job in Luton. I have to take it, yes?' He grabbed her hand to slow her down.

'Of course you should. You'd be stupid not to.' She stood with his chest against her back and gazed at the sand, so smooth and liquid that solitary figures and their dogs in the distance appeared to be walking on water. She could taste salt on her tongue, feel the crust of it in her hair. She let him kiss her neck for a while until the wind gusted again, and she ran across the sand, her feet slapping and spraying up clumps of it over her calves. She slowed when she came to the gulls, watching them rise one after the other as though on a string, their yellow legs hanging above her, their beaks screeching in time with her breath, like the sound was being ripped from her own chest.

She thought of Lucio — how she would have loved him to see it, to feel it. She wanted to sit next to him in the dunes, listening to the pulse of the waves, sensing the burrowing worms in the sand, submerging herself in this first picture of the sea. With him.

Lying on the pews of St Margaret's and watching him work, she felt soothed somehow, distracted from the frightening sense of how small her life was, how ordinary it was to be. She wasn't sure why she never went to the church with Vittorio, or why she didn't mention her visits to him, only that she wanted the world of Lucio's paintings all to herself. She had studied his progress for long enough now to see that his style had altered since the early murals, that some new element or feeling had entered it. Perhaps this came with the greater freedom Mr Swann had given him over the remaining scenes, or perhaps Lucio himself had changed as he painted them. But far from the sad, brooding picture of the hare that he had left for the harvest fair, there was now a quiet joy in his work — a love, even — sometimes in the tiniest object, the simplest gesture, that made her disproportionately hopeful, made her want to show him this view, this day.

She thought Mr Gilbert had been right after all when he had described Lucio's paintings as *transcendent*. The wooded settings, the intricate naturalism, the forms and faces of his new figures took Connie to some richer, finer place. Mortality, decay, the passage of time — she sensed them all still hovering in the background, but now they served to heighten the beauty of what he painted, the triumph of it. Not in a religious way: his pictures were more sacrilegious, if anything, in that place of worship. For when she viewed them she realised she loved life not because of God, but despite Him.

Yet Lucio had just two or three months of work left on the church. He had said so himself, avoiding her eye as he told her. She didn't want to think about what was left for either of them after that: his silence made it clear.

She heard Vittorio's breath behind her. 'Connie, wait …' He was disappointed with her, impatient again.

'You should have made him come,' she said, her voice barely audible over the cries of the gulls. 'He'd have loved this.'

'Who would?' he said, and then almost straight away, 'Lucio? Why are we talking about Lucio? *I'm* trying to talk to you.'

'I think you should make him get out more, that's all. He is your brother.' She knew they rarely saw each other these days, and it bothered her that they could so easily dispense of one another when she would have given anything for that bond of family, of belonging to someone.

'I've tried, Connie. You know that. Is it my fault he wants to waste months of his life painting pictures no one will ever look at?'

He *had* tried, in his own way, she knew. Through a customer at the garage, Vittorio had found a job for Lucio at the brick-works in Benford. It offered nearly triple the salary Repton was paying. He'd been furious when Lucio had refused it. She knew he wouldn't leave his paintings; she could see that, even if Vittorio couldn't. But what she couldn't comprehend was why Lucio wouldn't break with his father as Vittorio had done, especially as he had all the more reason to.

'I still don't get it. Why is he so tethered to the farm ... and to your father?' she asked.

Vittorio puffed out his lips and shrugged. 'Gufo is ... Gufo.' It wasn't the first time he had said it, and she wondered whether he was fobbing her off or whether he had never really made the effort to understand his brother.

'Why do you always say that? What's it supposed to mean?'

He hesitated.

'Just tell me for once,' she continued, with a force that made him frown. 'I want to know.'

'Lucio and my father, it's not easy to explain.' He looked tired. 'He's never been what my father wanted him to be,' he managed. 'Lucio's more like our mother — quiet, lonely ... a bit wild even, people said ... I don't know.' He squinted against the glare of the water. 'Lucio reminds my father of her. Maybe that's the problem.'

'Why? Why would that be a problem?' She felt intrusive but her desire to know was greater. 'What happened to her?'

He crossed his arms and dug his toes into the sand. 'She died. In the war. She was sick, you know — weak. I wasn't there, but Lucio was.' He considered this before adding quickly, 'I think my father blames him for not taking care of her. He doesn't say it. But it comes out.'

'You mean the fighting and physical stuff?'

He wouldn't look up from his feet in the sand, as if he felt ashamed. But the shame, in turn, made him angry. 'Lucio's an idiot — he's still trying to please him, even now. If he wants to stay at Repton's, that's his problem. I can't live my life for him. We came here to move on, not live in the past, like he does.'

He bent down to squat on his haunches and shake sand between his fists. When he stood again, he brushed himself off, and the conversation with it. 'I don't want to talk about Lucio and my father. I want to talk about us. About Luton.'

She understood what was coming, then. She didn't want him to spoil the glorious day with the weight of it, but she listened anyway, guilty that she had already pushed him so far. Even as she heard the words he wanted to ask her, she knew she wasn't enough for him. He needed the noise of people, their approval, the attention of more than her. She'd seen it in his face, flushed and eager on the dance floor of the Roxy. But more disturbing than that, she knew he wasn't enough for her. And yet she let him reach for her waist and pull her back. Because what was left to her without him? Aunty Bea nattering away over her teapot? The interminable tick of the clock on the mantel? The endless hours of gossip at Cleat's? Even the candle in the south window of St Margaret's would be gone soon, Lucio's paintings nothing more than a part of Leyton, closed up between four walls. Beyond them she saw her bike waiting in the muddy lane, his silhouette as he drilled seed on the ridge, his bloody hands on the gatepost, with only the fields and hedgerows of Leyton ahead of them. And the thought made her wretched.

She laid her palm along Vittorio's jaw, feeling the muscles flex under her fingers as he spoke. For a second there was something different about him, an uncertainty. She watched him negotiate it — a feeling so commonplace to her, to everyone else, but so unusual in him — and she found herself putting her arms about him. Over his shoulder, the sea shifted and glinted with such vast secrets, such promise. It was the furthest she had ever been from Leyton.

When she nodded at him, his chest swelled, and the tremor

of doubt in his eye was gone. He grinned. All these months on, and she still couldn't believe she might be the cause of that grin. And she almost felt like she was doing the right thing.

Connie didn't even try to sleep. She sat fully clothed on her bed, waiting for the dimness of the summer night to overtake her room, for the bright day by the sea to be gone. On the way back in the car, she had smelled the fresh coastal air slipping away from them, overtaken first by the peaty rot of the fens, then the mud and manure of Leyton. And she felt herself filling with doubt, with conflicting, unfinished thoughts that rattled inside her, until all she wanted was the church and its peace, the escape that Lucio's paintings gave her, their conviction.

He had finished the view in the north transept, the centrepiece of the series behind the pulpit, and when she got there the scaffolding had already been moved to one side. He had spent the longest on this painting of any so far, for it depicted St Margaret herself, before her persecution and martyrdom, tending her sheep in the countryside under the watch of a nursemaid. Mr Swann had sketched in the scene and begun painting it some months earlier, returning to dabble about on it intermittently. But to Connie it was Lucio's in every detail. She stood in the shadows by the entrance and took in the mural, free of obstruction for the first time, as Lucio swung the stage lights about so she could see the full effect of St Margaret's figure flooded with colour in the dim church.

She didn't resemble a saint at all: she didn't have that pale passivity about her. She was shapely and strong-limbed, with large eyes and a mouth so full it made Connie feel sinful just looking at her, like she was staring again at the naked forms of Renaissance sculptures in Mr Gilbert's art books. The curls about her face and shoulders were thick, like the hair of Rossetti's women, which she had seen in a Tate catalogue in the Reptons' library, except St Margaret's hair was blacker than coal. And her skin was not rosy or translucent like those Pre-Raphaelite models, but warm and brown and smooth as a hazelnut. It was the same colour Vittorio's face had been that evening on the way home after only one day in the sun. Connie cocked her head at the painting, beginning to recognise other features in the subject, similarities that became more obvious the longer she stared. The brooding lips were just like Vittorio's; but the hint of a gap in her teeth, the direct and weighty gaze, they were unmistakeably his brother's. What finally made Connie sure was the angle of the saint's wrist, held to her forehead, nudging back a lock of hair, a mannerism that had become so familiar to her now. St Margaret was Lucio Onorati cast in female form — and it was then she understood.

She climbed the scaffold beside him. He was mixing paint for the last view, which would fill the neat recess perpendicular to the north transept. They stood side by side, studying the completed centrepiece.

'She was a very beautiful woman ... your mother,' Connie ventured.

Lucio shot her a look, but he didn't contradict her and she knew that her instinct had been correct. She pointed to the saint's mouth. 'There ... that's Vittorio,' she said, touching her own lips. 'But here,' she turned to face him and took hold of his wrist, bringing it to his forehead in the pose of his subject, 'this is you.' With her other hand she traced a line in the air, under his eyes. 'And they are yours too. Did you know?' She let her fingers rest on his cheekbone, where they felt charged, as if with the current of the stage lights. For a second they were very still, except for his focus inching across her face, her mouth, her hair, like he was reading something that had been written there. When it flickered away, back to the work he'd begun on the last view, she knew she had lost him.

She felt her stomach contract and her lungs empty of air. 'So, what happened anyway? To your mother?' she asked. Her voice was falsely flippant and not her own. He stopped mixing his paints and seemed to tense beside her. She knew she'd asked the question that might give him the most pain, but she wouldn't admit to herself it was in retaliation for her own.

'She died,' was all he said, and she realised he saw straight through her.

'I'm sorry.' She meant it now. Her cheeks were burning and the threat of tears made her step away, distracting herself again with the mural.

In the left of the view, St Margaret's nursemaid was feeding a newborn lamb from a bottle. She wore a burlap apron and her sleeves were rolled up. Unlike the saint, the woman was stocky: the arm holding the milk was brawny as any man's. She might have single-handedly sheared, branded and butchered the entire flock, as easily as suckling a cade lamb. She didn't appear to be modelled on anyone from the village, but the more Connie studied her, the more she began to sense a vulnerability about the nursemaid that was at odds with her build, a sense of foreboding in her expression. She sat in the foreground on a rock, gazing at the saint instead of the lamb, her lips parted, her cheeks raw and shining. Connie traced the solitary track of light that pooled under her ear as she tilted back her head, realising as she did that it was the path of a tear. Behind her was a tumble of discarded cloth, worn and grubby, and beneath the hem of her dress, one of her feet bore another trickle, this time of blood, snaking around her ankle and collecting between her coarse toes.

Connie searched the scene, looking for other odd, jarring details. She knew there would be more: there always were. She had often seen Lucio painting them in, only to arrive the following evening to discover them gone again, or something equally cryptic in their place. She found herself both entertained and saddened by these puzzles — they gave her the childish hope that the work might never end, and yet their significance disturbed her if she dwelled on them too much. She had given up asking Lucio what they meant. His responses were evasive; often he simply shrugged. They could certainly be overlooked among all the other intricate studies of nature that formed his backdrops: the robin with crooked head and liquid eye in the crystallised hedgerow, the ivy and elder that wound their leaves about the stonework, the hoarfrosted holly that immediately conjured the muted sound of the spinney after the winter's first snowfall.

Still, those veiled tokens played on Connie, drawing her attention against her will and bothering her unaccountably. They made the paintings seem unbalanced, secretive, just as the old bricked-up window in the dining room of Leyton House often did, closed as an eye in the symmetrical facade. She examined the figure of the saint again, the sensuality of her, the intimate beauty that made Connie feel she was somehow trespassing. How on earth had he caught that expression, transferred that feeling in paint? She remembered the day she'd found Mrs Repton by the window in the library — that sense of intrusion on an unguarded thought. And then she saw it: the twist of black velvet looped around St Margaret's forefinger, the ribbon's tail half hidden in the folds of her skirt, like she had at that second pulled it from her hair and been caught in that vulnerable moment of imagining another life, another place.

Connie adjusted the stage light back in line with the others so that she could see the final portrait Lucio was working on. St Dorothea was still as Mr Swann had begun her — the ghost of a figure sketched into the alcove, tucked away to the side of the pulpit. Lucio had started on the backdrop first, with a maythorn hedge whose white blossoms settled so thickly upon the boughs that they cast an almost grey glow, like snow in the depths of winter. She thought of that first day he had shown her the nightingale in the hedgerow at Repton's, how the maythorn had shed its petals as they parted the branches.

'Why are you finishing with this one?' she asked. 'I always thought the view of St Margaret would be the last, being the most important.'

He put down his brushes, stepped back to consider his work. It was late and he seemed pale, drained, as he stretched out his neck. 'It's not important because it's small?'

'I didn't say that —'

'You see this?' He described the alcove's arch with his hand. 'This frame, how it pulls your eye?'

'*Draws* your eye.' But she nodded.

'It draws your eye,' he corrected himself, 'even when you don't want it to.'

She imagined the alcove without the scaffolding. It was true. How many times had she sat through services to find her gaze resting there in daydreams? How many times had she settled herself under the arch as a child, rolling her marbles in its recess while Aunty Bea cleaned the church? It was a sanctuary within a sanctuary. And he had understood it straight away.

'For that, it's important,' he said. 'I was thinking about it a long time.'

He picked up his palette and brushes as she climbed down from the platform. She searched along the nearest pew, looking for his jacket. It had become his habit to leave it there for her, and she saw him glance down from the staging as she laid it over her shoulders. She breathed in his smell: the mineral fumes of paint, the tang of his collar where it rubbed his neck, the scent of the spinney in autumn that always seemed embedded in the cloth, regardless of the season. She watched the end of his brush twitch, the fractional incline of his head, his boots shifting on the platform. The buzzing stage lights became the hedgerow's hum, twigs cracking underfoot, and in her dreams she heard the nightingale creaking out its alarm.

When she opened her eyes, she felt hours had passed. The light was different. She thought it might be morning and panicked, until she saw one of the spots casting its beam towards the roof, causing a gentle glow to fall about the pews. Lucio was sitting on the platform, his legs hanging over its edge, his head and arms propped on one of the bars, looking at her.

She sat up quickly. 'God, how long have I been out? What time is it?'

'Four o'clock.'

She stretched. 'I was dreaming of the spinney ... of birds singing.' She stood and put a hand on her head. Her hair was still stiff from the salt air. 'I've got to get back.'

'It suits you.'

She laughed, thinking he was teasing, but he seemed serious.

'The sun,' he said. 'The sun in your face.' She felt the tight skin of her nose, a bit burned from the day at the coast, and looked away, as if he'd caught her out.

'We ... we went to the seaside,' she said, like a confession. 'You should have come. I wanted you to. You'd have loved it.' She put a hand in her skirt pocket and felt the gritty sand at the bottom, the hard curve of the shell she'd found winking on the shore. Her fingers were comforted by its solid smoothness, something to hold on to.

'You can't hide away in here forever,' she said. He got up and concentrated again on the unfinished view. She stepped onto a rung of the scaffold, wanting to hold his attention. 'You know, everyone says you're so different, you and Vittorio, but … sometimes I think you're as obsessive as he is, just as stubborn, only about different things.' She climbed up next to him, by the dense flowers of the maythorn boughs. She felt chilled. 'What are you going to do when it's finished?'

He pushed back his hair with his wrist. 'What are you going to do?'

She dug her hand deeper into her pocket until she felt a tiny crack of thread, of stitches breaking. She hadn't expected this reply. It was as though he had realised she was asking the question not of him but of herself, and she became angry that he knew her so well but allowed her to understand so little of him.

'Your brother wants me to marry him,' she said. She heard the arrogance in her voice and regretted it. He nodded, as if he'd been waiting for her to say it, and she felt her stomach sink again.

'What do you want?' he asked.

It was she who didn't answer this time. She felt her throat constrict, her eyes stinging, and she swallowed and blinked it all back, not allowing herself to wonder whether it was from anger or despair.

They didn't speak for a while. She thought that if she opened her mouth, things might come tumbling out, things that she could not take back. She glanced towards the south door and knew that beyond it were the fields, the squat houses and their grey hearths, the burnished letters of Mrs Cleat's window, all brooding in the dark, like hens biding their time until the first light, when they would rattle out their dull declaration of Monday morning.

He broke the silence. 'It's alright,' he said softly. 'I understand.' His expression had no accusation in it, as if he had simply watched the images that passed through her mind; had seen how she was trapped, and why she could force herself to do something against her own nature. She thought perhaps he really did understand, but she didn't want him to: she wanted him to rail against it, to confront her, tell her she was making a mistake. But he only picked up his brushes and continued his work.

'Lucio?' she said, but her voice was lost under the vaulting, his name a shush once more, and she climbed down the scaffold.

Before she left, she folded up his jacket and put it back on the pew, slipping the shell under its collar. Outside, the lychgate was a triangular silhouette against the nacre of the pre-dawn sky. She dug her fingers into her pocket and through the hole that was left there.

When she got home from St Margaret's the birds were stirring in the gardens of Grimthorpe Lane. She slipped off her sandals and climbed through the kitchen window, as she always did. There was an art to manoeuvring around the sink, lowering herself onto the lino, reaching for her shoes from the sill, all without making a sound.

'Very lady-like, I'm sure,' came a low voice. Connie started. Aunty Bea was sitting in the dim kitchen, her hands spread on the table, catching the light that had begun to slant through the panes. Connie thought of Reverend Stanton palming the lectern before a sermon.

'So, barefoot and through the window, is it now?' Aunty Bea's voice was flat, detached. 'You're lucky I didn't think you was a didicoy and take the coal shovel to you.' She sniffed and pulled a handkerchief from the cuff of her bedjacket. Her hair was tucked in its night-time pins, and the lines of disappointment about her mouth seemed chiselled in the kitchen's shadows.

'You're up early,' Connie said. She meant to provoke her, to get the inevitable row over with, but the sarcasm in her voice faltered.

'Seems like none of us has been to bed tonight.'

Connie went to the switch and flicked on the light. Its beam was invasive, but less disconcerting than seeing her aunt sitting there in the dark.

'We need to talk,' Aunty Bea said.

'Talk?' Connie gave a cool laugh. 'That's novel, I can't remember the last time we actually *talked*.'

'And that would be my fault, I suppose? Being as I'm the one who's always at the Roxy or the flicks or God-knows-where, coming home through the window at four in the morning?' Her aunt slipped into the usual recriminations, but the words seemed listless in her mouth, lacking their typical vigour.

'Oh, here we go,' Connie said anyway. She crossed her arms and waited, but Aunty Bea was silent, unmoving. 'I couldn't sleep. I went for a walk, that's all.' She took her aunt's sullenness to be a sign of the great storm about to break. 'If the *talk* is over, I'd like to get ready for work.'

'No, it is not over,' Aunty Bea said. She got up and moved to the sink, her breath laboured. Her eyes glittered at Connie as she turned, but their focus seemed strangely elsewhere. 'I won't be doing at the Big House tomorrow. I want you to drop in to the kitchen and tell Mrs Cartwright on your way to Cleat's.'

'What? Why can't you work?' But her aunt's expression, the tone of her request, seemed too weary to have any other agenda. 'What's wrong with you?' She was genuinely concerned now.

'One thing, I'm asking,' Aunty Bea said, with some of her old spark. 'Just this one thing, after all I've done for you. Can you manage it, or not?'

Connie nodded, half expecting a renewal of hostilities, but her aunt only reached for a dishcloth and ran it about the sink. She watched her hang the cloth over the faucet, pull the latch on the window, check the knobs on the stove — all the small, obsessive habits of her domesticity. And she frowned as her aunt slipped through the door and shuffled up the stairs, as though Connie had not been there at all.

She sat down at the kitchen table, the house about her feeling somehow skewed, diminished, like it was Aunty Bea's anger, her strictures, that kept firm its joists. Without it there was suddenly less for Connie to throw herself against, no bars she could rattle to justify her frustrations. How could her aunt be sick? Aunty Bea didn't believe in illness any more than crying; she always said she never had time for such indulgences. But there had been those visits by Doctor Bland of late. Connie had seen him getting into his car as she cycled up the lane after work. Her aunt had flapped her hand when she'd asked about it, mumbling about *women's affairs,* as if Connie herself did not belong to that sex.

She heard the dry bark of Uncle Jack's morning cough and switched off the kitchen light. When she went into the narrow hall, she realised the sound was coming from the front room. She creaked the door ajar and put her head around it. Aunty Bea had meant it when she said no one had had any sleep that night: she guessed her aunt would have tossed and turned sufficiently to keep Uncle Jack up too.

He was sitting in his chair, his head propped against the wing. There was no light on, and she was surprised to find one or two embers glowing in the grate despite the summer night. A book had slipped from his lap, and she went in and kneeled before him on the hearthrug, reaching for it. He was awake: she smiled at him and set the book on the side table. He straightened his head, coughing again.

'You need to get off the Woodys,' she said.

He cricked the corner of his mouth at her. 'Too much fresh air and me lungs'd pack up from shock.'

She had the sudden desire to curl herself onto his lap and lean into his chest like she had as a child. He used to read to her then, Jules Verne and Robert Louis Stevenson, while she brushed ash off the pages to see the pictures. Instead she settled on the floor, her head against the arm of the chair, and felt his hand on her hair. A bedroom door closed above them.

'You shouldn't mind her so much, Lizzie,' he said.

She lifted her chin and looked up at him. 'I don't. But she minds me, doesn't she? I wonder sometimes whether she even likes me very much.'

His breath whistled and his hand became heavy on her head. 'You're wrong there. I think she likes you a lot more than she likes herself. She sees in you what she might've wanted to be.' His voice was so quiet that he could have been talking to himself.

'What? She'd like to have been a shop assistant?' Connie couldn't help it, despite the rare confidence Uncle Jack was granting.

'Maybe.'

She thought about it. As someone who'd spent her whole life doing other people's cleaning, Aunty Bea might see a certain glamour in working behind the counter at Cleat's. Still, it wasn't what Connie wanted to hear, and she leaned away from him to put the grate across the fire.

'I think it's more she looks at you and she sees someone open to things ...' He paused and ran his hand across his mouth. 'Someone willing to take a risk, like. Passionate, even.'

It was a lot of words for Uncle Jack, surprising words that she wasn't used to hearing from him. They made her uncomfortable, and she fobbed them off by joking. 'Steady on now, Mr Farrington! What kind of a girl do you take me for?' She cocked her head, expecting to see his smile, but there was only an edge of disappointment at his mouth.

'Can you not see it in yourself, Connie?' he said gently.

She shrugged, taken aback at the sound of her name, the seriousness of it coming from him.

'Them Eye-talians you're so keen spending time on, you suppose they only see the Hayworth hair and them skinny white spokes of legs?'

She'd wondered at this herself — what it was they did see in her, especially Vittorio, who could have had any girl he wanted. She could believe Lucio knew her: he always seemed to peel away the skin of everything with those eyes. But it didn't count for much: the night had proved that to her.

'I don't know what they see,' she said sharply, uneasy with the conversation.

'I do,' he persisted.

'Well, you're biased.' And she tried to laugh him off again.

He reached for the book she'd set on the table and took out a card he'd been using as a bookmark. When he handed it to her, she saw it was a photograph. She held the image up to the glow of the coals in the grate. She could make out a pier at the seaside. A youthful Uncle Jack, barely her age, was leaning against the railing, his hair thick under the cap he'd pushed back on his head. He was looking at a girl sitting on a wrought-iron bench before him. One of her hands was blurred at her neck and her face was animated with laughter, her hair loose and windswept about her shoulders. Had it not been for Uncle Jack behind this figure, she might not have recognised Aunty Bea. In the foreground another man seemed to have just completed a cartwheel: his legs and arms were out of focus, but the fringe of his hair fanned across his face.

'That's Bill,' Uncle Jack said. 'Always clowning about at some such acrobatics.'

She peered at their faces, tipping the card closer to the firelight. 'You're all so young and ... happy.'

Uncle Jack's breath whistled through his nose again. 'They were, I suppose. I were always tagging along, me. Chaperoning. That's what we did in them days.'

'Do you mean Aunty Bea was with —'

'Oh yeah, she were Bill's girl alright.' He tapped one heel on the toe of the other foot, as if to shift some grit from his slipper.

'What happened?' she asked.

Uncle Jack gave a low grumble, like he was dragging the memory from the depths of him, reluctantly. 'He always had his heart set on going overseas, Bill, even when he were young. America. Didn't have the class system holding a man back, he reckoned.' He drew his mouth into a pout. 'Maybe so. Anyway, he up and did it. Well before the war, this was. Your aunt was supposed to join him once he were settled. But she never seemed to get round to it, even though he kept writing and asking. And somehow, in her mind, the fact that she didn't go turned into him leaving her, hankering after something more, as if he'd got beyond himself. That's the version she likes to tell, anyway.'

'Did she love him?'

Uncle Jack lifted his chin in a faint acknowledgement.

'So you think she was too scared to leave? You know, to take a chance on a better life?'

He paused, considering. 'I think at first she hoped he'd come back with his tail between his legs. But after a while she gave up waiting … that's where I came in.' He shrugged but wouldn't hold her gaze. 'Like I said, he ended up with the Yanks in Italy during the war and that's where he stayed. Maybe she thought she'd made the right decision, then. I don't know …' He tilted his head back against the chair again, his eyes closed. 'Feeling justified only patches up a broken heart,' he said. 'It don't mend it.'

She considered the photo again: Jack looking at Bea looking at Bill.

'You know, I never could decide whether she married me to spite him or to spite herself,' he said, and he reached out his hand to take the photo back from her. She watched him slip it away inside his book. 'She were a stubborn little thing, our Bea. Still is, I reckon.'

Connie made a soft huff of agreement as she mulled over it all.

'Bea likes a fight, sure enough,' Uncle Jack said, 'and most of all with herself.' She glanced up at him when he said it, his expression knowing in the firelight. 'Not so unlike someone else I know.'

Her cheeks were burning as she got up, but the embers in the fire were nearly dead, and the air in the room smelled ashen and old, like the great atlas in the library of the Big House, something that was becoming nothing more than a memory of childhood.

Montelupini
1943

Under the pergola of the osteria, Fagiolo was roasting chestnuts in an oil drum. Their woody sweetness wafted through the night every time the innkeeper tossed them with his paddle, and Lucio, pacing the battlements above, felt his empty stomach creak louder than his boots on the freezing stones. Above the range, the sky was clean and brittle, the stars glinting sharp as grit. The procession to Montemezzo would be slow that night, the track icy and treacherous the higher they got. He jammed his hands under his armpits and breathed warm air into the upturned collar of his jacket.

Padre Ruggiero had named him a litter-bearer for Santa Lucia's effigy. He felt the responsibility of it, the silent resentment and reproaches of the village weighing heavy in his bones, like he was coming down with the flu. It made him miss his brother more than ever. Vittorio would have done it: borne the saint's litter as well as the talk of the village, dispatching both with the easy swagger of his walk, a single hook of his eyebrow. It was Primo they wanted to see, Primo who could silence them, not him. He blew on his numb fingers and remembered a joke Nonno Raimondi loved to tell on the saint's day. His grandfather would stand in the doorway of the osteria as the weary procession fogged through the piazzetta in the early hours of the morning, bringing the effigy back from the mountain to the church in the village. 'Just imagine,' he would slur to the litter-bearers, 'if you'd chosen a saint with a name day in July, you'd have peaches for balls instead of little frozen raisins.' Nonno Raimondi always said the midnight trek in the depths of winter was the greatest testament to Montelupini's stupidity. And yet his grandfather went along with everyone else to gaze at the saint as she was raised to her dais in San Pietro's.

The villagers were filling the piazzetta now, gathering with their lanterns and candles for the start of the march. But they kept close to the walls and huddled about each other, and Lucio knew it wasn't only from the cold. The Germans had lifted the curfew for the saint's feast, but the Montelupinese were awkward, already suspicious of a freedom they had so recently taken for granted. Maybe Vittorio was right: they were a village used to being told what to do. Perhaps it was in their nature, he thought. Perhaps it was in his.

He had done what Otto had told him to, without question. He had taken the money and scoured Cori to buy whatever supplies he could, while his mother tried the villagers for news of Vittorio. But neither food nor news was easy to come by these days, even if you had money. In a side alley off the town's piazza they had found an old woman who sold them a dry finger of pecorino. 'Madosca!' his mother said as Lucio handed over a thousand lire. 'What is it, gold?'

'No, signora.' The woman's hands were as desiccated as the cheese itself, and her laugh rasped like a death rattle. 'Have you tried eating gold?'

Lucio had taken the cheese and put it in his pocket carefully. The woman sucked on her toothless gums and shook her head. 'Wouldn't keep it there, if I were you.'

'Why not?' his mother asked.

'Eat it now. Better in your stomachs than the gruppo's.' And she cracked phlegm into the back of her throat and spat it into the gutter. They ate the cheese while she grumbled to them about the thugs who hid in the woods and looted the villages and vineyards all around them. They wore the red scarf, she said, but their highest ideal was nothing more than filling their bellies until the war was over. Lucio and his mother listened in silence, asking no more questions. When they left, they didn't speak to each other about what she had told them. Neither of them wanted to consider that a little power, a gun and the semblance of a cause might be enough for Vittorio.

When they got home from Cori, it seemed like half the village was waiting for them in Vicolo Giotto — the scabby Carozzi twins asking to play with Viviana even though the curfew had sounded; Maria Ventuzzi, with her crusted eyes, who hovered silently below their window as her mother had told her to; and the ancient Ardemira Ippoliti, sweeping their steps. That was how the villagers manoeuvred around their pride: sending hungry children or old women to perform unnecessary favours in return for a mouthful from their table. Neither he nor his mother had the heart to send them away. He watched her bending to them at the door, her bones moving under her dress like the alley cat's did under its loose skin, and he had wondered that the baby could still cling inside her.

In Cori they had spent every penny Otto had given them, but it bought them nothing more than a sack of army flour, some maize, a few rotten potatoes. They shared the food around and eked it out as best they could, but it didn't stop his stomach from grinding its complaint to the night every time Fagiolo tossed his chestnuts. He listened to them crackle softly in the drum, the murmur of voices below.

'But what's so wrong with that? Why shouldn't the boy carry the litter?' he heard Fagiolo ask, his voice rising indignantly above the others. Through the pergola, he could see Professore Centini warming himself at the brazier. 'Why shouldn't Gufo stand in his brother's place? Would you rather have Berto the goatherd tripping over the cobbles?' Fagiolo wasn't speaking to the mayor but to the two women beside him, solemn as bats in their black coats and black crocheted shawls.

'I'm sure the blessed saint doesn't mind being carried by a mute, but it's his family I have the problem with. Do they really deserve the honour?' It was Signora Mazzocchi. Lucio recognised her voice — quick, pinched and begrudging as always. Fagiolo and Professore Centini gave her warning looks. She simply shrugged and made a half-hearted attempt to whisper, glancing at the soldiers of the Wehrmacht who stood smoking at the edges of the piazzetta. 'I mean, a family of Fascist loyalists and German collaborators.' She sniffed pointedly at the mayor, who made a non-committal mumble. Lucio thought he had an air of uncertainty about him, only natural for someone whose own Fascist Party uniform was still wrapped in mothballs in his closet. And yet they all knew how loosely about the waist that blue cummerbund would sit these days. The war had made everyone change their opinions, but only some people allowed themselves to remember just how much. The mayor stood on one leg, bending the knee of the other several times and wincing, as if he hoped to divert the conversation to the much safer topic of his sciatica.

Signora Mazzocchi would not be dissuaded. 'Yes, German collaborators, that's what I said. *I* dare accuse Letia Onorati of it if no one else will.' Fagiolo raised a stern face to her, and she bent a little further over the drum of chestnuts. 'How else, tell me, has she been able to come by those supplies? How is it she always seems to have flour, or potatoes for gnocchi? Everyone in Vicolo Giotto goes begging to her, you know. They say she does ... well ...'

'She does what exactly?' Fagiolo snapped. Professore Centini wiggled his leg again and sucked air through his teeth noisily. Beside him, Signora Centini sighed and elbowed her husband in the arm.

'Come on, signora,' the innkeeper insisted, 'why don't you tell us what you think she does?'

'What who does?' It was Polvere. Lucio had seen the baker sidle up to the drum, taking the paddle from Fagiolo and giving the chestnuts a poke.

Signora Mazzocchi considered the two men, her cheeks red and shining in the light of the embers. 'Letia Onorati. She performs favours for the Germans, *intimate* favours. It's obvious. Don't you see? That's why Primo ran away to the Cori gruppo. He couldn't bear seeing what his own mother had become.' She unburdened herself with such effervescent relief that Lucio was reminded of the juice bursting from a rotten tomato. Acid bubbled in his stomach, a gripe of hunger and nerves, stirred by disgust.

Fagiolo snatched back his spatula from Polvere and shoved it so roughly into the drum that one or two chestnuts bounced over the rim and rolled about Signora Mazzocchi's feet. She caught her breath and glared at him, before her expression softened into something more complacent, knowing.

'Ah, that's right, Fagiolo,' she said. 'I forgot. You always did have a more *noble* appreciation for her, didn't you? Always carrying her books after school, making up songs for her on your guitar. You must be very disappointed.'

Fagiolo changed the paddle to his other hand, gripping it as he might a weapon in his fist. 'If Letia does anyone favours it's your relatives, signora.'

'And what is that supposed to mean?' she asked.

'Isn't Ardemira Ippoliti your aunt? And those grubby twins who are always being sent home at night by the Germans, aren't they your nieces? Didn't you know they go to Letia for food? I guess that makes your family German colluders too, Signora Mazzocchi. Doesn't it?'

'Well now, what time is it?' Professore Centini interrupted, smiling inanely in the direction of the soldiers.

Everyone ignored him, particularly his wife, who hurried to add her own views to the discussion. '*I've* heard from reliable sources out of town' — by which everyone knew she meant Pettegola — 'that things are not quite so black and white.'

'That's the very nature of war, my dear. Nothing ever is black and white,' her husband announced, as if this platitude might round off the topic.

But she shook him off. 'What I've been told is that Letia Onorati started colluding with the Germans so she could provide information to the Cori gruppo. And that's why Primo joined them. It makes sense, doesn't it? She's like a *double agent*.' She articulated the words with relish, and Lucio almost wanted to laugh at how his mother could push their imaginations to such heights.

'That's even worse!' Signora Mazzocchi barked. 'The gruppi deserve to be hanged. They're nothing more than thugs — gangs of Communists and deserters hiding in the hills and taking our supplies in the name of liberation. I can't see any actual resistance around here, can you? Between the gruppi and the requisitions of the crucchi,' she glanced over at the soldiers again, lowering her voice, 'we'll all be dead from starvation before the Allies ever get here. We can't live on chestnuts alone.' And, with disdain, she kicked one of the fallen nuts.

'Do you seriously think, signora,' Fagiolo hissed at her, 'that the Allies have a chance in these mountains without the help of the gruppi?' The mayor placed a hand on his arm and cleared his throat, as though to remind him that Signora Mazzocchi wasn't worth the risk.

'All I know is that those bandits have landed us where we are now,' she replied. 'It's their attempts at sabotage that have brought about the German curfews, random searches and threats. If it wasn't for them, the mountain passes would be safe to walk again and our blessed saint wouldn't have to be carried down Montemezzo at the gunpoint of a Nazi guard.'

'Well, you know, signora,' Fagiolo said, struggling to keep the emotion from his voice, 'you certainly can blame that on Letia Onorati. Without Letia, we wouldn't be having a procession at all.'

'Don't be ridiculous. We've had this procession come snow or storm for longer than anyone can remember. I hardly think tonight is all *her* doing. Padre Ruggiero came to an arrangement with the captain.'

Fagiolo stepped back, feigning surprise at her lack of knowledge. 'Oh, but it is her work, signora. You see, the captain insisted on maintaining the curfew, tradition or no tradition … that is, until Letia Onorati offered him two bottles of Raimondi Gold. Apparently they were the last ones left in the entire village.'

There was truth in what Fagiolo said, but Lucio thought of the mayor's platitude: it hadn't quite been so black and white. Padre Ruggiero had come to their kitchen late at night, uncomfortable with the condescension, the red tassel trembling awkwardly on his biretta. 'The captain has a taste for the grappa, you see,' the priest had told Lucio's mother. 'It really is all I have left to bargain with for the procession.'

'You mean it's all *I* have left to bargain with,' she replied.

'And must Santa Lucia always come before our bellies, Padre?' Her voice was flat. Lucio knew she didn't expect an answer.

But the priest had approached her, cupping a naked hand towards the curve of her stomach under her apron. 'You, of all people, ask me that?'

She turned away from him and sent Lucio to the cellar. In the dimness he had paused, breathing angry lungfuls of the musty air, his mind racing. He looked guiltily at his grandfather's empty chestnut barrels, and as he picked out the last bottles of Gold from the shelf, he'd felt the urge to smash them — one, two on the flagstones — to feel the glass shatter about his feet, the liquor splashing his ankles, the satisfying sting of alcohol in the cuts and nicks, a salve to his frustrations. And he imagined he'd heard Nonno Raimondi's laugh again, rough as splintered glass and just as sharp.

But he had returned to the kitchen with the necks of the bottles in his fists. He handed them not to Padre Ruggiero but to his mother, catching the doubt that scudded across her face: losing the grappa was more than losing a trade for food to last them through the spring; it was their only medicine, the one pain relief she might have for her delivery. She blinked at him slowly and he understood what she was doing: she wasn't giving in to Padre Ruggiero; she was giving in to the whole village. She intended to give them their procession, to allow them their prayers and ceremonies, the empty traditions that rang with the dim echo of who they once had been. It was her penance, of sorts. But Lucio also understood the villagers of Montelupini. He had been watching them for long enough now. The more she paid for her sins, the more they would damn her for them.

She had taken the bottles and set them down on the table, forcing Padre Ruggiero to help himself. It was then that the priest announced jovially, 'I want you at the head of the saint's litter, Gufo. It's what your father would want.' Lucio caught the uncertainty in his tone, a doubt that had not been there when he had made the same request of Vittorio. He nodded to Padre Ruggiero, but his focus was on the outline of his mother standing at the window. It was for her, he reminded himself; he was doing it for her — not the priest, not the village, not his father or brother. It was the least he could do. It was what she wanted.

Under the pergola, Fagiolo had returned to tossing his chestnuts. 'Are you saying she gave up the last bottles of Raimondi Gold just so we could have our procession?' Signora Mazzocchi asked. She glanced at the mayor to confirm Fagiolo's story, and at his nod she fingered her shawl as if grasping for purchase. 'Then the woman truly is a simpleton,' she said with satisfaction, 'giving the last of our precious tonic to a Nazi!' She pinned the shawl under her chin and swept through the piazzetta, ominous as a storm cloud dulling the crystal night.

Professore Centini winced. 'I'm afraid Letia Onorati will never be able to do anything right for some people in this village,' he offered pointlessly.

Fagiolo let out an angry grunt and Lucio saw him limp away towards the door of his osteria. Once alone, he hesitated, his hand on the doorknob, throwing his head back upon his shoulders. He seemed furious, but as much with himself as with anyone else. He cursed softly into the night with the fervour of a prayer: 'Damn them ... and fuck them all!' There was always a price to be paid for loving his mother, Lucio understood. He had seen it in his father, and he suspected he saw it now in Fagiolo.

It was a slow and arduous journey back to San Pietro's, shoulder-ing the saint's litter through the raw night. Lucio had wanted to feel uplifted, to gather some sense of meaning in the task of carrying his namesake, of being so close to the beauty of the statue he admired so much. But Professore Centini ambled stiffly behind him, blowing like a mule, and the other two bearers were skinny boys whose shoulders barely reached the handles and made the dais wobble between them. Lucio was forced to bear the brunt of its weight, steadying it down the uneven path. He thought of the boar he had carried along the same track with his father when he was not much taller than those boys. Before the procession began, the mayor had sized him up, marvelling that he was surely Aldo's height now, perhaps even taller. But Lucio doubted whether anything could ever be balanced between himself and his father. Especially now.

He craned to look behind him at the saint's face. She had become pale in the glow of so many lanterns and candles all about, blanched of the skin tones he always liked to study. The gold leaf painted into the red of her robes caught the naked flames in the night, and now seemed ghoulish and grotesque. He shivered and began to search for his mother among the marchers.

As the procession neared Rocca Re, he caught sight of her. She stood some way back from the lines of women chanting Lucia's prayer and thumbing their rosaries alongside the litter. She focused on him as he passed, and her mouth formed the shape of a word, sending it up into the night in a burst of white breath. Was it a prayer, the name of the saint? Or was it his name she offered up as he passed? He couldn't tell. He only knew, as he shouldered the weight of the dais, that all he cared about now was her. Her and the baby inside her.

She didn't come to Mass at San Pietro's. He searched for his mother along the crowded pews, but she hadn't followed. When the service was over, he went home to find her, but she wasn't there either. He climbed to the battlements, waiting to spot her walking up Via del Soccorso or coming from Fabrizia's house, but the silhouettes of the last villagers saying goodnight in the piazzetta were not hers. At the church, he saw the shapes of Padre Ruggiero and Captain Schlosser talking on the front steps; down its side alley, Fagiolo was pulling up the collar of his jacket against the freezing draught; and further on he caught the shape of Fabrizia scuttling past the fountain, her footprints small and neat in the thin snow that had begun to settle.

And then he thought he saw her, his mother, passing the vestiary door at the rear of the church, the glimpse of her shadow against the cobbles, the briefest hesitation as she glanced back in the direction of the fountain. But she dissolved into the darkness as quickly as she had appeared, leaving him wondering whether he really had seen her at all.

The news of the theft of Santa Lucia's crown whistled through the village like the winter winds that blasted up Via del Soccorso. It swept all manner of debris with it — ancient superstitions, old vendettas, wild speculation — and collected, as all news did, in fierce eddies of exchange at the osteria, where it was honed into its most potent form.

When Lucio passed the tavern late the next afternoon, Fagiolo called to him. He was clearing snow from the cobbles, and through the open door behind him, Lucio could see clusters of heads drawn together at the bar and about the tables, not all of them belonging to men. He had only ever seen women at the osteria on a handful of occasions: the day King Vittorio Emanuele III became the Emperor of Abyssinia, Italy's victory in the World Cup, the declaration of war. He knew then just how grave matters were.

'Did you see anything, Gufo? At the church last night?' Fagiolo asked.

Lucio shook his head.

'And Padre Ruggiero still hasn't found anything else missing? Only the crown?'

'Nothing else,' he answered.

Fagiolo eyed him painfully, as if regretting what he was about to say. He leaned his spade against the wall and took Lucio by the arm, pulling him away from the osteria door. 'I think you should go home and warn your mother.' His voice had lost its gruffness and seemed to waver. 'You know they're blaming her, don't you?'

Lucio shrugged. He knew, but he wouldn't nod, as though the action would somehow acknowledge his mother's guilt.

Fagiolo shook his head, tiredly. 'I'm sorry, Guf. I tried to tell them it's most likely to have been the crucchi. They've taken everything else from us, after all.'

Lucio thought back on the previous night. He desperately wanted to believe it wasn't his mother. Captain Schlosser had been busy talking to the priest on the church steps, hadn't he? He might have ordered any one of his men to slip into the church and take the crown. And he had seen Fabrizia hurrying across the piazza; even Fagiolo himself had left the church at around the same time. Either one could have been the thief too: everyone was desperate enough for food, for something to trade. And yet his mother was the first suspect. She always was.

'You know the Montelupinese as well as I do,' Fagiolo continued. 'They can't punish the Germans, can they? And they want a scapegoat, someone they can whip for all their other frustrations.'

'Whip?' Lucio repeated. The word seemed so extreme, so physical.

'Look, Gufo, La Mula's not going to let this drop. I've heard her carrying on.' Fagiolo raised his chin towards the bar. 'She's been telling the Fascist loyalists that Letia stole the crown for Vittorio's gruppo; and she's stirring up the partisan supporters to think your mother took it for the Germans. Even those who don't care about politics believe the stupid woman when she tells them Letia's brought down the evil eye on the village by offending the saint herself. She's got an argument to cover all bases.'

Lucio imagined the unrelenting signora listing her points for the prosecution, thrusting her chin towards the men at the bar with each accusation, like a hen pecking its way further and further up the dung heap with the cocks. *Who could bring themselves to steal from the saint on her very own name day? Barilotto's daughter, that's who! There was never any love lost between the Raimondi and the Church. She wasn't even in Mass last night. Why do you think she bribed the captain to let us have the procession in the first place? So the saint would be unlocked from the grotto, of course. Even Fagiolo said as much. Why wouldn't she sacrifice two measly bottles of her father's Gold if she could get her hands on that crown?* Her mulish voice became his own inside his head, his doubts heaping one on top of the other as he remembered his mother's shadow at the vestiary door. Had he been mistaken all along about her reasons for giving the villagers their festival?

'Do you think she did it?' he asked Fagiolo.

As if from nowhere, he felt the cuff of a hand burning across his ear. 'Don't ever let me hear you say that again,'

Fagiolo whispered. 'I know she didn't. And so do you.'

Lucio pulled away, but the innkeeper stepped towards him, regretful now. 'Gufo, don't you see? It doesn't matter who took it. Any one of us is hungry enough to do a lot worse. And the gold sitting on that statue's head is about as useful for filling our stomachs as the communion wafer. It was just a matter of time before it disappeared. And your mother was always going to be the culprit.'

Lucio pushed back his hair with his wrist and eyed the innkeeper. He knew Fagiolo was right. It didn't matter now. His cheeks seared from the slap and his own shame. 'What should I do?' he asked.

'Get her away.'

At that moment, the door of the osteria clattered and Professore Centini stood on the threshold, bending and straightening his knee, his face pained, grey as old snow. He winced at them and Lucio knew it wasn't from his sciatica. He thought again of the mayor's platitude before the procession. It was true: nothing was black and white anymore.

When he got home, Lucio found his mother making gnocchi. Fabrizia was at the table, her face flushed and focused, her mouth set hard, like she had been kneading the dough herself. His mother didn't greet him as he entered, still preoccupied with the conversation he had evidently interrupted.

'So, which am I, a Nazi colluder or a freedom fighter? Can't they decide?' His mother gave an empty laugh and rubbed her nose irritably in the crook of her arm. Fabrizia's gaze hovered on Lucio, who had begun re-tying the bag of flour propped against the cellar door. 'My God, Fabri, don't tell me you actually believe them?'

The butcher's wife looked away. 'What do you expect me to believe?' she lashed out. 'You start feeding half of Vicolo Giotto, you stop coming to Mass, you act as guilty as a fox among the chickens —'

'Does it really matter where the food comes from, as long as we can eat?'

'*I* don't care where it comes from, but they do. And soon they're going to see behind that apron. We're all starving, Leti, but you're the only one whose stomach's not getting any smaller!'

His mother stopped kneading and they fell silent. She put the heel of her hand to her temple, her fingers lacing her hair with flour so it seemed she had gone grey in the matter of a moment. Lucio came to stand behind her. Fabrizia reached across the table for her hand, as if to show them whose side she was on.

'They need someone to blame, Leti. You've always been good for that, but especially now ... now they suspect ...'

'They suspect what?'

Fabrizia adjusted her stance. He had never seen her struggle for words. 'Well, if they suspect you're already ... *lost*.'

'Lost?' His mother pushed herself from the table and began to pace about the confines of the kitchen in sudden bursts, like a bird trapped. '*Lost*.' She repeated the word to the window, where a shaft of pale sun hit the glass. 'I was lost to them years ago, wasn't I? Before I was even old enough to do anything wrong?'

Fabrizia didn't say anything more, but the tears that she wiped away made his mother stop. She went around the table and put her arms about her friend's shoulders. 'Come on, Fabri. I'll weather it. Don't I always?'

The butcher's wife shook her head. 'Not this time. This time it's different. I heard La Mula threatening this morning that she was going to the captain. I think she's going to name you as one of the Cori gruppo's links.'

His mother's arms dropped to her sides. 'What? Why would she do such a thing?'

'Because of Primo.' Fabrizia pulled down the corners of her mouth as if she had tasted something sour. 'And because the gruppo raided her brother's barn near Carpeto. She's still fuming because half the stores they found hidden there were hers. She was storming all round the village saying the gruppi are no better than bandits and it's time someone stood up to them.'

'So? How will she prove the connection? She's got no proof Vittorio's even with the gruppo.'

Fabrizia touched her fingers to the flour dusted across the table. His mother put her hand on the dough as if she might continue to knead, but went to a chair and sat down instead, losing the will. They all understood. 'And what if I tell the captain my supplies didn't come from the Cori gruppo but from one of his own soldiers? From money he gave me?'

'That might be even worse,' Fabrizia said. 'Don't you see, Leti? If the Allies push through, that could be an even surer noose about your neck. Fagiolo thinks —'

'You spoke to Fagiolo about this?'

'I didn't need to. He came to me. He's not an idiot. He doesn't quite know how serious things are,' she nodded to his mother's stomach, 'but he still thinks you'd be safer to leave.'

'Leave the village?' Lucio had already begun to suspect this was Fabrizia's mission as well as his own, but his mother's voice was incredulous. 'No! They won't force me to leave. Anyway, where would I go? There's Lucio to think of.'

Fabrizia raised her head to him. Her gaze roved over his

hair, his shoulders, before settling on his face. She was about to speak, but he stopped her.

'They say the Nazis are rounding up boys younger than me,' he said. 'Sending them off to the front or to factories in Germany.'

'Who says that? Who? Pettegola?' his mother barked at him, desperately. 'In Rome, it might be true, but not here, not in the mountains.'

'Fagiolo says it's happening even in Valmontone,' Fabrizia cut in. 'Boys as young as thirteen. It won't be long before they come to the villages.'

His mother stood up and rocked on her feet. She pressed her lips between her teeth, and her eyes flashed their accusations at Fabrizia, but she said no more.

Outside in the alley, the butcher's wife grabbed him by the arm. 'He was right,' she whispered. 'He said she wouldn't leave unless it was for you. Fagiolo knows her too well. And so do you.' Her eyelashes shone, and the dew under her nose glistened in the grey alleyway. 'Take care of her, Gufo,' she said. 'Make sure you take care of the both of them.' And she darted away across the cobbles that winked with melted snow.

Leyton
1950

Connie didn't go back to St Margaret's that summer. She wouldn't let herself. Rather, she focused on Vittorio, seeing him off for Luton in late September. She set a condition on her joining him: he had to be settled and established there before they announced their plans. She didn't exactly swear him to secrecy, but she knew he had told no one, for she was not eyed or baited any more than usual when they gossiped about him at Cleat's, and Agnes went back to overlooking her with genuine indifference. Other girls might have been angry at Vittorio's willingness to comply with these demands, suspicious even, but she was grateful that it bought her extra time, although for what she didn't know.

She continued to go to the Roxy on Saturday nights, enduring Tommy and the other boys on the bus, just to listen to Bobby's band play the interval, just to escape the morbid evenings of perky radio in her aunt and uncle's sitting room. But had she been honest with herself, she would have admitted it was the cycle home from the bus stop that she anticipated the most, allowing her to see the lit-up church, to feel the thrill of finding the candle still burning in the south window. Sometimes she'd even pedal across the commons as far as the lychgate, and sit on the bench, listening to the creaking of the cypresses, the sigh of beech leaves across the gravestones. But she wouldn't let herself scratch again at the oak door. Instead she waited for Vittorio to telephone her at the shop on Tuesday afternoons when Mrs Cleat was out, trying to conjure, in the tinny distance of his voice, the line of the road leading south.

She continued to freewheel down the rise on her way to Cleat's, but it no longer gave her the same pleasure. She noticed she applied the brakes more now, as if it was the future racing towards her that she was trying to slow. One morning she stopped at Lucio's gate and let her bike fall into the verge. She had been back to Leyton House once since returning Mrs Repton's shoes, but only to call Aunty Bea's message through the kitchen window to Mrs Cartwright. Now her aunt was out of sorts again, and she'd come to let the cook know.

She took the shortcut through the fields and across the back courtyard of the house. As she negotiated the mud in her wellies, her shoes in her satchel, she thought of Mrs Repton's white heels and the disappointments of that meeting. She hoped she would find Mrs Cartwright in the kitchen and be gone as quickly as she could. The Big House held little for her now. With Luton ahead of her, it seemed a relic of the past, a place of childish hopes and fantasies, and she couldn't help a certain scorn tempering the sadness she felt for it.

The cook wasn't in the kitchen when she arrived. Connie stood by the trough sink, casting around for a paper and pencil to leave a note. Through the open window she heard the clip of horseshoes on the cobbles: it was Fossett, bringing Mr Repton's hunting bay into the yard. The mare was a looming, nervy beast, sidestepping and rattling the bit. Someone called to the animal, scolding it, and Connie noticed its ears twist expectantly, its nostrils flare. Mr Repton strode from the stables in his hunting pinks, his polished boots — a streak of splendour in the dun-coloured yard. Behind her the door from the scullery opened, and she turned, preparing her message for Mrs Cartwright. But it was Mrs Repton who stood in front of her, pulling on green kid gloves. She stopped as she saw Connie, her hands held midair.

Mrs Repton said her name. Her eyes seemed to brighten and she gave a hopeful smile. She was wearing a tweed jacket with a vented skirt nipped into her waist, which would have made it seem she was about to join Mr Repton on his ride, had her hair not been pulled into an elaborate chignon that was partially hidden by the stole of a thick fox fur. Connie was fascinated by the pelt: rusty brown and flecked in black, so thick and alive that she imagined Mr Repton had just come in from the chase and draped it about her neck.

'I've come to … my aunt has a message … for Mrs Cart-wright,' Connie said, faltering. 'Or for you.' Mrs Repton set her gloves on the kitchen table. A pained expression crossed her face, but she came towards Connie and took her hand, as she always used to. Connie felt the urge to snatch it away. She didn't want to be drawn back to those times, to be lured into hope by praise and admiration, only to have Mrs Repton lay out before her the messy, unhappy compromise that was life. It wouldn't be that way for her, she promised herself. She pressed on. 'She's had to have the doctor, you see, and won't be in today.'

'Of course.'

They were silent for a few seconds.

'We should talk,' Mrs Repton said. Connie pulled her hand away. 'I've heard you might be leaving?'

She didn't answer. Vittorio must have told Mr Gilbert: she assumed that was how Mrs Repton knew.

'I just want to be sure you're making the right decision.'

'I am.'

Connie felt herself being studied and turned her face to the window. She heard Mrs Repton take a few paces across the kitchen.

'There are other ways of leaving Leyton, you know.'

The stone of the trough sink was hard and chill against Connie's hip, strangely comforting.

'Do you love him?' Mrs Repton asked.

The hooves of the bay skittered across the courtyard, as if eager to be off. 'It's the Hamerton Hunt this morning, isn't it? I forgot,' Connie said, wishing she had remembered and come later.

Mrs Repton sighed. 'Yes. Henry's riding out. I'm to join the ladies at Stoke House in the car.'

'You look very nice,' Connie said blandly.

Mrs Repton laughed, and the fox fur shivered under her breath. 'Yes, I'm good for that at least, aren't I?' She said it as though she was merely voicing Connie's thoughts.

Connie didn't take the bait. 'I should go before I make us both late.'

'Wait.' Mrs Repton took her arm. 'The mural project's finished. Did you know?'

She nodded.

'Harvey told me Swann's done the heraldic crests and the scaffolding's all down.' Mrs Repton cocked her head. 'You haven't been in to see them lately, have you?'

Connie stiffened. 'I've been busy. I expect I'll see them at the dedication service along with everyone else.'

Mrs Repton looked down at her boots. She seemed to be struggling with something. 'I just wanted you to know that a little money has changed hands recently. For Lucio, I mean.' She glanced through the window towards her husband. 'Not enough,

I know, but I've done what I can for him. It might allow him to work on his art for a while. Between us, Harvey and I were thinking we could help him get an exhibition together, introduce him to our connections in the art world ... well, eventually, anyway.'

Connie studied her beautiful face, the face she had watched in private whenever she'd had the chance as a child. Up close she saw now the unevenness of her pale skin, the particles of powder that glistened across her nose, the slight bleed of her lipstick. She felt she should say thank you, but she couldn't find it in her. Her thoughts kept going back to the murals in the church, how they went beyond Leyton, how they spoke to something bigger and better than the meagre approval of Mrs Repton or Mr Gilbert, the condescension of their *connections*.

'He still won't get any credit for St Margaret's, though, will he?' she said. Mrs Repton took a breath to speak, but Connie interrupted. 'I don't mean money.'

'Perhaps not now, no ...' Mrs Repton hesitated. 'But who knows how the truth will out in the future? Besides, as I understand it, Lucio doesn't want any acknowledgement. He's been quite adamant about it.'

'That's only because his father doesn't approve. And he doesn't want to cause trouble with the parish.'

'Is it?'

Connie didn't answer. She wasn't sure that was truth of it, after all. There was so much she wasn't sure of.

'Some things are better for everyone if they're kept a secret.' Mrs Repton picked up her gloves and slipped one on, smoothing her thumb over the soft leather. Outside, the bay beat out another syncopated rhythm on the cobbles as Mr Repton mounted. She touched her fur and straightened, as though readying herself for some onerous task ahead.

'Who knows?' she continued brightly, raising her chin and smiling with the face of another person. 'Perhaps in decades to come the experts might trace the parish murals to the early work of the famous Lucio Onorati.' She gave a piping laugh that Connie imagined she reserved for the ladies at Stoke House. It seemed to be the saddest thing Connie had ever heard pass her lips: yet another of the pretty delusions Mrs Repton draped about herself. And perhaps Mrs Repton felt this too, because for an instant she seemed utterly lost again, as she had when Connie had found her barefoot in the grass on the night of the harvest fair.

When they said goodbye, Mrs Repton kissed her and whispered, 'I'm sorry.'

Connie felt the stole brush against her cheek and was reminded of Mrs Repton's Siamese, the sheen of its fur in the twilight, the dark undercoat glimpsed like a secret beneath. Fromit, a series of disparate images rippled outwards in her mind: her mother's red shoes clicking down the lane, Mr Gilbert's arm around Vittorio through the bull's-eye pane, photographs slipped inside the pages of books, a seashell in a pocket, a stub of candle in the window. Perhaps they were all guilty of those small self-deceits, as cosseting as a second skin, the fears and the disappointments hidden underneath. And Connie understood she was as guilty as anyone.

'Won't be long before the whole village migrates south, I reckon,' Mrs Livesey was telling Mrs Cleat. She crossed her arms under her breasts when she saw Connie and eyed her suspiciously. Connie's heart jumped to her throat. She hadn't told Mrs Cleat her plans. To do so would be to reveal them to

Aunty Bea, and she wasn't ready for that battle yet. 'Leyton's not good enough for the young anymore,' Mrs Livesey continued. 'Seduced by the big smoke, they are. Although why they'd want the dirty, crowded, bombed-out ruins of London over fresh air and fields is beyond me.'

Mrs Cleat ignored her customer and continued slicing the ham. Mrs Livesey scanned the back shelves as if for something more colourful to inspire her. 'I've heard it's not a coincidence Mr Gilbert and Agnes are moving back to London at the same time.' Connie saw her run her tongue over the rogue tooth that pressed against her lip.

'For goodness sake, Janet, Harvey Gilbert's old enough to be her father,' Mrs Cleat said.

'Only just.'

'Well, it wasn't but a few years ago she were pulling up her socks in his playground. I hardly think he's been seduced by Aggie Armer's womanly wiles just yet.' Mrs Cleat took out the ledger and slapped it on the counter. 'I'm sure two people from the same village can share a carriage to St Pancras without announcing the banns!' She licked her pencil and held it above the page officiously. 'Will it be anything else today?'

Connie thought how much Mr Gilbert would have laughed at the seeds of this scandal being sown. She missed him. Every time she heard his name, the shame of their last exchange flared up in her all over again. She wanted to apologise, but he hadn't been into the shop since, only coming in on her afternoon off, and she was still building up the courage to go and see him. But it appeared that her time had come: not long after Mrs Livesey left that morning, Mrs Cleat sent her to the schoolhouse with Mr Gilbert's newspaper, clearly wanting reassurance her nose for scandal was still finely honed.

She entered the gate of the yard as the children were

bundling out of the classroom for morning play. Inside, Mr Gilbert was dusting the chalkboard.

'I remember when that was my job,' Connie called out, leaning against the doorjamb. He glanced at her before going back to the task. 'I used to be so proud to be the one to do it.'

'I remember,' he said. He turned back and held the felt out to her. She crossed the room and took it from him, beginning to dust where he had left off.

When she'd finished, she said, 'I'm going to miss you when you go.' He was silent. 'I just … I wanted to come and say —'

'Let's not, Connie. There's no need. Everything you said was true. And I should thank you, really. That's partly what made me realise I needed to go back to London, to city life. There's nothing here for me. I'm hiding from the truth if I think so.' His expression showed less sorrow than relief.

He didn't say any more, but held out his hand. She slipped her fingers inside his and felt his affectionate squeeze. 'I hear you're planning to leave yourself,' he said.

She nodded and saw that he didn't smile or frown, that he didn't make any judgement at all. He released her hand and took a piece of paper and a pen from his desk, scribbling something down. 'My address in London,' he explained. 'If you ever want to come and see me — for anything — you know where I am.'

She felt herself flood with gratitude, the consolation of knowing he still wanted the best for her, perhaps still believed in her, even after everything.

'And this,' he added, bending to open a drawer. 'I found it when I was packing and kept it for you.' He handed her a small fat book, bound in red and somewhat tattered. *Baedeker's Rome and Central Italy*, the gilt letters of the title read. 'It's a bit well thumbed, but I wanted you to have it. You might need it one day.'

She held the book in her hand, not daring to look at him

because her eyes were starting to sting with the terrible tears of uncertainty and self-doubt.

'Do you think so?' she barely managed to ask.

'I hope so,' he said. He came to her and put his hand on her shoulder. 'You know, Connie, sometimes it's a relief to give in.'

'What do you mean?'

He pulled away from her and reached for the brass bell on the shelf behind his desk. 'Go and look at the murals. You'll see.' And he strode to the edge of the yard and began to ring, the sound clattering through her bones and making her sigh as it used to, when the school day was over and all she had left was the damp walk across the fields to Grimthorpe Lane and Aunty Bea.

She left Cleat's that afternoon with the dark already settling in. She pulled on her gloves and hat and wheeled her bike from the alley. Vittorio had telephoned when Mrs Cleat was at her Christian Ladies meeting. He was buoyant with news: he'd found a club that made the Roxy seem like a barn dance; she would need new clothes; he'd already met someone who could get meat and sugar on the black market; the flat above the garage had no proper kitchen, so he'd put his name on the list for a terrace in Overington Street; it had an indoor toilet and they could walk straight to the pictures and the shops; there was even a park over the road where women with children met in the mornings.

She felt almost dizzy, not from excitement but from the sudden clarity of the images he cast before her: keeping house, cooking, shopping, scrubbing shirts and, one day, nappies. She stood on the pavement next to her bike, peering through the dusk until she could no longer see the slow curve of the high street, the fields shaken out across Bythorn Rise. All she could make out before her was a row of terraced gardens, square and aligned as postage stamps, the limp lines of washing, the prams under the kitchen windows.

She didn't hear the ringing of the bell along the high street until it was right upon her. 'That'll be Mrs Jellis, I 'spect,' Mrs Livesey said, standing beside her in clodded wellies and peering after the ambulance that was heading for the rise. 'Been in labour since yesterday morning. Should've called the midwife last night. Never usually takes her above a day to have a baby. Fancy calling the ambulance, all the way from Benford! Never heard anything so ridiculous.'

Connie left her murmuring her disapprovals to the others who had gathered on the street to see the spectacle of the ambulance. She felt a rankling in her stomach the whole ride home, a watery uncertainty that wasn't just about Vittorio and the prospect of Luton. She told herself it was the smell of diesel hanging over the road, or the smoke from distant bonfires that always clung to the open fields at this time of year. But when she got home, the ambulance was pulling away from the lane; and the small crowd of women on the verge, the kids playing Walk the Plank, all turned their chapped cheeks towards her. No one spoke. The only sound was a newborn wailing from Mrs Jellis's open window. Connie dropped her bike in the road and ran inside to find the house dim, her call echoing through the empty rooms.

It was Aunty Bea who came home that night. Connie watched her at the coat stand, reaching to take off the hat that wasn't on her head. She had never seen her aunt leave the house without a hat, or a headscarf at the least, and her tired pillbox was still hanging next to Uncle Jack's trilby on their hooks. Aunty Bea straightened, her lips parting, her hands falling back to her sides. She seemed shrunken, misplaced, standing there in the narrow hall, so childish that Connie could not help remembering herself hovering in that very spot, her coat half unbuttoned, her mother's cheap perfume lingering about the mirror while she'd swallowed hard to fight back the tears. She crossed the hall and put her arms about her aunt, but she was stiff as a china doll, her face as white and unyielding. She pulled away from Connie, clamping tight her mouth, as if terrified something might fall from her lips.

'Aunty?' Connie asked, holding on to her wrist.

But Aunty Bea started to climb the stairs. 'There's so much to do,' she muttered. 'He's left me with so much to do.'

Montelupini
1943–1944

They did not go to the caves beyond Cori, to the places they had heard other families were hiding their boys, the places where refugees from Rome had settled in makeshift camps. Instead they preferred to keep to themselves, to stay in the grottos they knew around Montemezzo, the familiar hunting grounds Lucio had traversed with Otto and Viviana, where they could descend sometimes and look down on the village far below.

They arranged their camp inside a cavernous chamber, near a spring that dripped through a crack in the mountain. An overhang allowed them to keep a fire burning, sheltered from the rain and wind and snow. Lucio spent the first days foraging for dead wood, which he chopped and stacked against the walls of the cave, partially insulating them from the stony chill and providing a store of dry firewood. But at night they woke shivering when the embers had died, and huddled for warmth on either side of Viviana. He would gaze out at the black sky then — sharp as ice, the stars curdled against it — and listen to the endless gush of water, the bats chattering from somewhere deep within the network of caves, the lonely lament of a wolf high in the range.

When their food stores began to run out, he went further

and further into the mountains to hunt with Viviana. Fabrizia had given him Urso's pikes, but he most often used them as walking sticks, never coming across prey big enough to justify their use. It still wrenched his stomach from time to time to pry the bloodied, shivering creatures from Viviana's paws. He strived to the beautiful accuracy, the calm kill that Otto had shown him, but hunting was an art, like the precision of his pencil: one bad stroke and the essence of a thing was changed, the whole turned ugly. And yet it sickened him less now than returning with nothing and seeing his mother's pale face, the hollow of her cheeks, her animal eyes as she scanned him for food. So he trekked further into the range, sometimes leaving her for days at a time, laying traps and following tracks, not able to bear the emptiness of her smile at his empty hands.

Sometimes, on clear nights, when the moon was full and bright as a coin in the pool of the sky, he descended towards the village, even as far as the stable at Collelungo. On occasion he discovered eggs or potatoes wrapped in a waxed cloth and left on the chicken roost — by Fabrizia or Fagiolo, he assumed. He replaced them with a spinosa quill or a pheasant feather, some useless, innocent token to show they were alive. That Fabrizia did not try to find them told him enough about the state of affairs in Montelupini: she was being watched. Everyone was watching everyone.

His mother's advancing pregnancy seemed to bring on her seizures more and more, visiting her both day and night. He would sense her waking up, catch her fingering the spittle encrusted around her mouth, unable to find the energy to lift her head even though she had slept the entire night. She said it was the baby, but he blamed himself for not finding her enough food, for not keeping her warm, for her worries about Vittorio, whom he had done nothing to dissuade from leaving. Each time he waited for her to come around, he would study her face, the colour of the chalk tracks that criss-crossed the mountains; the lines that, even in this forced sleep, cut into her forehead and around her mouth; the ridges of blue veins mapped along her hands. And it seemed that each time she opened her eyes, she came back to him a little less, as though, despite the life growing inside her, death was claiming her bit by bit.

He tried his best to distract her, to distract himself. He hummed the old brigands' tunes she used to sing, or recounted the tales of their exploits that she had told him as a small boy. Using charred sticks, he drew for her in the journal that Otto had given him, or on the walls of the cave. She would lie under her blankets then, her dry lips parted, and he'd feel her grow still, her hunger and fatigue overtaken for a time by concentration, the same way he lost himself in the task of creating the pictures: the body abandoned to the imagination.

But by the height of winter they were living mindlessly, alive to nothing but the need to eat and keep the blood from freezing in their veins. They spent days hunkered about the fire, while winds or snowstorms sucked and buffeted at the cave's entrance and Viviana howled. They ate stewed herbs and dandelions, and the boiled cracked bones of animals, hunted weeks earlier, some of which even Viviana had already discarded.

The sketches on the cave walls took on a life of their own. They seemed to Lucio to have been made by someone else, someone open to the minute form and shape of the world. He felt drained of that sensibility now, bled of it, as cold and calcified as the cave itself. The days passed, and it was like everything before had been sloughed like a skin, and he could believe they'd always lived there, there in that prehistoric time, before the war, before the village, when everything was reduced to the barest pulse of life.

After the storms had passed and he could go out to hunt again, he no longer saw the blood on the snow from the mice he gutted, the dun feathers he plucked from a trapped sparrow. He only saw his mother sleeping through the day, or her wide glassy eyes as she stared at night across the frosted valley, so clear she might throw a stone and shatter it like her own reflection on the thin ice of the lake. They barely spoke. There seemed nothing to say.

Spring arrived in slow increments. The gush of the mountain jangled in his dreams, the pale sun lingered above the lake where the first insects began to shiver, the forest's soft grind and crack seemed suddenly noisy to him. He started to grub for snails and slugs, sprouting arugula and chicory, eventually birds' eggs. Viviana unearthed warrens densely packed and warm, writhing with insistent life. Their bellies complained at being filled again. But in the evenings Lucio sat on the rock ledge and watched such spring storms as he had never seen before: the flares of light that changed night back into day, the delayed response of mortar that grumbled under the surface of the earth and jarred his bones, loose in his skin.

All through the winter, he had felt the cough of distant explosions in his chest, had seen the planes cutting the skies as effortlessly as migrating birds over the range. He'd heard the boom of jettisoned bombs, and in their wake the heightened peace that made him flinch at every sound — the quarrel of the birds in the trees, an ox lowing at plough, an axe starting up again in the valley. Afterwards it all felt so ordinary, so timeless, that the drone of the engines seemed destined for some other place, some other war, far away. But now this dull shelling that shook their nights without relief had become purposeful in its stealthy encroachment, as predictable as two dogs, pack hunting, inching in on their kill.

The baby came too soon and too fast, as if it sensed the urgency about them. Lucio was hunting to the south, but Viviana had had no luck the whole day and his traps were empty. Unable to face returning with nothing, he slept the night in a mossy basin under an overhang of boulders. His redemption came in the morning, when he found a patch of wild strawberries, tiny and perfumed like violets, ripened in the sunny lee of the rocks. He gathered them in his pockets, imagining their redness in his mother's hands. But when he called out to her at the mouth of the cave, she didn't answer. As he entered, he could hear her breath, gradually made out her prone form clutching at the slick of a baby, blue and waxy as a hatched chick, already bringing its wide mouth to her nipple. Next to her lay one of Urso's pikes, which she had used to cut away the cord. She was marble white, her hair clinging wet about her neck, her mouth slack with exhaustion. But her eyes, as he drew close, seemed too intense, alive and burning with determination in her face.

'A girl,' she said. He squatted by her and she gave the baby to him, surrendering it like she had only been waiting for him to come. He took the shrivelled thing — hardly more than a handful of flesh — to the light outside so he could see her. Pink suffused the blue of her skin as she grimaced and mouthed her silent wonder. And he felt like he had woken from a night terror, or the place where his mother went when she had a seizure, the fearful strictures of his heart loosening and letting the blood pulse through once more.

Later he took the bloodied clothes and blanket and washed them in the lake. The afternoon light had already ripened between the trees, and the busy forms of insects were caught in it as if in syrup. The pollen of the chestnut catkins touched the surface of the lake and made it shudder like Viviana's skin.

He wrung out the blanket, aware of the dog's tail in the under-growth, twitching from time to time. He spread the washing across the bushes at the lake's edge where the next day's sun would catch them, and then he called to Viviana, clicking his tongue in the way Urso had always done. She didn't come, but over the incline away from the lake he heard her start up the baying that told him she had something in her sights.

He ran towards the sound, a chill flashing through him as he began to recognise, between the dog's barks, the unmistakeable grunts of a boar. Viviana was crouching on her haunches in the shade of a great chestnut, her paws spread, unmoving, monochrome in the dusk, as if she was rendered in ink or marble, caught in the scene of Urso's famous bookplate. He called her name and his hand went to the skinning knife at his belt. He remembered the neat stroke across the neck of the boar cradled at his father's chest; Valeriana's head lolling over Urso's shoulder; the curl of the snake's carcass, like a question mark in Otto's hand; the badger's blood anointing Vittorio's cheek in the light of a lantern. He gripped at the knife, but even now it felt cumbersome in his hand, too large as he kneaded his palm against its handle, trying to discover its groove, its fit. It still felt wrong, like using someone else's scythe at harvest. His failings smarted in him as if he had scored the knife along his own flesh. He snatched at Viviana's collar and yanked her back, calling her off. The boar shredded through the undergrowth, squealing out its taunt. Lucio stood panting, staring after it as the ferns thrashed between the whispering trees.

Leyton
1950

Uncle Jack's wake, like his life, was quiet and unremarkable, dogged only by the stubbornness of Aunty Bea. She refused to set foot in a public house, obliging the villagers to run up and down the high street in the bitter November wind, ferrying pint glasses and sherry between the memorial hall and the Green Man. As a result, most of the mourners went home more sober than when they'd started. Bobby gave a rather stiff and awkward rendition of *Abide with Me* on his clarinet, which left everyone dry-eyed and her aunt nodding approvingly. And even when Connie, escalating between helpless grief and carefully guarded rage, was spotted sitting in Vittorio's car at the edge of the green, no scene ensued. Instead a fraught calm settled between her and her aunt, exhausting them both with the weight of avoidance and the fermentation of things left unsaid.

Uncle Jack's ashes arrived, disappointing in their drab little urn, observing them from the mantel beside the ticking clock. And still they skirted around each other, their movements slowed, their voices muted, as if the house was submerged in water. Two weeks passed and they barely left Grimthorpe Lane, Mrs Cleat insisting that Connie stay at home to grieve and comfort her aunt, when all she wanted, in fact, was the paltry distraction the shop could provide. She felt like she might suffocate in the house, the days marked only by her aunt clearing and blackening the grate, then building and lighting the fire again. The flames did nothing to warm them, but Connie was grateful for a focal point at least, the hypnotic relief they provided from the grey that engulfed her.

'What'll you do with the ashes?' she asked Aunty Bea eventually, when she could bear their silence no longer. The urn seemed to blush in the firelight, reflecting the embers as they both looked up at it. Connie curled her feet up into Uncle Jack's chair and leaned her head against the wing, smelling him in it.

'Enough, now,' her aunt said, dismissing Connie's sobs as though she was still a child, snivelling over a grazed knee.

Connie felt anger rising over her grief. 'Well, what are you going to do? Just sit and stare at that jar every night like he's still here?'

Aunty Bea stood and set the guard about the fire. She pulled back her shoulders. 'He'll be put in the Farrington plot as soon as St Margaret's is re-opened.' Her voice was calm and matter-of-fact, as though she was outlining a plan she'd been making for some time. 'I'll see Reverend Stanton about a service. Jack's can be the first memorial in the newly dedicated church. He'd have liked that.'

The self-satisfied expression on her aunt's face shone with something akin to zeal. 'What do you mean he would have liked it?' Connie said. 'He wouldn't have given a damn! He never wanted anything to do with that church. It's what *you'd* like, not him.'

Aunty Bea spun around from the mantel. 'And what would you suggest? Scattering him in the potato or spinach beds? Or better still, we might sprinkle him in the shed.' Her true voice was coming back to her, and Connie was almost glad.

Her aunt's sarcasm was at least familiar, a lifeline of continuity in this terrible flux, and she clutched at it.

'Only you could belittle everything that was important to him,' she said. 'Even now you're still talking over him, making him small.'

'Oh, that's right, I forgot,' Aunty Bea threw back. 'You know so much more about him than I do. I was just his wife, after all.'

'I know enough to understand this isn't about him. It's about you. He gave you everything you asked for. But it was never enough, was it? He was never enough. But you didn't have the guts to go after what you really wanted.'

Aunty Bea blew a sharp burst of air through her teeth. 'You don't know what you're talking about, girl.'

'I'm talking about Bill,' she said.

Her aunt's mouth slackened. She stared at Connie, and then glanced at the urn with an unmistakeable look of betrayal. She gathered up her lips again, as tightly as if they were on a drawstring, and pulled her bedjacket about her.

'Yes,' she said, as if certain of her mind now. 'I'll go and see Reverend Stanton tomorrow.' And she reached down for the poker and broke up the embers in the grate, replacing the guard and turning her back on the room.

Montelupini

1944

Lucio didn't go back to the cave for three nights. He was haunted by the memory of the boar and the raw helplessness of his sister's gaze, milky as the stars lost in the lake. He wouldn't go back empty-handed to his mother. Instead he took Viviana further south, deeper into the scrubs and forests where he saw no other tracks or traps, where he might have imagined himself the last hunter alive were it not for the earthy rumble of mortar, the dull cough of the mountain beneath him, the engines' drone mingling with the night wind in the beech canopy.

On the fourth day, he was descending through a glade of chestnuts, their new leaves flapping like flags above him, when the breeze brought him the scent of a fire. He heard voices in the dell below and he caught Viviana's collar, squatting next to her to listen. They were men's voices, guttural, strangely swallowed, their cadence even more alien to him than when he had first heard German spoken.

He backed Viviana up the incline, getting a safer view of the camp from above. There were twelve soldiers in the clearing, mostly sitting on their haunches or lying about the fire, where they were roasting the carcasses of what looked like squirrel and rabbit. Ammunition pouches criss-crossed their chests, and their striped coats were long and rough as blankets. They wore turbans about their heads, and grubby cowls hung behind their necks or were used to shade their faces while they dozed. Alongside the assortment of rifles and knives strung across them or lying by the fire, they resembled the warrior monks of some heathen sect, like Saracens stepped from the battlefields of the Crusades. Those whose features he could see wore wiry beards, and he thought he had never seen such dark faces, even on Sicilians. There was nothing about them that caught the light, not even their dented helmets painted with crescents like the new moon. They seemed of the elements, the bare toes in their sandals tough and brown as bark, their cheeks and noses pocked like volcanic stone. They might have blown in on a sirocco wind, the desert dust still upon them. Only their eyes were bright, glinting like damp pebbles within the wells of their sockets.

There was one pale-skinned man in their company. He sat at their edge, leaning against the trunk of a Turkey oak. His face was the only one shaven under the tall cylinder of his grubby white cap. Lucio watched him pick at a hole in the sole of his boot. He gave a command to the soldier next to him, in a different language again, the sound of the words this time familiar to Lucio from the radio at the osteria — French, Fagiolo had told him. But these were not the Allied troops anyone had been expecting. As the turbaned soldier stood to obey, Lucio caught a metallic flash at his earlobe, where several large silver hoops were threaded, weighted with leathery pendants, like shrivelled pieces of cured meat. The whites of the man's eyes, scanning the trees, were tinged yellow, a goatish quality about them, which made Lucio back away as if he had chanced upon something devilish deep within the cover of the woods.

He became panicked. He thought of his mother alone in

the cave and started back along his route without stopping. But he had to break the trek when Viviana rooted out a doe and then its kits, not more than a week old, squirming in their warren. He strung the rabbits up, the mother and each tiny baby, recompense for the boar he had passed over: even that pitiful game was better than an empty bag.

Near dark, when he reached the camp, he saw the fire dying under the overhang, the cooking pot empty. All was silent, save for the forest settling into its night-time sounds. He called his mother, but Viviana answered instead with a creaking growl as she took off towards the bushes before the lake. He followed her and found two figures rising from their hiding place in the scrub. One shouted at the dog to hush; the other hurried towards him. His mother threw her arm about his neck, the bundle of the baby slung at her chest.

'Where were you?' she whispered, her voice tight with worry. 'See, Lucio? It's Fabrizia. She's come.'

The butcher's wife looked him over. 'Madonna,' she said, her lips hardly moving. 'The state of you.' He became conscious of his muddy clothes, the dirt and blood ingrained in his hands, his matted hair. 'What have you been doing, running with the wolves?' She came to him and stood over the carcasses he had let fall to his feet. The mound of fur parted under the nudge of her toe, revealing the gutted rabbit, its six babies strung by their hind legs.

'It was all I could find.' His apology seemed lost somewhere in his throat.

'Good enough.' Fabrizia nodded. 'We'll be fine,' she breathed, as if to herself. She picked up the game and headed for the fire. 'We'll be fine. The Allies will be here soon.'

They sat on logs and Fabrizia built up the flames. The baby began to cry. He watched his mother loosening the swaddling, opening her clothes to feed, her face softer than he could remember in a long time.

'The Germans have left the village,' Fabrizia told him. 'They went towards Artena, but they say some got cut off by road and took to the mountains. I came to tell you. When we heard someone coming we hid.' She thrust her chin towards the scrub by the lake where Viviana had found them. 'They destroyed half the town hall. Centini's heartbroken. Loaded whatever stores they could take with them and torched the rest.' She slit the skins of the kits and tugged them from the flesh like she was pulling gloves from children's fingers.

'The Allies will come any day now, you'll see. Any day. They say there's already nothing left of Cisterna, half of Cori bombed. The roads are jammed with American jeeps and tanks. It's all anyone is talking about: *when the Americans come, when they bring the food, when they clear the roads and fix the wires and reconnect the water* ... Ha!' She brought down her knife upon the legs of the doe. 'What do they think? The Allies bomb us for months and then they're going work miracles overnight? A few bars of chocolate, some cigarettes thrown through the streets of Cori, and even La Mula believes their shit won't stink!' Underneath her bluster, Lucio could see she was as full of hope as the rest of them. 'You know, Pettegola told Centini some of those Americans are as big and black as the devil himself! Others even speak Italian. They have family here.'

'My brother?' Lucio interrupted her. 'Have you heard anything of him?'

Fabrizia darted a look at his mother, who was preoccupied with the baby, and shook her head. 'I wouldn't worry about Primo. If he's with that Cori gruppo, he's probably one of the few round here with a full stomach. They've become as bad as the crucchi, taking everything they can get their hands on.'

He saw his mother shift. She glanced away into the dark beyond the fire, but whether it was at the mention of the Germans or of Vittorio and the self-styled partisans, he couldn't tell. They weren't the only ones with torn loyalties, he knew. There were plenty of families in the villages whose fathers still wore the Fascist uniform while their sons hid in the hills, wearing the red scarf.

Fabrizia palmed the raw meat. 'Still, we've survived, haven't we?' she said, her tone brightening. She began to bone the rabbits. Her fingers were strong and sure, as business-like as if she was back behind her chopping block in the shop. Lucio was lulled into such comfort watching her that, for an instant, all the questions and uncertainty pushing in on him were held at bay. He felt exhausted, so relieved by her presence that he would do whatever she told him.

'Now fetch that pot so we can get this into your mother,' she said, nudging him with her elbow. 'She can't feed that baby on love alone.'

Leyton
1950

Connie sat under the lychgate at St Margaret's, feeling the night getting colder, smelling the frost in the air that would settle before dawn. Her fingers and toes were numb, but it was nothing compared to the stony chill of the house in Grimthorpe Lane, petrified by Aunty Bea's very breath, her unrelenting righteousness. Unable to sleep, Connie had ended up at the church. It was nothing but habit, she told herself. She sat under the lych for a long time, believing that simply being close by would give her the clarity of mind to think over what she needed to do. But when she heard the south door rattle, the key in the lock, she stood up quickly. She knew Lucio's walk even in the dark, and her relief at the sound of his step made her finally admit she'd been waiting for him all along.

The beam of his torch along the path picked her out. He stopped and switched it off, standing opposite her. She couldn't see his face, only discerned the clearing of his throat. 'I'm very sorry,' he said. 'About your uncle.'

Hearing the words from him, more than from anyone else, nearly broke her. She had to reach for her bike, for something to hold on to. He asked if she was alright. She nodded but kept her mouth shut.

When she thought she could control her voice, she said, 'Will you come with me? Will you help me to do something? Right now?' She rushed her words, frightened she might regret them or, worse, pour out all her frustrations and fears in a confused mess before him. He didn't answer. Without even asking her the details, he reached to switch on her bike lamp and take the handlebars from her.

They were quiet as they walked across the freezing commons. She led him all the way to the centre of the village green, the hardened grass cracking under their feet, the bicycle wheels drawing a line between their footprints. The bowling crease had its winter growth, but she could still make out where Uncle Jack had pressed it in the summer, the exact places he had sunk the stumps. She reached into the basket of her bike and unwrapped the towel she had wound around the urn.

Lucio turned to her uneasily, perhaps sensing she wasn't sure. But before she could change her mind, she had thrown out her arm and shaken the ashes across the crease. They fell lumpy and graceless, an ugly pile of dust dulling the grass of its glint. She held her breath and felt a rush of confused emotions: remorse, vindication, the terrible ordinariness of it all, the finality of her loss. She ran to the clubhouse and sank onto its step, trying to catch the special smell of the place, of Uncle Jack through the locked door. But all felt frozen now in the metallic air of winter.

After a while, Lucio followed her, and the way he stayed beside her, so still and patient, without judgement, made her cry even more — hard sobs of grief, of doubt and confusion, until he pulled her to him and put his arms around her. Everything felt infinitely better then. Infinitely better and so much worse. Her mind was full of Uncle Jack: his habits, his expressions, his jokes — and his death, his ashes there on the green. Was that it? Was that the sum total of him, of a life quietly lived in Leyton? She forced herself to push away from Lucio, and she didn't want to see if it hurt him as much as it hurt her. She picked up her bike and cycled across the green without looking back.

Montelupini
1944

They didn't return to the village straight away. Fabrizia told him she was still frightened of the strafing, which had plagued everyone's movements in the valley for weeks, making them jump and cover their heads at every banging shutter, at every broom handle clattering on the cobbles. But Lucio knew she was thinking not about gunfire but of the fallout that would rain upon his mother — and her baby — the moment she returned to Montelupini.

They stayed in the cave, and he continued to go out early each morning with Viviana to hunt, not returning until the afternoon or evening, when he had checked and reset all his traps. As the weather warmed, he would stop by the lake to swim, sometimes finding his mother and Fabrizia there, washing clothes or the rags they wrapped about the baby.

It was later than usual when he climbed down to the lake that afternoon, the cicadas thickening the air, the itch of summer in his throat. He'd had mixed luck that morning: one of his traps offered him a large buck, fresh and intact; another only a severed paw, already alive with flies. It wasn't the first time he'd seen it — an animal turning on itself, simply to survive. But the residual image always griped at him throughout the day like a bad dream, an ill omen.

He laid the hare at his feet and stripped, diving into the green water and staying there, submerged, his toes buried in the silt between the silky weeds. Below the water the engine of his own pulse sounded in his ears, like the sea in the shell Fagiolo kept on his bar. He had never seen the ocean up close. He thought of his father's journey from Africa to England and tried to chart his route across the seas, based on his memory of the world map pinned by the chalkboard at his old school. He tried to picture his father's face, to conjure him at some task, cutting maize or spraying grapes in the Vigna Alba. But he could not. In nearly five years, he had become as much a number to him as he was to the Allies, the number always written on his sporadic postcards and letters: *POW 27366*.

Floating on his back, he felt weed brushing his hand and tangling between his fingers. He stood up to find it was a cloth, a grubby length of cotton. At first he thought it was one of the baby's rags, drifted loose from his mother's washing. But as he lifted it, trailing it behind him to the water's edge, he saw it was too narrow, too long, and he knew it wasn't theirs. He studied the colour of the fabric, the loose weave as it fanned in the water at his knees, and he remembered the scarves wound around the necks of the turbaned soldiers in the woods. He lowered his hand and dropped the cloth in the mud, feeling cold, despite the warmth in the air. He began to grapple with his clothes, stepping into them wet. Across the water he could see the overhang of the cave through the variegated shadow of the trees. All seemed serene and silent: too still. No smoke rose from the fire, which had burned down to its embers, and the pot that hung above was upturned in the scree. He saw two ravens land to forage and peck in the spill of its contents.

He wasn't sure how much time passed as he stood watching.

He couldn't seem to move. He didn't want to move, didn't want to look. He only heard the sound of the water, its cool murk stirring, calling him back to the quiet depths so he wouldn't have to see, wouldn't have to remember. But the ravens interrupted, mocking him, and he heard Viviana's incessant bark somewhere in the scrub, until he forced himself to go, edging around the lake to the place where she was waiting.

He found Fabrizia squatting against a holly oak, clutching at the neck of her dress with one hand and pulling her skirts over her legs with the other. He stopped and half spun away, thinking he had come upon her doing her business or about to wash herself in the lake. But her expression was vacant and her eyes seemed to have become so small, the pupils were no more than pinpricks in her face. Slowly he understood the swelling of her cheeks, the blood on her teeth, saw where her earrings had been pulled from her ears. A red trickle glided down her neck, glossy in the afternoon light. He lifted his hand to her, but she flinched from him and went to her hands and knees, her dress falling open as she did so, turning loose a brawny breast.

'Don't look,' she hissed at him. 'Don't look at me. Go away!' He stumbled back as if she had struck him, and began to trample aimlessly through the scrub, suddenly remembering his mother. Panic took hold of his throat, so that he couldn't call out to her, could barely breathe. He found her under a burst of yellow broom near the lake's edge, her skirts still snared on its branches, its petals shaken through her hair, reminding him of the fireflies in the meadow at night, the swing of lanterns answering each other on the ridge.

She was sleeping, he told himself. She'd had a seizure and was climbing through that tunnel back towards the daylight. And soon she would wake up and find her head in his lap, her mouth wiped clean. But try as he might, he couldn't wipe away the marks from her neck, or staunch the blood that ran from her ears and mouth, that smeared her thighs and saturated the hair between. He pulled down her skirts and stroked her head and whispered to her, waiting for the relief of her open eyes. But it didn't come. Not this time. And as the dusk started to settle around them, he began to understand, to tell her to sleep, to sleep on. He took off his shirt and wrapped it about her breasts, where blood and milk had curdled, and she felt all wrong, pliant in his hands, heavy and slack, already just the carcass of something.

It seemed a week or a month or a year might have passed before he felt Fabrizia squeezing his wrist in her fingers, mouthing something through her split lips. Perhaps he didn't hear the words, or perhaps no sound came out. All he knew was that he stood too quickly and the blood banged in his ears like a blow to the head. He lost his sight for a second, and the exploding darkness became the flares and shelling that lit the cave at night, his sister's milky stare, the bright petals trapped in his mother's hair. His tongue was dry and felt too big for his mouth. When his vision returned, he had the sensation of shrinking, of everything becoming distant, so that when he saw the bundle of rags in the shallow water beyond the brush, it seemed he would have to walk very far to get there. Fabrizia was already ahead of him, standing over it, a cloud of silt billowing about her calves. He tripped into the water, pushing himself in front of her to reach the baby first. He fished her out and held her to his chest, showing his back to the butcher's wife so she couldn't see. Couldn't see the mud on his sister's cheeks, the silt clogging the tiny hollows of her nose, the weed that threaded about her ear, like a question mark or a lock of his mother's hair when she nursed her.

The night that came was clear. He felt naked and numb under it. He washed his mother and sister slowly, carefully, working over them with fingers that seemed to belong on the hands of someone else. Fabrizia kept the fire stoked and helped him wrap them in a blanket, the baby curled upon his mother's stomach as if she had never been born. They kept a silent vigil, until the din of his thoughts became too much to bear.

He stood up and Fabrizia rose too, as if she had only been waiting for him to move. They began to walk, aimlessly at first, but then with a purpose that seemed inevitable, across the plateau to the grotto of Santa Lucia.

Lucio stood next to the butcher's wife as she peered through the locked grille, squinting at the glowing outline of the effigy inside.

'They brought her back up the mountain strapped to a mule — Berto the goatherd and Polvere,' she muttered, like she was talking in her sleep. 'The Germans wouldn't allow a ceremony this time.' She didn't take out her rosary or kneel to pray as he had seen her do so many times with the other village women before the shrine. Instead she turned her back to the chapel and pulled her shawl about her shoulders. 'Strapped to a mule,' she said again. 'Like firewood.'

They stood on the rock ledge. The valley below brooded in darkness, devoid of lights now that the powerlines had been bombed. Montelupini clung grimly to the mountain. Far down the range, the intermittent beam of headlamps from a jeep convoy followed the scribble of the bends past Carpeto. And, beyond that, flares blossomed from time to time, like so many green sunrises.

'She gave up on us,' Fabrizia said. He thought she meant his mother, but she said, 'Lucia. She deserted us, didn't she?'

He was silent.

'Maybe your grandfather was right all along. Barilotto always knew she was a fraud. And we were never special. We just wanted to believe we were.' She gave a grunt or a laugh; he couldn't tell which.

A breeze stirred up from the valley and the trees behind them sighed. He heard the beating of wings, caught the sulphurous flash of an eye in the darkness.

'She always knew,' Fabrizia went on. 'Your mother always knew it was nothing but wishes and superstition.' Lucio tried to make out her expression in the light of the lantern hanging at his side, but her face was veiled in shadow. 'That's why she took the crown,' she whispered. 'Took it to feed us. She gave me supplies before you left.'

His gut cramped and the weight in his lungs felt doubly heavy now, as though he was sinking under the accumulation of grief, of regret, of realisation. He'd never wanted to admit that his mother had stolen the crown. The stores of food they'd bought with Otto's money had been used up so quickly, and the old folk, the children kept coming to their door in Vicolo Giotto. She had never sent them away, had she? It occurred to him now that of everyone in the village, only she was fearless enough, stealthy enough, practical enough to do such a thing. Only someone who owed Santa Lucia nothing, who had already died a hundred deaths before and seen the emptiness beyond, who knew that life was something to fight for at all costs, only a person like that would have had the courage to do it. Even so, he found himself wishing it hadn't been her: he wished it had been him.

He thought of the paw left severed in his snare that morning and he began to understand. It was all they could rely on, after all: their own desperate will. Not God's, not a saint's or a foreign army's, but their own. Even if what life had dealt pushed them to their very limits, made them into something they were not.

Fabrizia reached into her skirt pocket and took out a bundle of cloth: it was the scarf he had found in the lake. The skein of it was so much more recognisable now as those worn by the soldiers he had seen in the woods. He heard the rosary fall from her other hand into her pocket. 'No one's coming to save us,' she said. 'We've just got ourselves now.' He watched her handling the cloth, twisting and untwisting it as if she wanted to wring it clean. 'The Allies haven't delivered us. They've brought us down the final steps to hell.' And she spat on the ground, her cut lips shining wet and broken in her face.

She unwrapped the scarf and took something from it, pressing it into his palm. Her breath was fast and close beside him. He snatched back his hand and squinted at what she had put there, bringing it nearer his face so he could better see it: the hoop of a silver earring, nestled now in his palm. He wanted to ask her what he was to do, wanted her to put words to it so he could be certain, but she had already started back towards the cave.

In the hours that he sat alone on the rock ledge, waiting for the morning to reveal the blue sediment of the hills, to drain night from the valley, he made himself understand. And he wondered whether there would ever be a sunrise again that could drain the darkness now settled in his heart.

He didn't remember how long he spent climbing through the mountains, sleeping when he was tired, scavenging with Viviana when he was hungry. He found it difficult to think of time, the future or the past, of anything but his body's immediate needs, as if he had returned to that winter existence in the cave, his mother still expecting his return with a squirrel or a rabbit to skin. But he knew he was following them, for he would find himself standing in circles of flattened ferns while the rain dripped down from the broad canopy, or lighting a fire from their embers, even tossing Viviana bones already picked over and discarded in the ashes.

The husk of a new moon was low in the sky on the night he caught up with them. He could smell their camp: the foreign pungency of their fire, their piss and meaty sweat. They were sleeping when he saw them, all but one, who was squatting, his knees crutches to his arms. His hands hung limp, illuminated by the fire, surprisingly small and shrivelled, like a pair of bats nesting in the trees. He rocked on his heels, and Lucio could hear his moan, more a keening than a song.

Viviana started up a whine, as if in accompaniment. He clamped her muzzle with his hand and led her back through the forest, tying her up at some distance. When he returned to his vantage point, the soldier was pacing with a torch from the fire, his striped hood lowered from his turban. Lucio drew back towards a tumble of limestone boulders. They teetered on top of each other like the petrified eggs of some vast prehistoric creature, and he climbed them, wedging himself in their gaps, where the moss and lichen were hairy under his fingers, the stone so cold he found it soothing. Below him, the camp flickered between the black totems of the trees. The watchman sat again at the fire and began his ruminating song, otherworldly, strangely meditative. Lucio felt time slow, felt his senses strain to every tiny stimulus of the night. He heard each pop and spit of the fire, each breath catching in the throats of the sleeping men, the phosphorous flare of the watchman's match, the first crackle and singe of tobacco in the bone of his pipe. He felt the night air on his neck, the wind that rose over the precipice to his right and made the leaves flutter and clap. And at a distance, he could pick out a fox's rasp, and the pennywhistle piping of an owl over the ridge.

Finally, dawn broke above the mountain. The sun's rays sliced through the trees, and the sleeping men stirred and woke almost as one. Lucio could see them stretching and dressing and wandering through the undergrowth to piss. He scanned each one until he spotted the French officer in the dirty white hat. He was tipping his head to drink from a flask, and beside him the same yellow-eyed soldier was rolling blankets. He watched this man's lithe body as he packed up his camp, the efficient purpose of his dark hands. Lucio caught the metallic glint at his ear, saw where one of the rings had been torn. He felt for the silver hoop lodged upon his thumb and twisted it.

A distant barking started up over the ridge, and the men began to look towards the sound. Viviana, tired of being tethered, was calling him. The officer walked back towards the rise and listened, as if debating whether to retrace their steps and investigate. After a minute, he gave an order and the men continued to clear the camp. When Lucio turned back, the earringed soldier was gone. He searched the group, his chest tightening, until his vision began to blur and falter with panic. He heard the swish of undergrowth below, a loose scrabble of rocks. He lowered himself between the hunks of limestone, gripping with his bare feet like something wild. The top of a turban became visible as he peered between the boulders. He pressed himself against the stone, barely breathing, thinking he had been seen. But when he peered out again, the man had his robes hitched up like a woman's skirts, his baggy pantaloons pulled down, and he was squatting to shit in the seclusion of the rocks. Lucio saw the scratches of fingernails upon his neck and under his ear, still angry and raw. A cuckoo called smartly across the dell. The light fell in living shafts between the rocks. And he felt the moment crystallise into what Otto had once described to him as the hunter's gift: the perfect coincidence of prey at its most vulnerable, of hunter at his most focused, the beautiful inevitability of it.

The soldier's head nudged back on his neck with a compliance that shocked Lucio as he grabbed it, as if he was handling a child. He pulled him against his chest, heard the surprise lodge in the man's stretched throat. He felt him stiffen for the fight, but it never came: there was a soft rending hiss, like the piercing of overblown fruit, and then the slap of liquid on rock. And for the first time Lucio felt Urso's skinning knife become an extension of his hand, the contours of its handle in harmony with the muscles of his fingers and palm. He realised that it wasn't just his father's skill that had sliced the jugular of the boar so cleanly: the knife had become a part of him. He felt it now.

The soldier fell backwards, pinning him to the rocks. For a moment the body jerked against him in a strange syncopated rhythm of its own, until Lucio wrapped his arms about the man's chest and held him there, breathing in his ear until he quivered no more. And they were both as dead weights against the cold stone, the only sound the cuckoo, painfully alive in the new morning.

Leyton
1950

Connie's night was troubled and full of dreams half begun. She woke feeling confused and regretful, but not about what she'd done with Uncle Jack's ashes. Her conviction on that count felt so complete in the light of morning that it threw into relief all her other uncertainties, all the other doubts that loomed before her at every turn. She dressed while it was still dark, thinking she could cycle away her mood before the shop threatened to cement it into place, but her bike led her instinctively to St Margaret's, as it so often did.

The paintings were complete, the bulk of the scaffoldings removed now, so she knew there was little hope of finding Lucio there, losing sleep over them. But still she did, especially when, propping her bike against the lychgate, she saw that the oak door was unlocked and off its latch. She hesitated, not wanting to run into Mr Swann or, worse, Reverend Stanton, and have to explain herself. But it was too early for either of them. The grey clouds were still gilded by the first light, and she couldn't help going inside to see if Lucio might be asleep on a pew, as if nothing had changed.

She slipped in the door and crept into the nave, but her breath seemed the only life in the stony lung of the church.

She stood for a while before the crossing: she had never seen the paintings in natural light, away from the stage spots, and they seemed to have matured now, the colours ripening with the cast of shadows, enhancing the mystery of the scenes to her, the secrets they held. The figures surprised her all over again as she scanned them: Joanna and Salome outside the tomb; John and Peter in Gethsemane; Lazarus's sisters, Martha and Mary; Saul; Moses. She watched how their expressions changed with the growing light that shafted down the chancel and crept into the nave. And she stopped her breath, feeling like even that tiny sound might disturb the perfect transfiguration of the moment. That was when she sensed it — another presence in the church.

She turned to see a head bowed low in a pew of the north transept, before the mural of St Margaret. 'Lucio?' she called. The figure spun around, standing up as he did so, and she saw the angular features, the drawn cheeks of Aldo Onorati. Her first instinct was to leave, to run out of the church, but she held her ground, breathing through her mouth and not daring to move, as if she had just woken something dangerous, an old dog that might bite. She saw him clutch at the back of the pew but realised his grip was more for support, to steady himself on his feet. When she risked a look at his face, she saw his eyes were red and wet, his open lips setting tight, his initial surprise knotting once again into something closed and private.

He sat down heavily and bent his head, considering his hands spread across his knees. He seemed weary to her, as if he had been there all night.

'I'm sorry,' she offered at last, feeling she should say something, anything. 'I didn't mean to disturb you.'

'You didn't,' he said. His voice was surprisingly soft.

'I was looking for —'

'He's gone.' He didn't glance around, and she thought she might back off then, take the chance to slip away, but she stayed — out of ingrained politeness, perhaps, but also curiosity. He wasn't what she'd expected at all: there was something a little broken that was at odds with what she knew of him, something that reminded her too much of Lucio.

'Your son is very talented, isn't he?' she heard herself say. Her tone was pointed, a challenge in it. It sounded like the voice of someone older, a more collected, assured version of herself.

Aldo Onorati raised his head and considered the mural before him. She thought he was about to contradict her, but he began to nod. 'Yes,' he said. 'Yes, he is.'

Connie was thrown off-kilter. She realised she'd been expecting an argument, had been preparing herself for one — even wanted it, perhaps. She tried to think of a response that might cover her surprise, but all she saw was St Margaret surveying them knowingly. 'She's very beautiful,' she said. She came closer to the edge of his row, closer to the portrait. At his silence, she cleared her throat, the sound ringing awkwardly.

'I'm sorry,' she said, too loudly. 'I should have introduced myself. I'm —'

'I know who you are.' His weight shifted in the pew with a crack of wood. 'He told me.'

She nodded. 'Vittorio.' His name always seemed a statement, never a question. But Aldo Onorati shook his head and stood up to leave the pew by the opposite end, where he indicated to her the niche within the north transept. He waited while she approached the mural, set in the alcove where she used to play as a child.

The painting of St Dorothea was the only one she hadn't seen finished. She remembered the night after her trip to the seaside, the maythorn Lucio had been troubling over. As she drew closer, she could see that the bush filled the entire foreground of the view, as if it was the subject. Its flowers weighted the branches, thick and luminous as newly settled snow. And just at eye level, through the thicket, Connie made out a nest, the eggs inside green as olives, the wide beak of the nightingale hen on her stump nearby. She could almost hear again its creaking alarm as Lucio pinned back the branches for her to see.

By the time she looked up to Dorothea's face, she already knew who she would find there. She didn't need to trace her thin calves, nearly hidden behind the foliage, the copper curls that twisted about each other down her back, their stark counterpoint against all that white. Heat rushed to her face, doused by an icy flash as she thought of the eyes of the village on her, upon the very feature that singled her out, announcing her like a beacon right there to the side of the pulpit where Reverend Stanton preached. But as she stared at herself captured there on the wall, she found she was most bothered not by what the village would think, but by the way he had conceived her: her hair so prominent because she was walking away, leaving, glancing back over her shoulder, as though at someone who had just called her name.

She heard Aldo Onorati stirring behind her, the scuff of his boots on the flagstones. He came and stood next to her in the recess, and she wiped her cheeks quickly with the heel of her hand.

'He's talented, yes … but he's a fool,' he said.

She frowned, bracing herself for the argument that might yet come. She wanted to contradict him, to ask why he would say such a thing, how he could bother to understand his son so little. But all she managed was a feeble 'Why?'

The reflected brilliance of the maythorn seemed to brighten his sallow skin, giving it an odd intensity. 'He watches,' Aldo Onorati muttered, as if to himself, 'but he doesn't act. He won't fight. He never has.'

'Fight?' she asked. 'Fight for what?'

'For what he wants.'

She turned to him, but he was already backing away down the aisle, one hand clutched about his cap, the other deep inside his pocket. He stopped at the door and she caught him glance once more at the painting of St Margaret.

She listened to his footsteps on the gravel outside, each one driving something home to her. He was wrong. Aldo Onorati was wrong. She examined the study of St Dorothea again. Lucio had fought. He fought in the way he knew how, the way that was truest to himself: the painting showed her that. It was she who was the coward. She had never fought for what she'd wanted. She looked at her figure among the maythorn blossoms as Lucio saw her, the departing version of herself, so full of promise. And her heart felt as raw as the morning call of the crows among the gravestones — as raw, but as bold and as certain.

Montelupini
1946

The world had been at peace for more than ten months when his father walked back into the village. They had started to believe he wasn't coming home at all. Lucio spotted him making his way along Via del Soccorso with measured steps, past the missing shutters and falling plaster, the gaping roofs, the charred shell of the town hall. He crossed the piazzetta at the end of the day, as if he'd just returned from a trading trip to Cori. Fagiolo greeted him on the steps of the osteria, and they clasped hands and embraced.

'Still here, Fagio?' his father said.

'Still here, Capo. Still here.' But Lucio heard the innkeeper's voice crack and shift registers like a boy's. Fagiolo cleared his throat. 'You're fatter!' he declared.

His father breathed an uncertain laugh and seemed to grip Fagiolo's arms a little harder, shaking him affectionately. But he didn't answer. He didn't speak of what Lucio knew he saw and felt — the innkeeper's gaunt frame, the hollow facades and buildings, the lessening of everything he had left behind. His boots shifted on the cobbles as he looked over his shoulder. His eyes traversed the piazzetta, the dark entrance to Vicolo Giotto and back up over the battlement walls, where Lucio sat.

'Some things are still the same, though,' his father said. 'Some things never change,' he lied.

And it was Fagiolo's turn not to answer.

Vittorio had written to tell their father of their mother's death. Once the war was over and the Cori gruppo disbanded, he had come back to live in the village. Lucio didn't need to read the letter: he knew it wasn't the truth. Only he and Fabrizia knew what that was, and he hadn't spoken since the day he'd found his mother by the lake — not a single word, not even to his brother. The version of their mother's death that Vittorio knew was of Fabrizia's making. When they came down the mountain with the body, Lucio let her do the talking for both of them: Letia Onorati had had a seizure and fallen down an escarpment, she told the village. She'd scrambled down the scree to reach her, she said, touching her own cuts and bruises. But Letia had never woken up.

It was almost too plain an ending, too uneventful a punishment for the thief of Santa Lucia's crown, the Nazi whore, the partisan spy. The women crossed themselves and muttered their prayers, but they could not hide their hard mouths, their secret disappointment that Letia Onorati should have come to such an end, after all the turmoil she had caused them. And he watched the men's expressions soften and glaze still as they remembered her swaying skirts, her graceful neck as she carried her baskets. 'What a waste,' was all they said, as if this had not been true of the entire war. 'What a terrible waste.'

If there were rumours about a baby, Lucio didn't hear them. Fabrizia had wrapped his sister tightly and hidden her inside his mother's funeral clothes, only letting her tears fall when the coffin was finally sealed on them both. Perhaps Padre Ruggiero suspected his mother's infidelity, but if he did, he gave no sign of it.

'Better such an accident than what might have been,' he said to Fabrizia, on the steps of San Pietro's after the funeral service. She glanced at Lucio nervously. 'I mean the reprisals of the Allies, of course. Against Nazi collaborators.' His last words were an ominous whisper and he made the sign of the cross, as if he had named Lucifer himself. 'There were such reports of the forces who came up from the Aurunci — French colonials from Morocco and Africa — black faces and even blacker deeds, all manner of iniquities. Padre Tommaso tells me three women in Frosinone took their own lives rather than live with the shame of it.' The priest shook his head sadly, but his eye was hard upon them.

Lucio took Fabrizia's elbow in his hand, felt her weight shift.

'Evidence again, is it not, of Montelupini's singular blessings?' Padre Ruggiero held two fingers up towards Montemezzo and Santa Lucia's grotto, running his other hand over the crucifix on his chest. 'Not one of our women touched, thanks to the saint.'

'Not one, Padre,' Fabrizia repeated. But when Lucio led her away, he saw her eyes were opaque and flat, unblinking, as he had seen sometimes in animals resigned to the snare, the life in them all but extinguished.

Fagiolo was right. His father was stockier, stronger, like some of the men Lucio had seen return from working factories in the north before the war. At the osteria, they joked that being a prisoner suited him, but not everyone laughed. His father remained quiet. Lucio understood why when he saw what else he had brought home.

In their kitchen the next morning, his father reached into the pockets of his jacket and brought out a gold watch and a gold chain. He laid them on the kitchen table.

'How did you get them?' Vittorio asked, picking up the watch and examining it.

'Farm wages … cutting hedges, weaving bulrushes,' their father muttered.

Vittorio whistled. 'Ma-donna.' He weighed the chain and crucifix in his hand. 'So you're saying the English are smart enough to invent machines for the harvest, for drilling seed and threshing, but they'll pay good money for someone to weave them a basket?' He pulled in his chin sceptically, but Lucio could see he was hanging on every meagre word their father dropped about life in England.

When the Cori gruppo had disbanded, Vittorio, like so many of his comrades who had had their fingers in the flow of supplies and requisitions, took to profiting from the burgeoning black market. His brother was a natural, always scouting for the next deal, for anything American or English, making connections as far afield as Montemezzo, Valmontone, even Rome. Lucio continued to work their land without complaint, knowing his brother could put more food on the table with one carton of Chesterfields, one shabby and oversized Montgomery, than he was able to after months of labour in the fields. For Vittorio, everything about the war's victors was superior: their cigarettes, their alcohol, their food, their clothes. He could tell now how desperately Vittorio wanted to hear more of that land of industrialisation, of opportunity, the place where he believed the future lay. Lucio wanted to hear it himself, to believe it too, but if it was so, then why had their father come back? Why hadn't he simply sent for them?

Vittorio let the chain fall to the table, and it rattled like rain on the corrugated roof of the stable. 'Gold is good. It will hold its value,' he said. 'You might as well light a fire with the lira, but we can do a lot with this.'

'Can we?' their father said. His voice was a monotone, but his eyes were restless as spring flies. 'But what *I'm* going to do is go to Monteferro.'

'What for?' Vittorio asked.

'I want to trade them.'

'Already? What do you need?' His brother was clearly disappointed that this first taste of finery was to disappear as quickly as it arrived. But Lucio also saw Vittorio's eagerness to show their father what he had become. 'I can get things for you, you know. I've got connections now, Papa. I know a lot of people.'

'Really? You can get things?' Lucio remembered the way his father had of making people question themselves. The war hadn't changed him that much. Lucio's disappointment felt suddenly heavy in his stomach.

'Well … I can get cigarettes, some liquor, coffee,' Vittorio persisted. 'Tell me what you need.'

'What I need? What I need is a headstone. You think they sell those on the black market?'

They were silent. Their father looked up, but it wasn't Vittorio he had in his sights. Lucio felt the weight of his gaze fall upon him now, perhaps for the first time since he'd returned.

Through the window above the sink, where his mother had liked to stand, he could see the old spinster, Ardemira, beating a threadbare rug over her balcony. Her hands were almost blue about the broom handle, and as the dust rose up the alley, he felt each blow in his bones like a release. When she stopped beating, the absence of it was like a great void growing in his chest.

He pictured the polished squares of marble in the cemetery, the sepia photographs of the dead strangely alike, rows and rows of them under the cypresses, and the seal of raw cement behind which his mother lay. After the funeral, he had seen the attendant scratching her name in slow, laborious cursive with a stub of chalk: *Onorati, L.* Rain had started to fall. Nothing more than a brief summer cloudburst that unsettled the dust and made a smell like iron filings. *Onorati, L*, the attendant wrote again, so there were two strokes over some of the letters, like the memory of another name. Letia Raimondi, Letia Onorati, Rondinella, Leti. So many names after all, he thought, but did anyone really know her? He thought of the baby, the sister he had held in the morning light outside the cave, her milky stare. Nameless and unknown. Did it make any difference?

'I won't have the family name chalked on the cement like some pauper's,' his father said, his lips barely moving as if his mouth was seized with disgust. 'We'll do that for her, at least.' He fought to keep the accusation from his voice, but Lucio saw it in his face every time his father looked at him. He watched him run the chain into his cupped palm and close his fist over it. 'Whatever's left, we'll use towards replacing the saint's crown.'

Lucio knew then that he had heard the rumours. But how many of them his father believed, he could only guess.

'Do you mean you're going to use all this to buy a crown for some statue?' Vittorio asked.

Their father was already making his way towards the door, his back to them, a sign that the conversation had ended. He reached for his hat. Vittorio had removed the watch and was dangling it on two fingers, shaking his head. 'You don't understand,' he said. 'You can't until you see how much we've lost, how much we could recoup with this.'

Their father stood with the door handle in his fist. Lucio studied his back, straight and stiff, the muscles of his neck that ran in two proud cords, so rigid he seemed unable to turn his head to them. He remembered his mother's back at the window as Padre Ruggiero took the last bottles of Raimondi Gold from the kitchen table. Lucio understood what his father was trying to do, the desperate, flawed reasoning of it, his own form of penance. But did he truly believe it would buy back their honour, atone for what his mother had done, silence all the rumours — Otto, the money and supplies, the saint's crown — sins to which Lucio had also been a party? He wanted to show him his mistake, laugh in his father's face as Nonno Raimondi would have done, or shout out the whole brutal reality of what had been. But he didn't. The truth of it only floated in his head and drifted away, settling again somewhere deep and silent within him, like the silty sediment in the lake.

Each night, he sat on the battlement walls, witnessing his father knock on doors and shutters, collecting what paltry treasures he could from the villagers to trade and sell, making up the shortfall for the crown. He came back with religious medallions and broken communion necklaces, long-hoarded crochet work and linen raided from wedding chests, cosseted medals from the last war — all the hidden things that even the Nazis, the gruppi, the Allies wouldn't have wanted had they found them. He made a mendicant of himself until he had enough. Enough for Padre Ruggiero to commission a goldsmith in Rome, enough for the Bishop of Segni to come for the consecration on the saint's day that winter.

But even then it wasn't enough for his father. Perhaps it was just Lucio who noticed it. His father prayed to the effigy in San Pietro's that December night, expecting to find some sense of atonement, some resolution there. But all Lucio saw in the candlelight was the shadow of his father's cheeks, hollow and angular once more, the uncertainty of his open mouth. He watched his eyes casting about the altar, hard and restive, and saw there was no peace in them, only regret and yearning.

He'd once overheard someone at the osteria saying his mother had made Aldo Onorati a lost man. He hadn't understood at the time what they meant, but now he thought he did, and he knew they were wrong. Seeing his father there in the church, Lucio sensed that without her, he was more adrift than ever before. Replacing the crown had been a distraction and, now it was done, Lucio realised that even the saint couldn't help his father stop loving his mother, bitterly and in spite of himself. And he knew that, like the rest of the village, his father needed someone to blame. When those dark eyes settled on him, Lucio felt every inadequacy, every failing and disappointment of his life, as if he was living each one all over again.

Leyton
1950

All day at Cleat's, Connie found she was revisiting old images of herself, as though the painting at St Margaret's had flicked a switch in her, flooding light along a dim and dusty corridor that showed the approach of someone she'd thought had gone for good. After work she cycled home slowly, preoccupied, and when she got back to the house in Grimthorpe Lane, she nearly tripped over something left sitting in the hallway. She put on the lamp and saw it was a suitcase. She'd never seen it before and was surprised her aunt had call for such a thing, when she hardly ever stepped foot beyond Leyton. She went into the kitchen and found Aunty Bea sitting at the table.

'Whose case is that in the hall?' Connie asked, leaning against the sink to rub her shin. But the instant the words had left her mouth she knew the answer. Her aunt wouldn't look up, only poured the tea into a single cup and returned her hand to an envelope lying next to the milk jug. She tapped its edge along the table, business-like, aligning the contents. She'd been waiting.

'Sit down.'

Behind her, on the dresser, Connie saw the urn.

'Mrs Livesey brought it back,' her aunt said with manufactured calm. 'Found it lying on the green.' Her face flushed as if beyond her control, and then she hissed, 'Janet Livesey ... of all people!' Her words were barely a whisper. She almost seemed frightened of her own rage, wrangling it like some unwieldy, amorphous burden that bulged and seeped out in unexpected places.

'Is that what you care about?' Connie said. 'Not what I did, but what people might *think*?' She refused her aunt even the compliance of sitting. 'Well, I don't regret it. I'd do it again if I had to.'

Strangely, Aunty Bea began to nod. She turned to Connie at last, and her smile was thin and forced. 'I used to say things like that at your age. But, you see, you *do* regret — that's the very nature of getting older. That's what you're left with.'

Not me, Connie wanted to throw at her. *You, perhaps, but not me*. But all of a sudden she was full of doubt; she couldn't be sure. They were silent. The faucet let out a dribble of water that made Connie shiver. Half of her wanted to bury her face in her aunt's neck; the other half wanted to take it in her hands and squeeze as hard as she could.

'You'll take this with you — down to Luton. Use it to get yourself set up.' Aunty Bea slid the envelope across the table like she was dealing Connie a hand of cards. She could see it contained money. 'He left it to you ... in his will.' Her aunt waved her hand in the direction of the sitting room. 'And them books by the wireless. You can take those, too.'

Connie sat down, the shock of it settling in her limbs. 'So you know about Luton?'

Her aunt stood abruptly, the tea things rattling on the tabletop. 'D'you think so little of me?'

'I could have thought so much more, if only you'd let me.'

The clock on the mantel took up where the soft clink of the cups ended. Connie thought she saw a genuine sadness creeping into her aunt's face.

'That's where we're different, then,' Aunty Bea said. 'Because I always thought so much of you, regardless.'

Connie reached for her aunt's hand. 'Aunty Bea …'

But she turned to the door and shook her head, her hair the colour of autumn leaves against a winter dusk. 'Just go.'

Fossett found her at the bottom of the rise. He'd pulled up at the gate in the farm's truck after feeding the birds in the spinney. She'd struggled down the hill in the half-light, balancing the case on the handles of her bike, all her plans teetering as precariously now, her mind swimming with regret and doubt. When she reached Lucio's gate she couldn't help but sit there until the dark came, watching the copse by the brook, scanning the ridge and across towards the Big House, until she'd given up and the tears had come.

'Now then, what's this?' Fossett asked, ducking his head to catch her eye. 'Off somewhere? And so late? You waiting for someone?'

When she didn't answer he helped her down from the fence and opened the passenger door of the truck. 'Well, come on now, lovely. En't no one coming down here this late.'

She sat in the lumpy seat and listened to him lifting her bike and the suitcase onto the bed of the truck. She pressed the heels of her hands into her face before he got behind the wheel and started the engine.

'I can't go back,' she said, afraid he was going to swing the truck around and back up the rise.

'Oh, I see.' She heard him make a noise at the back of his throat, a soft chuckle. 'I can understand that.' He grimaced at her, conjuring the image of Aunty Bea. 'Still, don't mean he's coming.'

'Who?'

'Your young fella what you sat here waiting for all them months.'

His words drenched her with humiliation. Had even Fossett read her better than she'd read herself?

'I give him a lift to Benford train station this morning. Said there weren't nothing to keep him in Leyton anymore.'

She felt as if he had knocked all the air out of her.

'I 'spect now he meant you, going off to Luton, like ... with his brother.' He was watching her expectantly. Perhaps the whole of Leyton had seen through her.

'Oh, for goodness sake, did someone put up a notice on the parish board?'

He laughed. 'Not that I seen, but you know Leyton.'

'Well, where was he going? Lucio, I mean. What was he going to do? Did he tell you?'

'Whoa! Steady on.' Fossett ran a hand over his chin. 'Let's see now. He said that Mr Swann had offered him some work in London.'

'Really?' She didn't know whether she was surprised or disappointed, more relieved or angry. 'Really?' She fidgeted in the seat. How could he have gone without telling her, without saying goodbye? But then she realised that was exactly what she had once intended to do.

'No great loss, I suppose. Someone had already tipped him off on the price of them cony skins. I were on a tidy wicket there for a while.' He winked at her and she shook her head at him, struggling not to smile.

'Where are you taking me, Fossett?' she asked. She had the suspicion he was enjoying himself.

'Mrs Cleat's, of course,' he said. 'She'll know what to do.'

Fossett was right. Perhaps he was instinctive about people in the same way he was about his dogs and birds. He seemed to know that Mrs Cleat only needed to be needed to bring out the best in her. Connie felt ashamed at not seeing it before, not going to her earlier, after all their years of working together. She took Connie under her roof unquestioningly — even at the expense of a renewal of hostilities between herself and Bea Farrington, another schism in the Christian Ladies — and managed every angle of village gossip in her indomitable way.

'I had a room to rent and Connie wanted to be nearer the shop,' she fired off over the counter in the days that followed. 'Simple as that,' she added, her steely eye implying that further questions on the matter would reveal the utter stupidity of the asker. Despite her loyalty to St Margaret's, she took a surprisingly romantic view of Connie's scattering of Uncle Jack's ashes on the crease, even going so far as to motion the parish council to erect a plaque on the side of the clubhouse, which read:

In Memory of
Our Keeper of the Green
Jack Farrington
1900–1950

And any detractors of the much-anticipated mural project, particularly those quick to voice their disdain at St Dorothea being portrayed as a well-known local redhead, found themselves quickly silenced at Cleat's. 'Why shouldn't Mr Swann want to paint a head of hair like that, tell me? Artistic types see the beauty in what others might find … well, a little brash and confronting. That's the nature of art, is it not?' Connie couldn't help but think Mr Gilbert would have been quite proud of the *old girl*.

But most of all, Connie was surprised by Mrs Cleat's help in another matter that weighed more heavily on her mind. Her nights were often restless with it, and when she got tired of fighting her pillow and the satin eiderdown that kept slipping from the bed, she would descend the creaking stairs into the shop, pacing the unlit shelves, running her hand over the Formica, cocking her head at the moon that rippled through the bull's-eye pane. The counter always smelled of Parma Violets these days. Mrs Cleat called the rolls of purple sweets her *one indulgence* and said they were the true sign the war was over. Their intense musky perfume had trailed behind her ever since supplies had become more regular, but Connie knew they also wreaked havoc on her digestion.

Late one night in the shop, she heard a rustle of paper behind her and turned to find Mrs Cleat dissolving a Beecham's into a glass of water.

'I thought I heard the stairs,' she said. The rags in her hair caught the moonlight as she tossed back the drink with a shudder. 'Come on, now. Let's have a cup of tea.'

They sat in the back kitchen and she felt the shopkeeper studying her, waiting less for the tea to brew than for her to speak. When she didn't, Mrs Cleat said, 'Well, are you going to tell him you're not coming, or will I have to do it?'

'Tell who?'

'Prince Charming, of course! Who d'you think I meant?'

Connie had to close her mouth.

'I do answer my own telephone sometimes, you know.' Mrs Cleat swilled the pot gently. The slosh of the tea inside was comforting to Connie.

She sighed. 'There's just so much more I want, Mrs Cleat. So much more I want to see and do than ending up —' She stopped. It felt such a relief to say it to someone, but she didn't want to belittle the shop, or indeed those things that Mrs Cleat might at one time have wanted for herself: love, marriage, a family.

'Course you do. Don't you think I seen that? Soon as you explained them Berkel compression scales to me, I said to myself, *Make the most on her, Eleanor, 'cause you won't have her for much longer. She's going places on her own steam, that one.* And I told your aunt only the other day, *Did you expect she'd be slicing government cheddar all her life, Bea?'*

Mrs Cleat took her hand. 'She'll come around, you'll see. In the meantime, I suggest you stop leaving this lying around and actually do something about it.' She reached to the chair beside her and took from its seat a brochure. It was an admissions booklet for Avery Hill Teacher Training College in Greenwich. Mr Gilbert had sent it to her after she'd written to tell him she was living with Mrs Cleat.

'Do you really think I could?' she said.

'Mr Gilbert seems to think so, and he'd be the one to know, wouldn't he?' Mrs Cleat sniffed and poured the tea, glancing at Connie fingering the pamphlet. As she set down the pot, her face reddened and her eyes glittered. She pulled a handkerchief from her cuff.

'What? What's wrong?' Connie asked.

Mrs Cleat shook her head and fanned her face like she was having a hot flush. She tutted. 'No, nothing ... nothing at all ...' She balled the handkerchief into her fist and straightened the buttons of her housecoat. 'But I'll tell you one thing, Connie Farrington. It's times like this I realise it was all good for something.'

'What was?'

'The war, of course. For women like you and me.'

'What makes you say that?'

'You do. Just looking at you … and remembering myself.' Her focus softened. 'Course, in my day, a lot of it was nothing but dreams, but some of us still had them. You've got such opportunities now,' she said. 'Such possibilities.' And she licked her handkerchief and buffed at a spot on the table, before taking the pot to the sink.

When Connie finally went to bed, she thought of what Mrs Cleat had said. *Women like you and me.* Not many months ago, she might have been mortified at such a comparison. But perhaps it wasn't so far from the truth in some ways: she had never thought before then that Mrs Cleat had chosen the shop, her independence, above another husband, above children. As she creaked up the stairwell, the smell of Parma Violets lingered about Mrs Cleat's bedroom, and from within came the sound of ledger pages turning long into the night.

Over the next few days, she tried to telephone Vittorio, but she couldn't seem to catch him at the garage, and the messages she left went unanswered. When Mrs Cleat caught her hanging up the receiver for the fourth time that week, confused and almost teary with frustration, she insisted that Connie go to Luton the next day.

'Dear me, it's only common decency to break off with a chap to his face,' Mrs Cleat reassured her, as if this was a formality with which she herself had been repeatedly burdened. Connie was momentarily amused at the thought of Mrs Cleat dispatching suitors with the prickly courtesy she reserved for her accounts overdue. But the following morning, the dread of what was ahead of her had become physical, a heaviness in her limbs like she had already done a day's stocktake in the back store.

On the steps of the shop, Mrs Cleat picked lint from the lapel of Connie's mackintosh and thrust out her chin to indicate she should stand up straight. 'And be on your guard for diddies and pickpockets hanging about the stations,' she warned. She scanned Connie once more, giving her the curt nod of her approval, before hurrying back to her counter. 'I don't know. The young today,' she tutted to Mrs Jellis. 'What d'they think we done before the telephone, I ask you?' But she nodded again at Connie through the bull's-eye pane as she buffed the Formica.

The bus to Benford and the subsequent train to Luton seemed to take an age. She used to imagine this trip south so often, buoyant with the fantasy of escape, of her life beginning: the fields and cows and hedgerows through the carriage windows would melt into a blur behind her, and the solid lines of spires and rooftops, dense as trees in the woods, would greet her ahead. But now she was too preoccupied with the draw and tug of her stomach, sickened by the rocking carriage and the prospect of what she had to do when it stopped.

At Luton station, unable to face prolonging her agony with the confusion of buses and timetables, she hailed a cab. It was the first taxi she had ever been in, but her dread at visiting Vittorio dampened the small thrill of her extravagant independence. She couldn't truly enjoy the ride past the imposing town hall, down wide streets with their seemingly endless cars and buses, shops and cinemas, hotels and teahouses, the pavements of people. When she reached the garage on the other side of town, the cars on the pristine forecourt shone unnaturally bright in the winter sun, arranged in perfect angles to the street — ready to be driven away, to drive someone away. A wave of doubt broke over her: everything here seemed so busy and new and of-the-future, purposely other-than-Leyton.

Was she making the right decision? She watched the cab pulling off. No one came onto the forecourt to greet her. The office behind the rows of cars was empty. She walked up to the open doors of a workshop at the back. Inside, she found a Vauxhall on the jack, with a pair of overalled legs underneath it that did not belong to Vittorio.

'Victor Mature you're after, is it?' the mechanic said from under the car when she asked him. 'S'his half day, love.' He wheeled out and sat up, wiping his hands on a rag and eyeing her, not without interest. Her face must have shown her anxiety, for when she apologised and said goodbye, he followed her onto the street and called out, 'Look ... hang on. His new place's in Overington Street. S'not far off.' He gave her brief directions and then rubbed at his neck, a rueful expression on his face, as if regretting he had opened his mouth.

Overington Street was exactly as Vittorio had described it to her on the telephone. The row of terraced houses had for the most part been split into flats, small but newly painted and with a view across the park. She found the number and went through the gate. A net curtain downstairs quivered, and she saw an elderly hand retreating. Behind the upstairs window she heard voices, the sound of a door closing. A woman's laugh seemed to spiral down and settle before her, somehow random and at the same time inevitable. It wasn't just any woman's laugh, but one she knew, one she had felt the chill of many times before that morning. She dropped her hand from the knocker and turned to cross the street.

In the park over the road she sat down in the shadow of a laurel. She felt vapid, impotent, and the dampness of the bench seemed to seep straight into her as though she was blotting paper. A woman passed by, pushing a pram, the toddler peering over its side at the large spoked wheels making their *click, click, click*.

She thought of the noise her Royal Enfield had made when she first rode it from the shop. *This Roy-al En-field*. She remembered the way Vittorio had said the words. He had come so far, hadn't he? And she was sure he had so much further to go. She thought she might cry, but the whine of her vanity was fleeting, her injured pride brushed aside by the truth of it all, suddenly so obvious, such a relief in its admission: Vittorio and Agnes.

The door slammed shut behind them when they emerged, the loose scarf in Agnes's hand billowing against Vittorio's trousers in the draught. *Puce*, Mr Gilbert had called it. It wasn't puce at all, she saw, but brown, and it made her mouth twitch. She watched the way Agnes touched her hand to Vittorio's arm, pulling him up before the kerb so he would remember to open the door of the Anglia for her. She watched the way he swung her about like he might kiss her, only to point to something at her mouth instead. And she watched the way Agnes flushed and rubbed at her teeth with a finger, stooping down to the car's wing mirror to check her lipstick. Yes, she thought, they really were made for each other.

When Vittorio closed the door on Agnes and stepped around the car into the street, he caught sight of Connie as she sat there, on the park bench under the laurels. He stopped, his hand on the door of the driver's side, his mouth open, as though he might call to her. But Connie shook her head at him and got up to go. He spun around then, giving the roof of the car an edgy flick with his knuckles, before getting in and slamming the door. They pulled away, his arm along the open window, his fingers still thrumming. As they rounded the corner, the back of his hand went up briefly. But she couldn't tell whether it was a wave goodbye, or something more impatient — a sign that they were done, that he was moving on to something new.

'Get it over with, sharpish, and you could be back home by teatime,' Mrs Cleat had told her. 'I've managed a piece of brisket from Mr Jellis.' Connie closed the door of the taxi and stood at the entrance to Luton station. Her gratitude for Mrs Cleat's little indulgences, her veiled concerns, her choice of the word *home*, could not quite outweigh the depressing thought that such a day might end in nothing more than stew and dumplings in the back kitchen of Cleat's. She took her train ticket out of her bag and rubbed it between gloved fingers. It had been so easy after all, she thought. Not just Vittorio, but actually leaving Leyton: buying her return at Benford; the train journey south; the cab rides across town with the drivers barely noticing her, as if she was simply another somebody in a rush to get somewhere, rather than the runaway child she felt they might see. Something she had imagined to be so vast and weighty had shrunk to nothing more than a stiff piece of printed card in her hand, one of the many discarded tickets littered around the station dustbin.

She walked through to the platform. A train was already there, preparing to depart, the guard starting to close the carriage doors. 'Which train is this one?' she asked as he approached.

'Southbound, miss. Better hurry, if you're going to St Pancras.'

She turned to him in surprise. Did she look like someone who was going to London? She ran her eyes dubiously over her brown lace-ups. More doors slammed, a shout came from an open window, a whistle blew. She had the sense of time audibly escaping her.

'Miss?'

'Yes,' she answered. 'Yes, I'd better hurry.'

'Connie!' cried Mr Gilbert as he opened the door of his flat in Coleville Place. It was already dusk, and the starlings were making such a noise in the square across the road that she had trouble hearing him. 'My word,' she caught him saying, 'why didn't you call?' He glanced the length of the terrace, past the hollowed-out remains of the corner building, with its charred wallpaper still clinging for dear life. 'Are you here all by yourself?'

She nodded, finding that, despite everything she'd rehearsed on the train, she couldn't speak. The suddenness of her decision, the sheer size and confusion of St Pancras, her shock at the still-ravaged buildings, the final relief at finding him at home — it was as much as she could do to keep back her tears.

'Come on. Come inside,' he said, taking her elbow. 'I think it's marvellous you're here.'

'Do you?' she managed.

'Of course I do. Why else would I have sent the pamphlet?'

'It was that, you see. I had to know if you were serious … if you really thought …' The words tumbled from her as she fished in her bag for the dog-eared forms from Avery Hill.

'Yes, I am serious and, yes, I do think so.' He was smiling at her, and she noticed now that he was wearing his hat and scarf, as if he was on his way out, even though he was taking her own and hanging them in the hallway. 'Frankly, I wasn't sure whether I was being rather too pushy,' he said. 'But when you wrote to say you'd moved in with Mrs Cleat … well, we entertained some hope. It was Lucio who said I should try you again.'

'Lucio?' She felt she might have misheard the name.

'Ah,' Mr Gilbert said, his hand still clutching her coat on the stand. 'I thought he might have written to you.'

'Written? Why would you think he'd write and tell me anything?' She tried to mask the pique in her voice with flippancy. 'Tell me what?'

He frowned, but it seemed to be a cover for his amusement. 'That he's lodging with me — just until he's on his feet. We're looking into that scholarship again. I'm sure he'll want to tell you all about it himself ...'

She could smell the fire, felt the draw of it as Mr Gilbert threw open the sitting-room door. She hesitated, wanted to back away down the hall, but there he was, in a chair pulled close to the grate, bent over his journal. He stood when he saw her and the book fell to the floor.

Mr Gilbert cleared his throat. 'Sit down, Connie. Sit down. I'll make some tea.' He tossed his hat onto a dresser and hurried away before she could speak.

They stood opposite each other, listening to Mr Gilbert's footsteps down the corridor, the purposeful sound of the kitchen door closing. Lucio thrust his hands into his pockets. It was ridiculous, she knew, but he seemed taller, older, standing there before her. Perhaps it was his outline against the fire or that she wasn't used to seeing him in such an indoor setting — he appeared too big for the room. She wanted to turn away, to find a place to sit down on the sofa strewn with newspapers, or pace along Mr Gilbert's bookshelves: anything to have him take his eyes from her, but they wouldn't let go.

'I didn't know ... you ... I wouldn't have ...' she began, but everything she wanted to say felt wrong.

'You wouldn't have come if you knew I was here.' He bent to pick up his journal and stayed staring into the fire, as if disappointed.

'You told Fossett ... well, you made it quite clear you're moving on. You don't need to justify it to me ... of all people.'

'Don't I?' he asked her quickly. He had rolled the journal in one fist and was squeezing it. She turned away.

'I'm happy for you. I think it's fantastic. You know it was always what I said you should do. How do you like London, anyway? I can't believe you're here … I can't believe *I'm* here, for that matter.' She knew she was prattling, her voice so buoyant it teetered on the verge of collapse. He didn't answer.

She moved to the shelves and began to finger the spine of a book. She tried to think of what else she might say to show her goodwill, to prove her detachment, but feared that the more she spoke the more her words had the opposite effect. She pulled out a volume and busied herself with the title pages. She wanted to laugh: it was an E.M. Forster novel, but she didn't have the concentration to discern anything more. She smoothed her palm over the cover and slotted it back among the others.

'Connie.' With her back to him she couldn't be sure he'd said it or if she'd simply imagined it. She wouldn't look at him to check. She sensed his boot against the grate, his hand running along the stone mantel.

'I've offended you,' he said finally.

She thought of his study of her in the church and became self-conscious, knowing he must have been examining her, dissecting her all along, to capture her hesitation so perfectly in that instant of departure. And yet it had been him doing the leaving, not her. 'Why did you show me like that? Like I was going away?'

'Weren't you?' He didn't flinch.

'No! It was you who left,' she threw out. 'You didn't even say goodbye.'

'Neither did you.'

'I wasn't going anywhere.'

Her lack of honesty seemed to echo between them. She

recalled the last time they had seen each other, the night at the clubhouse, her running away without even glancing back. She felt the flush of the fire, now overwhelming. 'Well, I didn't leave, did I? I didn't want to … not then. But now' — she let out a long breath, like she was finally giving in, unburdening herself — 'now I really want to.' She felt the relief of the admission wash over her, a physical release in her muscles and bones. Mr Gilbert had been right about that. 'Now I want to do so much, Lucio, to see so much …'

Yet the moment she opened up and stepped towards him, his face fell, losing its warmth and closing against her.

'With my brother?' He was already nodding like he had expected it.

'No.' She attempted an exasperated laugh, only to find it was a sob. 'Not with Vittorio.' She shrugged and backed away. 'Maybe just me. On my own.'

But she made the mistake of looking at him, betraying the lie in her words: he crossed the room and stood in front of her, pressing his thumbs under her eyes where the tears had spilled. His mouth on hers was uncertain at first, as a bird at a fountain, but when she let him taste her relief, he drank it down, answering it with his own.

Mr Gilbert came back, rattling the tea things. They pulled apart, finding an intense fascination in the photographs on the shelves, the coal in the scuttle. He set down the tray on the table.

'Well, finally,' he declared, pausing deliberately before adding, 'tea!' But instead of pouring, he reached once more for his hat on the dresser. 'I dare say you two won't mind that it's stewed and black as treacle, but I think I'd prefer that pint with Swann at the Fitzroy, after all.' And he pushed his trilby to the back of his head, patted his pockets for keys and cigarettes, and went off with no attempt to disguise his broad grin.

Montelupini
1955

The church bell was ringing. Connie squinted up at the square tower. It reeled precariously against the pristine sky as if it might come tumbling down with each tuneless toll. Below the cobbled rise, the rooftops and buildings about the square seemed propped together like cards, some already toppled, only weeds and saplings sheltering in the vacant blocks, the occasional oblivious rooster. It was all just as he had drawn it, as he had warned her it would be: the old men at the bar who spat and cursed each other and eyed her silently over their cards; the women on the church steps, muttering with grim mouths at their rosaries; the grubby children who stared as she passed. But what he hadn't told her about were the baskets of figs or marrow flowers she would find on their doorstep, the herbs and bottles of pureed tomatoes; he hadn't told her of the barman at the inn who always bowed so solemnly and raised his hat, or of the daunting butcher-woman who waved her into the shop with a cleaver and thrust unidentifiable slices of meat into her hand. She prized these small gestures, springing up as they did from the air of watchfulness around her, in the same way she appreciated the village's beauty, couched in its ancient disrepair.

She descended the road that curved down to the washhouse, smelling the ripe alleyways warming in the heat — the scents she could distinguish now as mothballs and geraniums, cigarettes and overripe fruit, coffee grounds, garlic, and sewage. Collectively they were the smell of Montelupini. She thought of the *dear, dirty backways* favoured by Forster's Miss Lavish and breathed in deeply, smiling to herself. The Baedeker Mr Gilbert had given her was still on her shelf in London. The summer would be over soon enough, and she would be back in the chilly carbolic air of her classroom.

At the fountain by the washhouse, she came across the twins who filled casks with water and delivered them to houses on a cart. She liked the two girls. They were about the same age as those in her last class, and they had been the first in the village to speak to her, as if sensing she might understand them without the fluency of language. They rushed up to her now, offering to fill her flask. It had become a habit of theirs, and she secretly enjoyed the price they exacted: she was obliged to sit on the wall, sipping her water and waiting for them to finish trying on her new red sandals, her sunglasses, her headscarf; to finish brushing their fingers over her hair, while they whispered to each other in awed voices, 'Come capelli rossi ... come ricci ... come quelli di Santa Lucia ...'

By the time she had reached the plateau, the sun was beating down on her from high in the sky, and she was grateful for the water. Vittorio had been right: it wasn't like any water she had ever drunk. She could taste the mountain in it, the shade of chestnuts as she walked through their thick glades, the mossy boulders of the dell, damp to the touch. All about her, the wood cracked and ticked in the heat like the muscles that twitched in her thighs from the climb, and the cicadas pulsed in her throat, so that she could feel the place within her, moving under her skin. Between the trees a haze of insects shivered across the surface of the lake. She felt drawn to it, but her path was in the opposite direction, towards the bluff of rock, whitewashed in the sunlight.

As she broke through the trees and stepped onto the outcrop, the valley opened up before her, waiting to be read like the turned page of a book. She caught her ragged breath, let it settle. Far below, the village was wedged in the black sketch of the hills, the vineyards and terraces tacked on around it, a work in progress. The sky was cloudless and so blue, the mountains appeared as the silhouettes of great beasts panting against it in the sun. She heard the rumble of cartwheels on the chalk road far below, a donkey's bellowing complaints, the groan of old metal as the grille of the chapel opened behind her.

A hand took hers.

'Has the saint finished with you yet?' she asked, still gazing at the view. She could feel the heat of him along her damp back, his stubble grazing her neck, the mineral smell of paint closing about her.

'Nearly,' Lucio said. 'Just part of St Agatha's tomb to finish. Do you want to see?'

She nodded, but drew his arms further around her waist. 'In a minute.'

A bird was wheeling its languid circles down the ridge. She traced the clean dark span of it, the flutter of its wing tips. Below, the river was faint as a pencil line through the valley, a shed hair catching the light from time to time. All the details of his journals, of his paintings, were now familiar to her: it was the furthest she'd ever been from Leyton, and it felt like coming home.

Acknowledgements

I would like to name two books that were particularly helpful in my research for this novel: *Italy's Sorrow: a year of war, 1944–45* by James Holland and *Millions like Us: women's lives in war and peace 1939–49* by Virginia Nicholson. I am indebted to the kindness of Mrs Gillian Spokes, who opened the church of St Margaret of Antioch in Denton, Northants, especially for me to view the paintings of Sir Henry Bird and witness a beautiful example of twentieth-century mural work in a thirteenth-century church.

Thank you to the team at Scribe, especially Aviva Tuffield for taking a punt on a few thousand words and having faith that I'd deliver the rest (eventually). I'm so sorry I overshot my deadlines and you didn't get to see this book off into the world. It's still undoubtedly your baby, and your guidance was not just invaluable for the manuscript, it was the best kind of mentorship for me as a writer. Ian See, you were such a pleasure to work with and your judgement impeccable — thank you for all your effort. Thanks, Cate Kennedy, for being so generous with your time, for the gate-crashing, late-night karaoke, churros and all! Thank you to The Writers' House, Varuna, for a much-needed residency that helped break the back of the book, and to James Bradley, Kathryn Heyman and the inaugural Sydney Faber Academy participants for their feedback. But most importantly, to my wonderful writing group — Sam, Suzanne and Barbara, who were with me from the first: the time you dedicated to reading the endless drafts was such a gift. Thank you for getting me out of the house and keeping me sane.

While my story is entirely fictional, it owes a debt to many people in my family. My thanks go to my uncle and godfather, Luciano Riccioni, who some years ago took the time to record for me his memories of growing up in Italy and migrating to England. Uncle Luci, you have always been such a well of patience and love — thank you for your translation help and for letting me pick your brains with bizarre questions at the oddest of moments. To my dad, Albis, the embodiment of the immigrant work ethic and a great storyteller in his own right, thank you for passing a little of that on to me so I could finish this. You've always been a bigger influence than you can imagine. Aunty Angela and Aunty Mary — I loved listening to you, Nonna and Nonno during all those summers in Italy and apologise now for not telling you I was mentally taking notes. To my sister Sylvana, thank you for first putting the idea in my head with that pep talk when I still had nappy brain. 'You know, you should write,' you told me, and it was like suddenly being given permission. Thank you Big Sis, Suzanne, for keeping me going with long-distance encouragement and titbits of rural life, not to mention letting me live in Oakdene and introducing me to Watties shop all those years ago — a big influence. And Marcus, thank you for the lesson in hunting etiquette. To my gorgeous Lydia and Henry, thanks for never respecting the closed door and always keeping me grounded in reality — life, after all, is more important than novels. And finally my love and thanks to GJ, for never asking to read it, for never complaining about the 5 a.m. alarm and for never stinting in your quiet, unquestioning support, especially when there seemed no end and no dinner in sight. I couldn't have done it without you.

Cat & Fiddle
LESLEY JØRGENSEN

'Jørgensen steps so adroitly in and out of the heads of these wonderful characters that it's as if she's at your shoulder, the perfect travelling companion on the novel's journey: chatty, warm, compassionate and funny. An exuberant debut, bubbling with energy and insight.'
CATE KENNEDY

Cat & Fiddle centres on two families whose lives become entwined at the country estate of Bourne Abbey. While Dr Choudhury is busy advising Henry Bourne on the restoration of the abbey to its former glory, his wife's main concern is marrying off their three children, whose chances of good matches are dwindling by the day. Meanwhile, Henry is trying to keep the peace in his own family, but that's proving tricky. A delightful comedy about the cultural and generational clashes in today's society, *Cat & Fiddle* heralds the arrival of an exceptional new voice.

SCRIBE Seriously good books.
scribepublications.co.uk